PRAISE FOR [illegible]
BESTS[illegible]

A[illegible]

"Wild rides and pages [illegible]
—J. R. Ward, *New York Times* bestselling author

"Powerful romantic suspense . . . Hot enough to burn."
—*Romance Reviews Today*

Nalini Singh

"Craving the passionate and electrifying world created by the mega-talented Singh? Your next fix is here! Original and thrilling . . . Mind-blowing!" —*Romantic Times*

"Paranormal romance at its best." —*Publishers Weekly*

Virginia Kantra

"Virginia Kantra delivers intense paranormal suspense and intense romance. A perfect combination."
—Jayne Ann Krentz, *New York Times* bestselling author

"Lush writing, vivid descriptions, and smoldering sensuality."
—*Romance Novel TV*

Meljean Brook

"A read that goes down hot and sweet—utterly unique—and one hell of a ride."
—Marjorie M. Liu, *New York Times* bestselling author

"Meljean Brook . . . turns up the heat." —*Entertainment Weekly*

"[Brook] is truly one of the best voices out there. Sexy, exciting . . . A dark and sultry world."
—Gena Showalter, *New York Times* bestselling author

BURNING UP

Angela Knight
Nalini Singh
Virginia Kantra
Meljean Brook

BERKLEY SENSATION, NEW YORK

THE BERKLEY PUBLISHING GROUP
Published by the Penguin Group
Penguin Group (USA) Inc.
375 Hudson Street, New York, New York 10014, USA
Penguin Group (Canada), 90 Eglinton Avenue East, Suite 700, Toronto, Ontario M4P 2Y3, Canada
(a division of Pearson Penguin Canada Inc.)
Penguin Books Ltd., 80 Strand, London WC2R 0RL, England
Penguin Group Ireland, 25 St. Stephen's Green, Dublin 2, Ireland (a division of Penguin Books Ltd.)
Penguin Group (Australia), 250 Camberwell Road, Camberwell, Victoria 3124, Australia
(a division of Pearson Australia Group Pty. Ltd.)
Penguin Books India Pvt. Ltd., 11 Community Centre, Panchsheel Park, New Delhi—110 017, India
Penguin Group (NZ), 67 Apollo Drive, Rosedale, North Shore 0632, New Zealand
(a division of Pearson New Zealand Ltd.)
Penguin Books (South Africa) (Pty.) Ltd., 24 Sturdee Avenue, Rosebank, Johannesburg 2196,
South Africa

Penguin Books Ltd., Registered Offices: 80 Strand, London WC2R 0RL, England

This is a work of fiction. Names, characters, places, and incidents either are the product of the author's imagination or are used fictitiously, and any resemblance to actual persons, living or dead, business establishments, events, or locales is entirely coincidental. The publisher does not have any control over and does not assume any responsibility for author or third-party websites or their content.

BURNING UP

A Berkley Sensation Book / published by arrangement with the authors

PRINTING HISTORY
Berkley Sensation mass-market edition / August 2010

Copyright © 2010 by Penguin Group (USA) Inc.
"Whisper of Sin" by Nalini Singh copyright © 2010 by Nalini Singh.
"Blood and Roses" by Angela Knight copyright © 2010 by Julie Woodcock.
"Shifting Sea" by Virginia Kantra copyright © 2010 by Virginia Kantra.
"Here There Be Monsters" by Meljean Brook copyright © 2010 by Melissa Khan.
Excerpt from *Immortal Sea* by Virginia Kantra copyright © by Virginia Kantra.
Excerpt from *The Iron Duke* by Meljean Brook copyright © by Melissa Khan.
Cover art (man) by Vladmir Wrangel/Shutterstock.
Cover art (lightning) by Kellie L. Folkert/Shutterstock.
Cover art (tattoo) by Ferin/Shutterstock.
Cover design by Annette Fiore DeFex.
Interior text design by Tiffany Estreicher.

All rights reserved.
No part of this book may be reproduced, scanned, or distributed in any printed or electronic form without permission. Please do not participate in or encourage piracy of copyrighted materials in violation of the author's rights. Purchase only authorized editions.
For information, address: The Berkley Publishing Group,
a division of Penguin Group (USA) Inc.,
375 Hudson Street, New York, New York 10014.

ISBN: 978-0-425-23595-9

BERKLEY® SENSATION
Berkley Sensation Books are published by The Berkley Publishing Group,
a division of Penguin Group (USA) Inc.,
375 Hudson Street, New York, New York 10014.
BERKLEY® SENSATION and the "B" design are trademarks of Penguin Group (USA) Inc.

PRINTED IN THE UNITED STATES OF AMERICA

10 9 8 7 6 5 4 3 2 1

If you purchased this book without a cover, you should be aware that this book is stolen property. It was reported as "unsold and destroyed" to the publisher, and neither the author nor the publisher has received any payment for this "stripped book."

CONTENTS

WHISPER OF SIN

Nalini Singh

To May, Jennifer, and Kay ~ I couldn't have asked for better friends!

The San Francisco Gazette

August 2, 2072

CITY BEAT

Trouble in Chinatown?

Enforcement is refusing to either confirm or deny the rumors of a new organized crime family in the city. The word on the street is that this gang—known by the black "V" they scrawl at the locations of their crimes—intends to take over all illegal operations within San Francisco. So far, V has concentrated its efforts in Chinatown, but our sources say they plan to spread out across the greater Bay area.

Smith Jenson, the telepath who acts as PR manager for local government, has publicly stated that the threat from V is negligible. We beg to disagree. While Psy like Mr. Jenson and his colleagues stay safe in their high-rise apartments, humans and changelings on the ground are beginning to feel the effects of this new threat. There have been no deaths yet, but it's only a matter of time.

This reporter believes local government needs to step up to the plate. If they don't, San Francisco might just slip out of their grasp.

ONE

Her hose was shredded, Ria thought, staring uncomprehendingly at the bottoms of her feet. Where were her shoes? Lost somewhere in the alley where that bastard had tried to rape her as "down payment" on the protection money her family refused to pay.

Something fluttered over her shoulders and was tucked around her, warm and thick. A blanket. She gripped it tight, then winced as her bloodied palms made contact with the wool. Her hands spasmed open. Released, the blanket began to slide to the floor of the large paramedic van.

"I've got you." Following the deep voice, she blinked into a face she didn't know. The changeling who'd thrown her attacker against the wall had been blond and blue-eyed, reminding her of the cocky youth of her younger brother, Ken. This man . . . he was hewn out of rougher material, his jaw shadowed, his eyes the rich amber shade of aged whiskey, his hair thick and dark, a hundred shades of brown and gold intertwined. "Come on, sweetheart, speak to me."

She swallowed, tried to find words but they lost their way in the chaos of her brain, leaving her dumb. Instead, her mind filled with the terror of the lifetime she'd spent in that alley only minutes from her family home, in one of the streets surrounding the bustle of Chinatown. It had taken mere seconds for everything to change. One moment she was smiling, and the next, her excitement at finishing her final night class had given way to pain and shock as he hit and pawed—

A smooth burst of Mandarin, so unexpected, so welcome that it broke through the haze of pain and fear. She looked up again, astonished. This man, this stranger was speaking to her in the language of her grandmother, asking her if she was okay. She nodded, found the words to say, "I speak English." She rarely had to say that. Unlike her half-Caucasian mother, Ria had inherited little from her grandmother but her bones. Her hair was stick-straight, but a dark brown instead of jet black. Her eyes were faintly almond-shaped, but only if someone was really looking. She'd gotten the majority of her features from her brown-haired, brown-eyed All-American father.

"What's your name, darling?" A hand cupping her cheek.

She flinched, but this hand, though big, was gentle. And patient. She relaxed into the warmth after long minutes, reassured by the calluses that spoke of a man accustomed to working with his hands. "Ria. Who are you?"

"Emmett," he said, his voice holding nothing of laughter. "And I'm in charge of you."

Her brow furrowed, the real Ria fighting her way through the fog of shock. "Who're you to be in charge of me?"

"I'm big, I'm strong, and I'm pissed as hell that someone dared touch a woman on my watch."

She blinked. "Your watch?"

"Dorian's part of my team," he said, nodding to the blond man who'd turned her attacker into a sack of broken bones. "Wish he hadn't done such a good job—I would've liked to bloody the piece of shit myself."

Ria wasn't used to violence, but she knew without a doubt that this man was a changeling, that he could turn into a leopard with a single thought—and that the leopard had no problem with the most brutal kind of justice. When she looked into his eyes, she saw rage . . . and the flickers of something that wasn't quite human. "He can't hurt me." Somehow, she found herself trying to comfort him.

"But he did." An implacable statement. "And I'm going to sniff out the nest this little viper came from no matter what."

She glanced at her assailant's unconscious body. He was alive, barely. But he wouldn't be talking for a while yet. "He wasn't working alone?"

"Indications are he's with a new gang." Emmett tucked her blanket gently around her feet when it came loose. "Dark-River's done a hell of a lot of work to clear the city of this kind of scum, but sometimes, they pop back up."

Ria knew of DarkRiver. Who didn't? The leopard pack, based in the Yosemite forest, had claimed San Francisco as part of their territory when Ria had been a child—no other predatory changelings could enter the city without their permission. But in the past few years, they'd gone further and begun to wipe out human predators, too.

"I can tell you a little about him," she said, her voice gaining strength on a cresting wave of anger. "He came to my mother's shop, left an account number where she was supposed to wire 'protection' money. We thought he was just another thug."

"I'll get the number from you tomorrow. Right now, you need to be seen to." Sliding one muscular arm under her legs, he curved the other around her back, just below her shoulders, and scooped her up before she knew what was happening.

She gave a startled cry.

"I won't drop you." A soothing murmur as he shifted her deeper into the van. "Just getting you out of the wind."

She should've protested, but she was tired and achy and he was so warm. Resting her head against his heart when he sat down with her in his arms, she breathed deep. Her body sighed. He smelled good. All hot and male and real, his after-shave something clean and fresh. Though he clearly needed to shave more than once a day. His jaw rasped against her hair as he settled her more firmly on his lap. Not that she minded, she thought, her eyes fluttering shut.

Emmett stroked his hand over the hair of the mink in his arms. She was a little thing, and right now, she was at the end of her resources. Enraged at the thought that someone had dared harm her, he held her with conscious gentleness until he felt her begin to relax. When she sighed and snuggled closer, the leopard in him gave a pleased growl—right as Dorian looked into the van.

The blond soldier nodded at Ria. "She okay?"

"Where the hell are the paramedics?" Emmett snarled.

"With the piece of shit." Dorian shrugged. "I should've killed him."

The feral part of Emmett wanted to tell the man to go out there and finish the job, but he forced himself to think past the leopard's need to maul and tear. "We need any information he can give us on the Crew, so let's hope he can talk later."

"This is when a Psy would come in handy," Dorian muttered, referring to the psychic race that was the third part of the triumvirate that was their world. "One of the telepaths could rip the information right from the bastard's head."

"You guys are gruesome," said a drowsy feminine voice.

Emmett looked down to find Ria's eyes closed. "Yeah, we are." But he had a feeling she was already asleep, her lashes dark-moon crescents against skin so creamy, he wanted to taste it. Returning his attention to Dorian through sheer force of will, he said, "Did you find any emergency contact details in her wallet?" He'd left the young soldier to handle that while he took care of Ria.

"Yeah—parents are on their way." Dorian's smile was sharp. "Her daddy sounds like he's itching for a fight, so maybe you shouldn't look at her that way."

"Mind your own fucking business." He tightened his hold.

Raising his hands, Dorian backed off, laughing. "Hey, your funeral."

"Go get a paramedic here."

"I think Tammy just arrived—she can stitch up your girl."

The DarkRiver healer popped into the van on the heels of Dorian's statement. "Let me have a look at her," she said in a soft voice, putting her kit on the floor.

Ria's eyes snapped open at the other woman's first touch. Emmett ran a hand down her back in reassurance. "Ria, this is Tamsyn, our healer. You can trust her." To his leopard's delight, he felt her body relax almost at once.

"Call me Tammy." Tamsyn smiled. "Everyone does."

"I know you," Ria said an instant later. "You bought a chunk of jade from my mom's store."

"Alex is your mom?" Tammy smiled at Ria's nod. "I told her I needed something to threaten my mate with when he got blockheaded, and she said, why not a block for a block?"

"That sounds more like my grandmother."

Tammy grinned. "All women sound like their mothers after a certain age." A wink.

Ria found herself smiling despite herself. "Then I'm doomed." She held out her hands for Tammy to clean. "It doesn't actually really hurt anymore."

"Hmm, let me see. You got this falling on your hands?" Tammy was cleaning the dirt and debris from the wounds as she spoke.

Ria nodded, wincing at the sting of the antiseptic. "Yes."

The healer looked at her now clean palms. "No cuts that need stitching," the gorgeous brunette murmured. "Let me look at your face, sweetheart." Her hands were incredibly competent and careful, for all that she looked like a fashion model, with her height and her elegant bones.

Ria had always wanted to be tall. That was the one thing she hadn't inherited from her father. Instead, she was stuck with her mother's diminutive height—but not Alex's naturally slender body. No, Ria had gotten stuck with short and "curvy." *Hah, more like generously padded.* Her mother ate six dumplings in a row and had room for more. Ria ate three and put on five pounds.

"You asleep?" It was a rumble against her ear.

She shook her head. "Awake." Sort of.

"Your face is going to bruise some," Tamsyn told her, "but there's no permanent damage." She soothed something over the skin. "This'll help keep the bruising down."

"Xie xie." It came out automatically, a response to this healer's touch. Tamsyn had hands like her grandmother. Caring hands. Trustworthy hands.

"You're welcome." A smile she could hear though her eyes were closed. "Emmett, you need to leave us alone for a few minutes."

She felt the big body around hers tense. Forcing open her lids, she patted him on the chest, not quite sure where she found the courage. The leopard changelings were lethal when roused. But, in spite of the fierce scowl on his face, she had a feeling this cat would never hurt her. "I'll be okay."

"Tammy," Emmett argued, scowl darkening even further, "she's half asleep."

"I need to ask her some personal questions," Tamsyn said in that calm, capable voice, "so I can see if she needs any other meds."

Ria's fuzzy brain cleared. "He didn't get that far. Just knocked me around some."

A growl filled the air. She jolted upright, heart thudding at a hundred miles an hour. "What was that?"

"Emmett."

Blinking at Tammy's tone, she glanced at the man who held her. "You?"

"I am a leopard," he said, as if surprised by her surprise.

"Forget him," Tamsyn said, catching Ria's gaze as she disinfected the scratches on her knees. "You sure about what happened, kitten? No one's going to judge you."

It was impossible not to trust this woman. "I threw my handbag at him, kneed him in the balls. After that, he was more interested in hurting me than . . . you know."

Tamsyn nodded. "Alright, then. But if you ever need to talk, you call me." She slid a card into the giant handbag someone had retrieved and put in the ambulance while Ria hadn't been looking.

"That's—" Ria began when there was a commotion outside.

"Where's my daughter? You! Where is she? Tell me right now or I'll—"

"Mom." Ria felt tears rise for the first time as her mother entered the ambulance, pushing Tammy out of the way as if the other woman wasn't stronger and taller.

"My baby." Alex patted her all over, kissing her forehead with a mother's tender warmth. "That piece of shit."

"Mom!" Her mother never swore. When Ria's grandmother was feeling wicked, she called Alex a "tightass" simply to see her explode—her grandmother was a firecracker.

"You!" Alex fixed a gimlet eye on Emmett. "Why do you have your hands on my daughter?"

Those hands cuddled her even closer. "I'm looking after her."

Alex huffed. "Didn't look after her very well, did you? She got attacked right here, almost on the main road."

"Mom," Ria said, intending to stop the diatribe, when Emmett calmly nodded and said, "It was my fault. I'll fix it."

"It was not your fault," Ria said, but no one was listening to her.

"Good." Alex turned back to Ria. "Your grandmother's waiting for you."

"How did you manage to make her wait at home?"

"I told her you'd want her special jasmine tea when you got back."

Emmett had grown up in a strong and vibrant pack. He'd figured he could handle Ria's family. That was before he met her grandmother. Five feet nothing of pure fury and a tightly held rage that was all the more impressive for its control.

Ria came first, of course. Emmett would've allowed nothing less, even if her grandmother hadn't ordered him to carry Ria—who was protesting that she could "walk, for goodness sake"—into what looked like the grandmother's bedroom, so she could wash up and change. Soon as he'd completed that task, he was banished to the kitchen to wait.

Ria's father was still at the site, being restrained from giving the near-dead attacker even more of a beating. So was Ria's older brother. Which left him in the kitchen with Ria's mom and sister-in-law. Alex and Amber looked more like sisters than anything else. Ria's mom was a pretty woman, petite and graceful. Amber was cut in the same mold—even heavily pregnant as she was now, her features were delicate, her arms slimly fragile.

Emmett stayed very carefully in the chair where he'd been

ordered to sit. He was afraid he'd break one of them if he accidentally touched them. Now Ria, Ria he wanted to *handle.*

"Drink!" Something slammed in front of him.

He looked down at the puddle of jasmine tea around his little cup and decided not to mention Alex's temper. "Thanks."

"You think I don't see it?" She poked him in the shoulder. "You, the way you look at my baby?"

Nobody dared attack Emmett. He wasn't one of the more volatile leopards in DarkRiver, but he was beyond dangerous when riled. And wouldn't all his trainees just love to see him now, not daring to lift a finger for fear of bruising Alex. "How do I look at her?"

Alex narrowed her eyes. "Like a big cat with its food." She hooked her hands into claws and made as if she was shoving others aside. "Like that."

"You have a problem with that?"

"I have a problem with every man who wants to date my daughter." With that, Alex turned and walked back to the counter. "And her father, he has twice the problem."

Emmett wondered if Alex expected that to scare him off. "I grew up in a pack." He was used to nosy packmates, snarling fathers, ferally protective mothers.

Amber smiled when Alex sniffed and turned away. "They have problems with women, too," she said in a mock-whisper. "When I started dating Jet, Alex told me if I broke his heart, she'd beat me with a rolling pin."

Alex waved the very same implement in Amber's direction. "Don't you forget it."

Laughing, Amber hugged Alex. "She's okay, Mom. Ria will bounce back—better than you or I ever would."

That was when Ria's male relatives returned. Her father's first question was, "Who the hell is *he*?"

TWO

Ria sat back in the bubble bath her grandmother had drawn and sighed.

A light knock came moments later.

"It's okay, *Popo*."

Her grandmother came in. Though tiny, with a face that bore the million marks of a life well-lived, her stride was steady and her eyes clear. Miaoling Olivier had a whole heap of decades left in her yet, as she liked to say. Now, she walked in and took a seat on the closed lid of the toilet as Ria's father began yelling in the kitchen.

"Here we go," Miaoling said, rolling her eyes. "Sometimes, I think we accidentally opened our home to the inmates of an insane asylum."

Ria felt her lips twitch, her eyes water. "They're just angry and scared for me."

"Smart girl." Reaching over, her grandmother took one of Ria's ravaged palms and brought it to her mouth.

The kiss was soft, loving. It healed Ria from the inside out. "I love you, *Popo*."

"Do you know," Miaoling said, "you're the only one who calls me that. Ken and Jet both say nana."

"That's why they're not your favorites and I am."

"Shh." Miaoling's eyes twinkled as she put Ria's hand back down on the edge of the bath. "Did you thank the young man who found you? Maybe you should bake him a cake."

That made Ria smile. "Not interested," she told her ever-hopeful grandmother. "He's a little too beautiful for me." The blond DarkRiver male was clearly a highly trained member of the pack, but slender, looked more like a teenage surfer than a grown man. Emmett on the other hand . . .

Her grandmother sighed. "You go on like this, your female parts will dry up."

Ria snorted with laughter. *"Popo!"*

"What? I say only the truth." Miaoling's speech shifted, going from Harvard-perfect English to a rhythm she only ever used with those she was comfortable with. "Your age, I had your mother on the way."

"Times have changed—and I'm twenty-two, hardly shriveled up." She rested her head against the wall. "Tell me how you met Grandfather."

"Why? You know that already."

"Please." The story comforted her, and right now, she needed comforting.

"Alright, for my Ri-ri." A deep breath. "I was living on a farm in Henan Province and my family was trying to arrange my marriage. But, *ai*, I was a terrible one. I wouldn't marry any of the boys they brought around—too skinny, too fat, too stupid, too tied to his mama's apron strings."

"They let you get away with that?"

"I was only girl after three boys. I was spoiled." Said with a fond smile. "Then one day, my father comes home and says, Miaoling, today you dress nice, American doctor is coming to the village to check old people's eyes."

"Cataracts."

"Yes. My father says, maybe crazy American will want crazy Chinese wife who doesn't listen to anyone. Of course, that makes me want to not like American at all."

Ria giggled, as drawn into the story as she'd been as a child. "Then Grandfather came to the house for dinner."

"And I wore brown dress, ugly brown dress, with ugly

brown shoes." Her grandmother's hand stroked over Ria's hair, hair that Miaoling had once said held the silk of China but the lush chocolate shade of an entirely different culture. "But he's so handsome. Pretty green eyes, yellow hair. And he's nice. He laughs at me silently all night across the dinner table. He knows what I'm up to."

"But he asked you to marry him anyway."

"After one week. And crazy Miaoling said yes, and we came to America."

"So quick," Ria said, shaking her head. "Weren't you scared?"

"Pah, why scared? When in love, no scared. Only impatient."

"Don't say it, *Popo*!"

But it was too late. "Impatient to use woman parts!"

Emmett hid his grin in his jasmine tea. His hearing was leopard-acute. He could hear everything Ria's grandmother was saying—and damn if he wasn't half in love with the lady already. No wonder Ria's grandfather had married her.

Glancing up, he caught Alex's expression as her husband folded her into his arms. All her bluster aside, Alex really was worried about Ria. "No one will hurt your daughter again," he said quietly, rising to his feet.

They all looked at him for long minutes, until finally, Simon, Ria's father, nodded. But when he spoke, it was to say, "She's not for you. She's taken."

Emmett raised an eyebrow. "She's not wearing a ring." And if some moron had been stupid enough not to claim her when he'd had the chance, that wasn't Emmett's problem.

"She will," Simon said. "We've been friends with Tom's family, the Clarks, for years. The marriage proposal is a formality."

Emmett could hear Ria and her grandmother even now, giggling in the bathroom. Neither of them had mentioned this Tom in their discussion of utilizing "woman parts." The leopard gave a feline grin of satisfaction, though the man kept his face expressionless. "I have a feeling that nothing is a given with your daughter—she'll make her own choices." Of course, he had every intention of making sure she chose him, but no need to tell her parents that. Not yet.

Two hours later, after a quick meeting with the DarkRiver alpha and a number of other soldiers, Emmett rubbed at gritty eyes as he accepted the beer Nathan threw him. "I've got to head home, get some sleep."

"Take a few minutes to relax," the sentinel—one of the pack's highest-ranking soldiers—told him. "You've been taut as a bow all night. Everything go okay with the girl who was attacked?"

"Yeah." Emmett had no intention of discussing Ria further with anyone. Not tonight. "What was that Luc was saying about the Psy?" Changeling concerns rarely intersected with those of the unemotional psychic race, but from what he'd caught tonight, it might in this case.

Nate took a swig of his beer. "You know how they dominate politics. We've heard they might try to neutralize the Crew themselves."

"Why? They don't give a shit about human and changeling casualties." The sole reason the other race stayed in power—aside from the fact that their competitors had a way of withdrawing from the race after the publication of one scandal or another—was their ability to make money, money that did occasionally trickle down to the voters.

"We're starting to step on their toes," Nate said. "Psy like to be the top dogs in any given situation."

"Guess we'll have to move fast."

"We've got a little time." The other man put down his beer. "Apparently, not everyone in the Psy ranks is convinced we pose a credible threat."

Emmett snorted. "They really can't see beyond their ivory towers, can they?"

"Humans and changelings don't figure much on their radar." Nate's smile was distinctly pleased. "And while they're busy deciding whether or not to bother paying attention to us, we'll take this city."

Emmett raised his bottle in a toast. "To a successful campaign." However, right then, he was thinking less about DarkRiver's takeover of the city, and more about a very private campaign of his own. *Come on, mink, play with me.*

Ria lay in bed that night and sighed. She'd been cosseted, petted, and smothered half to death by her family in the hours since her return home. Most days, it would've made her certifiable. Today, she'd needed that warm blanket of love.

Warmth. Heat.

Her body softened, remembering what it had felt like to lie curled up in Emmett's lap. She'd never found herself in a man's lap before. Most of the men who'd dared run the gauntlet of her family's protectiveness to ask her out were nice boys from the neighborhood. She had nothing against them. But the thing was, she'd grown up with a father who was fierce in his care of his family, and an older brother who hadn't deviated far from the paternal mold when it came to looking after those who were his own. They ate those nice boys for breakfast.

Ria dreamed of a man who'd occasionally chew them up instead!

Hugging her pillow, she smiled at her own thoughts. You'd think she didn't like her family. That was far from the truth. But well, they were overwhelming. They kind of took over everything. How was she supposed to respect a man who let himself be taken over?

I'll be back to check on you tomorrow.

Emmett had said that right in front of her father.

Goose bumps broke out over her entire body. She wondered what those big, strong hands of his would feel like smoothing over her skin, all hot and—

Her phone beeped. She groaned when she saw the caller ID.

Tom.

Sighing, she went to answer, but the well-concealed devil in her made her turn off the cell instead. There was nothing wrong with Tom, except that he wanted to marry her. Her father liked Tom. Even Alex liked Tom. Ria had no problem with Tom. She just didn't want to marry him. No, what she dreamed of was a love story like her grandmother's—and Miaoling was the only one in the family who supported Ria's resistance to the "Great Match."

From Alex's and Simon's point of view, it truly was a great match. Like her, Tom was part Chinese. Like her, he'd grown up in the States, and had a very Western outlook on life, without having forgotten the other side of his heritage. Best of all, the Clarks and the Wembleys had been friends since before either Ria or Tom had been born.

It was all perfect.

Except Tom would never laugh with her over a secret joke as her grandfather had done with her grandmother. He'd never hold her with the furious tenderness with which Simon held Alex when he thought no one was looking. And he'd never pick a fight with her just so he'd get to make up, as Jet did with Amber.

Why couldn't they see that she wanted the same thing? All her life she'd been content to let Jet and their younger brother, Ken, take the spotlight. Being the middle child was actually kind of nice—she got the best of both worlds, and her relationship with her siblings was airtight. But with her man, with her husband, she wanted to be number one.

"Go to sleep, Ria," she muttered to herself, knowing she was obsessing because she was afraid of nightmares.

But when she did sleep, it wasn't to fall into a nightmare . . . but into the powerful arms of a man who looked at her with eyes gone cat-green.

Emmett studied his face in the bathroom mirror the next morning and scowled. It was a wonder Ria hadn't run screaming from him when he'd taken her into his arms. She was all soft and silky, a luscious armful. He, by comparison, looked like he'd had a few run-ins with both fists and walls. The fists were true, but like all changelings, he'd healed the damage fast. No, this was simply the face he'd been born with. It had never really bothered him before, but now he rubbed a hand over his stubbled jaw and decided he'd damn well better shave before he went to check up on Ria.

The shave and shower cleaned him up, but he was aware he still looked like a thug when he knocked on the door to her family home. He most definitely looked nothing like the pretty boy walking up the drive with a huge bouquet of roses.

Shit.

Why the hell hadn't he thought to bring flowers?

"Hello," the other man said in an Ivy League–educated voice. "I'm Tom."

Emmett held out a hand. "Emmett."

"Simon mentioned you on the phone," Tom said with a friendly smile that failed to hide the calculation in his eyes. "You helped Ria last night."

"You're a friend of the family?" Emmett asked to see what Tom would say, just as the door opened.

"No, he's my daughter's fiancé," Alex said, pulling Tom down for a kiss on the cheek.

Emmett glanced at Tom. "You don't believe in rings?"

"It's not official yet." The other man was calm, confident, clearly sure of his suit.

Emmett didn't smile, but the leopard snapped its teeth inside him. This human cub was about to learn that leopard males didn't recognize any claim not acknowledged by the female. And Ria didn't consider herself bound to this one. Even if he hadn't overhead her conversation with her grandmother, nothing about her had spoken of a commitment to another. She didn't carry Tom's scent . . . and she hadn't pushed Emmett away last night.

Saying nothing of that, he turned to face Alex. "Could I speak to Ria?"

"Why?" Alex's eyes narrowed, even as she pulled Tom inside and put her hand on the opposite doorjamb as if to bar Emmett's way.

"I need to see if she remembers anything else about her attacker." Emmett's leopard knew a worthy adversary when it saw one. Alex was one hell of a protective mama-bear. But Emmett had tangled with plenty like her in the pack. "It'll help us make the streets safer for all daughters." No, he wasn't above using emotional blackmail to talk his way in.

Alex dropped her arm. "Hmm. Come in—but if you upset Ria, I'll beat you up myself."

"I'm not fragile, Mom." A familiar voice, a familiar scent—soft, fresh, but with a lingering spice to it.

He drew the contradiction of it deep into his lungs, his leopard keeping careful watch as Ria hugged her mother, then took the flowers from Tom. No kiss. *Good.* His claws scratched inside his skin, wanting out, wanting to do damage. Pretty Tom with his slick hair and flawless skin irritated him.

"Emmett." Ria looked to him, all big brown eyes and hair. "We can talk in the living room."

As he nodded, Alex took the roses. "I'll put these in water. Tom can sit with you for moral support."

"On second thought," Ria said, making Alex freeze, "I think I'd rather go out for a walk—I can show Emmett where I was ambushed. Grandmother wants to talk to Tom."

Grinning inwardly at how neatly she'd cut off all options but the one she wanted, Emmett stepped out onto the drive and waited for her to join him. "You've done this before," he said when she came up beside him and they headed off.

"You have to grow a fairly strong personality in my family," she said, a smile flirting with her lips. "It's a survival mechanism." Reaching into the pocket of her coat, she passed over a folded piece of paper. "The account number."

"Thanks." He glanced at her features, frowning at the bruise she'd tried to hide under makeup. "Show me your hands."

She turned them palm-sides-up. "Healing okay."

"The bastard is in a coma," he muttered, cupping her hands so he could inspect the damage. The leopard hated seeing her marked up. So did the man. "You know a Psy we could chat up?"

"Well," she said when he forced himself to let her go, "my mother's accountant is Psy but I don't think Ms. Bhaskar is into interrogations."

"Pity."

"So, last night . . ."

"Can you talk about it?" He paused to look down into her face. "If it's too hard, we can delay it for a few days."

A hint of open irritation flared in her eyes. "What about making the streets safer for all daughters?"

"It's important," he admitted. "This gang, Vincent's Crew,

they're taunting us. If we don't get them out of the city soon, we lose the right to hold it."

"Really?" Lines marked her forehead. "Why?"

"It's about power," he told her. "A predatory changeling pack can only legitimately claim territory it can hold—and that means clearing it of all other predators. The Crew calls our authority into question. Another changeling group could decide that means we have no right to this area."

"And then blood would spill," she said, voice solemn. "The SnowDancer wolves?"

"Dangerous," he told her. "But they're holding a massive amount of territory already. Our intel says they haven't got the manpower to push us out."

"But they're not the only ones are they?" Sliding her hands into the pockets of her vivid red coat, Ria nodded left. "That's the alley where he grabbed me. I was walking home after a night class. My last class actually."

"Why were you alone?" he asked, a slight growl in his voice. "It was after dark."

"It was barely eight." Irritation sparked again—Emmett was starting to show the same overprotective tendencies as her parents. "And I'm an adult in case you haven't noticed."

A slow blink. "Oh, I noticed."

THREE

Heat curled up from her stomach, spread through her limbs, threatened to color her face. "Then don't patronize me." Steeling her spine against the impact, she met those gorgeous eyes of his. "My decision was a solid one. There were a lot of people around, heading out to restaurants or coming home from work. That excuse for a human being took me during a split-second respite in the foot traffic."

"Means he had to have been following you, just waiting for an opportunity." Emmett stared into the dark maw of the alley, his eyes narrowed.

She wondered if he'd even heard her first two sentences. "That's what I thought. I'm always careful when I get off the skytrain, but it's hard to pick up that sort of thing when so many people disembark at the stations." Last night, the mass of humanity had spread out as soon as they hit the ground, but there'd been enough of a crowd going her way that she hadn't really paid attention to anyone in particular.

"Until we neutralize the Crew," Emmett murmured, still staring into the alley, "you don't go anywhere alone."

Her mouth fell open. *"What?"*

"To Death," he said, turning to face her, "that's their motto.

They follow their quarry to death. They'll come after you again and again. It's a matter of 'honor.' " He all but spat on the street. "What the fuck kind of honor is it to hurt a woman?"

The unflinching conviction of his words reached straight through to the warm feminine core of her. But—"I can't sit at home. I have to start interviewing for jobs for one." Work was her ticket to freedom, a freedom she'd worked hard to gain. "And I take my grandmother to her appointments—"

"Who said you have to sit at home?" An intent stare.

Ria didn't react well to any kind of intimidation. "Well, if I can't go anywhere alone—and I'm not going to put my grandmother in danger—then what else am I supposed to do, hire a bodyguard?" The minute, the *second*, her father found out about this, he'd use it as an excuse to stop her from finding a job.

Simon and Alex Wembley loved their only daughter. They loved her so much, they couldn't bear to have the world put a single bruise on her soul. As a result, Ria had grown up being protected and cosseted. If it hadn't been for her grandmother, she might have turned into a spoiled brat. Instead, she'd grown up cherishing her parents' love . . . while understanding the sadness that lay behind its protective fervor. That's why she hadn't gone away to college like Ken—she hadn't been able to put that much worry in their hearts. But she couldn't live in a cocoon forever, not even for her mom and dad. It would never suit her—it would, in fact, destroy her.

However, her parents hadn't yet figured that out. In Simon's and Alex's minds, marriage to Tom would provide the ultimate protection—as a Clark wife, she'd be expected to do nothing more strenuous than look pretty and maybe arrange a few flowers. "Emmett?" she prompted when he remained silent.

"I'll protect you."

Her heart thudded. "How long?"

"As long as it takes."

She almost took a step back at the sheer untamed power of him. "You can't be with me twenty-four/seven. I won't say no to an escort from the skytrain at night, though." She was independent, not stupid.

"The Crew's been known to kidnap people off the street in broad daylight." His skin pulled taut over his cheekbones. "They intimidate any witnesses into silence, so their victims seem to disappear into thin air."

The need for freedom came up against the logic of what he was saying. "What about my family?"

"We've already posted pack soldiers at your mother's store and around your home. The Crew's M.O. is to hit the women in the family, so your mother, sister-in-law, and grandmother are most at risk."

"Amber's over eight months pregnant," Ria began.

"Really?" A teasing smile. "I thought she looked a bit different."

She felt a flush stain her cheekbones. "She hasn't been going out much anyway—if we tell her about the Crew's tactics, she'll probably be okay with staying inside for a bit."

"It would definitely make our job easier. Your mother?"

"No way. She'll go to work—she refuses to surrender to intimidation."

"I can't say that's exactly a surprise." He shook his head. "I'm not even going to ask about your grandmother. Just make sure she knows someone will be shadowing her every time she goes out alone."

"Knowing her, she'll get them to carry her shopping."

Emmett's eyes gleamed. "And you?"

"I'll be ignoring you," she said, feeling an odd sense of excitement in her gut.

No smile, no hint of softening in his face. "You're welcome to try."

Emmett finished fixing the computronics inside his mother's car and picked up his cell phone to call her. "I'll drop it off tomorrow morning. It was a short circuit, nothing big."

"Thanks, baby." His mom was the only one Emmett let get away with calling him "baby." The one time he'd tried to question her about it, she'd simply stared at him until he'd sighed and given in.

"Has Dad gotten in yet?"

"No," she told him, her voice holding a rare kind of clarity. "He's running an extra training session for some of the new soldiers. If things keep going the way they have been, I think there'll come a time when we'll have to take a stand against the Psy—we need to be prepared."

Since his mother was the pack historian, her words carried real weight. "What do you see?"

"I've been tracking the Psy Council's actions since I was a teenager," she told him, "and year by year, I see more and more darkness creep into their world. They're slowly going beyond cold, to a place that makes me scared for the Psy race as a whole."

Emmett felt no pity for the Psy—not given what he'd seen of their tactics, but his mother had always had a soft heart. "Lucas is obviously listening to you—I'm scheduled to teach more sessions as well." Somewhat to his surprise, he'd inherited his father's way with the younger members of the pack.

His mother chuckled. "I hear he gave you the ten- to fourteen-year-old crowd."

"They teach me patience." It was a deadpan comment.

"Oh, Emmett." Another laugh. "Why are you single? You're gorgeous, good with children, and you adore your mother."

Grinning, he fixed the timecode on the dashboard computer. "Not that you're biased."

"I get to be biased about my baby."

"There is someone," he found himself saying, "but she's being stubborn."

"I like her already."

Ria did try to ignore Emmett as she'd vowed. But ignoring six feet and a few spare inches of predatory changeling, especially one as quietly dangerous as Emmett, was not an easy task. She could feel his eyes on her even while he stood outside as she walked into a shop with her grandmother.

"Tea will take some time." Miaoling patted her arm. "Go and talk to that leopard who looks at you like you're food."

Heat rushed into her cheeks. "He does not." Though *she'd* found herself fighting the insane urge to stroke him . . . just to see what he'd do. Would he let her? The thought caused her stomach muscles to clench.

Miaoling made a face at Ria's response.

Ria kept talking, knowing she was protesting too much. "He's only protecting us because the Crew poses a threat to DarkRiver's control of the city."

"Pah!" Miaoling waved a hand. "I know when a man's hungry. And if you'd use your woman parts more often, you'd know, too!"

Thankfully, Mr. Wong appeared at that instant, eager to lead Miaoling upstairs to his apartment for their weekly tea-conference, as they called it. The two were as thick as thieves. Ria had no idea what they discussed at these conferences, but her grandmother always had a Cheshire cat smile on her face when she left Mr. Wong's.

At first, Ria had thought the two were . . . well . . . but her grandmother had put her straight with an unexpectedly solemn response.

"No, Ri-ri. I've loved only one man my whole life. I love the same man still."

The depth of devotion in that single sentence had brought tears to Ria's eyes. Her grandfather had been twenty years her grandmother's senior, and had taken his last breath when Ria was fifteen. His death had devastated Miaoling, but she hadn't ever broken down where Ria could see her. Instead, she'd used the memory of her love as a shield.

Miaoling still spoke to her husband as if he could hear her. Though she never did it when pragmatic Alex was nearby, she was open with it in front of Ria. Because Ria understood. Truly, when she was with her grandmother, she sometimes thought her grandfather was in the room with them, watching over the wife who, he'd often complained, had always made him wait.

Going to be slow coming up to heaven, too, aren't you, my darling?

Words her grandfather had said on his deathbed, his hand wrapped around his wife's. Miaoling had smiled and kissed him, teasing him to the last. Now, as Ria watched Miaoling ascend to the second floor of the shop, she felt her heart contract. "Grandmother?"

"Yes?" Miaoling looked over her shoulder, her eyes warm, full of silent encouragement.

"How long will you be?"

"Perhaps three hours. We're having lunch today as well."

"Then maybe I will go for a stroll."

Her grandmother smiled and continued on her way.

Heading out of Mr. Wong's, Ria found Emmett standing to her left, scanning the street. "Have you got someone who can stay here with my grandmother?" she asked.

"She's already inside," Emmett said. "Mr. Wong's planning to tell your grandmother she's his new assistant."

"The beautiful brunette minding the shop?" Her eyes widened. "She doesn't look dangerous enough to swat a fly."

"Not only can she swat flies, she can kill most men with a single blow."

Ria felt a sudden sense of inadequacy. "I wish I could do that."

"If you're serious," he said, looking her up and down in a way that was distinctly professional, "I can teach you enough self-defense that you won't ever feel helpless again. You're fit and you move well. You should pick it up quick."

Startled, she stared. "You'd do that?" A few tentative tendrils of hope wrapped around her heart—she'd begun to believe that Emmett was as suffocatingly protective as her father, but this argued differently.

"How much time do we have now?"

"Three hours."

He straightened away from the wall. "We can practice in a small basement gym members of the pack use when they can't get out of the city for a good hard run. You'll need workout gear."

Ria thought about it. "I'll buy some. There's a shop two blocks over." That way, none of her family would even know about the training. Not that their objections would've stopped her—but she didn't have time to have the argument.

Emmett slid his hand along Ria's arm, positioning her as she needed to be, and asked himself—for the hundredth time—why he was torturing himself like this. Even in the loose sweats and T-shirt she'd changed into, the woman who currently stood with her back to his chest set his body on fire. But the little mink didn't seem inclined to play—she'd been all business since the moment they got to the gym. The leopard wasn't pleased. Neither was the man. But no way was he going to push himself on Ria and make her uncomfortable. Not after what that bloody waste of space from the Crew had done to her.

"There." He released her. "Perfect. Now kick."

Ria brought up her leg in a forceful, fast kick. It wasn't graceful or poetic. It was hard, rough, dirty. Emmett didn't care about pretty. He cared about making sure she could protect herself. "I want you to practice for ten minutes while I go make a few calls."

Giving him a nod, Ria began to go through the beginner routine he'd devised. She was a fast learner, but as a human, her strength was much less than a changeling's. Added to that, she was small and female—so the next time they worked out, he planned to teach her to fight using anything at her disposal, as she'd used her handbag two nights ago. That is, unless she had the option to turn and run. A physical fight would never be the smart first choice for her.

Walking a short distance from where she moved that sweet little body with such focused determination, he brought out his phone and coded in a call to his alpha, Lucas. "Were you able to track the source of the hang-ups to Amber's cell phone?" Ria had told him about the calls this morning.

"Disposable." Lucas's anger was clear. "But we got another one of the bastards. He made the bad decision to try to shake down a couple while Clay was running patrol."

Emmett's leopard smiled, its teeth razor sharp. "Is he dead?" Clay didn't see the point in keeping vermin alive.

"Clay thought we might want to question him, so he only broke a few ribs. Man's refusing to talk, but I've had Clay prowling around him in leopard form—he'll break when those teeth get too close."

"What's your gut say—small fry or big gun?"

"Very small fry. He's not likely to know anything

important." A sigh of frustration. "Keep on the girl. They'll do anything to get to her, because the longer she remains alive, the more traction Vincent loses."

Emmett traced Ria's form with his gaze as she went through her routine. The curve of her butt was the perfect shape to fit into his hands. "I'm not letting her out of my sight."

FOUR

Having done two reps of the routine Emmett had shown her, Ria turned to see him walking back to her.

The savage edge in his eyes raised every hair on her body.

The man looked *hungry.* No one had ever looked at Ria like that. It was almost terrifying. But she stood in place, waiting, wondering.

"Ready for the next step?" His voice was deep, holding the beginnings of what sounded like a growl . . . a leopard barely contained.

She swallowed. "Sure."

He padded to a spot opposite her, still dressed in the jeans and T-shirt he'd been wearing earlier. It was obvious why he hadn't bothered to change—he hadn't so much as broken a sweat with what they'd done so far, while her muscles were starting to protest. Now, he crooked a finger. "Come on, mink, use what I just taught you."

She was so startled by what he'd called her that she completely lost her focus. He was in her face an instant later. "What the hell was that?" he growled. "If you blank out in a fight, you're dead."

"You called me a mink!" She refused to back off.

"Did I?" Moving at inhuman speed, he closed a hand around her throat before she knew what was happening. "Let's make sure you're not a dead mink."

Eyes narrowed, she reached up and tried to break his nose using the flat of her hand. He caught it using his free hand. Her knee was already aiming for his crotch, and when he blocked that, she leaned forward and sunk her teeth hard into his forearm.

"Fuck!" The hand around her neck remained in place, but he released her other hand. She immediately went for his eyes and his crotch again. Her knee brushed against something very hard, before he twisted away and swore. She kept going, kicking, trying to scratch, even attempting to break the pinkie of the hand he had around her throat.

He finally let go. "Truce."

Her heart was in her throat, exhilaration in her bloodstream. She knew he'd been playing with her—with his strength and training, he could've had her on the ground in one second flat. "How did I do?"

He glanced at his forearm. "I didn't teach you the biting." It was a snarl.

Or maybe he hadn't been playing the whole time. "I decided to add it on my own," she said, though in truth, it had been an instinctive response to his arrogant provocation. Her eyes went to the marks she'd made. Deep and red and perfectly formed. Guilt invaded. "I didn't mean to bite you that hard. But . . . I'm not sorry."

"Oh?" He walked over, slow, so slow. This time, she backed up. It was one thing to play with a predator who was keeping his claws sheathed, quite another to know you were prey. He kept coming. She knew the door out of the basement was only about a foot away. Making a quick move, she went to dart left.

Too late.

He was there before her and somehow, she found herself pasted up against the closed door, very aware she was all alone with a big, dangerous leopard in human skin. Except instead of fear, it was a vivid excitement that beat in her blood as he placed his hands palms-down on either side of her head and bent until their breaths mingled. "Boo."

She jumped, then wanted to slap herself for it. "Stop acting like the big bad cat."

A blink, and when he raised his lashes, the eyes that looked back at her were in no way human. "Mmm, I smell a pretty little human in my territory." A soft whisper against her lips, bright green-gold eyes daring her to respond.

Her breasts brushed his chest as he pressed closer, her breath coming in jagged pants. "You're behaving very badly." It was a husky reproach.

"You bit me." He angled his head a little to the left, and though she couldn't see those amazing eyes except for a glint through his lashes, she knew he was looking at her lips. "Say sorry."

She didn't know what made her do it. Parting her lips, she said, "No."

His mouth was on hers before the syllable ended. She found herself being kissed as she'd never been kissed in her life. He took over her mouth, slicked his tongue in, and tasted her like she was the finest candy and he was starving. Against her, his body was a hot, hard, impregnable wall. Her hands were somehow under his T-shirt and on his back, touching skin that burned with a wild fever that made her moan in the back of her throat.

A sound akin to a growl rolled up from his chest and into her mouth. Before she could process it, his hands were at her waist and he was lifting her up against the door. Wrapping her legs around him, she gave herself up to the possessive demand of his kiss. It fed fire through her body, a hot, pulsing storm. Then one of those big hands stroked down her back to squeeze her bottom.

She gasped, breaking the kiss.

He followed, taking her mouth again before she could do more than suck in a breath. *Oh, Lord.* He was stroking her butt, cupping and petting even as he devoured her mouth. It was wild, raw, primal. The heat in her stomach was matched only by the dampness between her thighs. Part of her was scandalized at her response, but that part was drowned out by the wild thunder of her pulse as pleasure sizzled through her veins, pure liquid flame.

Emmett broke the kiss just as her head was starting to spin. An instant later, she felt those delicious male lips along her jaw, down her throat. And that hand on her bottom . . . she swallowed, tried to think, lost the thread when Emmett shifted his hold so that his fingers brushed the heat between her legs. She cried out. "Stop."

A fluttering stroke that arced electricity right through her. "Please tell me you don't mean that." His stubble brushed her throat as he leaned in to nibble at her ear. "Come on, mink. Just a little more."

God, the man was a devil. And he smelled so good. A faint hint of sweat, the luscious warmth of male body heat, and the unique scent that was Emmett. She found she was kissing his jaw, fascinated by the contrast between the stubble and his skin. "Random sex isn't my style."

"Who said anything about random?" Another teasing brush, another rush of exquisite pleasure. "I plan to have sex with you on a regular basis."

The arrogance of the comment should have snapped her out of it. Instead, her mind bombarded her with images of naked limbs intertwined, a heavy male thigh pushing between her own. He'd be no gentle, easy lover. He'd demand and he'd take. He might even bite. "That's assuming an awful lot," she somehow found the willpower to say.

A press of his fingers this time, not a brush. She sucked in a breath, her eyes closing as she waited for it to pass. But he didn't stop. Instead, he lifted her until she was positioned just right . . . and began to rub himself against her in slow, grinding circles. She almost screamed. And then his fingers were on her again and she did scream.

Emmett caught Ria's scream with his mouth as he continued to tease her with his body—torturing himself in the process. But the scent of her damp heat, it was pure ambrosia. He wanted to sit her down—no, *lay* her down—on a sprawling playground of a bed, spread her thighs wide and taste. His cock pulsed, the leopard's hunger threatening to overwhelm the man's control.

Fighting the urge to tear off her sweats, he concentrated on driving her over the edge of pleasure. He hadn't needed her to tell him—he'd known instinctively that Ria wasn't a woman who took sex casually. He'd have to coax her into his bed. Taking her against the scarred door of a basement gym was hardly going to reassure her that her pleasure mattered to him. Mattered enough that when her body tightened, he grit his teeth and stroked her through the orgasm.

Her fingernails dug into his shoulders through his T-shirt—he wished like hell he'd taken the damn thing off. He wanted those marks on his skin, wanted to know she'd put them there. *Next time*, he promised the cat. *Next time*. "Beautiful," he murmured, nuzzling at her neck as she shuddered against him, her body going limp. "Pretty and soft and beautiful." *And mine.* The leopard bared its teeth at the thought, even as the man bit back a rawly possessive smile.

Finally shifting his hold from the gorgeous curve of her butt, he ran his hands up her sides as he kissed and petted her through the aftershocks of pleasure. Her eyes were still a little unfocused when she said, "Put me down." It was an order.

The leopard snarled, but he did as asked. She pressed her hands flat against the door and looked up at him. "You're . . ." Color streaked across her cheekbones.

He gave her a smile that he knew held a distinctly savage edge. "I'm thinking I want lots and lots of time when I slide into you."

"Are all cats as arrogant as you?"

He shrugged and leaned in close. "I'm the only cat you need to be thinking about."

Ria couldn't *not* think about Emmett. That night, as she sat across from her parents at the dinner table, she kept finding herself drifting off in the middle of conversations. Emmett's scent seemed to have become locked in her brain. She was fantasizing about burying her face in his neck, his strong body hard and taut against hers when Alex's voice penetrated.

"Ria!"

Jumping, Ria met her mother's eyes, hoping the guilt didn't show. "Sorry, what did you say?"

"Tom's popping by for coffee tonight. Why don't you change into a dress?"

Ria's fingers turned to iron around her chopsticks. Enough, she thought. And strangely, it had nothing to do with Emmett. Perhaps he'd pushed her to this point faster, but she'd always been walking toward it. "Mom," she said, putting down the abused chopsticks, "I have no interest whatsoever in Tom."

Utter silence.

Simon was the one to break it. "What's gotten into you, Ria? You and Tom grew up together—he knows you. He'll make a good husband." The tone of his voice said the matter was settled.

Ria looked into her father's face. "I love you, Dad, but not even for you will I marry a man who thinks I should be patted on the head once in a while and put in the corner like a good little girl the rest of the time."

White lines bracketed Simon's mouth. "That boy's only ever treated you with respect."

"He treats me like a dimwit," Ria said, skin blazing with temper. "Last week, he told me I wouldn't have to worry about finances when we were married, that he knows math confuses females."

Alex made a choked little sound that succeeded in ripping Ria's attention from her father's disapproving face. Alex's expression was a mix of outrage and disbelief. "He did not say that. You're making it up."

"Popo?" Ria turned to her right.

Miaoling ate a fried shrimp and nodded. "He said it. Then he smiled as if expecting praise."

Alex's hands clenched on the tablecloth. "And who does he think does the books for the shop, huh?"

"Alex." Simon closed his hand over his wife's. "We're getting off topic."

Taking a deep breath, Alex nodded. "You're right. Sweetheart, Tom is a very good match for you. You never had a problem with him before you met that disreputable leopard."

Ria supposed Emmett was disreputable—that stubble, those hands that had squeezed and petted, those eyes that told her he wanted to do all kinds of wicked things to her. But . . . "He's an honorable man." That core of honor was so much a part of him, she wondered if he was even aware of it. It was why it had been so easy for her to lose control in the gym today—she'd trusted Emmett to take care of her. And that, she thought, was a dangerous thing . . . the kind that could lead to a broken heart if she wasn't careful. "He's protecting our family."

"Exactly," Jet said, jumping into the conversation. "Maybe he's making time with you while he does this duty, but he won't marry you, Ria. Those cats stick together."

Ria's stomach twisted, because she knew her brother was right. "This isn't about Emmett. It's about me. I will, under no circumstances, marry Tom."

"Why not?" Alex asked, eyes flashing. "He's intelligent, handsome, has a good job, and brings you flowers."

Frustrated, Ria threw down her napkin and rose to her feet. "If he's that great, *you* marry him. I will *not* marry a man who hasn't even attempted to French-kiss me the entire year we've been 'dating.' "

Her parents yelled her name, but Jet's incredulous voice drowned them out. "Seriously? Not even a little tongue? You're right—dude is lame."

"JET!" It was Alex. She flew into a rapid stream of Mandarin.

Miaoling looked up at Ria and winked. "Sit. Eat."

And oddly enough, Ria did. The family fought through the entire meal, but now her parents were mad at Jet because he figured Tom had to be gay.

Alex glared at her son. "Maybe he's just being respectful of your sister."

"No effing way." A skeptical snort. "Men aren't that noble when it comes to women they want." Jet turned to his wife, his voice dropping. "When I saw Amber, all I wanted to do was—"

"You finish that sentence," Alex threatened, "and you'll be breathing fire I'll put so much chili in your food."

Amber grinned and blew Jet a kiss. "You know, it sounds to me like Tom's planning to marry Ria and get himself a nice, respectable wife, while having a bit on the side."

Simon's mouth fell open at this scandalous contribution from his flawlessly elegant daughter-in-law.

Miaoling ate another shrimp. "She's right. Like father, like son."

Silence. Deeper. More shocked.

FIVE

Simon cleared his throat. "Mother," he said, his tone that of a man who knows he's done for, "is that true?"

"You think I'm lying?"

"I think you'd do anything for your favorite granddaughter."

Leaning back, Miaoling actually cackled. "This time, I don't have to. Wait." She got up and headed toward her room.

Ria shrugged when all eyes turned to her. "Don't look at me."

"Eat some tofu," Alex said when they just sat there. "It'll go bad if we don't finish it tonight."

Everyone ate. But the instant Miaoling walked back into the room, all implements were abandoned, food forgotten. Wearing the same smile she always displayed when she came out of Mr. Wong's, Miaoling sat down and opened an envelope. Ria's eyes went wide when she saw the photograph in her grandmother's hand—Tom's father with his tongue down the throat of the woman everyone knew as his secretary. "Oh, my, God."

"Don't show me," Alex said, slapping her hands over her eyes. "I can't bear it. Essie's one of my best friends!"

Miaoling waved off the objection. "She knows. Doesn't

care—it keeps Tom Sr. from interrupting her hobbies. She's making lanterns this year."

"*Popo*," Ria said, choking, "how did you—"

"What do you think Mr. Wong and I talk about?" She turned her gaze to Ria's parents. "Want to know about the apartment Tom bought his mistress?"

Alex looked like she was about to keel over. "Mistress?" It was a thin sound.

A sense of fair play induced Ria to attempt to defend Tom. After all, she was now involved with Emmett. "Grandmother, no one has mistresses anymore. Tom was probably just waiting for the right time to tell me he'd fallen for someone else." Yes, he should've been man enough to stop the charade of their non-engagement soon as he met his girlfriend, but Ria wasn't going to beat him up about that. Chances were, he'd needed time to work up the strength to stand firm against familial pressure.

"I talked to her."

Jet whooped at Miaoling's words, while Amber shushed him and said, "How, Nana?"

"I'm a weak old lady, always need so much help." Miaoling's eyes gleamed. "Nice girl, too nice for Tom. She's so sad for him because he has to marry some plain, fat girl—"

"That snake!" Alex's hand clenched on a sharp knife as Ria's sympathy for Tom died a quick and permanent death.

"—but nothing's going to change between them after the wedding. Tom's set it all up so he can visit her on his way home every night. He's even promised to take her to Paris after he explains how things are to his wife."

Simon looked at Ria, a tic in his jaw. "If you even think about marrying Tom, I'll hogtie you and send you to live with my parents in Idaho."

"Yes, Dad." Grinning, Ria walked around to hug her parents. But she waited until she was alone with her grandmother to ask, "Was that in case I didn't get up the guts to pull myself out?"

"No, it was just backup." Miaoling's wrinkled hand was a touch of love against her cheek. "I always knew you'd find your voice. Don't ever let anyone take it away from you."

* * *

Pleased and frustrated in equal measures by his earlier encounter with Ria, Emmett forced himself to focus as he ran his early-evening class through some hand-to-hand combat moves. There were only four in this group—he preferred to spend more one-on-one time with the older, higher-level students.

"Jazz," he said, when the sole girl in the group smiled slowly at one of the boys before blowing him a flirtatious kiss—the poor kid lost his rhythm completely.

Emmett's cat found her little tricks amusing, but he put on a stern face, knowing if he didn't, she'd keep on doing exactly as she wanted. Female leopards were a handful—throw teenage hormones into the mix, and no wonder half the pack had sent him sympathy cards when Lucas put him in charge of this lot. The other half had offered to take him drinking.

"Yes, sir?" An innocent look.

"Unless you plan to beat your opponents with nothing but a smile and a hip wiggle," he said, "I suggest you work on your hand to eye coordination. It's off."

"It is not." Her back went ramrod straight. "I can move smoother than anyone else in this class."

He met her militant gaze. "Ten laps. *Now.*"

Swallowing at his unusually harsh tone, the ebony-skinned girl took off to do the required laps. Emmett turned back to the three boys who remained. "Gentlemen, you have something to say?"

One of them, a slender kid named Aaron, stepped forward. "She's right—she is better than all of us at the hand to eye stuff."

"Not today—she's too busy playing head games." Sending them back to their training, he waited for Jazz to return.

"Grab a drink and a seat," he said when she did, red-faced from having done the laps at full changeling speed as required. After making sure the boys had enough to carry on with, he walked over to hunker down in front of her. "Why do you think I made you do that?"

A shrug. "I was mouthing off."

"Yeah." And because he knew something of young female pride, he reached out to tug on one of her braids. "You *are* top of the class."

A small smile peeked out.

"But, kitten," he said, meeting her gaze, "that won't get you far if you can't hold your temper. You can still be Jazz, still be a smart-ass, too, if you want"—that got him another small smile—"but you need to learn to work within a hierarchy." Because that was how changeling packs stayed strong, though they were often far fewer in number than either of the two other races. And if his mother was correct in her predictions, that internal strength would become even more important in the years to come. These kids were all highly independent predatory changelings—his job was to start teaching them to work as a unit.

"I think I understand," Jazz said after a thoughtful pause. "It's how the sentinels and soldiers work to protect the alpha—they know they can always rely on each other."

"Exactly." Rising, he tugged her to her feet, "Go on, finish your training routine, and then we'll do some one-on-one combat."

A sharp grin. "I'm going to kick the boys' butts tonight."

Chuckling as he watched her slide easily into the graceful rhythm of combat, he wondered what Ria would think of the measures DarkRiver was taking to protect its future. Would she understand, or would she be repelled by the threat of violence, by the aggressiveness that was an inherent part of a predatory changeling's nature? Not that he had any intention of discussing those things with her—not as long as he could avoid it. She'd clearly been brought up in a sheltered environment—why ask her to worry about things she didn't have to? Protection was his job. His plans for Ria Wembley were all about pleasure . . . of the most decadent, delicious kind.

His entire body thrummed in anticipation.

Ria stayed home for two days after the explosive events in the gym, seeing Emmett only to say hi.

He scowled at her when she looked out the window on the

second day. She had a good feeling she knew what he was thinking—that she was running scared after coming apart in his arms—but tempting as it was to head out and put him straight, she stayed in.

Of course, that temptation wasn't the sole one where Emmett was concerned—her body wasn't letting her get much sleep. Now that it had had a taste of real pleasure, it wanted more. The sleepless nights left her frustrated in more ways than one, and she intended to punish the damn cat for it.

But first, she had to do something.

On the third day after he'd crushed her up against the basement door and kissed her senseless, she walked out dressed in a deep peach skirt suit teamed with a white silk shell. Emmett looked her up and down, then did it again . . . slow. Her cheeks felt like they matched her suit by the time he finished.

"I like it." A slow, feline purr.

She thrust a list at him. "Interview locations."

He raised an eyebrow as he scanned the list, but all he said was, "Hold on. I'll get cover for your home then we can go."

"Still no luck with tracking Vincent down?"

Sliding the phone into his pocket after rearranging his people, he shook his head. "Creep's laying low. He thinks we'll give up."

That, she knew, was simply not a possibility. "You haven't been sitting still." He'd only swung by her house in the mornings and at night. The other times, they'd had a rotation of both male and female DarkRiver soldiers.

"We have a bead on his base of operations." A smile that was openly feral. "We'll get him."

She nodded, but had the distinct feeling he wasn't telling her everything. *And why should he*, part of her pointed out. She was just someone he was protecting. Maybe he lusted after her, too, but Jet was right, the cats stuck together. She didn't know any DarkRiver people who'd entered into long-term relationships with humans—sexual, business, or otherwise. "Emmett," she began, intending to ask that question, then realizing he might see it as expectation.

"Yeah?"

"Nothing." She shook her head. "I think the first appointment is about a ten-minute walk away."

For a second, it looked like Emmett was going to pursue her aborted statement, but to her relief, he followed her lead and they headed off—with Ria sandwiched between the safety of the shop walls and Emmett's big frame. His constant alertness made her feel safe on the innermost level.

"What kinds of jobs are you applying for?" he asked a block from the first location on her list.

"Administrative," she said, then made a face. "I'd really love to run my own office—you know, be in charge of all the organizing for the boss, but that's going to be far in the future. First, I need experience—so I'll end up someone's lackey."

Emmett laughed at her tone. "I don't think you'll be a lackey for long."

"No, I won't," she said, and took several deep breaths. "Right, here it is. Wish me luck."

"I'll wish you luck inside." He pulled open the outer door.

"Emmett, I can't go into an interview with a bodyguard."

His eyes turned flint-hard. "Vincent knew when you'd be coming home from your course. Chances are high that he's worked out you'd now be applying for jobs."

She grit her teeth. "This is an established firm. I hardly think I'm going to be in danger from the sixty-year-old manager."

"You're not going behind a closed door with anyone."

Ria argued until she was close to the screaming point but he wouldn't budge. Predictably, her interviews didn't go well. The first manager was so affronted at the idea of being considered a threat that he booted her out without an interview. The next two were female and couldn't stop staring at Emmett long enough to listen to Ria. When one finally did throw her a crumb of attention, it was to give her a condescending smile and say that maybe she wasn't cut out for office work.

A babysitter didn't exactly inspire confidence.

Ria was close to tears by the fourth interview, but not from anxiety. From sheer rage. "Thank you for destroying my chances of employment," she said as they got off the skytrain near Chinatown, having circled the city for her appointments.

"Ria," he began.

She slapped up a hand, palm out. "I *am* cut out for office work. I do my mother's books. Not only that, I do the entire family's books. I make sure my father goes to his appointments and Amber sees the obstetrician on time, that Grandmother takes her medications and Jet doesn't forget to write New Year cards to our aunts in Albuquerque. I am *damn well* cut out for office work!"

"I never said you weren't."

The soothing tone in his voice made Ria want to bite him. "No, you simply stood there like I couldn't be counted on to take care of myself if someone tried to hurt me. That day, at the gym, it was all bullshit!"

His scowl was thunderous. "Take that back."

"I'm not talking about *that*, you idiot. I'm talking about the self-defense stuff. It was just to pacify me. You don't even trust me to scream." That had been the first lesson he'd taught her—scream as loud as you can and run. "You know what, I think that makes the other stuff bullshit, too."

"Hold on a fucking minute."

SIX

Ignoring him, she walked through the automatic doors of the medium-sized office building that was the location of her next appointment and strode up to the counter. "Hi," she said to the well-groomed woman on the other side, her skin a lush, flawless mahogany. "I have an appointment with Lucas Hunter."

The woman's eyes flicked behind Ria's shoulder, and something like surprise passed through them, but her voice, when she turned to Ria, was wholly professional. "Name?"

"Ria Wembley."

A warm smile. "You're fifteen minutes early, Ms. Wembley. If you'll wait here, I'll let you know when Lucas has finished with the current applicant."

"Thanks." She was walking toward the seating area when she belatedly realized she didn't know the name of this company. The ad had simply said that a small but growing construction firm was seeking administrative staff. Since that ad had been vetted by the college where she'd taken her course, she hadn't worried too much about the lack. But her ignorance probably wouldn't look too good . . . if this Hunter person even bothered to see her after learning about Emmett.

Turning on her heel, she skirted around Emmett to speak

to the receptionist again. "I'm sorry. I noticed that your doors don't have the company name on them."

The woman's gaze flicked to Emmett again. Ria fumed. But the beautiful brunette didn't seem to be checking him out. "Actually," she said after a small pause, "the name's still in discussions . . . er, the partners haven't decided on the order."

"Oh." That was odd, but not odd enough to make her run. Beggars, as they said, couldn't be choosers. Nodding, she walked to the comfortable arrangement of armchairs to the left of the reception counter, choosing a seat bathed in sunshine.

Emmett sprawled beside her. "What we shared was not bullshit. And I didn't know you even knew how to swear."

The joke just irritated her. "If you can lie about one thing, why not another?"

"Now, hold on. I never lied to you."

"Oh yeah? What do you call teaching me self-defense, then treating me like a brainless ninny?"

"Excuse me."

Ria jerked up at the sound of the receptionist's voice.

"Lucas is free now," she was told. "The interviews are taking place one floor up."

As she got up and headed across the lobby to the elevators, someone called out a hello. Since she didn't know the male heading out the front door, she assumed it had been aimed at Emmett. "Friend?" She stabbed the touchpad beside the elevator.

He wouldn't meet her eyes. "Yeah."

The elevator doors opened to reveal an empty cage and she could've sworn she heard Emmett sigh in relief. "Fear of crowded elevators?"

"Something like that."

They were on the next floor what felt like an instant later. The meeting room was obvious by its open door. The man who came to that door was beyond handsome—bright green eyes, dark hair that brushed his shoulders and savage clawlike markings on the right side of his face. He was young . . . yet not. Experience flickered in that striking green gaze, and Ria knew he'd sized her up in a single fleeting instant.

"Ria"—he held out a hand—"I'm Lucas. Come on in."

She shook and went to explain Emmett . . . except that her

self-appointed bodyguard had already grabbed a seat in the plush armchair outside the meeting room. Her mouth hung open for a second before she snapped it shut. What in the . . . ? This Lucas, with his aura of contained power, was undoubtedly far more dangerous than anyone else she'd met today and Emmett was okay with her being alone with him?

Deciding not to look a gift horse in the mouth, she walked in, aware of Lucas closing the door behind her as she took a seat on one side of a small table. There was something about his walk when he came to take his own seat . . . he reminded her of someone.

"Water?" At her nod, he poured her a glass and pushed it across. "I've read your resume. You've just completed studies in advanced office administration?"

She took a sip before answering. "Yes, at the top of my class. I've also had some on-the-job experience through the course."

Lucas nodded. "I have no doubt your technical skills are excellent. We checked with the college and with the people you put down as references."

The efficiency of it surprised and pleased her. "Your ad said you were seeking a number of staff," she said, finding herself relaxing in spite of her vivid awareness of his power. The woman who took on Lucas Hunter, she thought, would have her work cut out for her. "Could you give me more information about the positions—I could perhaps tell you which I might be best suited for."

"Actually, you're on the short list for a particular position already. That's what I want to discuss—it's in no way a normal administrative job."

Ria was intrigued. "No?"

"No." A smile that turned him from gorgeous to beautiful in a very masculine way. She appreciated the sight, but without wanting to jump his bones. Not like with Emmett. And that thought had no business interrupting her interview. Corralling her runaway hormones, she turned her attention firmly back to Lucas.

"How are you with chaos?" he asked.

"I love it." Her response was instinctive. "It gives me more to organize."

Lucas laughed. "What about constant interruptions, having to rejig meetings on a moment's notice, and a boss who might be impossible to track down at times?"

"If it needs to be done, it'll get done," she said, meeting those brilliant green eyes. "But I'll be honest—even though I probably shouldn't be. I'm likely to get a little short-tempered now and then."

"A temper might come in handy in this position." His lips tilted up at the corners. "This is a . . . family business. And that family will be in and out. Can you handle being the focus of their curiosity?"

It was a strange question, but her answer was easy. "Let's see—every Sunday without fail, my aunt Eadie calls to interrogate me about my life and offer 'essential fashion advice.' My paternal grandparents live in Idaho, but last week, they sent me a dossier on all the nice boys in town—just in case. Oh, and my normally very forward-thinking parents recently tried to arrange my marriage. I know how to handle family."

His eyes danced. "And the arranged marriage?"

Since she'd brought it up, she couldn't exactly avoid the personal question. "Not happening."

"That's what I thought." He rose to his feet, an amused curve to his mouth. "I think that's all I need from you, Ria."

Standing, she picked up her purse. "It's you, isn't it? The person I'd be working for if I get the job?"

A slight nod.

"Usually HR interviews applicants."

"I'm picky." He pulled open the door. "I need to trust the person I hire."

Smiling even as her stomach dropped, she stepped out. Emmett was up and waiting for her. They entered the elevator in silence and walked out into the street.

"How'd it go?" Emmett asked.

"Good."

He rubbed the back of his neck. "Still mad?"

"You think I should give you credit for letting me go in there alone?" She raised an eyebrow, wondering what he'd do.

"Er." His cheeks flushed. "Never mind."

She felt her lips twitch. "I know he was a cat, Emmett. The

way you leopards walk, it's a dead giveaway." They prowled, all soft and silent and lethal.

"Shit." He grinned. "I was hoping to score brownie points."

"So it's DarkRiver Construction?"

"Part of it. The building will also function as the pack's city headquarters—we outgrew the old premises."

All of which, Ria knew, meant she'd never get the job. Changeling packs looked after their own, sticking together like glue. Sure they'd helped clean up the city, making it safer for everyone, but as Emmett had explained, that had more to do with holding territory than anything else.

Tired, dispirited, and hungry, she walked into a neighborhood restaurant run by a family she'd seen at community functions, and grabbed a seat. Emmett took the chair opposite hers.

"You order," he said, scanning the room.

She was telling the waitress—who also happened to be the owner's daughter—that she wanted cashew chicken, when Emmett *moved* across the table to smash her and the waitress both to the ground. A split second later, she heard a loud pop followed by a scream. Emmett was already up and speaking on his cell. "He's heading out, past the candy shop—" He ran toward the door.

Getting up, Ria helped the shaken waitress to her feet. Emmett was back before she'd finished. "You hurt?" His hands swept over her body.

Aware of several interested glances, she slapped them off. "I'm fine." She turned to check on the waitress and got the same answer in response. "What happened?" she asked Emmett.

He pointed behind her. A large hole marred the previously pristine wall. "Bullet." His jaw was a brutal line, his eyes . . . his *eyes*.

Stepping instinctively closer, she put her hand on his chest. "Emmett."

He glanced down, those incredible green-gold eyes, *leopard* eyes, looking out at her from a human face. His hand cupped her cheek. "You have a scratch here." A thumb stroking gently over a hurt she didn't even feel, his gaze predator-cold.

She didn't know how she knew what to do. She just did. Instead of fighting off his hold as she had earlier, she leaned into him, slipping her arms around his waist. His own came around her at almost the same instant, and he squeezed her close, until she could barely breathe. But she held on, held tight.

She didn't know how long they stood wrapped around each other, but when he did finally release her, the fear in the restaurant had turned to speculation. Likely, her grandmother and mother would be hearing all about it in the time it took to type a text message. She didn't care. Because the leopard was gone from Emmett's eyes, his rage under control.

He tapped her cheek. "Grab your purse. This place needs to be looked at by our techs, and I want you safe at home."

Realizing he wanted to start tracking the shooter as soon as possible, Ria didn't argue. Emmett's eyes were hyperalert as they began to head out of the restaurant, his big body vibrating with protectiveness.

"Please!"

Startled, she looked over her shoulder. It was the waitress Emmett had taken down—the woman ran over, a bag of takeout containers in hand. Her smile was a little wary as it flicked to Emmett, but her gratitude clear. "Thank you." She shook her head when Emmett, the majority of his attention clearly on ensuring no more nasty surprises, went to grab his wallet. "It's a gift. My father was in the army. He says that bullet would've hit me first." She pressed the bag into Ria's hands. "Please take this."

Ria accepted it, understanding the family's need to give something back to the man who'd saved their child's life. "Thank you."

The woman smiled and looked up at Emmett. "You're welcome at our table at any time."

Emmett gave a short nod. Ria wondered if he understood the value of the invitation. She could've let it go, but that wasn't who she was—she asked him about it as they walked home at a rapid clip.

"I know," he said, his voice tense as he scanned the area. "We've been working on building relationships with the folks around here, but it's been a slow process. You're very insular."

"Talk about the big, fat charcoaled pot calling the kettle black."

An unworried shrug, no smile. "Didn't say we didn't understand."

"People like DarkRiver cats," she said, wondering why that damn arrogance was sexy on him. "You've cleaned things up so the shopkeepers feel safe."

"We're starting to get friendlier smiles," he told her, "but that's all going to be fucked to hell if Vincent and his gang of thugs start shooting holes in defenseless people."

"I have a feeling they don't know what they're up against."

A hard glance. "You got that right, mink."

She opened her mouth to respond but they'd arrived at her family home and Amber was waiting in the doorway, cell phone in hand. "She's home!" her sister-in-law said into the slim white device as soon as she spotted Ria. "No, she's safe. Emmett's with her."

All but lifting Ria inside, Emmett ordered Amber to shut the door. "And stay inside." He was gone before Ria could say anything else.

Blowing out a breath, she took the phone Amber was holding out. "Mom, I'm fine." She repeated that for the next ten minutes, until Alex finally calmed down. By that time, her grandmother had prepared tea, brought out two giant hunks of Mr. Wong's famous Divine Madeira Cake, and begun to make her special sweet black-sesame soup, one of Ria's favorites.

"Sit!" she said when Amber began to stand up as if to help.

Amber sat with a thankful groan. "The baby's kicking so hard. Want to feel?"

"Yes!" Ria scooted over. Amber was a great sister-in-law, but she was also intensely private. This kind of an invitation didn't come often. Placing her hand on Amber's abdomen, she stayed very still. Miaoling's future great-grand(gender unknown) didn't keep Ria waiting. She felt two very distinct thuds. "Wow, I think I felt the shape of a foot."

Amber laughed. "Probably. Baby Wembley has a future as a football player. Fitting really, given the family name."

"Don't tell Jet," Ria teased, biting into her cake. The

familiar taste was as welcome as a hug, soft and comforting. "He's hoping for a golf buddy."

"What about you, Ria?" Breaking off a piece of her own slice, Amber brought it to her mouth. "You thinking of popping out any golf buddies sometime soon?"

"Amber!" Ria fell back, laughing. "Where do you think I'm going to get the other half of the equation now that the Great Match is done for?"

"Oh, I don't know." Amber's eyes turned sly. "But I know a cat who looks at you like he wants to eat you up, then come back for seconds."

Ria was still gasping at the scandalous comment from her—usually—shy sister-in-law, when Miaoling began laughing. Slapping her thigh, she laughed so hard that Ria could do nothing but join in. "You heard"—she sobbed between bursts that left her stomach aching—"what Jet said. They don't get serious with humans."

"Who says?" Amber's eyes were shiny with humor. "Just because we don't know about any."

That cut off Ria's laughter. She sat back. Thought about it. Shook her head. "We'd have heard. I'd have heard at the college."

"Not necessarily," Amber argued. "They don't exactly advertise things. I'd say I'd never met a more closemouthed lot, but . . ." She waved a hand.

Ria blew out a breath. "I can't ask him. You know that."

"Why?" Miaoling asked.

"Because then he'd think I was hinting at something!"

Her grandmother gave her a gimlet-eyed glance. "If you don't hint, how's he going to know?"

Ria's mind flooded with the memories of her pressed up against that gym door, his hand stroking over her, his tongue in her mouth. "He knows."

"Yes," Amber said. "Changelings have a better sense of smell than humans. He can probably scent your you-know-what."

Ria stared. "Amber, what's come over you?"

Her sister-in-law picked up another piece of cake. "I'm going to blame it on the pregnancy." A slow grin.

SEVEN

Emmett's blood was at fever point. Returning to the restaurant, he caught the scent of the shooter and began tracking. Dorian and Clay had both picked up the trail while he escorted Ria home, but this was his hunt.

His fingers remembered the soft feel of Ria's skin, the delicate roughness of the scratch that shouldn't have been on her face. The leopard paced inside his skull, wanting out, wanting to do damage, but Emmett held on to his humanity. For now.

Minutes later, he found both Dorian and Clay standing frustrated at a busy intersection. "Fuck," Emmett said, sensing what they had. The shooter's scent simply disappeared.

"Probably someone waiting to pick him up," Dorian muttered, looking around. "No CCTV cameras in this area. We need to fix that."

Emmett narrowed his eyes, making a slow circuit of all four points of the intersection. It was clogged with people. "Can't have been a pickup. It'd be too hard to make a quick getaway," he muttered almost to himself . . . and looked up.

The old-fashioned fire escape ladder hung a few feet off the ground, just far enough up to confuse the scent trail with this many people around. Landing on the ladder with a single powerful jump, he began to follow the fading trail with the fluid grace of the leopard he was. No human could ever hope to match a predatory changeling moving at full speed.

Making it to the top of the building in seconds, he pursued the scent to the other side. Another ladder, this one looking down into a small parklike area thronged with elders playing what looked like a combination of mahjong and chess. Ignoring the ladder, he jumped straight to the ground, making several people scream. His cat ensured he landed on his feet, his body perfectly balanced.

Again, the scent was muddied by the number of people in the park. But worse, a few meters later it was overwhelmed totally by the strong disinfectant used to sanitize the nearby automated public toilets. Swearing under his breath, he did a circle of the park and came up with nothing. Frustration clawed at him. He was certain *this* was where the shooter had been picked up—on one of these narrow streets.

Thrusting a hand through his hair, he was striding back the way he'd come when an old man waved him over. "Here—he left his motorcycle parked on the footpath. Very rude." A piece of paper was put into his hand.

Opening it, he found a license plate number. *Hot damn.* "Thanks." His cell phone was in his hand an instant later. The elderly man waved away his thanks and went back to his game even as Emmett fed the tip through to the DarkRiver techs. Changelings had made it their business to be up-to-date on all technology known to man—because if the coldly powerful Psy had a weakness, it was that they relied too much on their machines.

But that technical knowledge also came in handy when DarkRiver needed to hack into Enforcement databases. Emmett had an address to go with the license plate five minutes later. Assembling a team took only a further three minutes—Lucas, Vaughn, and Clay, with Dorian holding a surveillance position. The young soldier was turning into one hell of a sharpshooter.

"How're we doing this?" Lucas asked as they got out of their vehicle a short distance from the shooter's home, his eyes cold.

"I want the bastard alive," Emmett said through gritted teeth. "We need to get Vincent's location." He glanced at Lucas. "We're skating way past the edge of the law here." Changelings had jurisdiction over crimes that involved their kind, but this shooter was most likely human. "It's daylight—we'll be seen."

His alpha shrugged. "Let me handle that."

Trusting his word, Emmett gave the signal and they fanned out, coming in at the suspect's dirty trailer from all sides. The bike sat near the back—and it was sticky with the scent Emmett had detected at the restaurant.

Even that close, no one shot out at them, and a couple of seconds later, Emmett's leopard picked up a new scent. Blood. Fresh and thick. "Goddammit," he muttered under his breath, knowing what they'd find. He was right.

The shooter lay slumped over a rickety table, the back of his head blown off execution style. "Vincent knew we'd picked up his scent," Lucas said, taking in the scene from the doorway beside Emmett. "I bet that blood is still warm."

They both stepped back out, Emmett's frustration making him want to kick something. "Think there might be intel in there that could lead us to Vincent?"

Lucas nodded at the neighbors in the surrounding trailers, a few of whom were openly staring. "We can't risk going in and giving the cops a reason to hassle us. As it is, these folks saw us open the door, stand in the doorway. No harm, no foul."

"I wouldn't let it bother you," Clay said, breaking his customary silence. "This guy, he was expendable. They'd have told him squat."

Emmett tried to believe that as he circled the trailer.

A hint of movement in his peripheral vision, prey breaking into a run.

He didn't even think about it, shifting into hard pursuit between one second and the next. The skinny guy in front of him didn't look back as he snaked through the trailer park. Not until he passed a group of children kicking around a dusty soccer ball. Emmett's gut chilled as the man's hand came up. "Get down!" he yelled, thrusting himself into an incredible burst of speed. Slamming into the shooter's arm, he pushed it up just as the man fired. The shot was silent, the bullet lost in the sky.

The shooter was already moving, using his body with the fluid grace of an experienced street fighter. His fist hit Emmett's cheek with enough force to jerk it back, but Emmett didn't let go of the man's wrist, holding the gun pointed up, even as he used his free elbow to hit the assassin's jaw. The bastard didn't go down.

Fuck it. Emmett squeezed the man's wrist, crushing his fragile human bones.

With a scream, the shooter dropped to his knees, the gun falling out of his hand. "Keep an eye on it," Emmett ordered Vaughn.

The jaguar nodded and made sure any kids who hadn't already scattered got the hell out. Emmett kept his hand around the shooter's wrist as the whimpering male knelt in the dust. This one, Emmett thought, would know something about Vincent. Dropping into a crouch, he met the man's shiny-wet eyes. "Tell me what I want to know," he said very quietly, "or I'll crush your wrist so badly, they'll never be able to put it back together."

The man spat at him. "I'll get a cloned replacement."

Emmett heard the faint sound of Enforcement sirens and knew he had a couple of minutes at most. Leaning close, he deliberately let his eyes go cat, his claws shooting out. Then he smiled. "You know, they're not very good at cloning eyes." He touched a claw to the very edge of the man's right eye. "Funny how a claw can accidentally blind a man during fighting."

Fear burned off the shooter, acrid and thick. "You can't do that. There're witnesses."

"Really?"

He watched as the man turned . . . to see only closed doors and shuttered windows.

"You threatened their kids," Emmett whispered. "Who do you think's going to come forward to save you?" He pressed in the claw until the edge actually touched the delicate surface.

The fear turned into sheer terror. "I'll answer your questions!"

Emmett asked them hard and fast. By the time Enforcement arrived, the Crew male was so grateful to see them, he confessed to the shooting just to get away from Emmett. The cops looked like they wanted to take Emmett in, too, but all of a sudden, there were twenty witnesses who'd seen everything—and who swore Emmett was a hero.

Faced with that many enthusiastic supporters, the cops gave up. One older female met Emmett's eyes. "You didn't have to crush his wrist." It wasn't censure, more a question.

Emmett raised an eyebrow.

She smiled and walked off. Right into Dorian.

The blond soldier grinned. "How about you let me buy you dinner?"

The cop laughed. "You're adorable. But I gave up cradle robbing a few years back."

Dorian was unabashed. Walking over to Emmett after the woman left, he folded his arms. "Sooooo . . . what happens if I flirt with Ria?"

"I use your ribs to make a wind chime."

"That's what I thought."

Emmett told the others what the assassin had revealed. "Vincent stays out of sight by living in a mobile home—it's a hover-truck, black, with constantly changing license plates. But it's shiny, all tricked out. The bastard likes living in style."

"That'll make it easier to spot him," Lucas said. "We'll start circulating the description. Someone will talk."

"He also said Vincent has a stockpile of weapons, so we need to be ready for what he might do when cornered." The bastard wouldn't care who he hit. "He's got connections to one of the big crime families up north—this is a test run. We don't kick him out, we're going to have more problems."

Lucas nodded. "It's not just the human gangs we need to worry about—we don't handle this challenge right, other changeling groups are going to start looking at our territory."

"Then let's make sure we take care of business."

Emmett spent the rest of the day ensuring his more shadowy

informants knew to look out for the truck. By the time night fell, there was only one thing he wanted to do . . . and only one person he wanted to do it with.

Unfortunately, though his split lip had healed with changeling speed, he still had a fairly impressive black eye. No way in hell would Ria's family let him in through the front door, especially at this time of night. If it had been his daughter, Emmett thought with a twist in his heart, he'd have done the same. But that didn't mean he was going to stay away from Ria.

Finding his way to the back of the two-story house that was the Wembley home, he nodded at Nate, on watch that shift, and looked up at the window that he knew faced out from Ria's bedroom. Nate gave him an interested look. "Wall's got no handholds."

"If I can hook myself up to that window," Emmett said, working out the mechanics, "I can get up."

The other man judged the gap. "Doable."

Decision made, Emmett backed up until he had enough distance, kicked himself into gear and jumped. The leopard made sure he caught the ledge he aimed for, and from there, it was a fairly simple climb. Holding himself up with one hand on the lower edge of Ria's darkened window, while his feet found precarious purchase on the slight ledge of the kitchen window below, he tapped on the glass.

Silence. Then a *shush* of sound, as if she was wearing something that trailed on the floor. His mind filled with a thousand erotic images, but the window didn't go up. Instead, he heard Nate's phone ring. Ria was being very careful. Smiling as he heard the sentinel answer, he waited.

The window went up a few seconds later. "Are you insane?" Ria hissed, sticking out her head. "How are you even staying up?"

"Not easily," he said with a grin, the stress of the day wiped away by the sight of her all sleep mussed and kissable. "Let me in?"

Pulling back, she waved him in. "Dear God, Emmett," she said the instant he was inside. "You could've fallen and broken your fool neck."

"I'm a leopard, mink. Climbing's my thing."

"I don't think leopards evolved to climb two-storied—" A gasp and she nudged his face toward the light coming in through the window. "What happened?"

"I didn't dodge fast enough." He pushed down the window, knowing Nate wouldn't be able to hear anything now if they kept their voices low. "My own fault."

Ria slapped a hand on his chest. "I want a straight answer. Talk."

He fingered the strap of her ankle-length satin nightgown. The material looked soft and utterly silky. He wanted to gather it up in his hands and bare something even softer and silkier.

"Emmett!" A low whisper, but her eyes were snapping fire.

Sliding his hands down her arms, he tugged her closer. "Who wants to talk?" He dropped his head, nuzzled the scent of her into his lungs.

Feminine heat and a delicate, exotic perfume.

Licking out to taste it was instinct. He wanted to know everything about his mate. The leopard smiled at the easy, absolute realization. Of course she was his mate. Why the hell else would he have climbed up that damn wall? Only for Ria. "I like your perfume."

She shuddered. "You're being bad again."

"Did you buy it for me?" He stroked his hands down her back, pressing her softness against the pounding heat of his cock.

"I-I had it from a gift set." She tangled her hands in his hair. "It said it's formulated for changelings."

"Mmm." Nibbling his way up from her neck to her lips, he took her mouth in a slow, lazy kiss. "Our sense of smell is so strong, normal perfume is too intense."

"I can't even smell this one," she murmured against his lips. "Guess you'll have to buy my perfume for me."

His cat purred, wondering if she realized what she'd just given away. "I'm going to buy you bubble bath, too."

"Emmett." A moan.

He kissed it away. "Does your door have a lock?"

"Yes." She pressed her lips to the pulse in his neck. "But it's not set."

Groaning, he swept her up into his arms and carried her to the door. "Do it."

"Say please."

He looked down into that teasing face and gave in to the urge to bite, sinking his teeth—very carefully—into the sensitive spot between shoulder and neck. She trembled, and he felt the lock turn. "How quiet?" he asked, licking over the mark as he carried her to the bed.

"My mother has ears like a bat."

Grinning, he dropped her lightly on the mattress, coming down on top of her as she finished the sentence. She was all soft and curvy under him, the satin of her nightgown delicious torture. He ran his hand down the side. It snagged. "Damn." His hands were rough, calloused, nothing like her creamy flesh.

"I love your hands, Emmett." It was an intimate whisper in the night-dark of her room.

He looked down into those intelligent eyes, and knew he was lost. Raising himself off her and to the side, he said, "I don't want to mess up your pretty nightgown. Pull it up for me."

She swallowed, but her hands moved to the satin, pulling it up with slow, sensual tugs. "I'm supposed to be mad at you."

"Hmm." He cupped her knee as it was revealed, waiting for more, for everything.

"You going to mess up my interviews next time, too?"

The sweet slope of her thigh. "Probably." He stroked his hand up, knew he'd have to taste.

A soft moan, her leg rising slightly, that knee bending as she rubbed her foot on the sheet. "How do you do this to me?"

Shifting his hand fully between her legs, he cupped her.

EIGHT

Her gasp was almost silent this time, her body rising in a sinuous curve. Tempted beyond measure, he leaned in to steal another kiss. "The same way you do it to me." She was so damp and hot under his palm that it was all he could do not to tear off her panties and slide his fingers into liquid-soft flesh.

Her hands tugged at his T-shirt. "Off."

He considered it. "I'll have to move my hand." And he didn't want to.

Ria's lips parted. "Your eyes have gone leopard."

"I can smell you, all slick and luscious and ready." He pressed the heel of his hand against the enticement of her, teasing, playing, caressing.

Her eyes fluttered closed. "Emmett"—a husky order—"if you don't get that T-shirt off, I'm not going to be responsible for my actions."

Moving his hand with reluctance, he pulled off the T-shirt, then got rid of the rest of his clothing—he wanted no more interruptions. Ria's eyes went wide as he came down beside her again, his hand closing over her thigh. "I want to rip off your panties."

Those gorgeous eyes went impossibly wider. "If you promise to buy me a replacement pair."

He froze, so aroused he could barely see straight. Burying his head against her neck, he breathed deep. It only twisted the coils more strongly around him. And those coils were soft, feminine, erotic beyond all measure. Fingers tensing, he tore off the scrap of fabric that had so tormented him.

Ria arched up and he took her mouth again, addicted to the sugar and spice taste of her. Under his fingers, she was pure feminine seduction, hot and slick with need. But he wasn't ready to end this. Continuing to play his fingers between her legs, he licked and kissed his way down her throat, and over the satin to the hollow of her breasts. Her chest rose and fell in jagged breaths, her hand sliding through his hair.

"Emmett." Her voice was husky, her passion unhidden.

Not yet, he told himself, and flicked his fingers over her clit, making her body jerk. When she tugged on his hair, he refused to go up. Instead, he closed his mouth over her nipple, sucking hard through the delicate satin of her gown. Her fingers clenched and unclenched convulsively, her entire body twisting as if it wanted to escape . . . and get closer at the same time.

Sensing that she was riding the fine edge of pleasure, Emmett slipped two fingers into her tight sheath, stroking her to trembling release. She bit his shoulder to muffle her cry, inciting the leopard to primal possessiveness. Petting her down from the orgasm, he moved to cover her body with his, one hand on the pillow beside her head, the other tangled in her hair as he tugged her back for an almost savage kiss.

She opened to him immediately, her arms wrapping around him. He nipped at her mouth and tore the straps of her gown, pushing down the material so he could close his hand over the sweet roundness of her breast. When he released her mouth, she pulled him back down. Growling low in his throat, he gave her what she wanted, molding her breast under his hand. She was so lush that he wanted to bite. Next time, he promised himself.

This time, his patience was at its limit.

Nudging apart her thighs, he nipped at her lower lip. "Put those pretty legs around my waist, mink."

An exquisite slide of soft feminine flesh as she gave him what he wanted. Then she gave him more, pressing her lips to his throat, nibbling on him with delicate possession as he fought not to thrust inside her in a single hard push. Shuddering, he ran one hand down her back to tilt her at just the right angle.

And then he was sliding in, the liquid heat of her almost scorching. Gritting his teeth, he clenched his hand on the pillow and pushed, slow and easy. "Next time," he choked out, "I get to go fast."

Gripping his biceps, Ria drew in a deep breath. "So long as you don't get any bigger . . . *Emmett.*" The last was a moan as he buried himself to the hilt.

He didn't move for several seconds, knowing he was a big man. But then Ria began to shift beneath him in slow rolling movements that drove him out of his mind. The leopard took control and he only just had the presence of mind to take her mouth in a kiss before he surrendered to the driving hunger to take, to mark.

Mine, he thought, *mine.*

A moment later, even that thought was lost.

Ria stared at the ceiling over the muscled slope of Emmett's shoulder. He was heavy, but she didn't mind being squashed. Not right now. Not when her body was so loose and sated, she felt like a big lazy cat herself. Which, she thought, was exactly what Emmett was acting like. He sprawled over her . . . inside her.

Her cheeks heated. How could she still be shy after what they'd done? But well, she hadn't expected him to start revving up for a second go so fast. "Fast recovery time?" she asked, not quite sure where she found the sass.

"Something like that." It was a rumble against her throat.

She ran her fingers through his hair, smiling.

"Ria?"

"Hmm?"

"Were you a virgin?"

The question made her cheeks burn. "Technically."

He sounded a little choked as he said, "Technically?"

"I'm twenty-two, Emmett. Just because I chose to wait for the right man doesn't mean I wasn't curious." She thought she might have shocked him when he remained silent for several long minutes.

She should've known better.

"Where do you keep the stuff you used to satisfy your curiosity?"

Her throat dried up. "Never you mind."

A squeeze of her hip. "Please?"

Her heart tumbled over. This man, she thought, could enslave her. "No."

"Next time?"

"No." She didn't know if she could survive the eroticism.

Emmett grazed her throat with his teeth. "I'll buy you some. And make you open them in front of me."

Her mind overloaded. She felt her body ready itself for another ride, and dear Lord she wanted it. "Less talk, more action, pussycat."

That got her a pinch on the butt, a low male growl, and all the action she could've hoped for.

Ria couldn't meet her mother's eyes the next morning. Not because she was ashamed—how could she possibly be ashamed of the glory of what she'd done with Emmett? The sex was one thing, but he'd been so affectionate afterward, not leaving until almost dawn. She'd felt petted and adored.

That was the reason she couldn't meet Alex's eyes. She was sure her mother would spot the bubbling joy in her, the certain knowledge that she was in love with a man who was almost perfect. And that *almost*, she thought with a frown, might yet be a big problem. She had more interviews lined up this week, and while Emmett had hinted that they were close to catching Vincent, that still left her with a bodyguard.

The phone rang as Alex was muttering about it being nine already. Since the shop opened at ten, she had plenty of time to get there, but Alex didn't like being late. "I'll grab it," Amber said, having just walked into the room. "Hello? Yes, she's here. One moment." She held out the phone to Ria, mouthing *DarkRiver Construction*.

Ready to hear the bad news, Ria took the receiver, not bothering to step out of the kitchen/dining room—Alex, Amber, and Miaoling would simply follow her. "Ria speaking."

"It's Lucas Hunter."

"Good morning." Her eyes narrowed. "May I ask a question?"

A chuckle. "No. Ask Emmett."

That was the problem, Ria thought. Emmett wouldn't answer her questions. His protectiveness was starting to get on her nerves—even the nerves that loved the bejesus out of him. "Then what can I do for you?"

"How about sorting out my filing system?"

Excitement shot through her . . . before coming to a crashing halt. "No, thank you."

A pause. "Ria, this has nothing to do with anything else. I'm an ice-cold bastard when it comes to business—I need an assistant who can deliver the goods."

"And the fact that I'd be protected at DarkRiver HQ is coincidence?"

"Yep. If you suck at your job, I'll boot you out after the probationary period."

Hearing that delighted her. "I," she said, starting to grin, "am very good at what I do."

"Then when can you start?"

Ria blinked. "Today if necessary."

"I'll see you when you arrive."

Hanging up, Ria looked into three pairs of avidly interested eyes. The symmetry of it struck her deep in the heart. Miaoling, with her wise, laughing gaze. Alex, so energetic and impatient. Amber, with both Miaoling's sense of calm and a slight wickedness it took even friends and family a long time to see.

Smile cracking her face, Ria pumped her fist in a victory salute before jumping over to do a little dance around the three most important women in her life. Alex opened up a bottle of champagne she'd secreted away—though Amber had to be satisfied with grape juice—and did a toast. "Here's to my daughter. Much too smart for that imbecile, Tom."

Emmett walked into Lucas's office area and winked at the assistant sitting primly at her desk. "Boss in?"

"You look like a hoodlum," he was told, before Ria got up and came over. "Did you even brush your hair after you showered?" She was threading her fingers through that hair as she spoke.

Emmett savored the feel of her so close. Hearing Lucas's door open, he bent down, picked Ria up, and planted a bone-tingling kiss on her lips.

She was panting for breath by the time he finished, her cheeks adorably red. "Emmett! I'm at work."

Shrugging, he met Lucas's eyes over the top of her head. His alpha held up his hands, his amusement open. "We ready to go?"

Emmett nodded. "He's parked about half an hour out of the city."

Ria looked between the two men. "Vincent?"

"Yes," Emmett said as Lucas made a signal that he'd be out in a minute and walked back into his office. "Bastard's ass is toast."

Ria put a hand on his chest. "Are you going in with lots of backup?"

"Don't worry about it, mink. I know what I'm doing."

"Emmett!" Her voice was a whip.

Surprised, he looked at her. "What?"

"Don't tell me not to worry! Don't pat me on the head as if I'm a brainless bimbo and tell me everything's going to be okay." She poked him with a finger. "If we're going to be in a relationship—" Snapping her mouth shut, she folded her arms and returned to her desk.

Stupefied, he prowled after her. "If we're going to be in a relationship, then what?"

"Nothing." She began to order papers on her desk. "Just don't get yourself killed. That would make me seriously angry."

He knew that wasn't it. Grabbing her arm, he pulled her toward him. "I'm not leaving till you tell me what's up."

Ria looked toward Lucas's open doorway. "This is not the time and place."

He waited.

She blew out a breath. "*Are* we in a relationship?"

"What did you think last night was?" This was one of those times when he didn't get women. Scratch that. When he didn't get *his* woman.

"Well, men don't necessarily equate sex with a relationship." It was a whisper, her eyes flicking to Lucas's door again.

Emmett decided not to remind her that Luc could probably hear everything anyway. "That wasn't sex, Ria. That was fucking-amazing-sex." He grinned at her blush. "And I equate everything I do with you to a relationship. Try going out with another man and see where it gets you."

She tried for a glare but a smile peeked out. "Go. Be careful." A tight hug. "We'll discuss the other stuff when you're back safe and sound. I'll be waiting."

He walked out with the scent of her bound into his very skin, her promise in his ears.

Ria found herself escorted home by an older man called Cian that day. "Any word?" she asked him as they reached the front door.

A shake of his head. "I don't think they'll move until a few hours after dark."

Something about Cian struck Ria as oddly familiar, but she was sure he'd never been on protection detail before. "Will you let me know if you learn anything?"

His eyes were warm when he looked at her. "Of course, Ria."

Nodding, she thanked him and walked inside. Her father had beaten everyone home and was at the stove, concocting his (in)famous secret spaghetti sauce. "Hey, Dad." She bussed him on the cheek. "Where's Amber?" she asked, guessing her grandmother was catching a nap as she sometimes did.

"She thought she might be having contractions—Jet came home and took her to the hospital."

Ria stopped in the process of taking off her coat. "Is she in labor?"

"Doctor thinks it's false, but he's keeping her there for a couple of hours to make sure." He touched his back pocket. "Jet's gonna buzz me if it looks like my grandbaby's going to come early."

Smiling, she hung up her coat and went to stand by his side, sliding one arm around his waist. "Smells good."

He put his free arm around her shoulders. "So, you involved with that cat?"

"Yep." She'd never lied to her father. Skirted around the truth maybe, but never lied. "I'm crazy about him."

A sigh. "Invite him to dinner."

"So you can grill him?"

"It's what fathers do." A squeeze of her shoulders. "I only want what's best for you. Have you considered how this man is going to support you?"

Ria didn't point out that she could support herself. That wasn't the issue at hand. "Well, when he's not acting as a Dark-River soldier, he has another job." She'd discovered that sometime last night—even now, the memory of Emmett's lazy voice murmuring the answers to all the little questions she had about him was enough to make her body flush.

"Oh?"

NINE

"Yeah." She drew it out, knowing it would drive her father crazy.

"Ria."

Laughing, she met his scowling eyes. "He's an engineer."

Her father's eyebrows climbed to his hairline. "Who does he work for?"

"DarkRiver Construction. He specializes in making sure buildings are built to withstand seismic events." That was how he'd put it, sounding far more academic than she'd expected. It had been obvious in that single sentence that he not only knew what he was doing, but that he loved his work. "He trained with Angus Wittier." Wittier was considered the premier expert on seismic-proof building in the country.

Simon nodded, his face contemplative. "Pass me the oregano and go get changed."

"Will the spaghetti be ready soon?" She wasn't hungry, her stomach in knots as she waited to hear the outcome of the DarkRiver–Crew showdown, but she wanted to keep the emotional temperature mellow for her father. Simon only cooked spaghetti when he was stressed—Amber's situation was clearly worrying him more than he'd admitted.

"Ten minutes."

"I'll set the table after I change." Walking up to her bedroom, she closed the door before calling Jet. "How's Amber?" she asked when her brother answered.

"She's okay right now, resting." His voice was soft. "Tell Mom and Dad not to worry—the doctor says everything's super with the baby."

"Hah," she said, with a smile. "You know how they are."

"You'll keep them calm, Ri-ri." Said with absolute confidence. "I'll call you as soon as anything changes."

Hanging up, Ria changed, and then did what Jet had expected her to do—she made sure everyone remained calm—though her own emotions had her feeling incredibly fragile beneath the surface. What if something happened to Emmett? *No*, she told herself, somehow managing to maintain her composed facade even when Amber suddenly went into labor and the entire family rushed to the hospital, escorted by a trio of DarkRiver soldiers.

They were walking past the emergency room when several ambulances came screaming in. Ria recognized the shock of white-blond hair on the stretcher they pulled out of the back of one vehicle. "Dorian," she whispered, looking for Emmett's big form. He wasn't there. But Dorian was bleeding, the red stark against the pale gold of his skin. *"Popo—"*

"Go." Miaoling squeezed her hand. "I'll take care of your mom."

Cian by her side, Ria ran to the fallen DarkRiver soldier, slipping her hand into his as the medical team worked around her. "Hold on, Dorian." He was unconscious, but she felt as if he knew she was there. She turned to Cian. "Tamsyn?"

A nurse pushed Ria out of the way as they wheeled Dorian into an operating theatre. Turning, she found Cian on the phone. "She's almost here," he told her, putting the phone in his pocket. Tiny lines of concern fanned out from the corners of his pale blue eyes.

Tamsyn ran in mere minutes later, a slender blonde female by her side. While the healer ran through to prep for the operating theatre, the woman halted beside Cian. The soldier immediately put his arm around her shoulders. "What're you doing here?"

"I was at Tammy's when the call came in," the woman said, pushing back her hair.

The instant Ria saw her eyes, all the pieces fell into place. The way Cian moved, the way he spoke, no wonder it had seemed familiar. "You're Emmett's parents."

"And you must be Ria. I'm Keelie." Emmett's mother's smile was wide, those whiskey-colored eyes she'd bequeathed her son as bright as diamonds.

Ria didn't even think about shaking hands. She walked forward and into open arms. The hug was tight. "Have you heard from Emmett?" Keelie asked.

Surprised that Keelie expected Emmett to call her first, Ria shook her head. "Not yet." Her phone rang at that very instant. Pulling it out, she put it to her ear.

"I'm on my way to the hospital, mink. Don't faint."

She felt her stomach drop. "What's wrong? Emmett, if you've been shot—"

"It's just a flesh wound. You can kiss it better." His tone was warm, a caress across her skin. "I'll come by after I stop in at the hospital—"

"I'm here," she interrupted him. "Amber's in labor."

"Problems?" Sharp concern.

Her heart clenched. "It's a couple of weeks too early, but the doctor said he didn't foresee any difficulties." She took a shuddering breath, trying to convince herself of that. "I'm in the ER. I saw Dorian being brought in."

"Is Blondie okay?"

"Tamsyn's in there with him."

"He took a bullet through the ribs—don't think it hit anything major. Hold on. Be there in a minute."

Closing the phone, she turned to share what he'd said with Keelie and Cian, but the couple shook their heads. "We heard."

"Oh, right."

"Emmett'll get you an earpiece," Keelie said. "It's what the other human members of the pack use when they want to have private conversations."

Ria's curiosity momentarily overwhelmed her worry. "You have human members?"

"Of course!" Keelie smiled. "I guess people must assume they're cats."

Ria opened her mouth to reply but something made her turn to the doorway. She was running toward Emmett before she realized she'd moved. He caught her with one arm, the other in a sling.

"Flesh wound?" She pushed aside his shirt to reveal the bandage. "That's an awfully large bandage for a flesh wound."

One big hand stroked over her hair. "It'll be fine as soon as Tammy has some time free. Gimme a kiss, mink."

"Emmett! Your parents are standing right there."

But he was already kissing her, and what could she do but kiss him back? She held on tight, so glad he was safe. "When did you turn into such an exhibitionist?" she whispered after he drew back, her cheeks nuclear-hot.

A small, wicked smile. "Just letting the others know you belong to me."

Her eyes widening in horror, she looked around his shoulder . . . to see the grinning faces of ten more DarkRiver soldiers. Including her boss. And a tall redheaded female who was giving her the thumbs-up. "Oh. My. God." She buried her face in Emmett's chest and felt the laughter rolling through his body. "I'm going to kill you." But in truth, all she wanted to do was stay pressed to him forever.

Dorian was pronounced stable half an hour later, and Tamsyn had enough energy left over to do a little extra healing. "How does it work?" Ria asked as the healer put her hand on Emmett's shoulder and closed her eyes.

"Some healers say it comes from within, but I think I act as a reservoir for pack energy." Tamsyn's forehead furrowed in concentration. "My body can only hold a finite amount, so if Dorian had been hurt too badly, I would've been wiped out. But he's a strong one."

"She's selling herself short," Emmett said. "Tammy directs and channels her energy so it does the most good—probably knows more about the human body than most doctors. Though she's one of those, too."

Ten minutes later, the sling was gone, Emmett's wound a soft pink. Ria ran her fingers over it, taking utmost care. "Does it hurt?"

"Naw, I'm tough. But if you want to kiss it better, I won't object."

Laughing, Tamsyn backed out of the cubicle. "Remember kids, this is a hospital." She closed the folding door behind herself.

Ria punched an unrepentant Emmett gently on his uninjured shoulder. "How did you get shot?"

"Aw, come on, mink, you don't want me to get into that."

Putting her hands on her hips, she faced him head-on. "Emmett, you know how we were going to have a conversation later?"

He looked a little wary. "Yeah?"

"Well—" she began just as her phone started to beep in a frantic pattern only the family ever used. "Amber!" She put the cell to her ear. "Mom?"

A fragile response. "Amber's in trouble."

Ria began moving, conscious of Emmett at her back. The maternity ward was in a completely different wing of the hospital so it took precious minutes to get there. She arrived to find Miaoling sitting down, her hand intertwined so tightly with Alex's her fingers had turned bone white. Simon sat on Alex's other side. No one said a word.

Ria's heart stopped. "What? What is it?"

It was her father who answered. "There was bleeding. Complications. They don't know if . . ."

"No one will talk to us," Alex said, sounding on the verge of tears. "They just rush in and out."

"Wait." Ria took a deep breath and grabbed the first nurse she saw.

Crouching down beside Miaoling, Emmett took her small, wrinkled hand in his as he watched Ria quietly and effectively intimidate a nurse into giving her the information her family needed. She returned several minutes later, a small fierce warrior. "They've got a fetal heartbeat. Amber's conscious and talking."

"The bleeding?" Alex asked, her voice breaking on the words.

"They're working on getting it under control." Ria looked up as another group burst into the waiting room.

Amber's parents, Emmett realized as Ria greeted them in a flowing burst of Mandarin, clearly trying to stave off their panic. The couple sat down on Simon's other side, asking Ria more questions. She shot Emmett a grateful glance as he continued to talk to Miaoling and Alex in a low voice, telling them about life in the pack, anything to take their minds off what was happening in the room only a few feet away.

They asked him all kinds of questions, but he knew they'd be unlikely to remember any of it come morning. Still he talked, giving them the distraction they needed, as Ria did the same with Amber's parents. Simon spoke to both his wife and mother-in-law, and Amber's parents, in turn, obviously trying to stay strong for his family.

But Ria was the glue, the quiet strength that held everyone together.

His leopard growled in pride.

Forty minutes later, there were tears of happiness, not sorrow. Amber was pronounced stable—though she'd have to stay in the hospital a bit longer than usual—the baby was a squalling ball of red-faced anger, and Jet was grinning like a fool.

"What're you going to call her?" Ria asked after everyone had piled into the room and reassured themselves that both mother and baby were fine.

"Joy," Jet said, touching one gentle finger to the baby's cheek. "That's what she is—our Joy."

"It's a beautiful name."

"Yeah. Amber wants to use Nana's name as a middle name." He drifted to his wife's side as if drawn there, curling his hand around hers. Though her face was lined with tiredness, Amber smiled. "Hey you."

Ria began to nudge everyone out of the room.

Half an hour later, Emmett used Simon's car to drop off Amber's parents, along with Alex and Miaoling, since none of them were in any condition to drive, before returning to pick up Ria and her father. Simon got into the passenger seat, as Ria slid into the back. Emmett could feel the older man's focus on him as they drove and it was no surprise to hear Simon say, "Ri, go inside. We'll be in in a moment."

Ria looked from one man to the other. Emmett shook his head in a slight negative when she went to open her mouth. Pursing her lips, she got out and entered the house. Emmett glanced at Simon. "I'll take care of her."

"She's special," Simon said, looking him straight in the eye. "We lost a baby girl to a late-pregnancy miscarriage a year after Jet was born. We weren't the same after . . . but then Ria came. She healed us. She's our heart."

Emmett nodded, fully comprehending the sheer depth of everyone's terror at the hospital tonight. "I understand." And he did. Because she was his heartbeat, too.

A pause. Then Simon opened the door and got out. "I'll send Ria to you. Save you sneaking up the wall."

Emmett winced. "Um . . ."

Simon's lips curved. "Ask me sometime about how I used to get into Alex's room when we were high school students."

Emmett was still grinning when Ria slid into the passenger seat. Before she could say anything, he started up the engine again. "Think your dad would mind if we took the car for a spin?"

"No, but where are we going?"

"For a little ride." Putting the vehicle into hover-drive, he took them out of the city, and through the red arches of the bridge that had been there so long, the world couldn't imagine San Francisco without it.

Ria sat back, releasing a sigh. "I'm so glad everyone's okay."

"Even me?"

"Even the idiot who got himself shot up when I specifically told him not to."

The leopard batted playfully at her sharp response, delighted by her. "Just checking." Passing the main lookout on the other side of the bridge, he drove up a "secret" route that all the high schoolers knew about.

"Hey, where does this go?" She twisted around. "I've never been up here."

"Mink, you must've been one hell of a good kid."

"I admit my nerdiness with pride." She made a choked up sound of surprise when she saw four other cars parked at the top, all of them a good distance from each other. "You brought us to a make-out spot?"

"How else was I supposed to get my hands on you?" Parking the car at the end of the dirt lot, he slid away the manual controls, then reached over and undid Ria's safety belt. "Come here."

Laughter danced in her eyes as she shifted over to straddle him, knees on the seat on either side of his thighs. "We are not making out in my parents' car."

"Yes, we are. That's the rule. You think those kids own those cars?" He nodded out the window. "Exactly."

Ria's smile softened, grew serious. "I was so scared for you, Emmett."

"Hey." He pressed his lips to hers. "I can't promise you I'll never be hurt, but I can promise that I'll do everything in my power to come back to you every day."

Her lips trembled. "If you don't, I'll come after you."

"I know." After seeing her at the hospital, he finally understood what she'd been trying to tell him all this time—Ria might be small and vulnerably human, but she was also strong enough to take anything the world threw at her, a warrior in her own way. It was time he started treating her like one. "You want to hear how it went down?"

A jerky nod.

"Okay, we have the truck surrounded, and we've blocked off the streets he could use to drive out, so he's a rat in a cage. We wait till nightfall." He unbuttoned the first three buttons on her shirt.

"Emmett!"

"It's to make the bad memories go away."

Giving a burst of stifled laughter, she thrust her fingers

through his hair as he pressed a kiss to the delicate skin between her breasts. "God, you're pretty, mink. I'm gonna kiss you all over next time."

"I like that song."

"Me, too." Another kiss before he straightened. "So, everything's going to plan. Problem is, Vincent's smart. He's got the immediate area around his truck set up with sensors. No way to get to the truck without alerting him."

"But you were sure he was in there?"

"We saw him come out earlier in the day—"

"How did you know what he looked like?"

Smart question. Nothing less than he expected from his mate. "No need. It was obvious he was the alpha dog."

"Go on."

He ran his finger down her bared skin, undoing a few more buttons along the way. His leopard rose to the forefront, possessive and oh-so-hungry.

TEN

Breathing past the desire to simply take, he continued. "It was clear we wouldn't be able to get into the truck even if we somehow got past the alarms—thing was armored like a tank. No windows, no visible vents. So we threw something at the back doors."

Ria blinked. "High-tech."

"All we needed was one of the goons to open the doors. Soon as he did, we shot in so many canisters of tear gas, they couldn't throw them all back." He'd finished unbuttoning her shirt, but she was too involved in the story to notice. The cat grinned. "Bastards had to come pouring out eventually. But the morons came out shooting, even though they couldn't see a target."

"You got shot by *accident*?" she asked, as if it was his fault.

"I got shot by *morons*." He bent to press kisses along the creamy upper curves of her breasts. "Aside from two lucky shots, they were useless. We had them down on their knees in seconds."

"What did you do to them?"

Looking up, he met her gaze. "I'm a leopard, Ria. I protect what's mine."

"I know." Absolute acceptance in her eyes, her face.

"I was the one to take Vincent down—and maybe he got a little banged up in the process, but we turned the whole lot of them over to Enforcement."

"Really?"

"Scout's honor." He smiled, letting the leopard out to play. "Turns out the Crew killed two cops in cold blood only a few hours before our takedown. Enforcement was *real* happy to take them in."

"Two birds, one stone," she murmured. "Vincent never again sees the light of day, and you make friends in Enforcement."

"And," he said, knowing she needed to know everything, "by taking down the Crew so completely, we gave notice to the Psy Council that we're here to stay."

Ria's eyes darkened. "They'll make trouble for you if they think you're a threat."

"Yeah."

"Good thing you cats are so tough." A soft whisper that told him she'd stand by him, no matter what.

Proud of her courage, he said, "We did let one goon go."

"Why?"

"So he could take a message to the *famiglia* up north. Anyone else comes down, we'll be sending them back in little tiny pieces. And then we'll come up and do the same to those who gave the orders."

"Would you really?"

"What do you think?"

"I think family comes first." She smiled. "You did something else. I can tell."

He began to slip her shirt off her shoulders. "We have some expert hackers. Maybe the big bosses found their data compromised and pictures of leopards as screen savers."

Ria's body began to shake as the shirt dropped to the floor. Her laughter was infectious—the leopard purred into her mouth as he took it in a slow, deep kiss. She kissed him back with an intensity that was pure Ria, then slid her mouth over his jaw and up to nibble on his ear. He was stroking his hand down to cup her breast when she screamed and jerked back.

He knew she was saying something, but he couldn't hear it, his entire body in agony.

Mouth snapping shut as her eyes fell on his face, Ria touched her fingers to a point below Emmett's right ear. "Oh, God." She realized his ears were bleeding. Her heart almost stopped. "Emmett?"

His eyes were hazy—he was clearly in pain. And still, she saw him turn to look for whatever it was that had made her scream. But the little spider on the headrest was long gone, scared by her stupid reaction. "Okay," she said. "Okay." A few contortions and she managed to get her shirt back on. Fastening a single button between her breasts, she slid back Emmett's door and half scrambled, half fell out of the vehicle.

Once out, she pushed at his shoulders, trying to get him into the passenger seat. He finally seemed to get the message and slid over, his movements nowhere near as graceful as usual. Instead, he slumped heavily into the seat and mimed writing.

Grabbing the purse she'd left on the dash, she pulled out the tiny notepad and pen she always carried. Emmett took it and wrote down an address, with the name *Tammy* at the top.

"Tamsyn." Nodding, Ria started up the car. The healer was a little ways out of the city, but if Emmett wanted to go to her rather than to Emergency, Ria wasn't going to argue.

It was the worst drive she'd ever made. Emmett touched his knuckles to the back of her cheek ten minutes into the journey, but his tenderness only made her feel worse. Fighting off tears, she drove as fast as she dared and made it to Tamsyn's just after one in the morning. Emmett slid back his own door and was out by the time she got to him. He swayed, as if he'd lost his center of balance.

Pulling his arm around her shoulders, she began to walk him to the door. It was wrenched open before they reached the first step. Nathan, who Ria had met during his watch on her parents' house, walked out, followed by Tamsyn. The healer was wearing a kimono-style robe in vivid blue, but it was her eyes that stole the scene, night-glow in the darkness.

"What happened?" she asked, coming to a stop in front of Emmett.

Tears streamed down Ria's face. "I screamed right next to his ear."

"Is that all?" Lifting her hands, the healer cupped them gently over Emmett's ears. "It won't take long to heal. He'll be extra-sensitive for a week, but after that, his hearing will go back to normal."

Ria felt Emmett squeeze her shoulders, his eyes already looking clearer. But she didn't breathe easy until Tamsyn drew back her hands and said, "There."

Emmett turned to Ria. "What was it?"

"A spider," she admitted, shamefaced. "Teeny, tiny."

"Scared of spiders, mink?" He drew her into his embrace.

"Very." Her eyes met Tamsyn's. "Thank you."

"No problem." Touching her fingers gently to Ria's cheek, she took the damp towel Nathan held out to her. "For the blood."

As Ria accepted the soft cloth with a murmur of thanks, Nathan jerked his head toward the house. "I'll leave the door open if you want to come in."

"No." Emmett shook his head. "I have to get Ria home."

The couple headed in with a wave. Reaching up, Ria dabbed away the blood with careful hands. Emmett bent his head and let her do what she needed to do. Only when his face was clear did he take the towel and put it on the hood of the car. "You gonna look at me anytime soon?"

She shook her head. "I'm so sorry, Emmett."

"Hey, it wasn't that bad." He tipped up her chin, forcing her to meet his gaze. "Excruciating, but otherwise not that bad."

Guilt threatened to crush her. Then she caught the glint in his eye. "Emmett, if I didn't love you so much, I'd kill you right now."

His eyes went night-glow between one second and the next. "What did you say?"

That was when she realized she'd given away everything. Her heart in her throat, she swallowed. "I said I love you."

Emmett cupped her cheek in his hand, those amazing, wild eyes becoming impossibly wilder. "Say that again."

She did.

Emmett's smile was slow, possessive, brilliant. "I love you, too, mink."

Her lips trembled. Throwing her arms around him, she let him pick her up and kiss the air right out of her. Sometime later, he said, "You're my mate. Think you can handle that?"

It was hard to speak with her heart bursting open. "Think you can handle me?"

"So long as you're gentle with me."

And she knew he was going to tease her about this for the rest of their lives. Her smile almost cracked her face, she was so delighted by the idea.

EPILOGUE

Of course Dorian flirted shamelessly with Ria at her and Emmett's mating ceremony. But Emmett didn't carry through his threat to eviscerate the younger man. Because Ria was his now, and Dorian, like every other man in DarkRiver, would rather die than cross that line.

His leopard smiled indulgently as the blond soldier danced Emmett's mate into a whirl, then caught her laughing form. Her eyes met Emmett's over Dorian's shoulder and she blew him a kiss. Smiling, he decided he'd shared his mate quite enough. "Go find another partner, Blondie."

Dorian released Ria with a mournful smile. "But I like your mink." Dodging Emmett's swipe, he walked off with a cocky grin.

"Is your pack always like this?" Ria asked, looking up at him, her arms wrapped around his waist.

"Crazy?"

"That, too. But so . . . like family."

"Yep. Pack is family."

A frown gathered between her brows. "What about my parents, grandmother, my brothers, Amber, and Joy—will they be shut out now?"

"They're family, too," he told her. "Sometimes, they might wish they weren't." Grinning, he directed her gaze to where poor Amber and Joy were being "looked after." The changelings weren't touching either mother or baby, but it was obvious they wanted to. Then Ria noticed the beautiful handcrafted baby blanket being held out to Amber. Her sister-in-law looked stunned . . . before a slow smile crept over her face.

"We like kids," Emmett whispered in her ear.

Pressing herself to him, she stood on tiptoe to whisper back. "Me, too."

He squeezed her close.

"How come you took so long to find me?" she asked.

"Stupidity." A nip of her ear. "But now that I have you, I'm never letting go."

Ria smiled and kissed the edge of his jaw. "Who says I'd let you?"

Laughing, Emmett spun her off her feet and around in a dizzying circle. Ria met her grandmother's eyes halfway through the first rotation. Miaoling was holding court with the young ones, but her smile was just for Ria. And Ria knew her grandmother understood.

Emmett was it for her. Forever. No matter what.

It was, she thought, looking down into eyes gone cat in joyful play, perfect.

The San Francisco Gazette

January 1, 2073

CITY BEAT

A New Wind

It seems that certain statements made in this column last year were prescient in the extreme. According to every person we spoke to during our research for today's column, the real power in San Francisco is no longer seen to lie with our elected representatives, but with a group of leopard changelings. Perhaps it's these cats who should be sitting in local government?

Lucas Hunter, the DarkRiver alpha, had this to say when I put the point to him: "We have no desire to stand for office. But we consider San Francisco our home—and we take threats to that home, and to the people within it, very seriously."

Bravo, Mr. Hunter. As far as this reporter is concerned, DarkRiver has proven both its determination, and its right, to hold the city. San Francisco is unequivocally a leopard town.

Blood and Roses

Angela Knight

ONE

The vampire knew how to sit on a horse. He rode with an easy muscularity despite his armor, achieving an effortless rhythm with his huge black stallion. A helm covered his head, red plumes floating in the wind, and gleaming plate mail sheathed his big body, so that he moved with the creak of leather and the scrape of steel on steel.

He was surrounded by a small troop of mounted men who maintained an alert, professional silence, their armor glinting in the light of the floating spell globes that danced over their heads. As befitted humans riding so close to Varil territory, they rode warily, with hands on sword hilts, crossbows, or spears.

They were still doomed.

Brooding, Amaris watched them ride through the wooded valley below. She and the three with her were shielded by a spell designed to conceal them from human or vampire senses. Their targets had no idea they were being watched.

Feeling her gorge rise in a sick wave, Amaris swallowed hard. The sense of evil surrounding her made her skin creep. *I should warn them. I can't just sit back and watch them all die.*

A male hand clamped over Amaris's knee with a force

that made her kneecap creak and the leggy roan mare dance beneath her. "If you betray us," Tannaz said, serene as a priest, "I will see Marin's soul feeds the Orb. It will be a very slow death." He smiled, all chilling charm. "And I will slit your eyelids away and make you watch."

"Get your hands off me, murderer," Amaris snarled, as much in fury at herself as her captor.

Another mocking smile flashed white through the visor of his helm. "Is that any way to talk to your beloved father?"

"'Beloved?'" She let her loathing fill her eyes. But he was right, damn him. Anything she tried to do for those poor bastards would get Marin killed. She'd sworn to her mother's ghost to protect her sister, a vow she would not break.

The two Varil raiders who stood to either side produced the grunting hiss that served their kind as laughter. They were massive creatures, bodies roped with muscle under iridescent reptilian scales, eyes glowing orange as coals in the darkness. They smelled like snakes. They wore no armor, and needed none with their thick hides. Clawed hands carried battle axes with blades the size of a warrior's shield.

It was said they'd once been human. Amaris doubted it.

What in the name of all the gods am I doing here?

Raniero rode in wariness, vampire senses alert for any attack, mystical or otherwise. Though the kingdom's magical barriers should keep Varilian raiders out, sometimes the vicious bastards got through. And considering the king's suspicions about Wizard Lord Korban, Raniero was not inclined to take chances.

"Do you think Korban really is working with the Varil?" Gvido asked. The boy rode at an easy trot beside him, his visor up, revealing a rawboned, freckled face in the light from Raniero's illumination spell.

"I know not," Raniero told him. "And I will draw no conclusions until I investigate further."

"But how could any border wizard work with the Varil?" Gvido shook his head in disbelief. "Remember what they did to that village? What was it called, Kessel? Men, women, children—ripped apart and eaten. I have evil dreams about it still." He had been Raniero's squire for almost a year now, an earnest sixteen-year-old with a merry smile and a pleasant tenor voice. He wore his long red hair tied back in a queue. His chin was covered by a thin orange scruff he stubbornly refused to shave; he was determined to grow a proper beard.

"Sorcerers," Olrick grunted from Raniero's right. A tall, muscular man with an impressive belly, he was a skilled and wily warrior. Yet after twenty years fighting at Raniero's side, his braided beard and long blond hair were dulling into gray. He would retire soon, and Raniero was not looking forward to it. "All wizards be mad. Years of sniffing potions and playing with spells. 'Tis no wonder their wits fly."

Raniero lifted a dark brow. "*I* work spells." His magic was not as strong as that of the border wizards, but he was no powerless peasant either.

"Ye be a vampire," Olrick said, unperturbed. "Of course ye be mad."

Suppressing a smile, Raniero flicked a rude finger at his friend. Olrick brayed his distinctive laugh and replied with a gesture even more obscene.

Raniero's chuckle faded into a frown as a feeling of waiting evil brushed his vampire senses. He straightened in his saddle and drew rein as he scanned the surrounding hills. Bakur, his black warhorse, danced in unease, as if he, too, sensed a threat. Alerted, Raniero's men pulled up and peered around.

At first his keen night vision detected nothing but the forested hills that surrounded them, silvered by moonlight and splashed with shadow.

Until something shimmered in a there-not-there flash that told him someone was moving behind a shielding spell. "Draw weapons!" Raniero bellowed, pulling his own great blade from its saddle sheath as he jerked Bakur to face the threat.

The attackers exploded into view—two Varil raiders afoot and one mounted fighter, all three plunging down the hill toward them. Raniero's gut clenched in dread. Though the odds seemed to favor his party, the reptilian raiders were far stronger than humans—and far more vicious. Ten men were not enough to bring two Varil down.

With a hard jerk of one shoulder, Raniero shrugged his shield off his back and into his left hand, spurring his stallion forward. He had to take the Varil out quickly if his men were to survive. Bakur squealed an equine challenge as he broke into a pounding gallop up the hill.

To Raniero's startled rage, the two raiders veered away from his charge. Before he could spin his horse after them, the third fighter bore down on him, bellowing a war cry.

Raniero swung his shield up to block the other's sword as the horses collided with a meaty thud. His enemy's blade struck the shield so hard Raniero felt the impact to his teeth. The man couldn't be human, not with such strength.

Another vampire. He'd be no easy kill.

Behind him, one of Raniero's men screamed, high and thin with agony and fear. The shriek died in a gurgle.

Raniero bared his fangs and swung his sword with all his supernatural strength. His foe caught the blow on his own kite-shaped shield, long sword arcing for Raniero's head. Raniero ducked and kneed Bakur aside. The two mounts wheeled, slashing at each other with sharp hooves and snapping teeth.

Another death scream. It sounded like Olrick.

Fury and grief sizzling through him, Raniero forced himself to concentrate on his enemy—and prayed he'd finish the bastard off in time to save the rest of his men.

As she'd been ordered, Amaris hung back on the hillside, waiting for Tannaz's signal. Her vantage point gave her a good view of the fight.

A bit too good, in fact. She really didn't want to watch what the raiders' axes were doing to those poor humans, so she focused her attention on the vampires.

Physically, the two were well-matched. Tannaz was a bit taller and thicker through the shoulders, but Raniero made up the difference in speed and agility. He clung to his beast by knees alone as the black warhorse battled Tannaz's bay destrier.

Tannaz rose in his stirrups to better bring his blade down on his foe's head. As Raniero blocked with his shield, his charger lunged and sank his teeth into the throat of Tannaz's bay. The horse threw up his head and reared to escape, blood flying. Tannaz lost his balance, tumbling from the saddle to land on the leafy forest floor with a crunch of armor and bone.

"Ha!" Delighted, Amaris rose in her stirrups for a better view.

But her murdering sire had already rolled to his feet, scuttling away as his bay fled the black's teeth and hooves. Wheeling the stallion after his foe, Raniero rained relentless blows down on Tannaz, forced the vampire to duck behind his shield and retreat. Steel rang on steel like the steady clang of a blacksmith's hammer.

Amaris! Curse your eyes, aid me! Her father's mystical voice bellowed in her mind.

Die and be damned, murderer, Amaris thought back.

If I do not return, Korban will slay Marin.

Amaris's lips curled back from her teeth.

Raniero used his shield to block the vampire's attempts to drive his sword into Bakur's glossy black chest. Spotting an opening, Raniero brought his sword down in a furious overhand blow.

One of his men shrieked in mortal agony, but he didn't dare look away from his enemy. A flash of white fluttered in his periphrial vision, but Raniero ignored that, too.

So when the beautiful woman suddenly appeared behind his opponent, he almost fell out of the saddle in sheer astonishment.

She was slim as a river reed, dressed in white silk so thin and fine, he could see the shadow of her nipples in the moonlight. Her hair fell around her shoulders in a cascade of dark curls, and her large eyes glowed a luminous green in her fine-boned face, like spring leaves illuminated by the sun.

A tattoo of a rose bloomed on the high rise of her cheek. He recognized the design instantly. What in the Red God's name was a Blood Rose doing *here*?

Raniero's vampire foe spun, spotted the Blood Rose, and leaped for her. Acting on sheer instinct, Raniero swung a leg over Bakur's side and dove, plowing the vampire into the forest floor before he could grab the girl.

As they hit the ground, Raniero lifted his sword, meaning to end the bastard right there.

He did not see the Blood Rose lift her delicate hands and send a spell blast slamming into his helmeted head.

Blackness descended like a swinging fist.

Tannaz jerked free of the vampire's dead weight and bounced to his feet, raising his sword as if to cleave his foe's head off his shoulders.

"Korban wants him alive!" Amaris shouted, readying a stun spell if he did not heed her.

Her father hesitated, spat a curse, and aimed a kick at Raniero's armored ribs instead. Panting, he gave her a smug, triumphant grin. "Well done, daughter."

"I was tempted to let him kill you."

"Vicious little harpy," Tannaz said, almost fondly. "I shall have to teach you respect."

She snorted contempt. "Oh, aye—when the Red God takes up needlework."

Ignoring that, Tannaz looked around at the Varil. The two raiders had settled among Raniero's fallen men to feed. Amaris refused to follow his gaze. The smell and sound of their feast was enough to make her stomach heave as it was.

"Feh," he spat. "They'll not be finished any time soon. We will move on ahead. I would have this one in a cell before your spell wears off."

She nodded grimly and summoned the horses with a wave of her hand. The spell to bring the vampire's black destrier under control took a bit more work, but soon the stallion was ambling along beside them, his master hanging bound and bewitched across his saddle.

At least it was over, Amaris comforted herself. She could take Marin and go.

If Korban kept his word . . .

TWO

Tzira Castle occupied the rocky heights of the Korban Mountain Range, named for the wizard clan that had held this stretch of the border for the last three hundred years. The clan had been good caretakers for generations, maintaining their section of the mystical barrier that protected the kingdom of Ourania from its neighbor, Zahur, land of the Varil.

They'd known the price of failure all too well. The humans of Zahur had been hunted to the brink of extinction to feed the Varil's vicious appetites.

Clan Korban had accordingly built Tzira into a sprawling fortress, its black stone seeming to grow from the granite flanks of the mountain, all massive, blocky towers and curving walls, riddled with arrow slits and glowing with torch spells. Even Amaris had to admit the place had a stark kind of beauty.

Too bad the latest Korban wizard had turned to treason.

Amaris strode into the great hall of Tzira Castle, her belly tight with a sickening combination of eagerness and dread.

Eagerness to see Marin again. Dread of what Korban might have done to her while Amaris was gone. *If she's dead, I will blow this castle to fractured stone and pave the road to hell.*

She would not survive the effort—Korban was too powerful—but she would make him regret his betrayal.

Heart in her throat, Amaris stalked through the mass of cowed servants and swaggering men-at-arms toward the dais where Korban sprawled on his lord's seat. He smirked at her as she came, probably because Tannaz strode at her heels, carrying Raniero draped over his shoulder like a slain buck.

"Ama'is!" The little voice piped across the babble of voices in the hall, high and incredibly sweet. Her knees went weak with relief. "Ama'is!" Marin couldn't yet manage the *r* in her name.

The child raced out of the crowd as Amaris dropped to her knees and spread her arms. Dark curls flying, big green eyes wide, the little girl flew into her hug with a force that rocked her back on her heels. "Ama'is!" she gasped. "Take me home! I want to see Mama!"

Amaris closed her eyes at the grief that stabbed her as she hugged her little sister close. Marin was too young to grasp death's finality. "I know, love. I do, too."

Raniero hit the ground beside her with a thud as Tannaz dumped him from his shoulder. Her father had stripped the warrior of his armor, weapons, and clothing, leaving him naught but his breeches—and the bespelled chains that leached his strength and kept him unconscious.

Tannaz sneered down at them, and Amaris gave him her best bloodthirsty glare in return. Marin burrowed into her shoulder, tiny body quivering. The child had watched him murder their mother but a month past, and she feared him with a black terror.

She might not understand death, but steel and blood were clear enough.

"Poor child." The voice was beautiful, warm and soft as deep velvet. A big male hand reached down toward Marin's gleaming curls.

Marin screamed and cowered.

Amaris jerked her sister away and surged to her feet, the child wrapped in her arms. Summoning a shielding spell, she glared at the wizard. "Back. *Away.*"

"Ahhh, Amaris, my sweet." Korban spread his arms in

the fine robes that draped his lean body in silk. Embroidered runes covered the red fabric in intricate spells of protection and power enhancement. The thread shone bright with gold—except where darkened with the blood of the robes' tailor, slain to enhance its power. His face was long and pale in the torchlight, a beard darkening his angular cheeks and framing his dissolute mouth. "You wound me."

"Not yet," Amaris snarled, "But I will if you do not keep your promise." She jerked her chin at the unconscious vampire. "I captured Lord Raniero, as you demanded. Now, release us."

"In time."

"Now!" Amaris demanded through clenched teeth.

Marin's little legs curled tighter around her hip. "He thinks 'bout killin' me to feed that ball of his," the child whispered fearfully. "I see it in his mind. All the time."

Korban's eyes rested on the back of the child's head, greed in their pale depths. "So much potential power for one so young. And you say she is but three years of age?"

"Her age is of no matter to you, wizard." Heartily sick of his games, Amaris spun toward the great hall's double doors. She'd left her horse saddled, Marin's few things packed in saddlebags. They could make Clefton in three days of hard riding. "We are leaving."

"No."

All around the hall, warriors looked up at his tone. Swords left scabbards with a sinister metallic slither.

Amaris stopped short as the point of one fighter's blade rose toward Marin's thin back. The child's arms and legs tightened around her with a strength born of sheer terror. Drawing in power desperately, Amaris reinforced the magical shield around them.

But it could not protect them against every man here.

"I've decided I need one further service from my Blood Rose."

Amaris whirled toward him, hot words on her lips. They died on her tongue at the sight of the crimson globe that floated above his palm. The sheer evil emanating from the thing made her skin crawl in revulsion.

The Blood Orb.

"I have a small problem," Korban told her absently, his eyes fixed on the Orb with lustful fascination. "I can kill King Ferran's errand boy, of course." He jerked his chin at Raniero, sprawled in muscular insensibility on the rush-covered floor. "But when he does not report back to his master, Ferran will consider his suspicions confirmed. And since the king maintains a well-trained and rather impressive army that includes a respectable cadre of wizards—well, I would as soon they did not pay me a visit."

"What has that to do with me?" Amaris snapped. "I cannot defend you from an army."

"No, but you can woo yon vampire into a more receptive frame of mind." He smiled. The expression might have imparted a certain beauty to his triangular, foxlike face, if not for his soulless eyes. "Receptive enough to send a magical message to his master that I am a true and loyal servant. Delay Ferran's attack just a bit. A month, perhaps even two, while I complete my work."

"You mean your mad plot to drop the barrier that protects us all from the Varil. Whereupon they'll roll over us and feast on our bleeding corpses." She turned to the nearest warrior. "Do you want to fill the belly of one of those monsters? I don't. One wonders why your master does."

The warrior winced and looked away.

Korban's pale face reddened with rage. "The Varil are my allies, bitch. They will give me power beyond your conception—power enough to make me king." He shot a dark look at the flinching warrior. "And those who are *loyal* to me will reap the benefits."

"Oh, aye," Amaris sneered. "I wager they will—as crows pick their bones for what scraps the Varil leave behind."

His fingers tightened around the Orb as his free hand lifted, trembling with his fury. Power heated the air around it into a hot red blaze.

Amaris fed more magic into her shields and readied herself to fight, clutching her sister close.

Then the glow faded from Korban's fingers, and the rage in his eyes drained into calculation. He rolled his shoulders back and lifted his chin. "You will not goad me so easily. You *will* lie with Raniero, and you will persuade him to cooperate. Or your sister will pay the price."

"I fear you overestimate my skills. Lord Raniero is famous for his incorruptibility."

"True. It's said he's refused some very impressive bribes." The Orb's light flooded Korban's face in crimson, like a mask of gore. "But none of those bribes included the attentions of a Blood Rose."

"I am not your whore, Korban."

"You are whatever we tell you to be, Amaris!" her father snarled.

"Ama'is!" Marin whimpered.

"We frighten the child," Korban said, his voice gently cruel. "But there is no need. All you must do is spend a little time with Lord Raniero. Look at him." He turned with a sweeping gesture, directing her attention toward the vampire. Raniero's profile looked as pure as a deity's in the light of the torches, his black hair spilling around bare, muscled shoulders. "Such a handsome man. What's a few nights in his arms? And then I'll free you, let you take Marin and go. I swear it by the Red God's blade."

"Ama'is," Marin whispered, staring at Korban like a bird gazing at a snake. "He's gonna feed me to his ball if you don't."

She was right. Korban was projecting the image of it into their minds, sharp and vivid as reality:

A knife flashed in the red light of the Orb, and the fantasy Marin screamed. The smell of blood filled the air, and the Orb brightened into a blinding crimson blaze.

The real child quivered against her and began to cry.

"Stop it, curse you!" Amaris spat. "I'll seduce your vampire for you. Just leave my sister out of your sickening plots."

Korban smiled, faint and satisfied. "I knew you'd see reason."

Pleased with his victory, Korban allowed Amaris to put her sister to bed. Usually, he permitted her only brief visits with the child, at the end of which Amaris had to surrender Marin to the nursemaid warden he'd assigned.

Even so, a pair of grim and wary guards followed her up the tower stairs to the small chamber where Marin was kept a hostage. Amaris's thoughts churned in anguished circles as she climbed, her sister sniffling fitfully in her arms. Though sweaty and tearstained, Marin smelled clean and sweet in the way of little girls. At least that wretched nurse was taking proper care of her.

For the moment.

Korban's promise to release them was, of course, a blatant lie. No matter what he mouthed, his plans for Marin were obvious. It would take a blood sacrifice of her innocence and magical potential to give the Blood Orb enough power to blow a hole in the kingdom's mystical barrier.

And Korban was determined to see the Varil invade, the Red God alone knew why.

I should have known Korban would break his promise to free us, Amaris thought as she carried the child up the narrow, winding staircase. *But I thought there was a faint possibility he'd keep his word. Now I will have to find some other way to escape.*

Fortunately, generations of wizards had spent centuries building and strengthening the Great Barrier, and a spell to unravel it was no easy thing to cast. Korban had yet to puzzle out how to do it, though 'twould seem he was close to his goal. Enough so that he thought he needed to allay Ferran's suspicions for but a few weeks more.

They reached the top of the stairway, and Amaris paused to let her guards unlock Marin's door. She carried the child inside.

The nurse looked up from her sewing. At first glance, one might mistake Hetram for a motherly woman in her cheery blue gown, given her ample lap and round, rosy cheeks. But her watery gray eyes were as chilly as a frozen lake, and the line of her mouth was thin and humorless. She had power, too, a sullen snake of magic Amaris could see in her heart, enough that Korban trusted her to control Marin's burgeoning talent.

It was probably no real challenge. In happier days, Marin

had tested their mother's patience with her mischievous magic. She'd had particular talent with an invisibility spell; she'd loved nothing better than popping out and startling her unsuspecting mother and sister. Now the child's misery made it hard for her to concentrate enough to work even the simplest magic.

"I'll take her." Hetram stood and reached for Marin.

"Nay, I'll do it." Amaris shouldered past her toward the little girl's narrow cot. She undressed her sister, taking pleasure in the homey task of pulling off Marin's wool kirtle and chemise and slipping a clean white smock over her head. Exhausted by fear and tears, Marin was asleep almost before she finished. Amaris tucked her limp little body into bed, then covered her with the thin blanket she'd been allowed.

Finished, Amaris sat still a moment, brooding as she studied Marin's pale, delicate features in the candlelight. *She looks so much like Mother.* Tears welled at the thought, and she quickly swiped her hand across her eyes, lest the nurse see her crying.

I will get her out of here, Mama. Somehow. I will not let that monster use her soul to feed that cursed Orb.

Which meant doing what she'd been doing all along: pretend to cooperate with their captors and watch for an opportunity to take her sister and escape. Pray gods the chance presented itself soon. She was running out of time.

And now she had to romance a vampire.

Something popped, and Amaris looked up, alert. But it was only the fire. Her eyes met the suspicious gaze of Marin's warden, who sat with a half-darned sock in her wide lap. Amaris pointedly turned her gaze toward the fire and made no move to leave, despite the woman's evident desire to see the back of her.

Gazing into the leaping flames, Amaris began to plan. She had to buy time, and there was only one way to do it.

She was going to have to make love to the vampire.

THREE

Amaris's stomach coiled into a sick ball at the thought of taking Raniero into her bed. She glowered at the fire, impatient with herself. *I'm a Blood Rose, curse it. Making love to them is what we were created to do.*

When it became obvious the Varil were a threat to the kingdom, the first great wizard king had transformed human champions into a race of vampire knights. To ensure the knights did not likewise become a threat, the king had then transformed his most talented female sorcerers into Blood Roses with the magical power to seduce and tame them.

Though vampires could sire vampire sons with mortal women, Blood Roses were born only to Blood Rose mothers. By law, the king alone could grant a Blood Rose's hand in marriage, and he granted that boon only to those he considered most deserving. Since drinking a Rose's blood made a vampire stronger, his allies had the advantage over any would-be vampire rebels.

Like other Roses, Amaris was well-versed in the Arts of the Rose. Her mother had sent her to one of the best Gardens in the kingdom to learn the traditional skills: how to charm, how to flirt, how to use her mouth and hands to bring her vampire lover pleasure.

Unfortunately, vampires could not be trusted. Her father was proof of that.

And Orel, of course.

For a while she'd actually believed all the silly songs the troubadours sang in the Garden. Songs of gallant vampire warriors romancing their lady Roses, sweeping them away to lives of love and passion.

She should have known it was all utter rot.

As a child, Amaris had watched her father torment her mother until Sava finally had enough and petitioned the king for a divorce. Ferran had been so scandalized that any vampire would beat a Blood Rose, he'd granted it on the spot. The king had even issued a royal order that Tannaz keep his distance on pain of death. The vampire hadn't dared break it.

At least until he'd fallen in with Korban and grown bold. Bold enough to murder both his former wife and her lover, Marin's father.

And then there was Orel, handsome, seductive—and insanely jealous. Amaris had met him while she was still at the Garden, and had promptly believed herself in love.

Until the day he'd seen her smile at another vampire.

Once back at the house they'd shared, Orel had ranted at Amaris like a madman before knocking her senseless. She'd awakened with him on top of her, beginning a rape. Terrified, enraged, she'd fired a blast of magic into his face. He'd fled, burned and screaming.

That experience had left her determined to never be so vulnerable again. She'd begun combat training with Basir, who was both her mother's lover and a skilled swordsman and sorcerer. After two years of hard work, Basir had pronounced her capable of defending herself.

But Orel's attack had taught her something else as well: vampires could not be trusted. No matter how loving they might act, they were predators, no different from the Varil. Any Rose who let down her guard with one would rue it.

Now Amaris had to lull her captors into believing her cowed

and cooperative. She felt confident that given enough time, she'd spot an opportunity to rescue her sister and escape.

But to buy that time, she was going to have to seduce Raniero. So she'd give the vampire her body—but never her trust.

Dawn was breaking when Amaris returned to the cramped chamber she'd been given in one of the castle's towers.

Moving quickly, she swung the door closed and hurried across the room to fling open the wooden shutters. The edge of the sun was just peeking over the horizon, painting streamers of rose and violet across the sky. Beneath them, the Korban Mountains lay in thick black shadow.

There wasn't much time.

Amaris took a deep breath and drew a long, thin dagger from the sheath that hung from her embroidered belt. Concentrating fiercely, she angled the knife point up, so that the rays of the sun poured over it. Gathering her will, she began to chant as the rising sun warmed her face. Magic swirled around her, flowing into the dagger, making the thin blade blaze.

Raniero woke half naked in a bed far more comfortable than the ground he so often slept on as the king's investigator. Blinking, disoriented, he tried to roll off the bed, only to discover two things: he was weak as a babe, and his wrists were chained to the posts of the bed.

Rage lengthening his teeth into fangs, he jerked his head around to stare at his wrists. The manacles that encircled them were covered with magical runes he read with a wizard's ease.

A draining spell. 'Twould sap his strength and magic, keeping him from breaking the chains.

Peering down the length of his body, he saw he wore naught but his breeches. His ankles, too, were chained.

With a growl, he dropped his head back on the feather pillow.

Who the six hells gave a prisoner a feather pillow?

The thought made him scan his cell in narrow-eyed suspicion.

It looked more guest's chamber than prison. The room was clean, with fresh rushes on the floor, and a fire burned in the fireplace, reducing the autumn chill. Two chairs sat before the fire, and there was a small bedside table on which an unlit candle stood beside a golden goblet. No window, but vampire that he was, he was rather glad of that. At least his captors couldn't cook him with the sunrise while he was helplessly chained to the bed.

What the six hells happened?

The last he remembered, he'd been about to take that vampire's head in an effort to keep the bastard from attacking the Blood Rose who had appeared in the middle of the fight.

The Blood Rose.

Raniero ground his teeth in rage as the truth burst upon him. *She'd been working with the vampire.* They'd gulled him with their playacting, and he'd swallowed the bait whole.

Fool, fool, fool! And by now his men were likely all dead, bodies devoured by the thrice-damned Varil.

He closed his eyes, sickened. Poor Gvido had so feared those monsters after seeing the aftermath of one of their raids. Raniero had often been woken by the boy's nightmare cries. How he must have suffered, dying at their hands.

And Olrick. He'd planned to retire and spend his last years surrounded by grandchildren while playing slap and tickle with his wife. Raniero would have to tell Gavina he'd gotten her man killed.

And then there were the others: Kellar, Favdo, Jacil, Magar, Brothan, Lor, and Shaco. Good men, brave men, all loyal king's warriors. He would have to tell their wives, children, and parents. And the king, who would be deeply grieved.

At least his majesty would see the families were paid a death pension. They would not be left impoverished.

Just grieving.

Raniero's eyes narrowed. His captors would rue this day. Which raised the question: why had they left him alive to seek vengeance?

He considered his prison again. It appeared someone was entertaining fantasies that he could be bought.

The idea was infuriating. But galling as it was, perhaps he

should pretend to play along, that he might gain an opportunity to escape.

And make the bastards pay.

Amaris paused outside Raniero's cell, ignoring the hot gazes of the four guards. She had dressed as carefully as ever she'd been taught in the Garden. Her gown was white silk, belted with a girdle embroidered with tiny roses, and she'd perfumed her skin with ambergris. A hint of kohl darkened her lids, and she'd rubbed a lemon on her lips to redden them. Her hair had been brushed into a gleaming fall of curls that tumbled to her hips. She carried a silver pitcher filled with honey mead.

Squaring her shoulders and drawing a deep breath, she nodded at the guards. "Unbolt the door."

The oldest of the four, a grizzled warrior with his long beard in braids, curled a scarred lip at her and made no move to obey. She met his gaze and lifted an icy brow, letting power leap in her eyes like a flame. Realizing how close he was to suffering a painful magical jolt for his contempt, he hurried to unbolt the door and give her a carefully respectful bow. Satisfied, she sailed past.

If she could make the guards fear her, they might hesitate at a crucial moment. She could construct an escape from such small strategies.

"I wondered when they'd send you." The vampire spoke from the firelit dimness, his voice rumbling and deep, almost touchable, a velvet seduction that seemed to stroke her skin.

The door swung closed behind Amaris with a bang. The iron bolt scraped home as the guard locked it. She managed not to jump at the harsh sound and lifted her chin. "Perhaps I come of my own accord."

"Do you?"

"Oh, aye." Forcing a smile, Amaris moved toward him, giving her hips the gentle sway she'd been taught. The pressure of her slippers sent a rich, green scent into the air. She'd ordered fresh herbs scattered among the rushes.

As Lady Taria said, *You must seduce a man's senses before you touch his body.*

Moving with deliberate grace, Amaris picked up the golden goblet on the wooden bedside table and filled it with honey mead. "Do you thirst?"

Dark eyes dropped to her throat. "Oh, aye." His purr made it clear he craved something other than the contents of her pitcher.

Not likely, vampire. Drinking her magical blood would strengthen him, perhaps enough to break his enchanted chains.

She took a slow and deliberate sip from the goblet, by way of demonstrating the drink had not been poisoned. As she swallowed the mead with its rich traces of lemon and berry, she let her gaze rest on his face.

Studying him through lowered lids, she had to admit Korban was right. The vampire was a handsome man. The firelight played over sculpted features: cheekbones carved high enough to leave hollows beneath, a stubbornly jutting warrior's chin, a straight and arrogant nose. His upper lip curved over a plump lower lip that seemed to invite a woman's bite. He wore no beard, though a night's growth shadowed the planes of his cheeks. His hair was dark, shoulder-length, as gleaming and thick as a woman's.

Half unwilling, she let her gaze drift down his body. He wore nothing but breeches so tight, he might as well have been naked. Muscle lay across his broad, bare torso in thick swordsman's slabs, rippling and bunching as he pulled at his chains. His legs were long and brawny, as befit a man who sat a horse so well. She could see his sex bulking heavy beneath the breeches.

It stirred under her gaze.

Fighting the urge to jerk her eyes away, she raised her chin and met his stare. He lifted a thick black brow, his eyes hot and narrow. And deeply cynical. He was no fool, this agent of the wizard king. An ally, then?

His lips parted, and she glimpsed the white gleam of a fang.

No, she'd trust no vampire. If it were only her own life, she might take the risk, but not with Marin's soul at hazard.

Amaris dropped her lashes and met his gaze under their thick fringe. "Would you have mead?"

His lips quirked. "Only if that's all you offer."

"It is." She let her own mouth curl. "For the moment."

There it was again, that cynical curve of the lip. "Mead it is, then."

Amaris stepped closer and bent over him. He lifted his head and let her press the goblet to his lips. She tipped it, and he swallowed with obvious thirst. The strong cords of his throat rippled up and down. His lids lowered, and for a moment sensual pleasure lay stark on his face. She watched, half bespelled, as he drained the cup.

"You *were* thirsty." Her voice sounded so hoarse, she silently cursed the desire it revealed.

He lay back, rolling brawny shoulders on his pillow. "A prisoner never knows when his needs will be met. Best to take advantage of any"—his lids dropped again—"opportunities."

"Far be it for me to leave you wanting." Despite the sophisticated quip, she could feel heat blooming across her face.

Blood Roses do not blush like virgins, curse it.

Raniero again drained the goblet the Blood Rose held to his lips. Even as he drank, he cursed himself. Her scent flooded his head, far more intoxicating than the mead. Ambergris, woman, magic—and blood. His fangs ached savagely.

Damn her to the six hells. If he could but drink from her—not much more than a goblet's worth—the magic of her blood would strengthen him enough to shatter the enchantment that held him. He could take care of the guards in the hall and be gone before his foes knew what he was about.

Which was why she'd never allow him to taste that long white throat.

Unless . . .

Raniero considered her through narrowed eyes as he drank in her scent. There was more than a little desire wafting from that long, elegant body. And other emotions too: fear, rage . . . And was that despair?

No, surely not. Why would she fear him, when he was so thoroughly bound and drained by his chains?

Unless it was someone else she feared . . .

FOUR

The idea of her fear was enraging. Even knowing Amaris was a traitor to her own people, Raniero could feel the tugging need to protect her. That compulsion was part of a Blood Rose's seductive magic, and he could no more fight it than he could refuse to breathe.

To most vampires, the hand of a Rose was a much desired prize, since her blood would strengthen both one's magic and one's might. Many were the drunken dreams he'd heard vampire courtiers spew of "A Rose and a fief."

Raniero wanted only the fief. He'd get his sons on mortals, thank you. Lusty peasant wenches spun far simpler schemes.

His stepmother had been one of those scheming Roses. She'd wanted her own son to inherit, so she'd told his father Raniero had tried to force himself on her. Raniero, who'd been all of sixteen, protested his innocence, but Fulk had believed Eiriene. He'd beaten his son near to death and left him outside the castle walls. Luckily, Raniero had been able to find shelter with the neighboring lord who'd fostered him when he'd been a boy. Landless, homeless, he'd fought to earn a place at King Ferran's court.

But he'd never forgotten the way a Rose could twist a man's mind.

That this Rose was scheming, he did not doubt. But what, and why?

In any case, it appeared Ferran's suspicions about Korban were confirmed. Why else would Raniero's party be attacked the moment they crossed onto Korban's land? And by a vampire and two Varil raiders, yet.

Why had his captors allowed Raniero to live, while slaying his men? Korban apparently thought he could buy Raniero's cooperation. And he thought he could do it with the bribe of a Blood Rose.

Whatever spies Korban obviously had at Ferran's palace—and he had at least one, if he'd known Raniero was coming—they weren't as good as he thought. Raniero's wariness of Roses was well-known.

But if Korban and his Rose knew it not, perhaps Raniero could pretend to yield to her wiles. Discover the wizard's plans, and find a way to foil them. It was certain outright struggle would do him no good, not in these chains.

"More?" the Rose asked, candlelight painting dancing gold highlights over the tattoo blooming on her cheek.

"Actually, there's something else I crave," he said, deliberately staring at the plump and tempting curve of her lips. "A taste of you."

Green eyes widened, and that luscious mouth parted. "Oh." A pretty blush brightened her high cheeks.

Red God's Balls, she did flustered innocence better than any sheltered virgin he'd ever met.

Slowly, almost unwillingly, she leaned down. He watched the hesitant movement. Ridiculously, his heart began to hammer. The scent of mingled fear and desire strengthened.

Why does she fear me?

The Rose's lips touched his, only the merest brush at first, warm breath tasting of honey mead and a hint of lemon. She kept her eyes open, almost as though she didn't trust him enough to close them. He forced relaxation into every hungry muscle and let her lead the way, keeping his mouth soft beneath hers.

She brushed her lips across his, once, then again. Hesitated like something small and wild eating from his hand. At last she deepened the kiss, slipping her tongue into his mouth, a shy, soft stroke. When she drew in a breath, he felt the tips of her breasts touch his chest. She sighed, and slowly, oh so slowly, her eyes closed as she leaned deeper into the kiss.

It took him a moment to realize he'd closed his own as well, the better to concentrate on the delicate sensations of her swirling tongue, her gently moving mouth. He could feel her heartbeat in her breast, a rapid thump that seemed to echo his own pulse.

One soft, slender hand came to rest on his chest, cool against his heating skin. She used it to push herself upright. They stared at each other in the candlelit darkness.

Again, he watched that curious fear leap in her eyes. For a moment, he expected her to whirl and run away.

Instead she squared her delicate shoulders. Her hands went to the laces of her white gown, began to pluck at them until they fell untied. He caught his breath as she drew it off over her head and dropped it in a silken pile on the floor. Her body gleamed in the candlelight, elegant and slim, breasts pale, perfect handfuls, nipples tight and pink. She had the legs of a horsewoman, long and strong, and her arms had a kind of delicate strength, as though she did more than needlework. Her green gaze had gone bright with defiance now, as if daring him to make some cutting comment.

But speech was beyond him. He felt his cock rise, hot and hard against his breeches, balls heavy with the weight of desire.

Her gaze dipped to the broad length against his belly, and her lips parted. As he watched, her eyes dilated into a shadowed forest green, dark and wild.

"Free me," he managed at last, his eyes on the tight pink tips of her breasts. "Let me touch you."

She shot him a wary look, then seemed to remember herself and added a seductive smile. "Wouldn't you rather I touch *you*?"

He laughed in a harsh bark. "At this moment, I would have you any way I can get you."

The Rose stepped closer to the bed and balanced on one long leg as she slid a thigh across his belly. He caught his breath in lust at the sensation of soft skin sliding over his in a wave of silken warmth. Slowly, so slowly, she sank down to straddle him. To his raging frustration, he could feel the cloth-covered head of his cock brushing the curve of her bare bottom.

"Ahhh." Her lids dipped and lifted, revealing the green of her eyes. The pink tip of her tongue crept out to wet her lips, and she swallowed. A very faint smile curved that tempting mouth. "You make a solid mount, my lord."

"And you make a lovely rider," Raniero rasped, though the courtly words were almost beyond him as lust stormed his brain. His eyes dipped down to the soft delta of her sex, the lips full and pouting behind raven curls. He wanted to see those lips close around his cock. He could imagine how they'd feel, swollen and wet, gripping him deliciously.

The Rose considered him, her head tilting. Her slender hands came to rest on his chest, long fingers stroking. Her nails were short and serviceable, and her palms were just slightly rough with calluses.

Raniero frowned in momentary puzzlement. Her hands were slim as a maid's, but rough as a swordsman's. No stranger to battle, this one.

Then the thought flew out of his head as she bent, green eyes locked on his. The tip of her tongue peeked out at him, and he stiffened in helpless anticipation.

She licked him. A quick little flick over the tight ridges of his torso, wet, impossibly tempting, a maddening promise of more. Her head lifted, and a smile flashed, quicksilver mockery.

God, he wished his hands were free. He'd show her need. He'd make her writhe.

But his hands were bound, and she was the one with the freedom to inflict delicious torment. She bent again, and he inhaled sharply, helplessly.

Raniero's nipples were her target this time. He'd never considered them particularly sensitive before—certainly not like a woman's—yet the rake of her teeth made his cock jerk like a rearing warhorse. She settled down to lick, gently, sweet teasing circles with the occasional application of a nibble or two. As if those desperate little points were candy.

Red God's Balls, he wished she'd do that to his cock.

As the Rose nibbled, she stroked her hands over his torso, traced each ridge of muscle with tapered fingers that suddenly curled into blunt little claws. The teasing rake of nails over ribs made him want to writhe.

Green eyes watched him, shadowed by thick lashes, dwelling on his face as if fascinated. Her nostrils flared, scenting him like a cat.

His cock jerked again, brushing the velvet skin of her bottom. Raniero couldn't quite suppress his moan.

Amaris was beginning to understand why poets spilled rivers of ink in praise of passion. The vampire lay spread under her like a feast, all frustrated power, arms bunching as he fought his chains. Yet he seemed scarcely aware of them, so utterly was he focused on her, on every tiny thing she did.

His face fascinated her. There was a muscle in his jaw that leaped and bunched each time she flicked her tongue over his nipples. He really was a handsome man, his face all jutting bone, deep hollows and uncompromising angles. It was a warrior's face, one that could have been sculpted by the Red God himself for the battlefield—designed to lead men and bellow orders and snarl as he swung a sword in lethal arcs.

And he had a warrior's body as well. His bunched upper arms were round as melons and near the size of her head. Each of his thighs appeared the width of her waist. Given the vampire strength within all that muscle, he'd be a formidable force on the battlefield.

A killer.

What if she could make him *her* killer? Amaris eyed him, considering the thick strength surging under her body, the wild black heat in his eyes.

A solid mount indeed.

Could she ride him? Could she trade him her blood for Marin's freedom? Did she dare?

Black eyes stared into hers, highlighted with candlelit reflection in flashes of liquid gold. The male hunger in that dark gaze demanded her surrender with a trace of savagery, as if he eyed her while riding at the head of an army.

Not while he himself was bound and helpless.

Raniero's lips parted in invitation. His breath smelled of honey mead. Unable to resist, she bent closer and kissed him again.

His mouth was soft, tempting, tangy with lemon, sweet with berries and honey. Amaris sighed, deepening the kiss, slipping her tongue into his mouth, exploring the sensuality he offered.

Something sharp pricked her tongue, and she frowned faintly, wondering. Until realization struck.

It was one of his fangs.

He was a vampire. In the storm of emotion and heat, she'd almost forgotten.

Luscious as he was, so powerfully seductive as he lay there in pretended submission, he was a predator. And worse, he was a trapped predator. If she were stupid enough to offer him the magical blood he needed to break his chains, he'd be gone like a ghost at dawn. And she'd be left alone to confront Korban's fury.

Vampires could not be trusted.

Anger surged in her, hot and sudden, spiked with helplessness. "Well," she growled down into his startled eyes, "there's one way I can use you."

She rose onto her knees in her simmering frustration, scooted back, grabbed the waistband of his breeches, and jerked downward. His cock sprang free, its strong length shading into delicious pink, its head ripe as a plum.

Amaris grabbed that tempting thickness in one hand, rose over it, and impaled herself in a single breathless rush.

Sensation ripped away her breath. He felt incredibly thick in her slick inner grip. She hadn't even realized she was so wet, so swollen with heat and need. Teasing him had aroused her as much as it had him.

Damn him to the six hells.

Bracing her hands on his chest, Amaris rose, teasing

herself with the juicy slide of his cock. Rolling her head back, she sank, acutely aware of his deep, rumbling groan.

She told herself she no longer cared what the vampire felt. No longer cared if he moaned as she rode him. Cared not if his hungry black gaze lingered on her face, if his big hands clenched in desire, if his feet twitched in helpless reaction to her jogging strokes.

All that mattered was the impaling heat between her legs that spun such sweet pleasure every time she rose and fell. The vampire ground his teeth and rolled his hips to meet her, adding his fierce power to her strokes. But that didn't matter. She wouldn't let it. Wouldn't let *him* matter.

Vampires couldn't be trusted. They lied. They hurt.

And they killed.

FIVE

Raniero ground his aching fangs as she rode him, head tossing until her curls teased his thighs. Amaris felt as deliciously wet as any fantasy he'd ever had, gripping him in a tight vise of feminine flesh. Each time she moved, jolts of pleasure surged straight up his cock and into his balls, drawing them tighter, hotter, until the raging need to come whipped him into a ferocious, heaving gallop beneath her.

Red God's Balls, what she'd done to him.

Gripped in a fist of lust, Raniero watched her—the sweet, seductive bounce of the breasts he was dying to taste as they danced beyond his chained reach. Her torso rolled as she rode him, all elegant, slim curves, the long muscles of her thighs working as she jogged in easy strength. Her tattoo seemed to glow in shades of red and green on her cheekbone beneath the green flash of her eyes, and her lips pouted at him, inviting kisses he couldn't reach her to give.

It was maddening to be so utterly at her mercy, driven to climax by her luscious body, gripped so intimately, yet unable to touch.

Orgasm struck him like a spell, a ferocious blast that convulsed his thighs and curled his hands into helpless fists. He arched beneath her, surging upward, her core sheathing his cock in slick, sliding heat. His seed exploded from him in a wave of fire that emptied his balls and dropped him back on the bed, bound and panting.

With one last high, sweet shout, she collapsed on top of him, panting, sweat slicking her skin.

For several long, stunned moments, they lay together like storm survivors. Raniero's muscles quivered and jumped in helpless spasms. He was more than a little satisfied when he felt hers do the same.

At least he wasn't the only one left wrung out and shivering. It had been the most amazing fuck he'd ever had, yet he found himself resenting it. Resenting her. She'd *taken* him like a camp whore in a ruthless possession.

He was the one who did the possessing, dammit.

She rose from his body, his drained sex slipping from her tight inner grip to plop on his sweating abdomen like a dead bird. Face averted, the Rose searched out the shift she'd tossed on the floor and shrugged it over her head. She tied the laces with hands that shook.

"Are you just going to leave me with my cock hanging out?"

She looked around at him as she stuffed her feet in her shoes. Her gaze dropped to his reddened, sticky organ. Blushing like a schoolgirl, the Rose reached down to drag his breeches up until he was decently covered again.

A moment later, the door banged shut behind her hem. He listened to the patter of her footsteps on the stone.

One of his guards said something he couldn't make out, and the other men laughed in a nasty, knowing little chorus of chuckles that made Raniero's face heat.

Bitch.

But Red God's balls, he'd never had better.

Amaris fled down the stairs as if a squadron of Varil was on her heels.

She hadn't even known her body was capable of . . . that. An explosion of ripe carnality so intense, she felt dazzled, as if she'd stared too long at the sun. Except she'd done the staring with every sense she had. Echoes of the vampire jolted through her body in hot pulses. She could still taste him on her tongue, hear his groans, feel the hard muscled heat of him between her thighs—and deeper, buried in her core, long and thick, an erotic invasion that made her shudder at the memory.

It was one thing to swive some vampire, another to imprint him on your soul. How had he done it? One fuck, and he'd driven himself impossibly deep, like a dagger between the ribs.

Bitter experience warned her to stay away from him. Yet Korban would demand she go to him again, use all her Blood Rose skills to seduce him into betraying his king.

She rounded the curve of the stone stairway—and almost slammed into a massive reptilian body. The Varil raiders hissed at her, evidently on their way up. In her agitation, she made no reply, instead turning sideways and slipping between the two, barely avoiding the claws that darted out in search of her flesh. They cursed her as she fled.

She reached the bottom of the tower stairs and escaped along the snaking corridor of the keep until she found her chamber. It was far from comfortable—a thin layer of rushes on the floor, a pallet that made her back ache in the morning, and a rough wooden bench before the fire. But as it also served as a vivid reminder of her status, it suited her just as well.

She poked up the fire and tossed on another log. As the room took on a dim glow, she collapsed on the bench to stare blankly into the flames.

What was she going to do about the vampire?

Sergeant Milric Lio Ony straightened warily when the two Varil raiders appeared at the head of the stairs. Wizard Lord Korban might trust the reptilian bastards, but he did not.

"You are dismissed," the larger of the two Varil said, his words spoken in a hissing accent that was nigh incomprehensible. A pair of iridescent blue stripes ran the length of his body from eye to tail. "Lord Korban has assigned my *kevil* and me to watch the vampire."

Milric exchanged a wary look with Camar, his second sword. The two men had worked for Korban for ten summers now, and barely had to exchange a word to know each other's thoughts. Their fellow guards shifted in unease. "I received no such orders." Milric let his hand fall to his blade hilt.

Lids veiled glowing orange eyes. "Is the Wizard Lord in the habit of consulting thee on such matters?"

"If he had been, I would have told him to stay away from you scaly bastards."

The second Varil sneered, the lifted black lip revealing stiletto-length teeth. Bits of his last meal rotted between them. "Then get thee gone, *git'fe*."

"You do not order us, lizard." Milric glowered at the hulking reptiles.

"Get. Thee. *Gone*." His four-fingered hand went to the axe slung across his shoulder as he bared those revolting teeth again.

Milric cursed softly. He had no doubt the bastard would use that axe if Milric didn't obey. Damned if he'd risk his life for the king's lickspittle vampire. Besides, there was mead in the kitchen stillroom, and he had a powerful thirst. He shrugged. "The post is yours."

Without another word, Milric headed down the stairs, his men hurrying at his heels.

"*Git'fe*," one of the Varil hissed. He didn't look around.

Which was why he didn't see the toothy grins the Varil exchanged before slipping into the vampire's cell.

Raniero looked up as the door opened—and felt his blood chill in his veins as the two raiders sauntered inside, spiked tail tips twitching in anticipation.

"Look, my *kevil*," the one with the blue stripe hissed. "A feast all laid out for us. Prime pork." He flexed his claws and bared a mouthful of stiletto teeth.

"And still alive to squeal." The other laughed, sending a fat goblet of spit flying.

Raniero eyed the two, clamping down on his instinctive terror with the skill of long practice. Fear was what these bastards wanted. "Korban has other plans for me," he said, his mind racing. A spell. His only chance was a spell. But given the way these chains drained his magic . . . "He will not be pleased to learn you've ruined his plans out of sheer pig greed."

Blue Stripe lifted his shoulders. "He will make other plans."

Which was the reason no sane man allied himself with the Varil. They were incapable of considering any concern but their own momentary whims. They made effective shock troops, but could be disciplined only through fear and the ruthless use of magical punishment.

Which meant they were going to slaughter him like the pig they'd called him—if he couldn't defeat his enchanted chains. Raniero took a breath and reached deep into himself, into the heart of his soul where his connection to the Magical All burned like a torch. The cool, bright flame leaped high at his mental touch, responding to his will.

As the warriors padded toward him, grinning like a pair of demons, he shaped that leaping light into a tight, glowing spear. And flung it at the spell that sealed his chains. If he could break the spell, the chains would be no match for his vampire strength.

The shining lance struck the spell—and winked out, its power sucked away.

Blue Stripe gaped his jaws, a rope of drool spilling from his dagger teeth.

Amaris's sated body purred, demanding sleep. Unfortunately, her mind raced in tight circles like a weasel in a trap. She fought to control its flight long enough for logic. So she had responded to the vampire. Well, so what? She was a Blood Rose. Making love to vampires was what Blood Roses did. All she had to do was . . .

A new thought shot through her preoccupation like a cork bobbing to the surface.

Why had those Varil raiders been walking up the tower stairs? There was nothing up there.

Except Raniero's cell.

Amaris stiffened on the thin pallet, her breath catching in horror. The Varil were notorious for their vicious appetites. They'd find a chained vampire as irresistible as wolves discovering a staked sheep. And with the enchantment binding him, he'd be helpless.

She bolted off her bed and grabbed the sheathed dagger that still lay on her bedside table after this morning's spell. It was little enough weapon against the likes of the Varil, but there was no time to run for the guard. She would have to summon Korban with a spell, and buy time until he could arrive. Assuming it suited him to keep Amaris and Raniero from feeding his lizards. Racing out the door, she sought Korban's black thoughts.

The vampire could be dying even now.

Raniero gritted his teeth as claws flashed down, raking shallow furrows across his bare chest. Blood welled and ran scarlet down his ribs. The reptiles were playing with him, looking to enjoy his pain and terror.

Damned if he'd give them any.

He could scream, of course. If he were lucky, someone might even come running.

But would that serve his king? If Raniero died now, whatever plot Korban had in mind would suffer a major setback. When no word came from Raniero, King Ferran would consider his suspicions confirmed. He'd likely give the situation his personal attention—with an army at his back.

With luck, Korban's plot would be foiled, and the kingdom saved. Perhaps.

All Raniero had to do was die without making enough noise to alert rescuers. Not exactly the act of heroism he'd prefer, but he seemed short of options . . .

Claws scraped his belly, slowly, cutting just deep enough to bleed him.

"He thinks he is brave." Blue Stripe licked his teeth with a pointed black tongue.

"That will not last, my *kevil*." His partner laid talons

against Raniero's bunched thigh, drew them slowly down. "He is *git'fe*. He will soon fill the air with his squeals."

"Go fuck yourselves," Raniero gritted, throwing all his strength against his chains, only to feel his power drain away in the spell.

Hissing laughter, the raiders reached for him again.

Raniero sensed the flare of magic just before the door blew open with the groaning screech of shattering bolts and breaking wood.

"Get away from him!"

The Blood Rose stormed through the door, a thin glowing dagger in her hand. She lifted it and snarled, "He is not food, lizards. Get yourselves gone, or die."

Oh, Red God's Balls, Raniero thought in horror as the Varil whirled to face her. *They'll rip her apart.*

SIX

The two brawny Varil towered over the slender Rose, yet there was no fear at all on her delicate face as she faced them. Her dagger glowed like a torch, sending the reptiles' shadows dancing like demons on the stone walls.

"Look, my *kevil*," Blue Stripe hissed, "a little treat before the feast."

"All you will eat is my blade if you do not get yourselves gone," Amaris snapped, brandishing her blazing knife.

It might as well have been a glowing toothpick against the raiders' power and size. Raniero could take no more. "Get out, Amaris! Summon help!"

Too late. Blue Stripe lunged at her, massive arms extended. She spun aside like a bull dancer, and the glowing blade flashed.

A splatter of green droplets rained through the air as the Varil howled in startled pain. "She cut me, Cari'f! The little *git'fe* cut me!"

But she had already made Cari'f her target, darting in with that ridiculous blade to slash the raider's fanged muzzle. He yowled and swiped a massive hand at her face. The blow would have taken her head if it had landed, but she spun aside. Bloody claws caught only one silken curl.

Raniero ground his teeth in frustration. Amaris was much faster than the Varil, but all they had to do was land one blow and she was finished. He threw himself against his chains with all his vampire strength, simultaneously knifing his magic into the draining spell. He had to get free before they killed her.

His magic died as the chains held firm. He cursed and gathered himself to try again.

Amaris buried her blade in Blue Stripe's thigh, then barely managed to yank it out again and dive aside before he could knock her into the nearest wall.

"What goes here?" a human voice bellowed.

Wizard Lord Korban stalked past the splintered door, half a dozen guards at his heels. "Cease!" he roared, flinging a spell globe at Blue Stripe. Just in time. The creature had finally succeeded in grabbing Amaris, and was about to rake her face open with his claws. The globe hit him in a splash of red light, and he yowled, releasing Amaris to paw at his burned shoulder.

"They were attempting to eat your captive, Korban," Amaris said.

"Nay!" Cari'f hissed. "It was . . . her! *She* tried to free him. We but stopped her."

"Which is, I suppose, why he is still chained and covered in the marks of your claws," Korban snarled. "Do not try to play me for a fool, reptile. You have not the wit for it. Get out of my sight before I slay you on the spot." A red glow gathered around his lifted hands.

"Have a care, wizard," Blue Stripe growled. "Our masters—"

"—Will be most displeased if I tell them the Great Barrier will not fall because you two got hungry." The glow blazed up in warning, bright as firelight. "Get you gone!"

Snarling, the two Varil limped out, hissing insults at the guards who brandished swords to speed them on their way.

Korban turned to Amaris, who was breathing hard, the bloody knife in her hand. Her thin gown was splashed with blood, both green and red.

Raniero tensed. She was hurt.

"It appears you saved my captive." Korban eyed her up and down, gaze lingering on the shadows of her nipples, visible through the thin fabric. "My thanks."

She curled a lip, her hand tightening on her knife until her knuckles went white. "I didn't save him for you. I would not see anyone helpless before those beasts."

He shrugged. "As you will." Turning to look down at Raniero, he studied the wounds that raked across his chest and arms. "You are fortunate she summoned me and came to your aid. Otherwise your injuries would have been far worse."

Raniero let his cold rage show in his eyes. He wouldn't have been helpless before those monsters if it hadn't been for Korban's plotting. "I am well aware of what I owe you both."

"Where were his guards?" Amaris demanded, a frown on her pretty face. "There were four human guards watching his door when I went downstairs, but they were gone when I returned. Yet their watch was not over."

The chill smile vanished from Korban's face, and his eyes narrowed. "That is a very good point. I believe I'll have a word with the guard captain." He turned, but before he stepped into the corridor, he looked back at Amaris. "Heal the vampire. He won't be able to take care of those injuries himself in those bespelled chains. And I'd as soon he doesn't die of bloodfever." Korban stalked out, the hem of his robe vanishing after him with a swish like a cat's tail.

His servants and hangers-on slipped out in his wake, leaving Raniero alone with the Rose. He eyed her in the firelight, frowning. "Why?"

She closed the door behind the last of the mob before turning to look at him. "Why what?"

"Why did you risk your life? You could have run for the guard."

Amaris shrugged as she crossed the room with a Rose's habitual floating grace. "I didn't think you had the time. I feared they'd rip you apart before I could bring help."

"Instead they might well have ripped us *both* apart."

Her green eyes sparked, magic flashing clear and blue in the depths of her pupils. "I am not so easy to kill."

"Still, you took a great risk." He studied her lovely face. "Thank you."

Amaris bent to examine the wounds raking across his chest. "As I told Korban, I would not see anyone at the mercy of those monsters." She touched delicate fingertips to his chest over a particularly deep set of claw marks.

Raniero caught his breath as her magic danced across his skin, delicate as butterfly wings at first, building to a rapid burn as she forced torn flesh to heal.

Amaris met his gaze, and desire shivered between them, lush and impossibly tempting.

The Blood Rose had saved him at risk of her own life. It made no sense. Roses schemed, lied, led a man around by his dick.

Look at his stepmother. Thanks to her lies, her son was now heir to the fief that should have been Raniero's.

Yet this Rose had put herself at hazard for one who could do her no good.

Raniero watched her, struggling with the mystery of it as her delicate fingers floated over his bloody flesh, healing his wounds with dancing waves of magic. His temples began to throb, a deep and sullen pulse.

Finishing at last, Amaris started to rise. And hesitated, her gaze on his face. She frowned. "Does your head ache?"

Raniero stirred in his bonds, gazing up at her warily. "Aye."

She made as if to go again, then stopped and sighed, as if yielding to a weakness. Cool fingers touched him between his gathered brows, and the pain drained away like water.

And that act, he knew, could have no other motive than simple kindness.

Again, the Rose turned to go.

"May I offer you pleasure in payment?"

Her lips twisted with such cynicism; it occurred to him that he was not the only one who doubted the motives of the other. "I need no payment."

"Then perhaps pleasure for its own sake?" When she started to speak again, he added, "I would offer you my mouth."

He could not have known.

Orel had been a selfish lover, though she hadn't the experience to realize it at the time. Cunnilingus was a pleasure he'd never offered her, though she'd heard much of it from the other Roses.

Her Garden mates had often rhapsodized about the sensation, comparing the tongue talents of this lover or that, until Amaris had been wild with curiosity.

No, Raniero could not have known. But once he'd made the offer, a dozen Varil raiders could not have dragged her from the room.

She hesitated, eying him. "But you are bound. How would you . . . ?"

Dark brows lifted. "You need only lower yourself over my head."

Oh, she saw how he could accomplish it now. And what a wicked idea. Unable to resist, Amaris plucked her bloodstained gown over her head and kicked off her slippers. Only to hesitate, suddenly flustered. "I am bloody."

He gave her a very male smile. "I care not."

Come to think of it, neither did she.

There was a moment's awkwardness as Amaris dealt with the problem of arranging her legs to accommodate his broad shoulders and bound arms. Then she settled down over his face, her own heating in self-consciousness.

Which she promptly forgot with the first molten flick of his tongue.

The sensation was startling in its intensity. Wet, hot, and piercingly sweet. Amaris settled down a little lower to give him better access, then raised up quickly, biting her lip. "Can you breathe?"

"Very well. Come back here." There was laughter in his voice.

She eased down again and was rewarded with a long, incredibly skillful lap that sent exotic sensations shooting up her spine.

And that was only the start of the delicious pleasure.

Sometimes he traced exotic runes over her jutting clit with the very tip of his tongue. Sometimes he lapped between her folds, or thrust deep into her sex in a maddening tease, or suckled her until the muscles of her thighs danced and quivered.

Amaris had thought herself experienced in the ways of passion, but Raniero taught her differently. He seemed to know her body far better than she did.

And he used that knowledge to whip her into an orgasm that rolled over her and drowned her in sweet fire.

Gods, what lush pleasure. The scent of the Rose flooded Raniero's head as her taste flowed over his tongue, astringent yet impossibly delicious, reminding him of a juicily ripe persimmon. Warm thighs clasped his head as slender fingers fisted in his hair, demanding and begging by turns.

Driving him mad with frustration.

He ached to touch her, to jerk free from his bonds and tumble her down and thrust his cock deep in that luscious peach of a cunt. But he was helpless.

Yet he'd never felt more powerful. Bound, he explored the power he could wield with only his tongue, his teeth, his lips. Nibbling, sucking, licking, he listened to her helpless cries of pleasure as his balls tightened into burning knots and his aching cock stretched up the length of his belly.

She'd fought for him. She was half his weight and a fraction of his strength, but she'd gone against those towering reptilian monsters to save his life.

Yet he was the one who was supposed to do the saving.

And now her delicate body quivered and jumped against his mouth, right there against his face—so frustratingly far from where he most wanted her.

She came again, her voice lifting in high, helpless cries of pleasure.

He dragged his chin up until he could gaze along the length of her beautiful body. "Fuck me," Raniero growled at last, unable to take anymore. "Red God's balls, fuck me."

She looked down at him with dazed eyes. And then she rose from his face.

For a moment he was afraid she'd leave him like this—aching, furious, his cock hard as a sword hilt.

But then she moved down over his hips and freed his sex from his breeches. He almost moaned in relief. Grabbing the thick shaft of his cock, Amaris impaled herself, sliding the length of him in one deliciously tight swoop. Raniero shivered at the sensation—tight as a cream-slick fist, hot and dazzling.

He threw back his head and ground upward, desperate for the climax that was just inches out of reach.

So damned close.

SEVEN

Raniero stuffed her with mind-blowing sensations, his cock a searing length buried halfway to her throat. Amaris tossed back her head and began to work her thighs, thrusting, grinding, driven by a burning whip of need.

Bracing her hands on his rock-hard belly, she gazed down at him as she rode. His face was drawn tight and stark with hunger, black eyes wild, fangs bared. His long hair tumbled around his bare and brawny shoulders. Sweat and streaks of blood marked his skin, muscles flexing in hard relief with each powerful driving thrust.

She wanted to free him. Wanted to experience all that feral passion, to know exactly what those black eyes promised. To feel his bite, his kiss, his hands on her breasts.

He shouldn't be any man's captive. Especially not Korban's.

Give him your blood, temptation whispered.

She imagined what it would be like—the stinging pain of penetration, the magical connection binding them together in drugging pleasure as he drank.

She could almost see his big body surging with the power of her blood, snapping the chains. The guards would have no chance against him. He'd free her and Marin, and they'd flee together.

Red God, she wanted to trust him. And every instinct she had swore he'd never play her false.

He surged upward so hard he lifted her clear of the bed, his body bending into a bow until only shoulders and heels touched the pallet.

Her climax hit like a ball of fire, blazing its way up her spine, detonating in her skull. She screamed, dimly aware of his roar of pleasure as he found his own peak.

Until she collapsed over him, both of them gasping, sweating skin to skin in a dazed heap.

Raniero had known Blood Roses—too well, in fact. His stepmother had only been the first. They might be beautiful and seductive, might even seem kind if it suited the moment's purposes. Yet their focus was always on their own advancement. Any vampire who forgot that was a fool who'd soon find himself paying the price for his gullibility.

As he had.

But none of those women would have risked their lives as she'd done.

Still, that left him with one nagging question. He asked it as they lay together, panting in the limp aftermath of passion. "Why do you work with Korban? Especially considering he seems to have formed some kind of alliance with the Varil."

She lifted her head off his chest and met his gaze, her sensual lips pulling tight. "He seeks a way to breach the Great Barrier. He's at work on the spell now. He believes his allies will make him ruler of Ourania after the conquest." Amaris snorted, a surprisingly indelicate sound. "More like he'll find himself king of rotting corpses."

"So why in the name of all the gods do you aid him? Even if King Ferran manages to drive the Varil back and repair the breech, hundreds will die. And without those peasants to work the fields, there'll be famine. Death will pile on death."

"I know." She rested her hands on his chest and propped her chin on them, her expression brooding.

"Then free me." Raniero lifted his head to meet her eyes in urgency. "At least let me taste your blood that I might free myself. I can alert the king and stop Korban before he destroys us all."

She considered his proposal for a long moment before she finally shook her head. "It's not so simple."

"But it is." He searched her face. She looked torn, as though she struggled with herself. "If you fear his threats, I can protect you. I have power, and the skill to use it. I would not be the king's investigator otherwise. I can get you away from that madman and his plots."

"It's not myself I fear for."

"Then who?" When her eyes slid away from his, he felt an inexplicable surge of jealousy. "A lover?"

Amaris blinked at that, and a quick, ironic smile flashed across her face. "Hardly." She took a deep breath, as if steeling herself to trust him. "It's my sister. She is but three years old, an innocent, yet she has great potential power. That's why Korban sent my father to kidnap her. Tannaz murdered my mother and stepfather and forced us to accompany him."

Suddenly too much became far too clear. "Breaching the Great Barrier will require vast magical resources. He means to sacrifice the child for the power it will give him."

She nodded tightly. "The Varil gave him a magical object called the Blood Orb, so called because it requires a death to trigger it. Fortunately, there's some part of the spell he still hasn't mastered. Once he does . . ."

"The child is dead." He flexed his fists restlessly. "Amaris, surely you see that I am the only chance you and your sister have. But we must act now, before . . ."

She bit her lip.

He ground his teeth. "You don't trust me."

"If you had my father, you would know why." She grimaced. "And my lover once tried to rape me. So no, I do not find trust an easy thing."

Raniero stared at her, appalled, unable to fathom a vampire who could so abuse any Rose, much less Amaris.

It was little wonder she was skittish.

Unfortunately, they couldn't afford her doubts. He met her

eyes, willing her to believe. "Amaris, I swear to you on my honor—I will free you and your sister, or I will die in the attempt. I will not allow Korban to sacrifice that child, not to power his spell, not for any reason. *I will not fail you.*"

Raniero's gaze was dark and utterly steady. He believed what he was saying. And she found herself believing him, despite the times she'd been betrayed.

He was no betrayer.

They had barely known each other a day, yet that didn't matter. She sensed his bedrock decency with a certainty that went beyond logic, beyond experience. It was a truth that rang in the soul.

Like magic.

Her heart began to pound, hard thumping lunges. "Feed, then. Take my blood." She sat up until she could straddle his chest and bend over him, pressing her bare, sweating breasts to his chest, her throat to his mouth.

Raniero froze as if unable to believe she was yielding herself. When he spoke, his voice sounded choked. "You will not regret your trust."

He kissed her leaping pulse, his lips lingering and tender.

And then he bit.

Amaris jerked at the hot sting. It had been years since she'd fed a vampire, since she'd dared let one get this close. She'd forgotten how it felt, the hot intimacy of trusting a man with her blood, the slide of fangs into flesh, the movement of lips and tongue.

And the surging tide of magic that rolled up from somewhere inside her, deep as bone and heart, a glittering tide that ran up her spine in shuddering waves.

He jerked, absorbing it, drinking the power in with every swallow. She gasped as he moaned against her skin.

Somewhere over the sound of her pounding heart, she heard a metallic crunch, the ring and rattle of chains.

Raniero's arms came around her, hard and sweating and strong. Somewhere in the back of her mind, she realized he'd broken his bonds.

Orel would have pushed her away, rolled to his feet, and gone for the door. Raniero cradled her as if she was something precious, his hands stroking over her skin, caressing her backside, exploring the dip of her waist, sliding his fingers into her hair.

Until at last he drew his fangs from her flesh with exquisite care, then ran his tongue over the tiny wounds. Amaris felt his magic dance across her skin, healing the punctures.

"Thank you," he breathed in her ear.

She straightened, drawing reluctantly back until she could sit up astride him and meet his dark gaze. Still he stroked her, sliding his hands along the curve of her thighs, cupping a breast, rasping a thumb across an erect nipple.

He gazed up at her with those dark, bespelling eyes. "You are so beautiful."

Simple words. She'd heard them before from other men, other vampires. So why did they have such power coming from him?

"We'd better go." Amaris licked her dry lips and tried to steady her voice. "If we're going to free Marin, we have to strike now."

Raniero let his hands drop away. Her skin felt curiously chilled without them. "I know." His gaze searched hers. "But later, when this is over . . ." He hesitated.

Her heart had slowed its frantic pound, but at those words, it leaped again. "When this is over?"

"When this is over, I want more of you." His eyes didn't falter as he stared into hers. "All of you."

Amaris couldn't seem to help her giddy smile. "You'll have me." Then she remembered everything that stood in the way—freeing her sister, fighting their way past the Varil, Korban's men, Tannaz, and Korban himself. "If we live."

Raniero's lips thinned with determination. "We'll live."

The door to Raniero's cell jerked open, and Amaris appeared around it, eyes wild, hair disheveled. "He dies!" She wrung her hands, staring at the four guards in the corridor. "Help me!"

They exchanged a wary look. "Judging from the sounds half a sandglass ago, he was healthy enough."

"I think it's some spell. Mayhaps Korban's enemies move against him." She glared at them, magic lighting her pupils with a warning glow. "Or would you rather go to Korban and tell him why you let his prize captive die?"

Considering their lord's reaction to the last guard unit's irresponsibility, that was a message none of them wanted to carry. "Very well, woman," the guard sergeant said. "You two, stay in the corridor. Kriso, with me."

Drawing his sword, he flung the door wide and stalked inside—where Raniero wrapped a length of broken chain around his neck and broke it with one ruthless jerk. Kriso fell to the magic blast Amaris fired at his head. She grabbed his sword from his hand before he hit the ground.

The other two guards shouted in alarm and rage, but Raniero was already in the corridor like a cat among pigeons, the sergeant's sword in his hand. He killed them both in the same smooth motion, cleaving one man's head from his shoulders before running the other right through the breastplate.

Raniero turned to aim a wild, glittering grin at Amaris. "I think the sergeant's armor will just fit."

She eyed the carnage. "I doubt he'll argue. But hurry—I want to get Marin away from her witch of a nurse before someone stumbles on these four."

But they found the nurse just leaving Marin's room, a bundle of possessions in her arms. She gasped the truth around the fingers Raniero dug in her fat throat. "Milord came for the child. He said he has no more need of me. He told me . . . he told me nothing more!"

"The Great Barrier," Amaris whispered in numb horror as Hetram fell unconscious to the steps. "Korban has finished his spell."

EIGHT

"Can you find her?" Raniero demanded, his black eyes glittering through the slit in the helm he'd taken from the guardsman. "Track her with magic, since she is your blood?"

The suggestion arrested the panicked reel of Amaris's mind, helped her think again. "Yes. I should be able to . . ." Biting her lip, she drew on her magic and reached out for her sister. It was an old, familiar spell, one she'd used a hundred times to keep track of an active child prone to disappearing. Sometimes literally; Marin had particularly loved using that invisibility spell . . .

There.

She felt the solid tug of the little girl's life, and her knees went weak with relief. Not dead, then.

Not yet.

"I've got her. Come on!" Amaris spun from the room and shot down the snaking stone hallway. Behind her, Raniero's booted feet rang on the stone, and his armor creaked as he raced after her.

"Which way?" he demanded as they ran.

"Up." She spotted a stairway and took them. "Feels like she's about fifty feet up, and maybe twice that far to the right."

"Battlements," Raniero grunted. "Makes sense."

"The Great Barrier is closest to the castle there." She knew the spot. Korban had once dragged her there for one of his mad rants. She'd listened to him go on and on about the power the Varil would give him, watching the glowing curtain of magic shift and glitter in the night.

If the barrier fell, his own people would be the first to pay the price, but Korban really didn't care.

Amaris reached the top of the stairs, but before she could charge out onto the battlements, a big hand grabbed her shoulder and dragged her to a stop.

"Guards," Raniero murmured. "Where are his guards?"

"I doubt there are any," she whispered back. "It's one thing for his people to know what he intends. But to work the spell in front of them, when they know they'll be the first the Varil will kill . . . Nay, he'll not want witnesses."

They slipped onto the battlements together, stolen swords in hand, Raniero with a guard's shield slung over his shoulder. The sky overhead was black with scudding clouds. The icy wind whipped Amaris's hair, carrying the sound of chanting to her ears. She didn't recognize the words of the spell, but something about the hissing alien syllables made the hair rise on the back of her neck.

"I do not like the sound of that," Raniero said grimly, shrugging his shield down onto his left arm. "Which way?"

Amaris indicated the direction with a gesture, and the vampire took the lead. She padded after his broad back, straining to hear any approaching enemy over the moan of the wind.

Abruptly Raniero jerked back and froze, lifting a warning hand. She stopped to peek around his brawny shoulder.

And caught her breath in dread.

The two Varil warriors stood just ahead, backs turned as they watched the scene ahead with snakelike intensity.

Tannaz held Marin pinned to a stone altar as Korban chanted, holding a glowing knife poised over the child's chest. The Blood Orb floated above her head like a demonic bubble, crimson energies swirling sullenly inside its glowing heart.

Amaris reached down into the core of her magic, felt its hot leap, and shouted a spell that sent it boiling from her fingertips. The blast hit Korban's knife and knocked it from his hand, spinning it over the stone wall.

Korban snatched for the blade with a shout of startled rage, but he was too late. Furious, his face going scarlet with rage, he whirled to glare at Raniero and Amaris. "Kill them!"

The Varil whipped around and charged, huge blades lifted, fangs bared. Amaris dodged between them, avoiding their flashing blades. She had to get to Marin before Korban could complete his spell. Behind her, steel clashed on steel as Raniero engaged the two reptiles.

"Oh, no you don't, you traitorous little bitch!" Tannaz leaped into her path, brandishing his sword. Behind him, Korban wrapped an arm around Marin and dragged her off the altar, ignoring the child's shrieking struggles. The Blood Orb floated after them like a dog begging for a promised meal.

Tannaz swung his blade in a furious stroke, obviously thinking he'd kill her quickly. Amaris ducked his overconfident stroke, her sword slashing across his armored ribs even as she sent a spell rolling down the blade. Her magical attack sliced through his armor like parchment. Tannaz howled in startled pain and clutched his side. Amaris spun, whipping the sword around to slice his thigh to the bone.

"Oh, you're going to bleed for that!" Ignoring the wound, he charged her with a vampire's flashing speed.

She sidestepped like a dancer, and he missed, though she felt his sword snag the fabric of her gown. It tore with a ragged sound.

Damn, but she wished she had her armor.

Being a Blood Rose gave Amaris speed and strength beyond human, but she was still no match for a vampire as powerful as Tannaz. He would inevitably wear her down and kill her . . . Unless she could goad him into stupidity.

"Mother always said you were a bully and a coward. She underestimated you." Amaris gave him a slow and vicious smile. "You're also a murderer and a traitor."

The rage that flashed over his face chilled her blood. He attacked, his sword slamming into hers with force enough to numb her arm to the shoulder. Before she could shake it off, he attacked again.

And again. And again. Amaris scrambled backward, parrying frantically as he rained blows on her, sometimes overhand, sometimes in flat, brutal arcs, sometimes targeting her thighs or arms. In minutes, she was bleeding from a dozen shallow wounds, though she managed to avoid anything more serious.

She was losing. Simply staying alive wasn't enough; she had to land blows of her own. Yet attacking him was impossible when it was all she could do to keep him from driving through her guard and gutting her.

As Amaris circled with Tannaz, retreating, parrying, trying frantically to stay alive, she got fleeting glimpses of Marin and Raniero. The child hung limp in Korban's arms, her eyes wide with helpless terror as he chanted, the Blood Orb hovering close.

Raniero's blade flashed in bright moonlit arcs, shield ringing as he blocked the Varils' massive battle axes. Blood streaked his armor, both vampire red and reptile green.

But Amaris didn't dare divert her attention from her father's murderous blade.

Then one thin slipper hit a pool of her blood, and slid. With a cry, she went down on one knee. She tried to throw herself backward, twisting away from the thrust she saw coming right for her heart.

Too late.

The blade slid between ribs and left hip and kept on going, right out her back. She bit back a scream of hot agony.

Tannaz grinned down into her eyes, fangs flashing.

An axe strike clanged against Raniero's shield as he spun, avoiding the second reptile's attempt to hack his head off. He retreated in a fighter's crouch, watching his opponents with narrow eyes. They prowled, attempting to circle behind him, thick lizard tails twitching hungrily. They were slower than he was, but they were also much stronger, as evinced by the dents they'd left in his shield and armor. He was surprised Amaris had held her own with them as long as she had; only her Blood Rose speed and agility had kept her alive.

The thought of Amaris made his gut coil into a solid knot of anxiety. The last he'd seen of her, she was fighting her father. Yet he couldn't see her now.

Unfortunately, he couldn't help her until he'd taken care of the Varil.

An axe thunked against his shield with a force that drove him back on his heels. Damn, the bastards were strong. He spun away from the blow, using the momentum to launch an attack at the other lizard. His blade crashed against Blue Stripe's axe, skidded along the steel, and bit into a scaled shoulder. The Varil hissed in pain and rage, jerking away as green blood flew.

Unfortunately, it was a shallow cut, not enough to disable the big lizard. And Raniero had collected some ugly wounds of his own, despite his stolen armor. His hands were slippery with blood, and a wound on his thigh throbbed in time to his pulse. His sword was growing heavy in his hands, and he knew he was slowing down.

And that could be the death of him, because vampire speed was all that kept him alive. He had to keep moving, or the lizards would trap him between them.

So he retreated, dancing away from his foes, darting in and out between them as he hacked at any target the Varil presented. He knew he had to wrap up this fight before Amaris or her sister died.

Then, as he ducked the brutal swing of a spiked tail, he glimpsed Amaris on her knees, her father's sword rammed completely through her body. And his heart froze in his chest.

It was a lethal moment's distraction. The two Varil saw it and lunged forward in simultaneous attack, one great axe swinging for his head, the other for his torso.

He sensed the twin attacks more than saw them. Throwing himself forward into a long, flat dive, he felt one blade skim past his ass as the other scraped one kicking armored shin. He landed in an acrobat's tumble and came up just in time to hear an anguished roar.

In missing him, Blue Stripe's axe had buried itself in his partner's chest. Cari'f fell, tail lashing in death throes.

Taking Blue Stripe's axe with it.

Blue Stripe lunged for Cari'f's axe, grabbed it out of the convulsing clawed fist, and whirled.

Too late.

Raniero heaved his great sword in a flat, furious arc that chopped into the reptile's thick neck with a meaty *thunk*. But even as he died, the raider swung his axe. Raniero deflected it with his shield, but the massive blade still struck his thigh a glancing blow. Blood flew, bright scarlet mixing with Varil green as Raniero went down.

"I'll wager that hurts," Tannaz purred as Amaris panted in anguish down on one knee. "Now, don't you wish you'd been a loyal daughter instead of a treacherous little bitch?" He levered up on the sword he'd driven between her ribs and hip.

The pain was a blinding scarlet screech that forced Amaris to her feet again. She dropped her sword to grip her father's wrist, trying to keep him from hurting her further.

He grinned down into her face. "Nothing to say, daughter? No viperous accusations, no vicious insults?"

"Why bother?" she managed as pain rippled through her side in nauseating waves. Her left hand groped for her belt, found the hilt of the slender knife she wore there. Her right hand spread against his armored side, found the chink just beneath his ribs. "You know what you are."

Rage lit his eyes, and he twisted the sword, ripping a scream from her lips. "And I know what *you* are—a whore, just like your mother."

Not close enough. She forced herself another inch up the blade, stepping full against him as she drew the knife from its belt sheath. "But did you know how I've met the sun every morning I've been your captive?" With a quick twist of the wrist, she drove her little knife right into the chink in his armor into the flesh beneath. It wasn't a deep wound given the length of the blade, certainly nothing that would kill him. Not by itself. Her lip curled in satisfaction. "Burn, Father!"

Before he could jerk away, she cast the spell that released all the morning sunlight she'd stored in her dagger for just this moment, sending it pouring into the knife wound on a river of magic.

Amaris jerked back, forcing herself back the length of the sword, reeling backward as Tannaz went up like a torch. The vampire howled in agony, the light pouring from the dagger to devour his magical flesh. He blazed bonfire bright until the fire finally went out, leaving his armor to collapse to the battlement stones, empty of all but ash.

Dizzy, weak with blood loss and the effort of casting the spell, Amaris reeled like a drunken woman. But before she could hit the ground, strong male hands caught her shoulders.

"I will have to remember not to make you angry," Raniero said, even as he sent a pulse of magic into her body. She added his strength to her own and healed the lethal sword wound, sighing in relief as the pain faded.

NINE

"We've got to get to Marin before he kills her," Amaris said grimly.

Raniero longed to tell her to stay behind, but her magic was greater than his, and he knew he'd need her if he was to have any hope at all of stopping the wizard. So he nodded silently and turned to lead the way as they went in search of Korban.

They found him bathed in the pulsing crimson glow of the Blood Orb. His eyes were wide and glittering with exhilaration in his pale face as he held Marin pinned against his chest. The child hung limp in his arms, the side of her face marked with a purpling handprint where he'd obviously struck her.

"You bastard!" Amaris snarled.

Korban smirked at them and kept right on chanting, the words coming in a fast singsong now.

Amaris exchanged a grim glance with Raniero, realizing he was coming to the end of the spell. Once that happened, all he had to do was break Marin's neck, and the Great Barrier would fall.

"We've got to get her away from him," Amaris whispered.

"Aye, but how?" Raniero hefted his sword and eyed Korban, who promptly lifted the child higher to shield himself. "Fucking coward."

Amaris's eyes widened with desperate inspiration. "Marin!" Her voice rang clear over Korban's chanting. "Remember our game!"

The child's despairing gaze met hers, but there was no understanding in them.

She tried again. "Remember that game you love to play? The one where I look for you?"

Marin's big brown eyes went huge. Then, thank the Red God, her little face screwed up with effort.

And she vanished.

Korban's chanting broke off in a startled yelp, and his hands jerked as if losing their hold. He flailed as if trying to recapture the child who'd just magicked herself invisible and squirmed from his grip.

"Hit the ground, Marin!" Amaris screamed.

The child instantly appeared, her body drawn into a ball as she lay on the stone floor. The wizard started to swoop down and grab her up again.

Raniero ran forward, swinging his sword in a furious upward blow. It cleaved through Korban's neck in one clean stroke, and the wizard's head went flying.

But even as his body fell, the Blood Orb flashed a horrifying crimson. A trail of red light started draining from the wizard's headless body into the globe, which began to pulse brighter.

Raniero froze in horror. "Red God's Balls! Korban's death has completed the spell!"

Her heart turning into a solid block of ice, Amaris realized he was right. Though the death of an innocent would have provided more power, any death at all would fuel the spell. In moments, it would activate and rip the barrier apart. And once it fell, the Varil would invade.

Unless . . .

"We've got to redirect the spell."

"It's too complicated—there's no time!"

"I can do it!" She stared hard at the pattern of swirling energies, reading them, finding the spot where the spell could be warped, turned to a new purpose. Throwing out both hands, she began to chant, sending her magic swirling toward the chink in the spell.

It was like trying to redirect floodwaters with her bare

hands. The spell roared along the channel Korban had constructed, ignoring her efforts to turn it in a new direction. Amaris gritted her teeth and kept trying. She was damned if they'd fall to the Varil after suffering so much, fighting so hard.

But even as she strained to turn the magic, she knew she simply didn't have enough power.

Until strong fingers wrapped around her shoulders, and a new stream of magic joined that rolling down her arms.

Raniero's.

The vampire joined his will to hers, reinforcing her magic, working to warp the spell into the new shape she willed for it. And slowly, reluctantly, the spell twisted, took on the form she demanded.

The mystical energies pouring through the Great Barrier began adding to its strength instead of weakening it.

Somewhere in the distance, Amaris thought she heard reptilian voices howl in rage. Perhaps it was her imagination.

But it made her grin anyway.

Even as she smiled, the Blood Orb hit the stones of the battlements and shattered.

Silence fell.

It was so quiet, Amaris could hear her own panting along with Raniero's deeper breaths. She felt dizzy, exhausted with blood loss and effort.

"Ama'is!" Her sister flung her small warm body against Amaris's thighs, almost bowling her over. "Ama'is, you saved me!"

She dropped to her wobbling knees and wrapped shaking arms around the little girl. "I had help." Amaris met Raniero's eyes, and let her own gratitude show. "I had a lot of help."

He leaned down and kissed her over the child's head, quick and hard. She smiled at him as he drew away, knowing a promise when she tasted one.

They limped into the great hall, where the guards and castle folk slept together on thin pallets. At the ring of Raniero's boots on the stone, Korban's warriors jolted awake and rose with a mass growl—only to fall silent in staring astonishment at the sight of their lord's head, swinging by its bloody hair from Raniero's right hand.

The left held Blue Stripe's decapitated skull by one long ear. Amaris carried Cari'f's head as her own gory trophy, a chilling grin of triumph pasted on her face.

Together, the lovers strolled to the dais through the stunned crowd, Marin walking solemnly behind them. Amaris's heart was knotted in her throat, but she knew that the castle had to be reclaimed for the king.

Besides, she was frankly too tired to run from these bastards anyway.

Raniero dumped his burden on the dais, then flung himself into the lord's chair. Amaris dropped the head she carried next to the other two, then moved to stand behind his chair, secretly bracing herself against it as the room spun around her. Despite the healing spell, she'd lost far too much blood. Marin leaned against his knee and gave the crowd a little smirk that warmed Amaris's heart. Despite everything she'd been through, the child's spirit was intact.

Raniero's deep voice rang across the stillness of the great hall. "I have a message from your king."

He gestured a spell, and a huge image appeared in the air over the hall. Ferran's face stared out from it, rage in his golden eyes, a muscle flexing in his handsome cheek. He wore full armor, and he spoke from horseback. "I ride to Tzira Castle with my forces. When I arrive, I shall investigate your lord's crimes. I expect you to give Lord Investigator Raniero your full obedience in the meantime." He paused and swept his gaze over the crowd, which visibly cowered. "Lord Raniero pointed out that many of you were simply following the orders of your lord. He urges me to mercy. We shall see if he is of the same opinion when I arrive."

The image winked out. Raniero contemplated the pale faces staring at him. "I trust," he said at last, "you will give me your full obedience?"

Heads nodded rapidly all the length of the room.

Leaning against the back of his throne, Amaris smiled in tired satisfaction.

TEN

Three Weeks Later

"A Rose and a fief," Raniero said, settling against the pile of silken pillows in the lord's bed. "I never thought to receive such a boon."

"Well, you did save the kingdom," Amaris pointed out, settling in next to him. "Naturally the king was grateful."

He gave her a look. "*We* saved the kingdom."

"So we did." She leaned into his warm, muscled side, and he wrapped an arm around her.

King Ferran had decided Tzira Castle was too important to be entrusted to anyone except a man he was utterly sure of. Which meant Raniero, though the king sighed that he was loathe to lose his best investigator.

It was not a gift Raniero was inclined to turn down.

Ferran had showered gifts on Amaris, too, in recognition for her efforts to prevent the loss of the kingdom. There'd been gold and jewels and bolts of fine fabric, but more important, he'd given her the pick of his staff. She'd selected a calm, experienced nurse from among them to care for Marin. The woman and Amaris's sister were now abed in the next chamber down the corridor, in an airy room full of the toys the king had presented to his "little heroine."

Now, for the first time in weeks, Amaris and Raniero were finally alone, without either the king to entertain or Marin to reassure.

Raniero cleared his throat, looking suddenly uncomfortable. "It strikes me that the king may have made too many assumptions."

Amaris looked up at him, lifting a brow. "Oh?"

"Yes." He swallowed. "The fief might have been his to give, but not the Rose. And I would not have you if it's but a matter of duty."

Amaris stared at him, incredulous. "Duty?"

He nodded, his eyes serious as he looked down into her face. "I know your sense of honor is strong, but . . ."

She stretched upward until her mouth met his in a kiss that blazed with all the heat and passion she felt down to her soul. His lips parted under the fierce assault, and she slid her tongue inside his mouth.

Stroked, licked, tasted.

When she finally drew back, she saw with satisfaction that Raniero's eyes looked a little dazed. "Did that feel like duty, my lord?"

He licked his lips. "No. It felt like . . ." He stopped and swallowed.

"Love." Amaris did not let her eyes drop, though a part of her wanted to flinch at the nakedness of the word.

But she trusted him. She'd learned out there on the battlements that Raniero was not like those who'd betrayed her. He was a man who could be trusted unto death.

So she met his eyes and said it again. "I love you, Raniero."

Light flared in his eyes, bright with relief and passion. "And I love you, Amaris."

Then his mouth covered hers, and he hauled her into his arms. As Raniero kissed her with starved intensity, his hands began to explore, cupping first one breast, then the other, thumb playing back and forth over the nipple that hardened hungrily under his touch. She kissed him back, a slow mating of tongue and lip and careful nipping teeth, reveling in the taste of him, male and magic.

"You drove me mad in that cell," he growled against her mouth, "touching me when I couldn't touch you, fucking me half blind while I was chained and helpless."

"Mmm," she purred, remembering those sweet, wild rides. "As I recall, you were well-revenged by that wicked mouth of yours. That sly tongue touched plenty. I thought I would lose my mind."

"Serves you right." Chuckling, Raniero danced his fingers down her torso, following the curve of her belly down to the soft nest between her legs. He rumbled a growl as he found her already growing slick and swollen. "You tasted so sweet." White teeth flashed. "In fact, I find myself hungering for more."

Amaris yelped a giggle as he tumbled her back on the bed and began to work his way down her torso, pausing for a nip here, a suckle there. Her breasts drew him into a passionate detour for a sweet eternity that was far too short, his tongue circling each nipple in turn, drawing wet runes that set her blood ablaze. She squirmed and sighed as he stiffened his tongue to flick and tease, then used his teeth with gentle ruthlessness until she quivered.

Finally he continued down her body, exploring the rise of her rib cage with kisses, pausing to swirl his tongue into her belly button. She laughed at the cool tickle, threading her hands into his long, dark hair.

But when he finally settled between her legs, she lost all urge to laugh. The width of his powerful shoulders nudged her thighs apart, and he wrapped his strong arms around her legs as he lay full length down the bed.

Amaris lifted her head to watch with breathless attention as he tilted his head, considering her sex. His dark eyes flicked up to meet her gaze, and he gave her a wicked white grin.

The first pass of his tongue between her swollen folds made her quiver in helpless need. He licked again, slow and lazy as a cat cleaning his paws, each creamy stroke sending jolts of pleasure sizzling up her spine. Gasps and whimpers escaped her lips as he tasted her as though she dripped honey, deliberate, maddening, spinning rapture over her like a spell. She could almost see the golden glow of his magic behind her eyelids.

And still his tongue worked, dancing over her clit, sliding between her folds, thrusting deep into her core. As though that wicked enchantment wasn't enough, he reached up around her thighs to squeeze and tease her nipples, winding the delight tighter and tighter.

The orgasm stormed out of nowhere, shaking her body, jerking the muscles of her thighs like lute strings. She screamed at the sheer sweet glory blazing through her mind.

When Amaris could see again, he was braced over her on one hand as he aimed his thick, hungry cock with the other. "Oh, yes!" She drew her legs wide in welcome.

Raniero entered in a slow, luscious slide, groaning in delight. "Red God's Balls, you're tight," he panted.

And he felt so deliciously thick, a tunneling pleasure that seemed to reach halfway to her waist. His withdrawal was just as careful, a sweet, silken delight. Dazzled, she looked up at him as he braced his arms to either side of her shoulders, biting his lip as if he fought to control himself. His dark eyes seemed to glow with feral need as he thrust in and out.

A need for something more than sex. A need she felt just as powerfully.

Hypnotized by that need, she stared up into his eyes, admiring the flush riding his high cheekbones, the sensual curve of his mouth, the white tips of his fangs showing between his parted lips.

Raniero picked up the pace, nostrils flaring like a racing stallion's. Each long thrust jolted her closer and closer to explosion. Gasping, she hooked her heels over his thighs and ground upward, meeting him with rolling hips.

The climax exploded in her core like a blast of magic, primal and savage. As she threw back her head to scream, he bent his arms, lowering himself over her, his black eyes wild and hungry. His lifted upper lip displayed the length of his teeth.

Knowing what he wanted, what he needed, she angled her head to offer him her throat. "Now, oh, now!"

The touch of his hot lips and the cool slice of his teeth kicked her climax even higher. Thrusting heavily, he began to drink. She fisted her hands in the silk of his hair, gasping with the feral intensity of her pleasure.

They lay together in the aftermath, panting, sweat sheening their skin in the moonlight that poured through the window. Amaris stroked his strong back slowly, feeling a sweet contentment she'd never known.

Until he raised his wrist to his mouth and sliced his fangs across the skin. Blood welled as he met her gaze, an odd vulnerability in his eyes. "Will you drink from me?"

Amaris blinked at him in dumbfounded surprise. She'd heard of this in the Garden, but she'd never expected a vampire to make such an offer.

For a vampire to share his blood with his Rose linked them in magic, heart to heart, soul to soul.

"Oh, yes," Amaris breathed, joy blazing through her like sunlight.

He tasted like love, and she smiled against his skin, knowing neither of them would ever be alone again.

Shifting Sea

Virginia Kantra

This one is for Kristen, to read in a hammock.
And to my wonderful readers—thank you!

ONE

Scotland, 1813

Major John Harris squinted between his horse's ears, willing himself to ignore the throbbing in his knee and the pounding like hoofbeats in his head.

He had survived the bloody siege of Ciudad Rodrigo. He would not die of a hangover now that he was home.

Now that he had a home.

And all his limbs.

He had not expected either outcome. He was a man used to dealing with life's harsher realities. But he could not be sorry that life, for once, had frustrated his worst expectations.

He lifted his face, letting the wind tatter the remnants of his nightmare and blow his hangover out to sea. The air smelled of earth and sea, brush and brine. Neptune jingled his bridle, bobbing his massive head in approval. The rawboned gray had carried Jack unflinchingly on the winter retreat from Corunna and through the long, blistering march to Talavera, but the Peninsular war against Napoleon had left the big horse scarred and past his prime.

Like his rider, Jack admitted ruefully. At least Neptune seemed to be taking the transition to civilian life in stride.

Lucky beast.

In the weeks since his cousin's lawyers had found him in a stinking Lisbon hospital, Jack had learned to walk again without a cane and to sleep again in a room with four walls. But he was as ignorant as the rawest ensign when it came to managing his unexpected inheritance.

He was a soldier, not a farmer, determined to carry out his duty to the best of his ability, grimly aware that his tenants' lives depended on his decisions as surely as his troops' had. He only hoped his best would be good enough.

The rutted road meandered over hills as worn as his bones. The land—his land, now—swept in a ragged curve around the harbor, anchored at one end by the peaked roofs and chimneys of Arden Hall and on the other by furrowed cliffs. Fishing boats bobbed in the shining flat water. A bleak, spare church, an unprofitable inn, and a score of small dark houses clung like mussels to the rocks, their inhabitants prickly as barnacles and closemouthed as clams.

Jack was used to bivouacking in hostile countryside. But Spanish bandits had nothing on these stubborn Scots. Almost a third of his tenants were Highlanders driven west by the Clearances and carrying a grudge against all things English.

Including their new landlord.

Jack closed his knees, urging his horse onward, leaving the village behind. His thoughts clamored, restless and strident as the seabirds haunting the cliffs. He could hear their plaintive cries slicing the air, the rush of wind drumming in his ears, the waves curling to shore like distant music, like singing.

Actual singing, he registered in surprise.

A woman's voice, husky and cool, rising and falling with the breeze, tangling him in lines of music, knotting in his soul.

He stopped, searching the shore below for the singer. Just beyond the reach of the tide, in a patch of tangled garden and blowing grass, a cottage nestled in the shelter of the rock.

Jack narrowed his eyes. Who would choose to live beyond the village outskirts, outside the protection of the harbor and neighbors?

A flash of white at the water's edge caught his gaze, a billow of movement like a sail.

Not a sail. A woman's skirts, a woman's hair, flowing loose in the wind, shining like seafoam in the sun.

His breath caught. Her song plucked his heart from his chest. She was all white and gold like an angel in a dream, a vision concocted of loneliness and spray and too much whiskey.

Neptune snorted, his ironshod hooves slipping on the rock.

Jack tightened the reins, collecting his horse, recovering his balance. The angelic vision became simply a girl without hat or shawl, singing a song he'd never heard in a language he did not know.

Who was she?

One of his tenants, he thought, setting Neptune at the descent. A fisher's wife, a farmer's daughter, a serving girl perhaps. No gentlewoman went bonnet-less and barefoot on the beach.

At the sound of their approach, the song ceased. The girl turned, pushing back her tumbled hair with one hand. The pose and the wind molded her gown to her body.

Lust slammed into Jack like a bullet.

She was tall and lovely, her breasts high and round, her skin as pale as pearl. Her face was almost savage in its beauty, her broad jaw and level brow balanced by a full mouth and strong cheekbones.

Jack sat like stone, his blood pounding in his head and his groin. Beneath him, Neptune stood like a monument, iron muscles quivering.

He should say something, Jack thought at last. Reassure her. He was a stranger, after all, and she was alone.

"Major John Harris at your service, ma'am." His voice grated on his ears.

She regarded him without expression, her eyes tarnished gold.

"From the hall," he said since she seemed not to recognize his name. "And you are . . . ?"

"Morwenna."

No surname. A servant, then?

He cleared his throat. He was not accustomed to the

company of women. But his years of military service had given him the habit of command and some small store of social conversation. "I saw you from the cliffs," he said.

And promptly plunged down the bluffs like a sailor diving after a mermaid's song.

She would think him mad.

Perhaps he was.

"You were singing," he added. As if that explained or excused anything.

"I was not calling you."

A dismissal, by God. She did not speak like a servant. Despite the absence of gloves, her hands were tapered and smooth. Her dress . . . Well, he didn't know much about women's fashions, but the fabric appeared very fine. Perhaps she was a gentlewoman fallen on hard times.

He should ride on. He could not stay, looming over her like the lord of the manor riding out to debauch village maidens.

She met his gaze boldly, like a woman willing to be debauched.

His blood thrummed. Before he could consider the consequences, he swung from his horse, landing hard and heavily on his right leg. He gripped the saddle and breathed deep and evenly, willing the pain to subside.

"You are injured," she said behind him.

Scarred.

He turned stiffly. "Nothing to signify."

She considered him, those strange golden eyes traveling down to his boots and up again, lingering in places no well-bred woman would look. He felt the stroke of her gaze like a smooth gloved hand.

She nodded. "We had better go to my cottage, then. There is a bed there."

Jack's mind reeled with shock and possibilities. She was a whore.

Or he was still stupid from a lack of sleep and a surfeit of whiskey. She looked nothing like the prostitutes he had seen on London's streets or the camp followers he had known in the army.

Yet she was living outside the village. She had invited him to her bed. Surely he had not misunderstood?

He attempted a smile. "A chair would suffice."

Her face lit suddenly with humor or awareness. "It might suit you," she said. "It would not suit me."

As if—the image fired his brain—he had suggested they engage in sexual congress on a chair.

He shook his head to clear it.

"Come." She smiled at him and turned. "This way."

She glided toward the bottom of the bluff, all billowing skirts and floating hair.

After a moment's hesitation, he stomped after her, alert as if he rode into ambush. His riding boots slipped and skidded on the shale. Neptune plodded behind.

Jack had spent the past week riding over the estate, trying to familiarize himself with his new duties. This was not the first time a cottager had invited him to inspect a chimney or a leaking roof, to listen to a list of complaints or take a cup of tea.

Surely she was offering more than tea.

Or was it only her beauty and his own soul-deep loneliness that made him wish for more?

The cottage garden was bright with gorse and heather. Pink roses nodded by the open door. Jack tethered his horse to the front gate and ducked his head to follow her inside.

The single room was cool and bare and dim. No lantern. No fire. Sunlight leaked from the shuttered windows to stripe the room's wide bed. The covers were tumbled.

He wrenched his gaze away.

A simple plank table teetered in the center of the flagstone floor. He took in the oddly bare shelves, the room's only chair. "You live alone?"

"Yes."

The single word dropped into the quiet like a rock into a pond. He felt the ripples to his fingertips.

But he must not misunderstand her. "There is no husband to help you with your holding?" he asked carefully. "No man in your life?"

Those full lips curved. "Many men. None that I would choose to live with."

Something reckless in him rose to meet the wicked challenge of that smile. But he was never reckless. He had been a careful officer, deliberate in battle, calm under fire, conscious always of the men under his command.

He glanced again at the empty hearth, the lack of furniture, the plain, bare walls. "Then you must tell me how I may be of service to you, ma'am."

She reached behind her back, her hair sliding forward over her shoulders. He watched as her gown fell away from her bosom and rustled to the floor.

Well. His lungs expanded. There was no misunderstanding that.

She was completely naked, her skin pink and white and gloriously bare. No shift. No stays.

The blood left his brain to pool hotly, thickly, in his groin.

He had never seen a woman more beautiful. He forced his gaze from her long, slim legs to the pale thatch between her thighs, up the curve of her belly to her high, full breasts. Beneath the flowing curtain of her hair, her nipples were pink and tight.

She tossed her head and smiled into his eyes, accepting his stunned silence as the tribute it was. "Serve me."

All traces of headache vanished. There was only this need pulsing like fire through his veins. He had almost forgotten the relief, the solace, the sweet forgetfulness to be found in a woman's body. *This* woman's body, naked and almost within reach. It had been so long. Not since his injury and his inheritance, long before his return to England.

But he was her landlord.

Jack had not been raised in the ways of the landed gentry. A poor relation without the means to purchase a commission, he had joined the Infantry as a gentleman volunteer, fighting with the enlisted men, subsisting on an enlisted man's rations, until an opening was created by heavy casualties in the officers' ranks. He did not know what his cousin, the expected heir of Arden, would have done in the face of such magnificent temptation.

But he did know a man of honor did not take advantage of his dependents.

Even if one of those dependents was a whore.

She lived alone, she had said, without a man to fish or farm for her. Did she fear for her living?

"You are not obliged to do this," he said carefully. "I will not turn you out. If you owe rent—"

"I owe no one. I please myself. Today I choose to be pleased by a man. By you," she said clearly, so there could be no doubt.

Inside him something rigid as a scar relaxed. She *desired* him. Although a woman in her profession must be skilled at making her clients feel wanted.

Her eyes laughed at him. "Unless you are not willing to offer your services after all."

She must know. She must see. Beneath his breeches, he was hard as a rifle barrel and as ready to go off.

"I believe," Jack said gravely, "I am up for the task."

She sank onto the low rope bed, bare feet flat on the floor, naked knees parted. Still smiling, she reached for him, hooking her fingers into his breeches flap to draw him close between her smooth, pale thighs. His heart pounded.

In a kind of fever dream, he stared down at the top of her head. Her lower lip pouted in concentration as she worked the buttons from their holes, the brush of her knuckles sweet agony. A bar of sunlight slid between the shutters, firing her white blond hair to gold.

A little hum—triumph or approval—escaped her throat as she freed her prize. The contrast between her slim white fingers and his dark, thick cock seared his brain. His erection jerked in her hands.

Jack closed his eyes, absorbing her feather touch as she cupped and explored him. His hands rested lightly on her head. How long since a woman had held and caressed him? He could not think. Like this? Never.

Liquid fire swirled. His eyes shot open. She wasn't . . . She couldn't. . . .

She licked her lips, tasting him. Apparently she had. With her tongue.

Dear God.

His collar and boots felt suddenly too tight. His mouth went dry. Of course she wouldn't . . . No woman had ever . . .

His knees nearly buckled as she fit her slick, hot mouth over the head of his cock. She was doing it, sucking him, swallowing him, sliding her full lips up and down his shaft, taking him deep in her throat. His mind blanked. His hips arched instinctively.

He was going to explode. He had to stop her. He would stop her. In a minute.

Or not.

His hands clenched convulsively in her hair. The strands slid cool and smooth as water between his fingers, against his belly. His gaze fell on the arch of her brow, the line of her back, the delicate bumps of her spine. He couldn't see her face. But, oh God, he could feel her. Her tongue . . .

She was naked, submissive, bending before him, totally focused on his pleasure and yet utterly in control.

It was unbearably erotic.

And oddly unsettling.

He slid his hands to her shoulders and pushed her firmly onto the mattress. Levering himself over her, he settled his weight against her, absorbing the damp heat of her flesh, the womanly softness of her body. His erection lodged against her stomach.

She lay back, her hair fanning over the pillow, watching him with half-lidded eyes, a faint smile on her lips. He wanted . . . He didn't know what he wanted. Only her.

Spreading her thighs wide, he mounted her with one strong, deep thrust.

Her sharp inhale echoed his own.

She felt so good, hot and wet and welcoming beneath him. Around him. Lowering his face to the side of her head, he inhaled the clean, salt tang of her hair. She smelled of sunshine and woman, of sex and the sea. For the first time in weeks, he felt he could breathe.

He hunched his back, stroking slowly in and out, feeling her inner muscles clench and quiver in response. But his right knee would not bear his weight for long. With a grunt, he reversed their positions, pulling and lifting her to lie over him while she laughed and rubbed against him like a cat.

He saw the red imprint of a button on her breast and frowned. He should take off his jacket. His boots. Any woman, even a whore, deserved that much courtesy.

But she required no preliminaries. Desired none. Quick as a fish, she straddled him, hot and gloriously wet. Taking him in hand, she impaled herself on his cock. Sensation bolted in a white hot arc from his balls to his brain.

Her name ripped from his throat. *"Morwenna."*

In the plain, dim room, she burned above him, her hair a wild halo around her head, her white breasts tipped with coral or with flame. Her smooth thighs squeezed his sides. She set a shallow rhythm, rocking herself, pleasuring herself. Riding him. Her head was flung back, her eyes closed as she ground her wet sex against him. He was buried in her as deep as a man could be, intimately connected and yet apart.

He wanted her *with* him. Body and soul. Cunny and cock.

Grasping her buttocks, he pulled her down hard as he thrust up.

Her startled eyes met his. Her rhythm faltered.

"With me," he said harshly. He pressed up, gripping hard enough to bruise. She gasped and tightened around him.

The connection shot him to the edge.

Grimly, he held on, his blood roaring in his ears, as he drove into her, hammered into her, forging links of loneliness, heat, and need. The wet slap of their coupling filled the room. His lungs labored like a bellows. Her lips parted. Her eyes glazed, golden eyes burning to the back of his brain. Hot. Close. The pressure built in his balls and the base of his skull.

So close. The intimacy nearly shattered him. But he did not want to go alone.

He had never knowingly left a man behind. Or a woman, for that matter.

Teeth clenched, he plunged inside her, clinging to consciousness like a dying soldier on the battlefield, until he felt her swell and surge, until he felt her spasm and shake, until she shuddered and came apart in his arms.

Relief swept through him. A single thought spun with him into the abyss. *Thank God.*

Relaxing his grip, he let the dark sweep over him and carry him away.

That had not gone at all as she had planned.

Morwenna sprawled over the man's hard chest like seaweed on the rocks, the ripples of her release receding like the tide. Her body floated in delicious languor. Inside, she felt pleasantly tender. Relaxed.

Uneasy.

She raised herself on one elbow. The buttons of his coat were imprinted on her breasts, round red marks like love bites. Morwenna frowned. She was accustomed to wresting satisfaction from her human lovers. She did not tussle with them for control. But this one . . .

She propped above him, studying him in the slatted light from the shutters. He had a pleasing face, she decided, strong and composed even in sleep. His brow was broad and faintly creased, his long jaw shadowed with stubble. A few strands of silver threaded among the brown, reminders of his mortality. With one finger, she traced the air above his face, following the etchings of pain beside his mouth, the lines of laughter lurking at the corners of his eyes.

Not that she actually touched him. Her kind did not. Only to fight or to mate, to demonstrate power or possession.

Yet as she hovered over him, absorbing his strength, breathing his breath, something in her stirred and swayed like kelp below the surface of the water.

His body was broad and solid between her spread thighs. He was still half hard inside her. With very little effort, she could take him again. Warmth bloomed deep inside her at the thought.

No. He had already served her pleasure. She was not a fish wriggling on the hook of sexual desire. Her body was her own. Her life, her own. She would not cede control of either to any male.

Which was why she had sex with humans.

The memory of the man's face as he pushed hard inside

her flashed across her brain, his dark, dark eyes, his hoarse command. *With me.*

She shivered. Definitely not what she had planned.

She slipped from the bed. Scooping the white dress from the floor, she pulled it over her head.

"If you are cold," his voice said, husky with humor or sleep, "I would be happy to warm you."

Blinking, she emerged from the folds of the dress. The man lay motionless on the bed, watching her with heavy-lidded eyes. She felt another inconvenient pull of attraction.

"I do not feel the cold," she said truthfully.

Even in this body, her blood kept her warm. But she smoothed the dress down anyway, a fabric barrier between her and the man, taking care to cover the parts humans usually kept covered. She noticed he made no move to do the same. His heavy shaft lay quiet against his thigh. As she watched, it lengthened and stirred as if aware of her interest.

She raised her gaze to his face. "You should go."

His dark brows drew together. "Go," he repeated.

She met his gaze, conscious of his seed wet between her thighs, the delicious tenderness of her own body. "Now," she said firmly.

He sat up in bed. "You are expecting someone."

Morgan.

With a shock, she realized she had not spared Morgan a thought since leaving the beach. Yet she had called him. He would certainly come.

"Yes," she admitted.

The man's jaw set. "Another client?"

She did not understand his question. "It does not matter. You must go."

"It matters." He stood, the top of his head nearly brushing the ceiling. He tucked himself and his shirttails away, his movements as carefully controlled as his voice. "To me."

He was jealous. Her heart jolted with pleasure and annoyance. Did he believe because he had been inside her body that he owned her?

"I am flattered." She smiled, showing the edges of her teeth. "Or I would be if you had any right to an opinion."

His eyes were grave and steady on hers. "Is it the money? I can pay you."

She was not offended. She knew humans equated value with gold. "I do not want your money," she said. "I laid with you for my pleasure. Now it is time for you to go."

"Come with me."

Her mouth dropped open. She had not expected that response.

"You don't have to live like this," he continued in his deep, earnest voice. "The hall is open again. I will speak to Watts, my butler. If you won't take money from me, there must be some work you can do."

He wanted to hire her as some kind of . . . servant? The idea amused and appalled her.

"I do not want to work at your hall."

"Come anyway," he urged.

The mad thing was, for a moment she was tempted. He was so very appealing, big and dark, stiff with honor and frustration.

She shook her head. "As what?" Over the past decade or so, she had learned enough about human affairs to know what he proposed was impossible. For both of them. "As your wife? Your mistress?"

He did not answer.

She took pity on him. "I am content as I am," she told him gently. "I will not give up my freedom. But I thank you for your offer."

He drew a short, sharp breath. For a moment she feared that he would argue or worse, try to force her.

He nodded once. "Then may I come to you here?"

She smiled at him in relief and approval. "You may."

Whether he would find her was another matter.

She followed him out of the cottage, watching as he climbed stiffly onto his horse and rode away without another word.

She was *not* disappointed.

Merely a little letdown.

She had not thought he would give up so easily.

She stood a long time staring out at the bright and restless sea, its surface scrolled by the wind.

A plume of vapor. *There.*

A round black swell broke the uneven water, its huge dark fin cutting the air like a sail.

Orcas did not swim alone, but she wasted no time searching for the rest of the pod. This was no ordinary whale.

It scythed through the water, too fast, too close, as if it would beach itself on the rocks. Her heart beat faster as the sleek black shape barreled toward the shore, its outlines blurring beneath the water. A wave crested and crashed. Spray shot skyward. Sunlight broke and glittered in a thousand dazzling drops, veiling the barrier between land and sea. The air shimmered.

Morwenna blinked.

A man rose hip deep from the water, tall and leanly muscled, his hair silver white as foam, his pale skin shining from the sea. Water streamed from his shoulders and wrapped his legs, forming itself into the black and silver garments of the finfolk. His chest was bare except for the silver chain and medallion of his office. Tossing back his dripping hair, he waded toward her.

Pale gold eyes met hers.

Morgan, lord of the finfolk and warden of the northern deeps.

Her brother.

Her twin.

"Sister," he said in greeting. "You called."

TWO

The next bright morning was market day in the village of Farness. The wind chased the clouds across the sky and harried the sparkling breakers of the bay toward the long stone jetty. A shepherd urged his flock of fat, *baaing* sheep along the narrow street between whitewashed cottages. Giggling children chased a lamb between the market stalls.

It was only up close that Jack could see the thatch on the cottages needed patching and the villagers lost their smiles at his approach.

His steward, Edwin Sloat, had urged him not to come.

"They're a surly lot, these Scots," he'd said, smoothing a hand over his thinning hair. "Liars and cheats, most of them. Let Cook do the shopping. Or the housekeeper, Mrs. Pratt."

But Jack was determined to gain a better understanding of this place and his new responsibilities. To do his duty, he must get to know his dependents.

So here they were, he and Sloat, stopping by a fish stall to survey the day's catch. The fisherman stood back, his gaze fixed on his cracked boots.

"Fine catch," Jack remarked pleasantly.

The man did not answer.

Sloat considered the gleaming row of fish. "That big one would do for our dinner. Send it to Cook in the kitchen," he instructed the fisherman.

The steward did not offer to pay for the delivery, Jack noticed. Nor did the vendor seem to expect him to.

"What do I owe you?" Jack asked.

The man gaped until he resembled the spangled salmon in his arms.

Sloat coughed. "No need to trouble yourself, Major. He'll put it on account."

Jack frowned. Some of the officers he had served with lived on credit. They owed tradesmen for everything, their boots, their shirts, their wine. But Jack came from trade on his mother's side. He knew the burden this placed on the vendors who depended on the gentry for a living. "Surely we can spare the ready better than he can."

"You're not in London any longer," Sloat said. "Or even the Peninsula. It will take time for you to understand how we do things here."

But as Jack watched Sloat stroll the market, patting, prodding, assessing, he thought he understood very well.

The steward accepted two pints in the tavern's silent taproom, helped himself to an apple from a stall. At the baker's, he poked holes in two loaves before deeming a third fit to eat. No one questioned, no one protested his actions.

Jack looked from the crumbs littering his steward's waistcoat to the baker's frown in his orange beard and laid a shilling on the counter.

The baker's gaze darted from the money to Jack to Sloat. "What's this, then?"

"Payment," Jack said.

The baker wiped floured hands across his wide middle. But he made no move to touch the coin.

Sloat swallowed his bread. "Our credit is good here."

"No longer," Jack said. "We pay ready money from now on."

Sloat's cheeks puffed. "I really cannot advise—"

"I am not asking your advice," Jack said. "Inform the other merchants in town I expect them to send their bills directly to me. We will settle our accounts before beginning business on the new footing."

"You will regret this," Sloat said.

"To me directly," Jack repeated. "By the end of the week."

Their eyes met.

The steward's gaze fell. Without a word, he turned and slammed his way out of the shop.

"Well," said the baker in the silence he left behind. "That's two things I never thought to see all in one day."

They were the first words anyone had directed to Jack all morning. He turned from the door. "Two things?"

"Woman came in before you," the baker said. "Wanted to buy a loaf with a pearl. Big as an egg, it was."

Jack's brows drew together. He was half convinced the baker was gammoning him. But why make up such a story? "Did you sell her the bread?"

"I did not." The baker picked up the shilling from his counter. "I had no change to give her for her pearl."

Jack met his gaze in acknowledgment. "Perhaps next time you will not have to send her away empty-handed."

The baker scratched his hairy jaw, half hiding a blush behind his floury hand. "Nay, I gave her a bun," he confessed. "Face like an angel, she had."

Face like an angel . . .

Jack's pulse kicked like a pack mule. "Morwenna."

"Who?"

He exhaled. "The . . ." But he would not call her a whore. "The lady who was in here."

The baker looked blank.

"From the cottage beyond the bluffs," Jack said.

"That cottage has been empty a dozen years or more."

"But she was here," Jack said. She must have been. *A face like an angel.* "You must know her."

The baker shook his head. "Never seen her before in my life."

Perhaps he needed an incentive to remember.

Jack pulled out sixpence and set it on the counter. "For her bun," he said. "Let's settle all accounts today. How much more do I owe you?"

The man rubbed his beard again, leaving matching white streaks along his jaw. "I do not do the fine baking up at the hall. Only bread for the staff. Say, six quartern loaves a week, one shilling sixpence?"

A quartern loaf weighed four pounds. The price was more than fair. Jack nodded.

"Then . . ." The baker's lips moved as he calculated. "Nine shillings a week for six months."

"Six months," Jack repeated. A slow burn ignited in his gut. "You have not been paid in all this time. Since my cousin died."

Since Sloat took over the management of the estate.

The baker nodded warily.

Grimly, Jack began to count out sovereigns on the counter.

A commotion in the street outside filtered through the stone and daub walls.

"Thief!" The cry penetrated to the shop.

Sloat's voice.

Jack's head shot around. Through the dirty windows, he could see his estate steward's broad, round-shouldered back nearly blocking the view of the street. And beyond Sloat, at the center of a tightening knot of villagers, was a woman in a sky blue dress with a cloud of hair pale as moonlight and floating like thistledown.

The fire in Jack's gut shot to his chest. *Morwenna.*

Dropping the money on the counter, he strode to the door.

"I am not a thief." Her voice rose above the crowd, clear and cool and edged with irritation like ice. "I offered to pay."

"With stolen coin," Sloat blustered.

"With gold, yes." She drew her shawl more tightly over her elbows. "I thought he would prefer it to jewels. The other man said—"

"And where does the likes of you get gold or jewels?"

"Enough," Jack ordered.

The word dropped into the crowd like a stone, sending ripples through the square. The villagers eddied and ebbed away, leaving him a clear path and a clear view of Morwenna. She stood in the street, straight as a Viking maiden at the prow of her ship, her loose hair tousled by the wind.

His heart slammed into his ribs. She was even more beautiful than he had remembered.

A face like an angel, the baker had said. Yes. But the cool perfection of her features only offset the wicked awareness of those eyes. She saw him and a slight, very slight smile lifted one corner of her mouth.

His breath stopped.

Sloat, the great, fat idiot, was too intent on his target to understand he had lost command of the situation. "Answer me, girl. Where would you get gold?"

She turned those wide, bright eyes on him. "I found it."

He sneered. "Stole it, you mean."

"Mr. Sloat." Jack did not raise his voice, but any man in his battalion would have recognized and responded instantly to his tone. "You have no evidence of a crime, only of an offer to pay. Which I understand is more than you have managed these last six months."

His estate manager flushed. But he did not back down. "No honest woman would have such a coin in her possession." He scanned the circle of witnesses before beckoning forward a dark, thin man in a shabby brown coat.

Jack recognized the shopkeeper. *Hodges?* Hobson, that was his name.

"Tell him," Sloat said.

The thin man fidgeted. "Well, she came in wanting some shoes, you see. I had some half boots ready-made. Not fine, but serviceable for a lady, and—"

"The coin," Sloat snapped.

"Right." Hobson looked once, apologetically, at Morwenna, before addressing Jack. "It was gold. And, er, old."

Jack held out his hand. "Show me."

"Er . . ."

Morwenna thrust her chin at Sloat. "*He* took it."

"For safekeeping," Sloat insisted. "The coin is evidence. It must be preserved until this woman can be brought before a magistrate."

"Let me see," Jack said.

Sloat dug in his waistcoat pocket and abstracted his prize.

Jack turned it over in his palm. Rather than the guinea he expected, the coin was roughly stamped on one side with a cross and on the other with two pillars. A Spanish doubloon, like the pirate treasure he used to dream of when he was a boy. He looked at Morwenna. "This is yours?"

She shrugged. "As much as anyone's."

Jack had a sudden vision of her confronting him in her cottage, the outlines of her body revealed through her loose white dress. *I do not want your money,* she had said. *I laid with you for my pleasure.*

"She's a liar as well as a thief," Sloat said.

Jack kept his hand from fisting on the coin. "I would not throw around public accusations of thievery if I were you. Go back to the hall. I want the household accounts for the past six months on my desk when I return."

Sloat wet his lips. "I only want to see justice done."

"So do I," Jack said grimly. "The accounts, Mr. Sloat."

Sloat's gaze darted around the circle of interested and unsympathetic faces. A soft catcall carried through the ranks of the villagers. A snigger. A hush. For months the steward had been the power here; it would take time to establish Jack as master of Arden Hall.

Sloat delivered a jerky bow and stalked toward their tethered horses.

The tension loosened in Jack's shoulders. He held out the gold piece to Morwenna. "I believe this is yours."

"His now," she said, with a nod toward Hobson. "He gave me shoes."

Jack glanced from her new boots to Hobson's avid face.

"It is too much," Jack explained. "Nor can he spend it here. I will pay him for the boots."

Such a fuss over a coin, Morwenna thought.

The children of the sea flowed as the sea flowed, free from attachments or possessions. What they needed they retrieved from the deep, the gifts of the tide, and the shipwrecks of men.

She regarded the tall, dark-haired human with the hard mouth and gentle, weary eyes, holding out the treasure from the sea. Her lover from yesterday. How amusing.

How adorable.

He had come to her rescue. Anyway, he thought he had, which was unexpectedly appealing.

Her brother had been right. There was much she did not understand about human ways. She had blundered with the pearl, she acknowledged. Floundered with the gold.

But she was right, too. She could make a place for herself among humankind if she chose.

She smiled as she took the coin like a tribute from her lover's hand.

She had her own ways of getting what she wanted.

She watched him confer with the shopkeeper; saw more coins exchange hands.

"Thank you, Hobson," the man said quietly.

The shopkeeper bowed deeply, clutching the money. "Thank *you*, Major."

His name was Major, Morwenna noted as he came back to her. She really must make an effort to remember it this time.

"Have you completed your errands?" the man—Major—asked.

She had purchased bread and shoes. Surely that was enough to prove to Morgan that she could function perfectly well onshore.

"Yes. Thank you," she added, because he and the shopkeeper had both used the phrase and it seemed like the right thing to say.

"Then may I escort you home?"

He was so stiff, so considerate. Something about that strong, composed face, those warm, observant eyes, got her juices flowing.

Her smile broadened. "You may."

"My horse must carry us both, I am afraid," he said, a rueful expression in his eyes. "I could lead you, but my leg would undoubtedly give out on the walk over the bluffs."

She regarded the great gray animal standing placidly in

front of the shop and felt almost breathless. He expected her to ride on *that*? And the animal would allow it?

This day was proving full of new experiences.

"Your leg and my feet," she said.

"I beg your pardon?"

She gestured toward her feet, already chafing in their laced leather boots.

His face cleared in comprehension. "Your new shoes."

Her first shoes, she thought, wiggling her toes cautiously. They were very uncomfortable. Very human. She could not wait to show them to Morgan.

Major mounted with surprising grace for a big man with a bad leg. He leaned down from the saddle. "Take my hand," he instructed. "And put your foot on mine."

The horse flicked an ear at her approach.

"I beg your pardon," she told it and took the man's hand.

"Steady." He tugged.

She felt the pull in her shoulders and gasped, more disoriented than alarmed as he swung her up and over. Somehow he lifted and turned her so that both her legs were on one side of the horse and her buttocks pressed his thigh on the other.

Morwenna had never been on horseback before. She clutched the man's coat as the gray horse tossed its head. The ground seemed very far away.

But his chest was hard and unbudging at her back. The warmth of his body, the strength of his arms, enveloped her.

"Comfortable?" his voice rumbled in her ear.

She nodded, her fingers relaxing their grip on his sleeve. The muscles of his thighs shifted, and the horse stepped forward.

She sat very still, absorbing a swarm of new sensations, most of them pleasant. He was so very close, touching her. Surrounding her.

"Hobson tells me he has not seen you in the village before," he remarked conversationally.

Morwenna straightened her swaying seat. She must remember not to get *too* comfortable. Her lover was human and male, which made him tractable, but he was far from stupid.

"No."

"So you are new to the area," he said, still in that not-quite-questioning tone.

She had no fixed territory. Unlike the selkie, who alternated between seal and human shape, the finfolk did not need to come ashore to rest. Their ability to take their chosen form in water gave them greater range and freedom than the other children of the sea. But their fluid nature made them even more susceptible to the ocean's lure. Dazzled by life beneath the waves, they could forget their existence onshore, losing the will and finally the ability to take human form.

Even her brother admitted that time on land kept them safe. Kept them sane.

"I am visiting," she explained.

"You must have friends nearby, then. Or family. You said you live alone."

She squirmed on her perch above the horse's neck. Most men were too distracted by sex to pay attention to anything she said. How inconvenient—how flattering—to find one who actually listened.

"Family." Was that enough to satisfy him? "My brother."

The horse lurched up the track that climbed the bluff. Water boomed in the caves as the tide rolled in.

"Older or younger?" the man asked.

Her brow puckered. She could feel his body heat through her dress along one side, his arm, strong and warm across her lap. Was all this chatter really necessary? He had not talked this much while they were having sex. Perhaps she should suggest they have sex again.

She eyed the distance to the ground and the cliffs that plunged to the sea. Perhaps not on horseback.

"We are twins," she said.

"You are close, then."

The children of the sea did not bind themselves with family ties as humans did. But she and Morgan were among the last blood born of their kind, fostered together in the same human household until they reached the age of Change. For centuries, he had been her playmate, her companion, her second self.

She nodded.

"This brother . . ." he persisted, following some linear train of thought, as men and humans did.

Morwenna sighed.

"He does not object to your living alone?"

She grinned. "Oh, he objects. Frequently. Recently. Yesterday, in fact."

The arms around her relaxed. "He was your visitor yesterday. The man you were expecting."

"Yes. Morgan thinks I should return with him to court to—" Whelp babies, she almost said. "To be with my own kind. He does not think I can make a life for myself here."

"So you went to the village today to prove him wrong." His voice was dryly amused.

"Something like that," she admitted. She turned her head to smile at him, pleased by his perception. His brown eyes were steady on hers, flecked with green and gold like the surrounding hills.

She felt a quiver in her stomach deeper than desire. Inside her something clicked like a key turning in a lock, like a door opening on an undiscovered room. Her heart expanded. Her breath caught in dismay.

Oh, no.

He did not know her. He could not know her. He was human and she . . .

"Tell me about your family," she invited hastily.

Get him talking about himself. Men liked to do that. She would rather be bored than intrigued by him.

"There isn't much to tell," he responded readily enough. "My father was a gentleman—a distant connection of the Ardens, as it turned out—who married a merchant's daughter. I was their only child. They died together of a fever when I was sixteen, and, having no other prospects, I ran off to be a soldier."

So he was essentially alone. Like her. She pushed the thought away.

"Do you like being a soldier?"

He was silent so long she thought he would not answer. She told herself she was not interested.

"I liked the order of it," he said at last. "The sense of purpose. The responsibility."

To have a purpose . . . She could hardly fathom it. "My existence would seem very frivolous to you."

"Ladies are more restricted in their occupations."

"I am not restricted." She saw the frown forming on his brow, the questions gathering in his eyes, and added, "But I can see the appeal of feeling a part of something larger than oneself."

"Yes," he said. "I did not always like my job. Killing is an ugly business. But I liked doing my job well."

How very odd he was.

How attractive.

The gray horse crested the bluffs. The sea sparkled to the western isles and beyond. Morwenna lifted her face, letting the wind snatch away her thoughts. The briny breeze mingled with the wool of his coat, the sweat on his skin, the scent of his horse. Sea smells, earth smells, animal smells, blended like water and wine. She drank them in, holding them inside her until the sky spun around her and she was dizzy with lack of oxygen.

She released her breath on a puff of laughter.

The man Major was watching her, a bemused expression on his face.

"What?"

"Nothing." He shook his head. "It's just . . . It's you."

She raised both eyebrows in question.

"You seem to enjoy things so much," he said.

"Things?"

He gestured at the sunlit hills and bright water. "Everything. Life."

She did not understand. "Is not existence meant to be enjoyed?"

"Not for most people."

"Not for you," she guessed.

He did not speak.

An unfamiliar tenderness unfurled inside her. She cupped his face in her hand, tracing the line beside his mouth with her thumb. "We must see what we can do to change that."

His chest rose sharply with his breath. He angled his head, brushing her mouth with his. He kissed her once, again, warmly, softly, sweetly enough to steal her soul through her lips. She trembled.

Assuming she had a soul.

He raised his head, a curve to his lips, a troubled expression in his earth brown eyes. "I did not escort you home to seduce you."

Her pulse pounded. As if he could, she thought with desperate pride.

"Then I suppose I must seduce you." She paused before adding wickedly, "Again."

Her heart lurched at his slow, wry smile. "I am at your service always."

She chuckled against his mouth.

They rode down the hill together, his arm holding her secure against him, the horse swaying beneath them. They did not speak. Morwenna felt oddly breathless. She was used to lust, to the rush to rut. There was something new and delicious about this slow, sizzling delight, this gradual buildup to the act of sex. Her blood hummed in anticipation. Riding cocooned against his strength, she had time to savor her arousal.

And his. When he helped her from his horse, she felt his desire for her hard against her stomach.

Drawing back, she smiled into his eyes. "Will you come inside?"

She cast a hasty glamour over the cottage as he pushed on the latch and opened the door, banishing sand and cobwebs, masking the disorder and neglect of years. Her body was sending her all sorts of urgent signals: *Him. Hurry. Now.* But the sweetness of his kiss stayed with her, warm and flowing through her veins like honey. Time itself slowed, trapped in this golden moment.

She sat in the room's only chair to remove her boots as he bent to light the fire. For some reason, her hands were shaking. The laces tangled.

"Let me," he said and knelt at her feet to deal with the knot.

Sweetness filled her heart to overflowing.

He picked at the laces and eased the boot from her foot. Angry red lines creased her toes and ankle where the leather had chafed her flesh. He cradled her foot in his hands.

"What are you . . . *oh.*" She sighed with relief, closing her eyes in pleasure as his strong hands pressed and rubbed all the sore and tender places.

"That feels . . ."

His hands stilled.

Her eyes opened.

"Oh," she said again and tried to pull away.

He held her foot trapped in his big hands, staring down at the faint, iridescent webbing between her toes.

THREE

Jack stared down at the pretty bare foot in his hands. Soft, pale skin. High, smooth arch.

Webbed toes.

They didn't even look human. The connecting skin shimmered like fish scales, delicate as insect wings.

His stomach cramped. He looked up into Morwenna's eyes, bright and opaque as the eyes of an animal. A primitive chill chased up his spine and lifted the hair at the back of his neck.

"What is this?" he asked quietly.

She snatched back her foot, curling it under the legs of the chair. "What does it look like?" she asked defensively.

He couldn't say. He could hardly think. Stories from his schoolboy days—Poseidon and the Nereids, Ulysses and the Sirens—raced through his head, mixed up with memories of Morwenna singing at the water's edge, her silver hair shining like seafoam in the sun.

Ridiculous.

He took a deep, steadying breath.

"Not like anything I've seen before," he said carefully. Or anything he believed in. "I was hoping you could explain."

She pursed her lips. "Must everything have an explanation?"

"In my experience, yes."

She stood, shaking her skirts down over her ankles. "Then you explain it."

"Morwenna, your toes are . . ." A gentleman did not discuss a lady's feet. But he had held hers in his hand, and her toes were . . .

Webbed. Shining with rainbow color like a soap bubble.

"Different," she supplied.

He seized on the word gratefully. "Different. Yes."

"And anything different must therefore be flawed."

He straightened warily. She was offended. Hurt? "I did not say *flawed*."

"Am I suddenly repugnant to you now?"

"No."

Her chin tilted at a militant angle. "But you wish to leave anyway. Because of my different feet."

He shook his head in baffled admiration. Like a practiced swordsman, she had reversed their positions, driving him on the defensive. "Of course not."

"Then what do my toes matter?"

He could deal with her anger. But the emotion glistening in her eyes caused a quick clutch in his chest.

"They don't."

"Ah." She held his gaze for a long moment, letting his words speak for her.

He knew he was being manipulated. He did not care. She was so beautiful with her flushed cheeks and that sheen in her eyes. Her quick passions had roused his. The memory of their last time together rose like smoke between them, firing his imagination, cutting off all oxygen to his brain. *Then* she hadn't faced him from half a room away. *Then* she had dropped her dress and sat on the mattress, pulling him to stand between her smooth, bare thighs. He wanted it to be *then*.

He dragged air into his lungs. How could he press her with questions when he could not breathe? He could have her again, he thought. In this room, on that bed, this very afternoon. His shaft hardened. All he had to do was let go of his questions and enjoy the moment.

Accept the moment.

Accept her.

Her challenge thrummed inside him like the beating of his pulse. *Is not existence meant to be enjoyed?*

Yes. Lust and longing surged together inside him. He wanted this for himself. He owed it to her. Yesterday he hadn't taken time to enjoy her properly, to do the things a man does for a woman he cares about.

There was more than one way to discover her secrets.

Very deliberately, he took off his jacket and hung it from the back of the chair. He sat down to pull off his boots.

She watched him, her chin raised another notch. "Do you wish to compare feet now?"

"No," he said calmly. He set his boots side by side under her table before looking up into her eyes. "I want to make love to you."

Her breath caught.

Slowly, slowly, her lips curved. She reached for the fastenings of her gown.

Thank God. He crossed the room in two quick strides. "Let me."

He gathered up her hair to lay over her shoulder, out of his way. It smelled like sea and sunshine. Her nape was as white and delicate as porcelain, as rich as salted cream. He untied the tapes of her gown, controlling himself with effort, determined not to grab or tear. Tugging the sleeves from her arms—no chemise, no petticoats—he pressed his lips to her shoulder, opening his mouth to taste the salt of her skin. She made a sound of impatience and turned in his arms, twining her bare arms around his neck. Her breasts pressed against him.

Need churned inside him, greedy, hot.

But this wasn't about greed.

He half walked, half carried her to the bed, made her sit while he stripped off his trousers and drawers. His cock jutted out like a tent pole against the long tails of his shirt. She reached for him, caressing him boldly through the linen fabric. He groaned in pleasure, thrusting forward into her hand. She knew him, knew his body, knew how to touch him and make him respond.

He wanted to do the same. To bring her that pleasure. To share that knowledge. To have that power over her.

He cuffed her wrists, pulling her hands from his body. Easing her back against the pillows, he pushed her thighs wide. She propped on her elbows to watch him, her lips parted, her eyes gleaming. *Beautiful.* His heart thundered. He traced a line with his fingers from her collarbone to her waist; ran his hand over her sleek belly to the roughness of curls between her legs. She was already wet. She smiled and arched her back, offering her breasts, offering . . . everything.

He could take her now. He was hard and aching. His blood pounded in his ears like siege guns.

But it was a siege he planned, an assault on her senses, an invitation to surrender.

He bent over her, his mouth roaming the trail blazed by his hands, wandering here, lingering there, getting to know her body. Her collarbone, her breasts, the curve of her belly, the crease of her thigh. She sighed and shifted, showing him the way. *There. More. Again.* He kissed and licked and suckled her, learning what made her flush and moan, what made her clench and sigh, reveling in her response.

She undulated under him, beautiful in her abandon, surging under his hand, against his mouth. Hot, wet woman. Heady. Ripe. He drank her in, her scent, her cries. He was drunk on her response, his head swimming, his control slipping.

Her arms came around him, stroking under his shirt, tickling his ribs. Her fingers danced along the ridges of his scars, making him shiver like a horse tormented by flies.

"Take it off," she commanded.

He shook his head, used his mouth on her. She gasped, she quivered, but she would not be distracted.

She tugged again at the shirt. "Now."

"No."

"Why not?"

Reluctantly, he raised his head. Her cheeks were flushed,

her eyes great pools of black rimmed with gold. He had never seen anyone or anything more beautiful. And he . . .

"I am scarred," he said bluntly. "Not just my leg, but my back. My side."

She found his face with her hands, touched his mouth, his cheek. "I want you. All of you." Her palms stroked down his belly and thighs, cupped his big, square knees, slid up under his shirt. "Naked."

His heart pounded. "It is not pretty," he warned.

"I want to see you." Her voice was a Siren's voice, lilting, irresistible. She reached him with her hands and with her words, her fingers circling, squeezing, moving higher. Her knuckles brushed his sac. "Let me see you."

He had never been a vain man. Or a coward. She deserved to see, to know who she lay with. That didn't stop his mouth from drying as he dragged his shirt over his head. He knelt over her on the bed, braced for her rejection, dreading her pity.

He did not close his eyes.

Neither did she. In the warm light that spilled from the windows, in the clean air that blew from the sea, she studied the damage to his body.

He had been lucky. The Ninety-Fifth had been caught in the breach, trapped between trenches laid with pikes and sword blades and the two big guns filled with canister shot. He had been fighting his way to the guns when the French fired the mines beneath the slope. The earth had vomited rocks and flame. The sky rained dirt and body parts. His world had exploded in death, in darkness and in pain.

But he had survived.

With one finger, she traced the jagged gouge high on his arm. She brushed the red pucker at his hip. She laid her palm against the twisted mass of purple scars where the surgeon had probed for shrapnel.

"This is what you men do to each other in war," she said.

He could not read her tone.

"Sometimes," he said stiffly. He fought an absurd inclination to apologize. For his gender? His profession?

She met his gaze, her eyes like tarnished gold. "You do not wish to talk about it."

He had left his shirt on to shield himself as much as to protect her. He did not want to go down into the pit again, into the pain, into the bloody surgeon's tent and the long, agonizing time before and after. "A gentleman does not discuss such subjects with ladies."

He sounded like a prig.

"Even a lady he is naked and in bed with?"

"Especially not a lady he is in bed with," Jack said firmly.

He did not want to bring those memories here, into this room, into this moment. He didn't want that ugliness to touch her.

Yet she continued to touch him, her fingers at once soothing and inflaming. She rubbed small circles against his chest, scraped her nails gently across his abdomen. His cock swelled, hard and eager, shameless at her approach. Her hands wandered over his torso, laying claim to him, to all of him, making no distinction between his damaged flesh and the rest.

He swallowed against the constriction in his throat. "You don't have to touch them."

Touch me, he thought.

Her smooth shoulders shrugged against the pillows. "Why not? Your scars are part of you. As my feet are part of me. Not the most interesting part," she added. Her teasing look set him on fire. She circled his erection with both hands, cupping him lightly. He gritted his teeth against the exquisite pleasure of it. "I am sorry you were hurt. But if we want each other, we must accept each other as we are, with all our scars and all our parts."

He wanted her. He ached for her, with his body and in his soul. He craved her joy, her acceptance, her unabashed appreciation of life.

"I want you," he said, his voice as raw as his need.

She smiled up at him. "Now."

Forever, he thought.

He lowered himself to her. They came together in comfort and in lust, her arms lifting around him, her hands sliding down his scarred back to grip his buttocks. Her legs twined with his. Holding him. Touching him. She felt so good, soft, warm, wet. He made a sound deep in his throat and thrust.

She surged to meet him. And despite their differences, or because of them, all the parts fit. As if he had found the other piece of himself, the missing half that made him whole. His mind blurred as they moved together, two bodies with one rhythm. One flesh. His breath shortened. His heart raced. Her body rose and strained beneath his, matching him thrust for thrust. He plunged and withdrew, plunged and held himself still inside her until he felt her tense and go lax around him, softening at her climax. He pressed harder, deeper. The tremors that took her shook them both.

She held him, held him close, as he turned his face into her hair and emptied himself.

Slowly, Jack returned to his senses. His knee throbbed like a sore tooth. His thigh ached with strain. He was exhausted and sweaty . . . and more content than he could remember ever being in his life.

He turned his head on the pillow. Morwenna lay half under him, her face perfect in the golden light, smooth and rounded, luminous as a pearl. She smelled like sex. Like sex and the sea.

Webbed toes, his brain reminded him, but he silenced thought and listened to his heart instead.

She was all beautiful. Beautiful and his. Every part of her was his.

He threaded his fingers through her hair, combing the white gold strands from her brow. "Morwenna."

Her lips curved. "Major."

Silent laughter swelled his chest. "Under the circumstances," he said gravely, "I believe you might call me Jack."

She opened wide golden eyes. "Jack?"

"Or John, if you prefer."

"Jack," she repeated. "I like it."

Tenderness raked his heart. He kissed her again, a long, slow, openmouthed kiss that stirred him all over again.

He cleared his throat. "Your brother was right, you know."

She blinked. "I beg your pardon."

"It isn't wise for you to live alone here. It isn't . . ." *Proper.* "Safe," he concluded.

His weight still pinned her to the mattress. But already he

could feel her withdrawing, regrouping, pulling away from him. "It isn't your concern."

"I am concerned," he said honestly. "You obviously haven't been responsible for managing your own household before. You need help. Protection."

Her quick frown gave her mouth a sulky look. "I told you once I will not live with you."

"Not with me." That would cause even more talk than her living alone. "Your brother is in the area, you said. You can stay with him."

"No."

"I will escort you."

"I am not one of your soldiers. You cannot command my obedience."

"I would call on him in any case."

Her eyes narrowed. "You wish to meet my brother."

"It is customary," Jack said carefully. "When a couple is . . ."

What? he wondered. Courting?

Could he seriously be considering making her an offer? An unknown woman of dubious background living alone on the edges of his estate?

Yes, his heart insisted.

"Getting to know one another," he said.

She wiggled under him, making him acutely aware of her naked body. "We already got to know each other. Twice."

He smiled. "Which makes my introduction to your family the next—the only—appropriate course of action."

"My brother would not agree with you."

"Then give me the opportunity to change his mind. Let me ask his permission to court you."

There. He had said it. Certainty settled into his bones and lightened his chest.

"That is not necessary," she said.

Not the reaction he hoped for.

Or, truth to tell, expected.

"I am well able to provide for a wife," he assured her stiffly. "My father was a gentleman. Aside from my cousin's estate, I have savings of my own which I am prepared to settle on you."

"Are you trying to persuade me of my great good fortune in attracting you as a partner?"

"No. Maybe." He rolled away from her, off the bed. "I sound like an ass."

"Merely human."

He turned.

She sat on the edge of the mattress, her hair tumbled over her smooth shoulders, watching him. "You would make a good husband, I think. For someone else. I am . . . fond of you. But I have no desire to marry."

She was rejecting him. His hands curled into fists at his sides. He did not understand. Every woman wanted to marry. What other options did she have?

"You must want security," he said. "A family, a home of your own."

"I enjoy my freedom. I wish to keep it."

He stared at her, baffled and frustrated. "What if you are with child?"

Her eyes were bright as the sun-struck sea. But underneath the golden surface, shadows flickered and swayed. "It is not possible."

"Of course it's possible." His voice was harsh. "We have lain together. Twice."

She raised her brows at his deliberate appropriation of her words. "And will do so again, I hope."

"Then marry me."

The offer slipped out, shocking them both. But he did not take the words back. He wanted this, wanted her.

"Because we pleasure each other in bed?" She tilted her head as if considering. His heart pounded in anticipation. "No. My life suits me. There is nothing you can give me that I do not have. Nothing I need or want."

Her rejection knocked the air from his lungs. He inhaled past his constricted throat.

He had narrowly escaped committing his life and honor to a woman he hardly knew. A woman without apparent wealth or connection. He should be relieved.

He was not relieved. He was hurt, confused, angry.

"Then I will bid you good day, madam."

Unfortunately, he could not even exit on that dignified note, bearing away with him his injured pride, his bruised heart, and his rejected proposal. First he must get through the awkward business of dressing. He could only be grateful that he was a soldier and not a dandy. At least he did not require her assistance to struggle into his boots and his coat.

She pulled the blue dress over her head and stood in the doorway of her cottage to watch him mount.

Her words echoed in his empty heart. *There is nothing you can give me that I do not have. Nothing I need or want.*

A child. He could have gotten her with child.

"You will inform me," he commanded, "if there are any consequences."

A flush rose in her smooth, pale, perfect face. "I will inform you."

With that, he had to be satisfied.

He pressed his heels to Neptune's sides and rode away.

FOUR

The rising wind rattled the library windows, pushing smoke down the chimney and into the room. The fire fought the gloom outside. Unfortunately, the red flames failed to lighten Jack's mood or to dispel the chill between him and Sloat.

The estate manager settled deeper into his chair on the opposite side of Jack's desk, stretching his thin shanks toward the fire. "Everything was done to preserve the wealth of the estate," he protested. "To protect your interests."

Possibly, Jack acknowledged.

And possibly Sloat, like a looter on a battlefield, would rob anyone too weak to beat him off.

Jack had spent the last four days reviewing the household accounts, responding to a flood of bills and grievances presented by local fishers, farmers, and tradesmen.

In the past six months, pleas for payment had been disputed or ignored. Improvements had been neglected or denied. Jack suspected some of the money that could have been plowed into the land had gone to line Sloat's own pockets.

He wouldn't trust Sloat at his back in a fight. But he had no cause to fire the man. After four days of searching, he could find no proof that the steward had stolen from the estate, no evidence that Sloat had exceeded his authority.

"I do not question your attention to the estate's profits," he said. "Only to its people."

Sloat smirked. "Your cousin never complained."

An old, sick man without any family about him, dependent on his steward and his housekeeper.

"My cousin is dead," Jack said. "You report to me now."

"His executors charged me to run his estate," Sloat said.

"While they searched for an heir." News of his inheritance had come as a surprise to Jack. Presumably it was a shock to Sloat as well. "The estate is my responsibility."

"You cannot manage without me."

"Let us hope," Jack said steadily, "that won't be necessary. Or are you proffering your resignation?"

Silence fell. A sudden squall lashed the windows.

Sloat sniffed. "You are, of course, free to do as you please."

No, he wasn't.

He was bound by his responsibilities, trapped by his obligations and a gentleman's code of behavior. If he pleased himself, he would overcome Morwenna's objections and carry her off to his bed. Instead, he was stuck in this smoky room with his hostile steward going over figures until his eyes blurred.

He plucked another bill from the pile on his desk, scanned another column of numbers. "Dougie Munro wants a hundred pounds for horse feed."

"He'll be lucky to get half that."

It cost more to feed a horse than to keep a servant. The stables at Alden housed four farm animals, Sloat's cob, and a couple of carriage ponies. "The charge seems reasonable to me," Jack said.

"He is a tenant. He owes rent."

"He cannot meet his obligations if we don't meet ours." Jack put the bill on the stack to be paid.

Outside, a bell rang, tolling against the storm, penetrating the rush of wind and rain.

Jack raised his head, glad of the distraction. "Who died?"

"No one. Yet," Sloat said. "They ring the church bell to guide the boats in to the harbor."

Jack glanced at the windows, where a hard rain streaked the glass. "The fishermen went out in this weather?"

Sloat shrugged. "It wasn't raining when they went out."

They continued to work with the rain beating at the glass and the fire hissing in the hearth. The bell tolled incessantly, jangling on Jack's nerves.

He drummed his fingers, glanced outside at the thrashing trees and turbulent sky. He thought of the men on the boats, braving the storm, and the families waiting for them onshore. "I'm going to the village," he announced abruptly. "We need to help."

Sloat huddled closer to the fire. "Why?"

He eyed his steward with dislike. "Because we can. Load a wagon with blankets, brandy, firewood. Have Mrs. Pratt make up some baskets and bring them down with you."

"Bring them where?"

Where did people gather in times of trouble? The church?

"The tavern," Jack said. "Hurry."

A wet and worried-looking groom led Neptune from the stables. Outside the yard, the wind pounced, shrieking, biting, pelting them with rain. The horse shuddered and shook his head in protest. Jack steadied him with hands and voice. Neptune responded to his reassurance, putting his head down, forging forward through the sucking mud. The rain slashed down like knives. Trees tossed and bent. Branches creaked and flew.

Jack raised his face to the slashing wind and rain. Despite the freezing discomfort, it felt good to be out, to be doing, to pit his strength against something as substantial as the storm. Neptune emerged from the illusory shelter of the wood onto the track that spilled to the harbor.

The ruthless wind, the brutal view, snatched his breath away. The ocean raged as loud as an army on the move, gray and violent as a battlefield. Huge breakers rolled between the swelling sea and the lowering sky, flinging themselves onto the rocks in a fury of spray and foam.

The shuttered houses clung to the rocks like a colony of oysters, dark and closed. Slits of yellow lamp light edged the tavern windows. The church bell tolled, *Come . . . back. Come . . . back.*

A boat spun and tumbled in the turbulent waves like a leaf in the gutter, beyond reach, beyond help, beyond hope. Half a dozen men clustered onshore, brandishing a rope in the wind. Their shouts rose thin and piping as gulls' cries. Jack watched as the weighted rope coiled over the water, fell short, and was reeled in again.

The small craft pitched and tossed without sail or oars, up and down, up and . . . A wave crashed down and drained away, leaving a single man inside clinging to the side of the boat.

Jack's heart thundered. He spurred Neptune forward, hooves clattering on the wet stone.

They reached the strand. The man in the boat had caught a wild toss and somehow tied the rope to the prow. The men onshore hauled and cursed, the wet rope yanking through their hands.

Jack slid from the saddle and stumbled down the beach into the teeth of the wind and the cold, cold tide. The air was thick with salt and fear. Water slapped his face, filled his boots, dragged at his thighs. He slogged through the churning surf and grabbed hold of the rope between two other men.

"Pull!"

The boat leaped liked a shark fighting at the end of a line. Jack's shoulders wrenched. His boots scraped shale.

"Pull."

A waved crashed over them, almost knocking Jack from his feet. The man in front of him went down. He hauled him up by his collar, wrapped white knuckles around the twisted rope.

"Pull."

They staggered back, fighting the savage sea and angry tide for possession of the boat. It wallowed and rolled, ungainly in the shallows, banging ribs and shins, smashing fingers. They towed it through the long white breakers and onto the shore.

The man inside sprawled against the bench, dark and limp as seaweed abandoned by the tide.

Jack's leg throbbed like fire. Blood crawled across his knuckles. He couldn't feel his fingers or his feet. He ran to Neptune, a big, gray shape against wet, black rocks, and led him to the men whipped by the rain, huddled around the boat.

"How many more?" he shouted against the wind.

A burly man with an orange beard—the baker—looked up. "All in. Jeb's was the last boat."

"Put him on my horse. We'll take him to the tavern."

Sloat would be there soon with a cartload of brandy and blankets.

Or he'd fire the bastard.

They limped and lurched from the beach, a sodden line of men buffeted by the gale and bolstered by their small victory over the sea.

The taproom enveloped them in warmth, noise, and light. Half the village of Farness crowded the bar or clustered around small tables. The smell of wet wool, smoke, and onions hung on the air.

Jack's head swam. He needed to sit down.

The rescued man leaned on his companions, stumbling across the wet plank floor to a place by the fire.

"Da!" A pretty, rounded young woman with swollen eyes rushed forward and threw her arms around him. She drew back, her gaze fixed painfully on his face. "Colin?"

Quiet fell on the taproom.

"Sorry, lass." Her father's voice was hoarse with salt and sorrow. "He's . . . He was trying to save the nets when . . ."

"*No*! Colin." Wailing, she sank to the floor.

"Whiskey," Jack ordered.

He was tired of death. He had sat by too many dying soldiers, stood in too many sitting rooms to deliver unwelcome news to grieving mothers and wives. Sliding an arm about the girl, he raised her from the floor. "Let me help you to a chair."

She sobbed noisily and collapsed against his chest. The tavern keeper reached for a bottle.

The door to the taproom burst open in a rush of rain and a gush of cold air.

Jack glanced up, expecting Sloat.

Morwenna materialized from the storm, framed by wet timbers against the stormy sky. Her fair hair was plastered to her head by rain. Her blue dress clung to her body. She looked like the figurehead on a sailing ship. Like a mermaid.

Jack felt a crackle like lightning zing along his nerves and lift all the little hairs on the back of his neck.

"I heard the bell," she said. "What is happening?"

No one answered.

She was not one of them, Jack realized. She shone among the villagers of Farness like a fine wax taper, slender, straight, and pale. She did not belong in this grimy taproom. How could he ever have thought she could belong to him?

Her gaze swept the room like a flame, lighting on his hand where it rested on the girl's back. Her brow pleated. "You are hurt."

He had forgotten his bloody knuckles. "I'm fine."

Morwenna took a half step forward out of the rain, toward him. "I could help."

Her offer seared him like the drag of the wet rope. *There is nothing you can give me that I do not have,* she had said. *Nothing I need or want.*

"There is nothing you can do," he said.

Her breath rasped like a match against the silence. Her gaze narrowed. "Who is that?"

He glanced down at the crying girl in his arms. He didn't even know her name.

The tavern keeper's wife crossed her padded arms against her bosom. "That's our Jenny Miller. She just lost her man."

"Lost," Morwenna repeated blankly. As if the young fisherman were a halfpenny or a sheep.

"In the sea," Jack said harshly.

She cocked her head, listening to the wind and the sad, deep notes of the bell: *Come . . . back.* "I could find him for you."

Jenny's father stirred by the fire. "He went down with the nets," he said dully. "He will not be found until this storm is past."

His daughter gave a muffled sob.

Jack's helplessness pushed like a thumb on his windpipe. "There's nothing you can do." He forced the words through his tight throat. *Nothing he could do.* "Nothing anyone can do."

She met his gaze, her eyes running with borrowed colors like the sea. Without a word she turned and walked into the rain.

The tavern keeper's wife sniffed. "She's a fool to go back out in this weather."

Jack stared at the closed door, his throat aching, his heart burning in his chest.

Yes.

And he was a bigger one for going after her.

Morwenna strode to the harbor in a welter of rain and unfamiliar emotion. The storm was raw and turbulent outside her, inside her, churning in her chest, pulsing in her fingertips.

The memory of Jack's dark, weary eyes, his hard, strained face, jabbed at her heart.

She had offered her help, and he had dismissed her.

She could not blame him. She had spurned him, after all. And he had no idea what she could do. What she was.

Once her kind had been revered, feared and worshipped. But as their numbers dwindled and they withdrew deeper into the wild places of earth, their encounters with humankind became less frequent. Reverence had faded to superstition and fear to unbelief. Now even the legends were fading from human memory.

Better that way, her brother insisted. Safer that way. There were so many of them . . .

And Jack was one of them, one with them, the men with their wet clothes and weathered faces, the girl with the red-rimmed eyes.

She lengthened her stride, unhampered by the pelting rain and gusts of wind. She was not *jealous.* What she wanted, she would have. She was an immortal child of the sea, part of the First Creation.

And yet . . .

Standing alone outside the circle of the fire, she had been achingly aware of something outside and separate from herself, the web of human experience. All those others in the taproom had come together in the face of the storm, bound together by some human need, united by a shared understanding of death and love and loss.

Humans died.

She would not die.

But she could do something they could not do.

She walked the long stone jetty that protected the harbor. Waves crested and crashed around her, pouring their might onto the rocks, sending up shoots and plumes of spray, drenching her hair and her skirt. The sea pounded through the soles of her feet and within her chest.

Dimly, she heard shouting behind her. She would not have chosen to reveal herself. She did not want to prompt questions she was not prepared to answer. Not yet.

But she would not let human considerations, human fears, distract her from her magic. She closed her mind to consequences and embraced the water's power. She breathed it in, licking it from her lips, absorbing it through her skin. She was drunk on the smell of brine, blinded and deafened by the beauty of the tempest.

Lifting her arms to the wind, she raised her face to the rain and sang in the storm.

Her notes pierced the heavy sky, soared like drops of vapor into the clouds swirling and combining high above the earth. Bright shards of music ripped from her throat and flashed like lightning among the currents of air. The energy of the storm pulsed inside her, welled inside her, spilled from her eyes and her heart like song. Like blood.

She felt the clouds shift and break, felt the sea surge and respond, and trembled in the marrow of her bones.

It was not enough.

Voices fretted her, plucking at her peace, stirring her to the depths like the wind moving over the waters.

She lost her man.

He will not be found until this storm is past.

There is nothing you can do.

Resolve stiffened her spine. She anchored her feet on the slippery wet stone and sang in the seals from the sea.

She summoned them by name and by magic, and they came, streaking dark and brindled out of the deeps, racing in response to her song. Leaping, diving, seeking, finding . . .

There. A young man drifting in a fisherman's smock and boots, his dark hair flowing like weeds. A heartbeat, thin and thready beneath the surface of the water. Her own pulse fluttered in response.

Rain spattered and sank on the surface of the ocean. She felt his breath rising like a chain of silver bubbles, barely linking him to life. Her lungs emptied. Was she too late?

In a burst of notes and panic, she sent the seals scything through the water to bring him up, to bring him in. They curled around him like cats, bumping him with their whiskered heads, prodding him with their flippers, rolling him on to his back like an otter. They turned his white face to the clearing sky and bore him up, making a raft of their broad, sleek bodies to carry him toward shore. She smoothed the waves in their path to a grumble, a ripple, a flourish of foam.

Her power was running out like water from a cup, leaving her emptied, her throat raw, her legs as heavy as wet sand.

She heard cries, raucous and indistinct as the kittiwakes on the cliff. The human inhabitants of Farness straggled along the seawall, watching the seals come in on the tide.

Jack . . .

Even from a distance she recognized him, his broad shoulders, his straight soldier's posture, and everything inside her shifted and flowed like the changing shore. As if he had power over the very landscape of her heart.

The young fisherman raised his head and coughed. Or was that the barking of a seal?

Her vision wavered. Her mind grayed. She blinked, watching as a figure with flying skirts and braids detached from the huddle onshore.

"Colin!" The girl dashed to the water's edge like a curlew darting in the tide.

Morwenna smiled.

Then the stones rose up sharply to take her, and the world faded away.

When she woke, she could not hear the sea any longer, only the murmur of human voices.

She recognized the smells of the taproom, beer and smoke, sweat and onions, and the clean soap-and-man scent that was Jack. His hard shoulder pillowed her cheek. His arms and legs supported her as if she rode before him on his horse. She felt cradled. Protected.

Off-balance.

"Never seen anything like it," a rough male voice pronounced.

Oh dear. She opened her eyes.

Immediately Jack's arms tightened around her. "Morwenna."

Only her name, but she felt another shift in her chest as everything readjusted. His lean, strong face was very close, his deep brown eyes concerned.

"Are you all right?" he asked. "What were you doing out there?"

More than she could ever tell him.

She sat up cautiously, aware of the villagers gathered around the fire. She recognized the baker with his curling orange beard, the dark and nervous shopkeeper, the nasty man with the crow's voice and the weasel's name. *Stoat?* Sloat, that was it. The young lovers cuddled in the corner, the fisherman's muscled arm around the girl's round waist.

Jack was waiting for her answer. They all were waiting. She was truly a part of their circle now, the focus of all eyes. She fought the urge to hunch her shoulders, to hide from their attention.

"I suppose I must have fainted."

Jack's mouth compressed. "Before that."

"I went outside."

"Into the storm," he said flatly.

She glanced out the windows to avoid meeting his eyes.

In the wake of her magic, the setting sun had painted the sky orange and rose. "The weather is clearing, is it not?"

"It is now," Jack acknowledged. "What about the seals?"

She moistened her lips. "They must have washed ashore. In the storm."

"Washed ashore." His voice was stiff with disbelief.

She smiled at him. "Like that lucky young man saved by the tide."

An old fisherman spoke from his place at the bar. "It wasn't the tide that saved him. It was the selkie."

Morwenna's heart beat faster. The seals she had called to her were ordinary harbor seals. But the old man's guess was uncomfortably close to the truth. The selkie were water elementals like the finfolk, all children of the sea.

Jack's brows drew together. "The what?"

"The seal folk. They live in the ocean as seals, see, and when they come ashore they put off their sealskins and walk around no different from you and me."

"Except better looking," put in another. "And naked."

"Superstitious nonsense," Sloat said.

The fisherman stuck out his jaw. "I've seen them out there in the waves. Guided me home once in the fog."

The young man, Colin, lifted his head from the girl's brown hair and looked at Morwenna.

"My grandda said if you find a selkie's pelt and hide it, the selkie must bide with you as man or wife," the second fisherman said.

Sloat sneered. "Your grandda was at sea too long. I knew you Scots had sex with sheep. But seals?"

Jack silenced him with a look. "It's a pleasant story."

Morwenna released a relieved breath. *Story.* He did not believe a word of it.

Colin left his corner and stood before Morwenna, fumbling beneath the open neck of his shirt. He wore a leather thong around his throat and the silver sign of the mortals' murdered Christ. He pulled the thong over his head and offered her the cross in his broad palm. "Thank you," he said simply.

The ache in her throat grew to a lump. She swallowed hard. "You owe me nothing."

Stubbornly, he held out his hand. "I know what I know."

She shook her head, aware of Jack watching them. But she could not spurn the young fisherman's earnest thanks. Nor could she take his offering and send him away empty-handed.

She curled her hand around the cross and traced a spiral in his palm, the sign of the sea. "I will treasure your gift and remember," she said. "Go in peace over the waters and return in safety to the land."

His smile almost blinded her with its brilliance.

"Now go back to your sweetheart," Morwenna told him. "Thank her, if you must thank someone, and hold her tight for the time that has been given to you both."

He ducked his head in shy acknowledgment and retreated.

"An interesting blessing," Jack observed quietly.

She shrugged, not daring to look at him for fear he would find the truth in her eyes. "It did not hurt me to say and may do him good to hear. Their lives will be short and hard enough. They should love each other while they can."

"Excellent advice," he said.

Finally she met his gaze. What she saw in his eyes made her pulse pound. Not distrust, not suspicion, but warmth and acceptance and desire.

"Oh," she said with a foolish lurch of heart, "do you think so?"

"Yes." He stopped and took her hands in his. Warm, steady hands. Strong, human hands. "Marry me, Morwenna."

Her heart turned over completely and her whole world shifted again. She felt grit in her eyes like sand in an oyster and blinked. A single pearl rolled down her cheek.

She smiled tremulously. "Perhaps we could start with dinner," she suggested. "You did say you would court me."

FIVE

"This charade has gone on long enough," Morgan said.

Her brother stalked the confines of Morwenna's neat little cottage like a shark trapped by the tide, all sleek power and frustrated energy. "How long has it been now? Four weeks?"

"Three," Morwenna said defensively.

Three weeks of this odd human process known as courtship. Dinner at Jack's house, with her hair piled up and a bewildering array of cutlery on the table. Sex at hers, sweaty, sweet, and satisfying. He took her for a ride in his carriage. She took him for walks along the beach. They even sat side by side in the church one Sunday morning while the preacher droned like a drowsy bee and the sun cast colored patterns on the stone floor.

Only three weeks.

Not that the actual number of days mattered except as a measure of her brother's concern. If Morgan was counting time by human standards, in weeks rather than seasons and centuries, he was worried indeed.

She watched him pace to the cupboard and turn. The once-empty shelves behind him were littered with items she had received since the storm, left at her doorstep or pressed shyly upon her when she walked into town: a pitcher of flowers, a package of candles, a loaf of bread, a shawl. She accepted the villagers' offerings as she accepted the gifts of the tide and gave them fair weather and good fishing in return.

Yet somehow the trade had become more meaningful than a simple transaction.

She tried to explain. "I have a place here."

Morgan threw her an impatient look. "Your place is on Sanctuary. Among your own kind. Not with . . . with . . ."

She raised her chin. "His name is Jack."

"Does he know who you are? What you are?"

She hesitated. She was venturing further and further from who she had been. Once she told Jack the truth, there was no going back. One way or another, their idyll would end. "He does not need to know. He accepts what he sees."

"Then he is blind. Or stupid."

"He is not stupid." She remembered the warm perception in Jack's serious gaze, the strength of his steady hands. "He loves me."

Her brother looked down his long, bold nose. "Humans fear what they do not understand. And what they fear, they hate. He is not capable of loving you."

His words touched her deepest fears. Her brother knew her too well. And yet . . .

"You do not know him," she said.

Morgan stared at her, baffled, and shook his head. "Say that he loves you. It cannot last. He is mortal. He will die eventually. That is his fate, his nature. And you will go on. That is ours."

"Unless . . ." She drew a shaky breath, daring at last to speak the possibility burning like a coal in her breast. Knowing her words would hurt and anger Morgan. "He has asked me to marry him."

If they married, if she lived on land with Jack as a human, she would love as a human. Age as a human. Die as a human.

"Wenna." Morgan's voice was shaken. Her throat tightened at his use of her old childhood name. He was her brother, her twin. In their carefree existence, in their careless way, they had always cared for each other. "You would give up immortality? You would give up the sea?"

Yes.

No.

"I do not know." She bit her lip. "I might."

"For what? For him?"

Could she give up the sea for Jack?

She admired him: his quiet strength, his bone-deep sense of responsibility, his constant heart. She *liked* him.

But more, she liked the person she became when she was with him. Someone softer, more open, more aware of others' emotions, more capable of feeling.

Less alone.

The children of the sea were alive to sensation. With Jack, she felt another part of her stir to life, like a long-dead limb responding to the pricks and tingles of returning circulation.

She sought a way to put her feelings into words, searched for an answer that would satisfy her brother. That would satisfy them both.

"For Jack, yes." The words came slowly, dragged from the depths of her consciousness, from the bottom of her heart. "And perhaps for . . . love?"

Morgan's face closed. "We are finfolk. What do we know of love?"

You love me, she thought.

The realization struck like a fishhook into her heart, barbed and unexpected. They never spoke of their bond. It was not their way. But if she turned her back on Morgan and the sea, he might never recover. Would never forgive.

She swallowed past the ache in her throat. "Enough to know how precious love is," she said quietly. "And how rare."

"Love does not last, Morwenna." Her brother's gaze met hers, golden and implacable. "Nothing lasts forever but the sea."

The sea shone as smooth as glass. Sunlight poured like honey over the green and gold hills as Jack handed Morwenna into the pony cart and walked around the horse's head.

She twisted on the seat to regard the basket packed behind her. "A picnic?" Her voice rose with pleasure.

Jack climbed up. Stiffly, because of his leg. "You said I should enjoy life more," he reminded her.

"And I am delighted you listened," she responded promptly. "But didn't you eat off the ground often enough as a soldier?"

He loved the way she laughed at him with her eyes. He picked up the ribbons, clicking his tongue at the pony. "Cook never prepared a basket for me in the Peninsula."

"Champagne and sweetmeats?"

"Meat pies and lemonade." He grinned. "I'm a man of basic appetites."

He had a simple soldier's desires. For a home, a wife, children. And after years of wandering, he was finally on the road to achieving them all.

These past few weeks with Morwenna he'd felt more at home, more at peace, than ever before in his life. Last night across the dining table at Arden, she had glowed in the light of the candles, her silver gold hair arranged in tousled curls. Like she *belonged* there, mistress of his heart and of his house. The servants all liked her. The villagers liked her.

And he . . .

He'd wanted to lay her down among the silver and china, between the puddings and the gravy, and lick her all over. He'd burned to take her upstairs to the master bedroom with its big, curtained bed and touch her, take her, own her.

Of course he'd done none of those things.

Sloat and the servants had been around to keep his lust in check. Whatever circumstances had driven her from her brother's home and protection, she was a lady. He would not show her less than respect in front of his dependents.

Now, sitting in the open carriage with her hands folded demurely in her lap, she gave him the slumberous look he loved. "If you wished to satisfy your basic appetites, we could have stayed at the cottage. I have two chairs now," she informed him smugly. "*And* a bed."

His blood heated even as he laughed. She might be a lady, but he was still very much a man. He was urgently, painfully aware that he could have her back at her cottage and naked in under five minutes.

But he wanted more from her than civilized dinners or stolen rendezvous.

He turned the cart down the narrow track that meandered to the cove and the boat he had waiting. He was sensitive to every shift of her body on the narrow bench, of her thigh warm beside his. Beneath his tailored coat, he was sweating, his body as hard as the brake handle.

But he would not be distracted again. Every time in the past few weeks he had tried to broach the subject of marriage, Morwenna had turned the conversation aside, diverting him with a look, a touch, a whispered invitation.

Not that he had been that difficult to distract, Jack admitted ruefully.

He had planned this outing with all the care of a general plotting battle strategy. Out-of-doors, where she was most comfortable. By the sea, where he saw her for the first time. On an island, picturesque and private. He gave instructions for the basket, the blanket, the boat. His mother's ring was in his waistcoat pocket. He had even directed Sloat to draft a letter to his lawyer.

This time everything was prepared.

Everything was perfect.

This time she would say yes.

Morwenna sat in the front of the boat, trailing her hand over the side. The water flowed between her fingers, rippling along her nerve endings, murmuring her name. Beneath the stiff fabric of her dress, her breasts peaked. Her toes curled in her tight new shoes. She longed to be naked in the ocean.

And yet she would not have given up her place in the boat for anything.

She looked at Jack, his dark hair lifting in the breeze from the sea, the sun reddening his nose and cheekbones, and felt a rush of love for him so intense her heart stumbled.

It cannot last, her brother had warned.

But didn't that make the present even more precious?

This moment must be enough. She would make it be enough for both of them. She would fashion a string of perfect moments like a necklace of pearls—her gift to him. He would never regret loving her. While she . . .

Her throat felt suddenly tight.

We are finfolk. Her brother's words echoed harshly in her ears. *What do we know of love?*

She had no experience with love, no example to guide her. Few pair bonds among their kind lasted through the centuries. Children were rare, grudgingly born and quickly fostered.

And yet . . .

She watched the muscles of Jack's arms bunch and stretch, his big hands grasp the oars, and she lost her breath, falling into the creak and the rhythm of the oars. His scent, soap and linen, salty sweat and clean skin, tugged at her senses. He rowed strongly if not particularly well, digging deep into the water. One paddle caught a swell and shot a plume of spray into the boat.

He grinned ruefully. "Army men are better in the saddle than at the oars."

"I love you in the saddle," she assured him, and he laughed.

The sound warmed her heart and eased her doubts. He was so different. Different from her, yes, but also unlike any man she had ever known before.

All the men she had observed over the centuries were seafaring men, Vikings, sailors, fishermen.

"You did not learn to row growing up?" she asked.

"Not in Cheapside. London," he explained. "My mother's family lived in Cheapside."

Over his shoulder, she could see the island rising like a green wave from the blue and silver sea.

She wrinkled her forehead, struggling to recall what she knew of London. "There is a river in London."

He glanced over his shoulder, angling the boat toward the narrow beach. "A very dirty one. Not for boys in boats and definitely not for swimming."

"You cannot swim?" She could hardly fathom such a thing.

"I can paddle. Or I could."

Before the injuries that scarred his leg, she guessed.

He turned back to her, his gaze lazy and amused. "I suppose you swim like a fish."

"I can swim," she admitted.

Her belly hollowed. *Exactly like a fish.*

The boat rocked in the shallow water. A tumble of gray rock protected a pale sickle of sand. Above the beach the hills swelled, covered in long grass and white and yellow flowers, yarrow and meadowsweet.

The paddles gleamed in the sunlight. The round hull scraped bottom. Morwenna stood, holding on to the side of the boat.

"I've got you." Jack swung her into his arms.

She clutched at his shoulders. "You will hurt your leg."

"You'll soak your hem."

"No matter. I—"

But he was already striding through the ankle-deep water. He set her gently on her feet, his broad hands lingering at her waist before he left her to fetch the basket.

She sighed and spread the blanket on the grass. The sun was very warm. She straightened, stretching her back, looking longingly at the bright blue water. She wished now she had waded ashore. Her dress chafed. Her boots rubbed. For a moment, she felt as confined by her human role as by her human clothes.

"Show me," Jack said.

The sight of him, dark and muscular in his tight blue coat, soothed her. Steadied her. "Show you what?"

"How to swim."

Longing surged under her skin. She resisted the temptation. "I cannot Change. Um. My clothes."

"You don't need to change." A smile creased the corners of his eyes. "We can swim naked."

Her heart tripped.

He had seen her naked many times. This was no different, and yet she felt curiously exposed. The ocean was hers, her life, a part of herself she had kept carefully separate from him. Now he was asking her to share it, to bring him into her world.

Jack stripped off his jacket and tossed it on the blanket. "There's no one to see."

He pulled his shirt over his head.

Her gaze traveled the heavy definition of his muscles, the pattern of his scars, the dark hair that fanned across his chest and narrowed to a line below his navel. Lust stirred, easy and familiar.

"We do not need to swim," she said.

He unbuttoned his breeches. He was already half aroused, dusky and thick. "It will be fun."

She did not need fun. She needed . . . She was no longer sure what she needed.

"The water will be cold," she warned.

Jack glanced down at his erection. "That's probably a good thing."

She smiled in acknowledgment, reaching slowly for the front closure of her dress.

"I can do that." His hands were there, between her breasts, slipping the delicate buttons from their holes. "Let me."

His breath was warm against her face, his expression intent.

She trembled, undone by more than his hands. "I can manage."

"You can do anything," he murmured. Her bodice sagged open. Her breath caught. "But let me."

He cupped the soft weight of her breasts, his thumbs skating over her nipples. "Let me take care of you, Morwenna."

Desire clenched her insides. An unfamiliar ache lodged in her throat. No one in her life had ever wanted to take care of her. Even Morgan knew better than to try.

Jack's fingers brushed her throat, traced her collarbone, found her wildly beating pulse in the hollow below her jaw. Sliding the pins from her hair, he combed the smooth strands over her shoulders, arranging them over her breasts, caressing her through the long curtain of her hair. His touch made her feel attended. Cherished.

Loved.

He nudged her dress from her shoulders. It pooled at her feet.

They stood together in the sunlight like the first man and

the first woman, naked and unashamed. His arousal brushed her stomach, silky and hot. She flushed with anticipation, her skin blooming.

He laced his fingers with hers. "Take me swimming with you."

Her heart hammered. She glanced down at the blanket, sideways at him. "Don't you want to . . ."

His smile lit his serious eyes. "There will be time later. Time for everything."

The memory of her own words haunted her. *Their lives will be short and hard enough. They should love each other while they can.*

How could she refuse him this? How could she refuse him anything?

She would not Change in front of him. But she could give him this much of herself.

"All right," she said.

They walked hand in hand to the water's edge, the boundary of her world.

Jack grimaced. "Damn, that's cold."

She laughed. "Better to go in all at once."

She ran forward, kicking up spray, and dived into the cold salt sea.

Joy.

The force, the shock, nearly forced her Change. Water enveloped her, embraced her, slid over her limbs, flowed through her hair.

She dived, free from gravity and the planes of earth, dizzy with freedom, feeling the magic bubble through her veins, wrap her sinews, stretch her flesh, soften her bones. Her thighs fused. Her toes spread. She opened her mouth to drink, to inhale, intoxicating briny gulps.

In the sea, she was free, she could be . . . anything. Anything at all.

"Morwenna!" A voice, louder than the cry of the gulls or the pounding of her heart or the rush of water in her ears. Jack's voice, calling her back to shore.

Disoriented, she drifted, caught between Change and thought.

Jack.

Her hair floated around her in a cloud. She righted herself, found her feet and the direction of the light. The surface. *There.* She kicked, feeling her legs, bone and muscle, respond.

Sunlight and air broke on her face.

She forced herself to breathe. To be. To be human.

She turned, blinking the water from her eyes. Jack stood waist deep in the cold water, his wet hair molded to his skull. Water ran down his chest, emphasizing the masculine shape of him, the sleek, hard muscles, the tension of his broad shoulders.

The tension evaporated when he saw her. His face relaxed. "You were under a long time."

Time. They had so little time.

She glided back to him. "I am here now."

Let it be enough, she prayed. Let me be enough for him.

They played together like otters or children, bobbing, laughing, splashing in the water. He chased her, shrieking, diving, until she let herself be caught. Breathless, she floated in his arms, twined around him like kelp. Her hands drifted over him, enjoying the textures of him, rough and smooth, under the water. In that moment she had everything she wanted, Jack and the sea. Inside she was melting, flowing, brimming with love.

He trapped her hands; held them. "Come with me."

"Yes."

"Lie with me."

Oh, yes.

They waded dripping from the water and lay side by side on the blanket, lacing their fingers together. Turning her head, she pressed her lips to his shoulder. His skin was cool and tasted of salt.

"You are cold."

He shrugged. "The sun will dry me quickly enough."

She rolled to face him, smiling, draping her leg over his hip. "I can warm you."

"Better than the sun." He turned on his side toward her,

combing her damp hair from her face with his fingers. His brown eyes were steady on hers. "My light. My love."

He covered her mouth with his. Soft and quiet, wooing her. Her heart lurched and then raced. He touched her gently and with purpose until she trembled in his arms.

He smiled. "Cold?"

"No."

Her skin flushed as he continued to touch her, to taste, trailing his fingers from throat to breast, from hip to thigh and everywhere in between. His hands left fires in their wake, a bone-deep glow, flash points of pleasure.

"*Jack.*"

He gathered her close, body to body, skin to skin, heat to heat. Their mouths met and explored before he grasped her hips and nudged forward. She gasped, her fingers biting into his shoulders. He thrust.

Ah. She shuddered, her teeth biting down on her lower lip. "Again."

He paused. "Are you asking me or telling me?"

She wriggled. "Which will get you to do what I want?"

"Either," he admitted frankly. His neck arched, the cords straining as she touched him. "Oh, God, Morwenna."

She melted against him. "Please. Do it. Now."

He surged.

She cried out in passion, in possession, in joy. He was in her, part of her, as she clenched around him and made him hers, as he thrust inside her and made her his, all their boundaries blurring, all their divisions melting away. They moved together, flowed together, fused together by sweat and heat and need.

One.

Tenderness cracked her heart.

"You are the first," she told him.

He focused on her face, his pupils wide and wild. "What?"

She touched his cheek. "My first love."

Her last.

Her only.

"Good," he said with masculine satisfaction and sank into her again.

The ripples began inside her. He held himself deep and still as she shuddered, as she shattered, feeling him everywhere inside her, surging inside her, in her blood and in her loins and in her heart. She wrapped her arms around him to hold him closer, wrapped her legs around him to bring him deeper, felt him push into her, pound into her, until he plunged with her into the heart of the whirlpool and they both were swept away.

They floated, drifting in each other's arms. The sun was warm on her naked hip, golden behind her eyelids.

He raised his head and kissed her so sweetly she shivered again in longing and delight.

"I am a plain man with ordinary needs. I want to give you my life and my love. To share a home and children with you. Marry me, Morwenna."

She felt the prick of real tears, hard, human tears in her eyes. She swallowed the lump in her throat. "Are you asking me or telling me?"

But his emotions ran too deep for teasing. His gaze was straight and serious. "Which will get you to do what I want?"

"Either," she answered honestly. "I love you."

His hands tightened. His eyes blazed. "Yes?" he demanded. "Say yes."

"Yes!"

Neither spoke again for a long while.

SIX

The sun slid toward the sea. Pink and purple clouds fled across the sky, herded like sheep by the wind. The tide rolled in, long, flat breakers edged with dirty lace.

Morwenna sat in the prow as Jack rowed the heavy wooden boat back to the mainland.

She loved.

And was loved.

The knowledge was a warm glow in her chest, radiating outward to her fingers and toes like the rays of the afternoon sun.

Jack hauled on the oars, his lean brown face open and relaxed despite the restive sea. She had done that for him, she thought smugly. She had erased the lines from his face and put that lazy, satisfied glint in his eyes.

She smiled.

"Wind's picking up," he remarked.

She could feel a shimmer of vapor in the air, a powerful current flowing from the west. "It must rain sometime," she said apologetically.

"We'll be home before then," he assured her.

Home. Such a round, firm, settled word. The warmth inside her grew.

"I want to go to Arden," she said.

He nodded. "I told Cook to prepare a special dinner for us."

She was touched by his thoughtfulness; amused by his appetite. "After that lunch?"

The empty picnic basket rested between the seats. She nudged it with her foot out of the water that had collected in the bottom of the boat.

"We should celebrate. I have something to give you," Jack said.

She looked at him, instantly diverted from the puddle at her feet. "What?"

"My mother's ring. A cabochon sapphire." He cleared his throat. "Of course you might prefer a different stone. Or a larger one."

She did not care about the size or the stone. The look in his eyes meant everything. "I would love to wear your mother's ring."

Pleasure shone in his dark eyes, but he only said, "Wait until you see it."

"Tonight."

"Actually, I have it in my pocket. I still haven't proposed to you properly."

She arched her eyebrows. "There is a proper way to propose?"

"Generally the man goes down upon one knee."

"I think I might quite like you on your knees. Just think of all you could do . . . down there. But the way you proposed was better."

He cocked an eyebrow. "Without ceremony?"

"Naked," she explained. "And inside me."

His gaze kindled. "Most *im*proper. But since it persuaded you to say yes . . ."

A *pop*.

A lurch.

A rush.

Morwenna stared, bewildered, as a black rag washed between

the seats. The bow dipped suddenly beneath Jack's weight. "What . . . ?"

Water gurgled in the bottom of the boat. The picnic basket listed on its side in a rapidly growing pool of water.

"Jack?"

A wave washed over the side. Her seat slanted under her.

"We've sprung a leak." His voice was calm and sharp. "Stay with the boat."

The water gushed to his boots. There was a hole, she realized. Under his seat. She was not frightened, only bewildered and annoyed.

"Hold on to the boat," Jack ordered. "The hull will float if—"

Another wave rushed the boat. He dropped the oars and grabbed for her.

She reached for his hands as the world went suddenly, wildly awry. The boat pitched, the bow plunged. The sudden weight of the water flipped the solid hull, throwing her into the cold salt sea. Brine filled her mouth, blurred her eyes . . . She heard a splash, a thunk, as her head bobbed under the surface. Sputtering, she raised her face, raking streamers of wet hair from her eyes. Her skirts mushroomed, billowing around her. And Jack . . .

Her heart clenched like a fist.

"Jack!"

He floated a few yards away, arms thrashing feebly. His eyes were open. Dazed. A great bloody gash streaked his forehead.

He was hurt. In danger. Something—the hard wooden edge of the hull as it flipped or the end of an oar—must have struck him when they capsized.

She kicked toward him, hampered by her skirts. Her legs were tangled, heavy, her half boots full of water.

He groaned. "Morwenna."

"I'm here," she called frantically. "It's all right. I am—"

Terrified.

His eyes rolled back in his skull. His head dropped forward.

He slid beneath the water.

"No!"

She lunged for him, reaching, reaching . . . Her fingers brushed something. His hair. His sleeve. She gripped tight and tugged, hauling him to the surface, turning his face to the sky. Was he breathing? His face was pale, his lips slack.

A wave smacked into the hull and broke over them. They both went under. Morwenna kicked her sodden skirts, struggled to support Jack's head. Her breath burst from her lips in an absurd staccato rhythm like a song or a prayer: *Please, please, please.*

Water was her element. But she was trapped by her clothes. Trapped in this body. Jack was easily twice her size and weighted by his boots. The gash on his forehead was red, wet, and open like a mouth. Her heart drummed in panic. She could call the seals. She did not have the strength to save him.

Or time to wait.

"Jack." She spoke sharply, urgently, into his ear, willing him to respond. "Hold me."

His lids lifted. His bleary eyes slid over her.

"Do you hear me?" She shook him. "Hold on. Hold on to me."

"No," he slurred. "Drag you . . . down."

"You won't."

Not if she Changed. Now. Quickly.

"You must hold on," she said fiercely.

His gaze found hers. "Love . . . you. Save . . . yourself."

He sagged.

Sank.

With a little cry, she seized his hand and pressed it to her shoulder. *Please.* His fingers fumbled. Squeezed. Her relief rose like a sob.

She had never attempted to Change like this, with clothes plastered to her body and shoes on her feet. With urgency beating in her blood and panic squeezing her heart. No plunge, no dive, no wild surge of spirit becoming one with the sea. She gritted her teeth, wrenching power from her uncooperative flesh, forcing magic along constricted veins and sinews.

It hurt.

Pain lanced through her, unexpected, shocking. She spasmed,

writhing like a fish out of water. Jack drifted beside her—breathing?—his touch a brand, an anchor on her flesh. Quickly. Now.

Her blood drummed in her ears as she Changed, as her muscles rippled and popped and her bones erupted and dissolved. Seams popped. Fabric tore.

Jack.

She nudged against him, glided under him, felt his hands slide and grip, felt his weight shift and roll.

Hold on, she said or thought or sang and carried him safely to shore.

He could not breathe. He was drowning. Dreaming. Delirious.

His head was on fire and his chest burned and his limbs were cold, at once heavy and weightless. His blood rushed in his ears.

Hold on, someone said, as they'd said in the surgeons' tent when they'd placed the pad between his teeth and probed his wounds for bits of bone and shrapnel. The world whirled as it had then, and the pain shot through his head.

They were taking him somewhere, carrying him swiftly, away from the battlefield.

Hold on.

So he did, clinging grimly to life. There was something he had to do, someone he had to see, some . . .

Morwenna.

The sea gushed and bubbled around him. The world fractured in a blaze of light, a blast of sound, a burst of agony. Air knifed his lungs. He gasped and choked. On blood? Or brine?

He felt a nudge, a shove, as he lay like a felled log in the surf, cold, hard sand under his cheek, water running through his fingers.

Morwenna. He turned his head to find her, struggled to push to his knees.

She was there—and not there—in the shallow water.

He closed his eyes. Opened them again. There was a dolphin. He saw it, the sleek barrel shape, the distinctive fin.

And there was Morwenna, shining like the mist, insubstantial as the foam, her wet hair around her shoulders . . .

A wave rattled in and drained away, taking the last vestige of the dolphin with it.

But the double image, Morwenna's face superimposed on the fin, the tail, seared the back of his eyes.

Better if he had not seen her at all.

She rose from the water and ran to him, her dress clinging to her in rags.

His heart pounded. She was safe. He was relieved. He was . . . He opened his mouth, but no sound emerged.

He tried again. "I didn't see you out there. In the water. I thought you were dead."

"Are you all right?"

"Hallucinating," he explained.

She kneeled beside him, her face inhuman in its perfection, beautiful in its concern.

He could not breathe. He could not think. His brain was on fire. "Are you . . ."

"I am fine."

"Morwenna?"

"Yes. Let me help you to the cart." She reached for him and he saw—he *saw*—the faint iridescent webbing between her fingers. Even as he watched, it faded, it melted away.

Turning his head, he threw up onto the sand.

He lay there a long time, his face pressed to the ground, listening to nothing but the rasp of his breathing and the water running over the rocks.

He raised his head, bile bitter in his mouth. "What are you?" he asked hoarsely.

Morwenna flinched. He was afraid. Disgusted. Disbelieving.

Or perhaps he had simply swallowed too much seawater after a bump on the head.

But the wary, searching look in his eyes, the memory of

Morgan's words, quickly disabused her of that hope. *Humans fear what they do not understand. And what they fear, they hate.*

She sat back on her heels and folded her hands, no longer trying to touch him. "What do you think I am?"

He shook his head. Winced as the movement jarred his wound. "You don't want to know."

His rejection jabbed like a sea urchin's barb. He was hurt, she reminded herself, the gash on his forehead still bleeding. Hurt and confused. "Let me help you," she said again gently.

"You helped me . . ." His eyes focused as he struggled to remember. "That was you in the water, carrying me."

She sighed. "Yes. Come now." She slid an arm around him, urged him to his feet. "We need to get you home."

He weighed on her, his arm heavy and damp around her shoulders, his body shaking as if with fever. "You're a mermaid."

She arched her eyebrows, injecting what she hoped was the right amount of amusement in her voice. "Half woman, half fish? There is no such thing."

She coaxed him a few steps toward the cart, water squelching from his boots.

He staggered and recovered. "But I saw . . . And your toes . . ."

He stopped.

She could not put him off forever, she realized with a sinking feeling in the pit of her stomach. She would not apologize for who she was or for what she had done. She had *saved* him.

Besides, he clearly wasn't budging until he had an answer.

"I am finfolk," she said clearly. "An elemental of the water."

He swayed. "I need to sit down."

Wonderful. Her eyes burned. Her throat ached. First she made him throw up and now he had to sit down. "We are almost at the cart," she said. "Lean on me."

They shambled toward the cart and the patient pony. Jack managed somehow to pull himself into the rig before collapsing onto the seat. Beneath his tan, his face was lined and bloodless.

"What is . . . An elemental, you said?"

She swallowed past the constriction of her throat. She did not want to quarrel with him. Not when he was injured, half drowned, and in shock. "We are the children of the sea, formed when God brought the waters of the world into being, the first fruits of His creation."

"Not . . . human?"

"We can take human form. The finfolk can take any form under the sea."

He was silent, staring at the horse's ears.

Her heart hammered. "Do you believe me?"

Jack stirred and looked at her, his eyes dull. "I don't know what to believe. You lied to me."

She untied the hitch with jerky motions. Of course he would see it that way. He was a man of rigid honor. He saw the whole world in black and white.

But she was not of his world. "I did not lie. Not really."

He frowned. "Misled me, then."

She raised her chin, driven on the defensive by hurt and guilt. She was responsible for her evasions. But he bore some responsibility, too. "You were eager enough to be misled. You did not want to see anything that did not accord with your notions of who I should be. The clues were there. You did not want to know."

His face was closed. Stubborn. "A man doesn't imagine the woman he's in love with is a mermaid."

"Finfolk."

He ignored her distinction, focused on his own human logic. "You should have trusted me."

"You said you accepted me. You said you loved me. Would my telling you have made any difference?"

"Of course it makes a difference. I wanted to marry you."

Ah. Pain pierced her heart. *Wanted*, not *want*.

She was a fool.

I am a plain man, he had told her when he proposed. *With ordinary needs.*

And now he did not need her. Did not want her. Could not accept her.

It was as simple, as devastating, as that.

She drew her ragged dress, her shredded pride around her, a shield to protect her broken heart. She was an elemental, one of the First Creation. She would not stoop to beg for his love.

"How fortunate for us both, then," she said, "that you never proposed properly."

She slapped the pony's reins across its broad back. The cart jolted as she turned swiftly away.

"Morwenna!"

Her vision blurred. She did not stop to hear. There was a roaring in her head like the sound of the waves and the bitter taste of salt on her lips.

Her brother was right. Love did not last. Nothing lasted forever but the sea.

She crossed the beach, shedding her clothes, and plunged into the ocean.

SEVEN

"The cottage was empty," Jack said flatly.

He stared out the library window, his mood as bleak as the sky, his back to the room. Against the glass, Edwin Sloat's image appeared, a darker shadow against the shadow of the trees. Jack's own reflection swam in the glass like a ghost, gray and hollow eyed, the illusion heightened by the bandage on his forehead.

He'd looked worse stumbling off the troop ship in London. But however terrible his injuries, however dubious his prospects, then he'd had hope.

Now . . .

"She has not returned," Sloat said behind him, his voice an unctuous blend of sympathy and satisfaction.

Jack's hands fisted at his sides. His eyes felt gritty and dry. "No."

He had been back to the cottage three times with increasing desperation and diminished hopes. Morwenna was gone as if she had never been. The air smelled like a deserted campsite, of ash and abandonment. Only the rumpled covers of the bed and scattered gifts from the villagers proved she had been there at all.

He felt her absence like an amputated limb, a phantom pain in his chest where his heart had been.

What had she said after she sang the young fisherman from the sea? *Go back to your sweetheart . . . hold her tight for the time that has been given to you both.*

Good advice.

So why the hell hadn't he followed it? He should have relished every day, every hour, every second he had with her.

Now it was too late even to apologize.

She had saved him from death. More, she had made him feel alive.

And instead of thanking her, he had accused her of not trusting him. Of not being what he imagined, when she was so clearly everything he needed.

No wonder she left him.

A cough recalled his attention to the steward standing behind him.

"Apparently no one has seen the girl since your, er, outing the other day," Sloat said. "It's caused some talk in the village."

Jack felt a prickle like a soldier's warning awareness of danger. He turned from the window. "What are you suggesting?"

"Nothing. Good heavens, nothing at all. Actually, I defended you."

Cold comprehension pierced Jack's fog of misery. "What do they think I did? Push her overboard?"

Sloat's tongue flickered over his lips. "Of course not. Even if, in a moment of passion, you were driven to . . . But no one would ever accuse you of such a thing. Certainly not to your face."

No one but Sloat, Jack thought grimly.

"Perhaps I should present myself to the magistrate," he said only half in jest.

"Oh, no, sir." The steward sounded genuinely shocked. "But perhaps . . . Might I suggest a stay in town would be in order? Only until the talk dies down."

"You are very careful of my reputation," Jack observed.

Even more concerned, he guessed, with his own consequence in the household and the neighborhood. Sloat's activities had been curtailed by Jack's arrival, his position further threatened by the possibility of Jack's marriage. The steward must want nothing more than for Jack to go away.

"A change of scene would do you good," Sloat urged. "The estate provides enough income to support a London residence. More income if . . . Well, enough has been said on that subject, eh?"

More income if Sloat were left in charge to carry on as he had before.

This was overreaching, even for Sloat.

"I will stay," Jack said.

Even if Morwenna never came back, his duty was here.

"Don't look for thanks," Sloat warned him. "These Scots are an ungrateful lot."

"Excuse me, sir." Watts, the red-faced butler, shuffled into the room. "There are several gentlemen . . . men . . . *persons* here to see you. From the village."

"I warned you there was talk," Sloat said. "Send them away."

Jack silenced him with a look. Whatever the accusations, he would face them. He nodded to the butler. "Show them in, Watts."

The butler blinked and wandered off, eventually returning with the delegation from the village: the shopkeeper Hobson in his shabby coat, the broad baker with his orange beard, and the old and young fishermen whose boat had been caught in the storm. They came in tugging their caps and stamping their feet, ill at ease as dray horses on a racetrack.

"Gentlemen," Jack said politely. "What can I do for you?"

Sloat sneered. "Isn't it obvious? They're here to extort money."

"I don't think so," Jack said, watching their faces. "Two of them have already presented their accounts and been paid."

The sharp-faced shopkeeper nodded. "That's right. That's why we came. Partly why we came."

"Because they want more. I told you how it would be," Sloat said to Jack. "Once they recognize a soft touch, they rob you blind."

The young fisherman flushed and took a step forward. "We're not thieves."

"Not like some," the baker rumbled with a dark look at Sloat.

"Why don't you tell me your business," Jack said in his command voice.

Hobson, apparently the designated leader, tugged on his waistcoat. "Young Colin here found something on the beach and he thought, we all thought . . ." Looks and nods were exchanged. "You should know about it."

"It's your boat, sir," Colin said.

"The boat sank," Sloat said.

Jeb, the older fisherman, nodded. "Aye, we heard. But there it was on the beach when we come in at the end of the day, whole and dry."

"Not whole," the baker said.

"Of course not," Sloat interjected. "It capsized."

"Sprang a leak on the way back from the island," Jack explained.

"This weren't like any leak I ever saw," Jeb said. "This was a big hole cut in the bottom of the boat, all nice and round and even."

The shopkeeper nodded. "I saw it myself. New hole. You could tell by the edges."

Jack narrowed his eyes, his soldier's instinct returning, sharper than before. "We had no problems rowing out."

"You wouldn't," Jeb said. "There was pitch on the edges of the hole with threads in it. Like somebody patched it soft, see, to hide it, maybe to hold it until you got out in deep water."

"A repair," Sloat suggested.

The young fisherman, Colin, snorted. "Nobody would be daft enough to repair a boat with a plug like that."

Jack didn't know anything about boats. But he understood barrels. "Wouldn't a plug swell in the water? Like a cork."

"A wood plug, aye," Jeb agreed. "But those threads . . . This weren't a proper plug at all. Just rag and pitch."

"And sugar, maybe. Or salt," the baker said. "Something that would dissolve in the water."

"You're suggesting someone deliberately sabotaged the boat."

"Someone with a grudge," Hobson said.

"Someone from the village," Sloat said.

The baker shook his head. "Major's liked in the village."

There were more shuffles, more nods.

"That's why we came," Hobson said.

Jack looked at Sloat, anger cold as a blade inside him. "You knew where I was going. I told you to ready the boat."

Sloat bridled. "After which it sat unattended for hours on that beach. Anyone could have tampered with it."

"Only one man did."

Sloat showed his teeth in a ghastly smile. "You can't do anything. You can't prove anything."

"I don't require proof to do this," Jack said and threw a hard right hook that knocked him to the ground.

The large, soft man sprawled on the carpet, his lip bleeding.

Jack stood over him, knuckles throbbing and face set. "Get up."

Sloat touched a hand to his bleeding mouth and shook his head.

"You deserved to be thrashed," Jack said. "For what you tried to do to me and for what you have done to others. But until this moment you were technically in my employ. Get up. Watts will stay with you while you pack a change of clothes. One of the grooms can drive you to the stage in Kinlochbervie."

"But my things—"

"Will be packed up and sent after you. Get out of my sight," Jack said in an even voice that had made hardened soldiers flinch. "If you are wise, you will stay out of my sight and off my land for the rest of your life."

The steward turned white and red and white again. Without a word he scrambled to his feet and lurched from the room.

"Nice hook," said the baker.

"And good riddance," Hobson added.

Jeb spat in the grate and then looked sheepishly at Jack. "Beg pardon, Major."

Jack was surprised to find himself smiling. "Not at all. I share your sentiments."

"He could have murdered you in your bed," Hobson said with more relish than the prospect warranted.

"I doubt he would go that far," Jack said dryly. "He obviously has little stomach for outright violence. He is a villain, but an opportunistic one."

"Cowardly weasel," the baker said.

"Still, I am grateful to you." Jack extended his smile to them all. "I am lucky the boat washed ashore as it did and even more fortunate in my neighbors."

Grins and nods answered him.

Colin stuck his hands in his belt. "It didn't wash up. The lady brought it."

Hobson looked embarrassed. "Now, lad . . ."

Jeb elbowed the young man in the side.

Jack's heart banged in his chest in sudden, wild hope. *The lady*. Morwenna. "Did you see her?"

"Nay," the young fisherman admitted reluctantly.

No, of course not. She had left him.

"But it stands to reason it was her." Jeb spoke up. "Boat was full of water at the bottom of the bay. It didn't empty itself and drag itself ashore."

Colin nodded, as if the boat being dragged ashore by a mermaid was somehow more plausible.

The baker scratched his jaw. "One way or another, things are better with the lady around."

"She's our luck," Jeb said simply.

"The luck of the village," the shopkeeper said.

They all looked at Jack then. As if he could do something to bring her back.

Too late.

He'd lost his chance when he'd thrown her confession back in her face. He had accused her of a lack of trust, when the true problem was his own lack of faith.

These men believed in her, he realized.

Could he do less?

She still cared enough to try to protect him. She had raised the boat and left it on the beach as a warning.

The question now was, what could he possibly give her in return?

* * *

The sun went down in a blare of color as bright as a trumpet blast. The sea shimmered silver and gold.

Jack marched the length of the jetty in the green coat and red collar and cuffs of an officer of the Ninety-Fifth Rifles, as well turned out as if he reported for parade, as grimly determined as if he rode Neptune into battle. His polished boots slipped and crunched on the weed-fringed rocks.

The villagers hung back at a respectful distance along the seawall, witnesses to his public show of faith.

Or spectators at his public humiliation.

His jaw set.

He stopped where the stone ended, where the land met the sea and the waves running along the rocks gleamed and foamed like Morwenna's hair. The march, the show, were for the watchers onshore and for atonement.

But his words, spoken quietly to the sea, were for her alone.

"You told me once there was nothing I could give you that you do not already have. Nothing you need." He swallowed against the ache in his throat. "But you took something of mine when you returned to the sea. You took my heart."

The wind sighed. The salt air touched his lips like a cool kiss, like the taste of tears.

He took a deep breath. "Everything I have, everything I am, is yours. My lands, my life, my love. My trust. Morwenna . . . Will you marry me?"

Long moments passed. The clouds moved swift and full as sails before the wind. A bell rang in the harbor, tolling a warning to lingering ships.

No answer.

Jack waited, his heart full and his gut churning, while the sea murmured and the sun slipped further in the sky.

Onshore, a few sensible folks stopped watching and went home to their chores or their suppers.

Still no answer.

Or perhaps her answer was No.

At long, long last he bowed his head, blinking moisture from his eyes. "You will always have my love," he told the tide. "And my pledge. Take this, and remember me."

Drawing back his arm, he hurled the ring over the ocean.

The last rays of the sun fired the gold as it plunged in a glittering arc to the sea.

Jack fell to his knees on the rock, a strong man undone by love and grief.

Later, when they told the story, the watchers left onshore argued about what happened next. They all agreed that a woman appeared out of the sea. Some said she was naked, and some saw a silver dress that sparkled like fish scales in the sun, and a few claimed she wore an actual mermaid's tail as she came out of the water. But all agreed she was the most beautiful sight they had ever seen, their lady, the luck of Farness.

Her long pale hair streamed over her shoulders as if carried by the tide. On her left hand she wore a gold ring with a blue stone that flashed in the sun.

She walked to their major and touched him on the shoulder, and he rose and took her into his arms.

She was here.

She was real and warm and back in his arms, her wet, sleek body pressed to his uniform coat, her wild, pale hair tickling his throat.

A wave of love and relief washed over Jack so great he trembled and felt her trembling in return.

She kissed him and drew back, gazing into his eyes.

"You do have something I want," she told him gravely. "Something I need and never had before."

He caught her hand, pressing his lips to her palm and then to his mother's ring gleaming around her finger.

"Your love." A smile wavered on her lips as he helped her to her feet. "Although now that you have asked me properly, you can never take back the ring. Or your proposal."

"I don't want to take it back," he told her hoarsely. "I meant every word. I love you."

Her golden eyes glistened with laughter and tears. "Then give me your coat, my love, and let us go home."

He took off his green uniform jacket and tenderly wrapped it around her. Together, they began the long walk over the jetty and home.

Here There Be Monsters

Meljean Brook

ACKNOWLEDGMENTS

Special thanks to Maili, because she made me realize that I was trying to spell "challenge" just by adding two letters, and this story is all the better for her feedback. And because, years ago, when I mentioned on my blog that I wanted to write steampunk romance, she knew what I was talking about and said she'd want to read it. So she did . . . and I'll always be thankful she got her hands on this one early.

ONE

By the time Ivy found Ratcatcher Row, a stinking yellow fog smothered the docks. She inched along the unfamiliar street, holding her right hand out to her side and using the buildings facing the narrow wooden walk as a guide. Though only an arm's length away, the thick mist dissolved Ivy's gloved fingers into ghostly outlines. On her left, the clicking, segmented shadow of a spider-rickshaw scurried by on the cobblestones, and the hydraulic hiss of the driver's thrusting feet seemed to whisper a single refrain.

Hurry, hurry, hurry.

Oh, she wanted to. Her humid breath filled the thin scarf she'd tied over her mouth and nose. Her heart pounded as if she'd sprinted through these streets instead of picking her way through the fog, stopping at each building to search for an identifying sign.

But at least she was moving. As long as she could move, she couldn't be taken.

Seven years ago, after two centuries under brutal Horde rule, the pirate captain Rhys Trahaearn had destroyed the tower that the Horde used to control the nanoagents infecting every person in London. For seven years, Ivy had been free to move as she wished, to feel as she wished—until earlier that night. Only hours ago, she'd been frozen in her bed with her eyes closed, unable to move, listening to strangers search from room to room through her boardinghouse. From blacksmiths to beggars, no one in that cheap tenement owned anything of value. But when someone had come through her door, stripped away her blankets, and prodded at her thighs and breasts as if evaluating her thin body, when the strangers had left and she'd seen the empty beds in rooms that had been earlier filled, Ivy had realized each sleeping person had been valuable—as workers, as slaves . . . which were the only uses the Horde ever had for them.

And if the Horde was returning to London with their controlling towers and paralyzing devices, nothing would stop Ivy from leaving.

A steamcoach waited in front of the next building, rattling and puttering, its gas lanterns penetrating the fog in faint glowing spheres. By the feeble light, Ivy found the establishment's sign, and almost moved on before her mind registered the painting on the wood: a compass.

The Star Rose Inn. She'd been looking for a picture of a flower, or even a woman, but it was a *compass* rose. A sailor wouldn't have mistaken it, but Ivy almost had—yet she was here. *Finally here.*

Her heart slamming in her ribs, Ivy rose up on her toes to peer through the small glass window. No lights burned within. She'd have to wake up the innkeeper—who'd likely turn Ivy away after taking a look at her—or she could break the lock. A lock hadn't stopped her when she'd been a child, raised in the Horde's crèche, it hadn't stopped her after they'd taken her arms, and it wouldn't stop her now that the Blacksmith had given her new ones. But even if she broke through the lock, she wouldn't know which room Mad Machen slept in.

Raising her fist, she hammered on the door. A minute later, a stout man wearing a nightcap and with gray tufts of hair growing behind his ears swung open the small, hinged window. He lifted a gas lamp to the opening. Ivy squinted against the sudden, bright light, and tugged the scarf down, exposing her mouth and nose.

She knew what she looked like. Soot from the day's work still streaked her face; fog and sweat dampened her red hair. The buckles at the waist of her long coat didn't hide the thread-bare nightgown underneath, and the trousers tucked into her boots had been old when she'd bought them. The satchel clutched to her chest was nothing but a shirt tied together, and held everything she owned. Her desperation must have hung around her as thick as the mist; she wasn't surprised when the innkeeper immediately lowered the lamp, swinging the window closed.

"We're full up tonight. You'll find rooms on the cheap at The Crowing Cock."

"Wait!" She curled her fingers around the window frame, preventing its closure. "Please. I'm here to see Captain Machen. I've come from the Blacksmith's."

She'd never used her connection to her mentor like this before. But two names in London would open almost any door: the Blacksmith's, and the Iron Duke's.

The innkeeper paused. "The Blacksmith?"

Ivy pulled aside her nightgown collar, exposing the guild's mark: a chain wrapped around her neck and a hammer poised to strike. When the innkeeper began to shake his head and close the window again, Ivy quickly stripped off her glove, exposing pale gray fingers and silvery nails.

"The mark is supposed to be around my wrist," she told him. "But my skin won't take a tattoo."

He stared at Ivy's hand before looking into her face again—perhaps searching for a hint of how she had managed to afford mechanical flesh. Finally, the innkeeper stepped back, opening the door.

"I'll tell the captain you're here."

Ivy waited to expel her sigh of relief until after he'd moved to a door at the back of the empty dining room and disappeared up a narrow stair. Cool and dark, with well-scrubbed walls and floors, the inn's open dining room appeared cleaner than any she'd ever lived, worked, or eaten in. She was accustomed to pubs like the Hammer & Chain: dank and crowded, stinking of soot and sweat, and where fights broke out more often than not. But she returned every night, because the Blacksmith's workers could buy a hot meal on the cheap, and she went home to a windowless room that smelled of smoke and mildew, and whose north and south walls she could touch with both hands outstretched. This inn smelled of lemon wax and a warm, yeasty fragrance—a scent that reminded her of walking past the bakery in the crisp early morning, while heading to the smithy in the Narrow.

This was a good place. It gave her hope. Her grip on the satchel slowly eased as her nervousness and fear began to subside.

She'd heard of Mad Machen before he'd come to the smithy. Everyone in England had. Born to a merchant family in Manhattan City, the youngest of four sons, he'd been a surgeon in the British Navy when Rhys Trahaearn had attacked his naval fleet. Mad Machen had been among those forced to join Trahaearn's crew—then willingly remained aboard. He'd been with the pirate captain when Trahaearn had destroyed the Horde's tower.

Unlike Trahaearn, who'd been given a duke's title—and the king's pardon bestowed upon all of his crew—Mad Machen hadn't reformed. After taking command of his own ship, *Vesuvius*, he continued pirating from the North Sea to the Caribbean.

But despite all of the stories of murder, insanity, and pillaging, the Mad Machen that Ivy had met at the Blacksmith's hadn't been a cruel man. Big and intimidating, with a thick coarse scar around his neck and overgrown dark hair, he'd been a gruff man—but not cruel. Every morning for the past week, he'd accompanied his friend Obadiah Barker to the smithy, and sat with him through the excruciating process of exchanging a steel prosthetic leg for a limb made from mechanical flesh. Mad Machen had borne Barker's curses and screams without anger; he'd offered a hand for Barker to squeeze—and more than once, to bite. And every evening, he'd carried his delirious friend to the waiting steamcoach.

Ivy had assisted the Blacksmith in the surgery, and attended the two men during the long stretches between sessions, waiting for the flesh to grow. She'd listened to Mad Machen and Barker talk of ships they'd taken and ports they'd visited—Barker speaking a hundred words in his lilting accent to every flattened word of Mad Machen's—and when Barker's dread and fear of the next session became overwhelming, Ivy had told him of her own surgery, painting herself as a ridiculous shivering washrag until Barker had begun to laugh. Mad Machen's gaze had met hers then, and she'd seen his gratitude and appreciation.

She hoped he still felt them now. Her heart began pounding again as the innkeeper returned. He led her across the dining room and up the dark, narrow stairwell. At the top, he opened the first door on the left, revealing a dimly lit parlor.

Though midnight had passed several hours before, Mad Machen wasn't in bed, as Ivy had expected. He sat in a low chair, a snifter in hand and his long legs stretched out in front of him, knee-high boots crossed at the ankles. He'd unbuckled his jacket. His pale shirt opened at the neck, exposing deeply tanned skin and the puckered white scar at his throat.

He froze with the snifter halfway to his mouth when she entered the room. His gaze swept over her, taking her in, pausing on the makeshift satchel in her hand. Slowly, his gaze rose to her face. Dark eyes locked on hers, he stood.

"Ivy," he said, in a voice deeper and rougher than she remembered. She realized he'd never spoken her name before.

And she expected him to grant her a favor?

Her nervousness came crashing back. Fingers twisting in the satchel, she glanced around the room. Mad Machen wasn't alone. On an armchair to her right, a woman with an angular face watched her with narrowed, cat-green eyes. A sapphire kerchief wrapped back from her forehead and tied at her nape, the blue tails tangled in the long black curls and tiny braids. Her short aviator's jacket buckled to her throat, and her hand hovered near the dagger hilt sheathed at the top of her brown, thigh-high boots.

To Ivy's left, Barker lay on a green sofa, bushy black hair falling back from his forehead. He hadn't bothered with a glass, but was drinking a deep amber liquid straight from the bottle. His boots and stockings were off, and he held his feet together as if examining them, pale gray against brown. He rolled his head to the side and looked at her when Mad Machen said her name.

"Ivy!" A smile broadened his mouth as he rocked up to sitting—and sat, swaying. With some effort, he focused on her again. "You've come all the way to the docks in this soup?"

"Yes." Her pulse racing, she looked at Mad Machen. His gaze hadn't strayed from her face. "At the Blacksmith's, you said that you'd planned to weigh anchor tomorrow morning. I wondered . . . I hoped that you would allow me passage on your ship."

His brows lowered, and the small movement seemed to darken every feature. "To where?"

"Anywhere." She didn't know. She didn't care. Just away. "The first city you put in to port."

He didn't immediately answer, and she became aware of Barker, no longer smiling. A grim expression had settled on his open face. In the opposite seat, the woman stared at Mad Machen, the gold hoops in her ears swinging with the tiny shake of her head.

Mad Machen either didn't notice them or disregarded them. He strode across the room, stopping only an arm's length away. Ivy had to lift her chin to meet his eyes.

"*Vesuvius* has no comfortable quarters. She isn't a passenger ship."

"I know. But I can't afford passage on a—" She broke off when his face darkened further. Hurriedly, she assured him, "I'll work. I can repair engines, prosthetics . . . or windups, if you have any automata. I can build anything you need."

"I already have a blacksmith onboard."

Panic began to take hold. She looked past Mad Machen to the woman, then Barker. "Do you know of any ship that needs one? A ship that departs soon? I won't ask for a wage—only for board. Please."

Closing his eyes, Barker shook his head. The woman didn't respond, only stared back at Ivy, her gaze cold and assessing.

In the quiet, Ivy's heart thundered in her ears. Smithing was her only trade. She owned nothing of value but her skill.

Nothing but her body.

Sickness roiled in her stomach, tasted sour on her tongue. She'd avoided this route for so long, but perhaps it always came to this. Feeling dull and worn, she lifted her gaze to Mad Machen's.

"I'm a virgin," she said.

His broad chest rose on a sharp breath. A flush swept under his skin, his jaw tightening. Though his companions had been quiet, now they were still and silent—as if waiting.

His response was a low growl. "*Vesuvius* isn't a slaver ship, either."

"I don't want to be sold. I want to be free when I get off your ship." She tried to gather dignity and courage. "I'm offering it as payment. Some men prize it."

His face continued to darken as she spoke, until the only lightness lay in the whites of his eyes, the tight line around his mouth, the rough scar at his throat. He looked . . . utterly mad.

By the starry sky—she'd made a horrible mistake.

Suddenly terrified, Ivy backed up a step, before whipping around and reaching for the door. "I'll find another—"

His hand slammed against the door, holding it closed. "You won't find another. You'll sleep in my bed. Not just once. For as long as you're on the ship."

Barker's bottle clattered to the floor, as if he'd lurched to his feet and it had dropped from his lap. "Eben, you can't—"

"Don't."

Barker fell silent.

Trembling, Ivy stared at Mad Machen's fingers, braced against the polished wood. More scars whitened his knuckles. How many people had he hit to accumulate those? Had any of them been women? Clenching her teeth against the scream working up into her throat, she swallowed it down. She strove for an even tone, but it emerged as a hoarse whisper.

"Will you promise not to hurt me?"

She felt him stiffen behind her, and the draw of a ragged breath. His right arm came over her shoulder, his palm flattening against the door, trapping her between. She squeezed the shirt and its few contents closer to her small breasts.

"We'll sail in the morning." His voice was low and rough against her ear. His hand dropped to the door handle. "Come with me."

Tension pulled her muscles tight when his left hand curved around the side of her waist. Stiffly, she stepped back, then hastily forward again when she bumped against his hard body. He guided her out of the parlor, and the only sounds in the cool hallway were their footsteps, her unsteady breath.

He caught her hand when she turned for the staircase. With a lift of his shadowed chin, he indicated down the length of the hall. "My bedchamber is this way."

Already? They weren't yet on the ship. She looked blindly down the narrow hallway.

Mad Machen watched her. "Did you intend to return home first?"

"No." Not there. Not ever again.

"We leave for *Vesuvius* early. You'll sleep in my bed."

The lump in her throat choked her. Tucking her chin down, she followed him to the last room on the right. Using a key, he unlocked the door and moved to the bureau against the far wall, where he sparked a small gas lamp. Ivy took in the wardrobe, its doors open and innards bare. The bed dominated the center of the floor, the mattress larger than her room at the boardinghouse. A blue counterpane covered the whitest linens she'd ever seen.

"Put your things in the wardrobe."

She wanted to hold on to them. But she wanted passage out of London more. Obediently, she untied the shirt, hung it on the hook. She stiffened as he drew near, frowning down at the items still in her hands.

"This is all you have?"

A pair of silk stockings, given as a gift from an aristocrat's mistress whose feet Ivy had rebuilt after her Horde prosthetics malfunctioned—and a small flange, dark with age, scarred and worn.

He picked up the iron disk, touched his thumb to the hole in the center. "Not a coin."

She almost laughed. No, she'd used her only penny to pay the steamcoach driver who'd brought her from Limehouse to the docks. English money wasn't worth anything in the rest of the world, anyway, whereas French currency—the trade currency—held its value in every port.

"It was my elbow," she said. "When I was a chimney sweep."

His gaze fell to her hands. "Why keep it?"

So that she'd never forget what it was to wriggle through hot, narrow shafts, when one slip could mean her death. So that she'd never take what she had now for granted.

She took the flange from him and brought it to her lips. "Because now I'm the only person in the world who can kiss my elbow."

Mad Machen didn't laugh. He didn't smile. His long fingers wrapped around her wrist and drew her hand to his face, until she cupped his rough jaw.

"Can you feel this?"

She could feel the heat he emitted and each short whisker that formed the scratchy stubble against her palm. And, almost imperceptibly, the electric charge of the mechanical nanoagents in his skin, beneath his skin—like tiny bugs working together to strengthen, to heal, to enhance.

"Yes." It was a whisper.

The skin beneath her hand warmed. "Good. You'll soon feel me everywhere."

Instinctively, she yanked her arm back—then froze, wondering if she'd just made another mistake. He stepped closer, and she fought not to flinch as his hands came up.

Catching her face between his big palms, he gazed down into her eyes. "Don't be afraid of me."

Too frightened to do anything else, she nodded. With a low groan, his eyes closed and he lowered his head. Ivy waited, shaking.

His lips brushed hers once, twice. She relaxed, for the barest moment—then his mouth was devouring, the strength of his kiss forcing her head back, hurting her neck. His hands gripped her bottom and hauled her up, and she felt him through her coat and nightgown, thick and enormous against her stomach. Terror began to rise, the reality of what he would do, what she'd agreed to do, and then she was on her feet again.

Mad Machen spun away from her, his chest heaving. He strode to the door and flung it open, pausing only long enough to say, "If you run away now, I'll come after you."

The door slammed. In shock, Ivy stared after him, holding her fingers to her lips. Already, she could feel her bugs working to heal the bruised tissues. *Sweet blue heaven.*

She'd traded one monster for another.

Eben headed straight for the bottle. Swiping the brandy out of Barker's hand, he tilted it back and drank, hoping to dull the need. And if the need wouldn't subside, drink until he passed out.

"Well," his quartermaster said. "Now you don't have to return here to court her."

Christ. Eben lowered the bottle, dropped into his chair. He'd have returned, and she'd have been gone. God knew where.

God knew what might have happened to her along the way.

Yasmeen came around, whacking her hand against Barker's new leg. Obediently, he pulled his feet up, gave her a place on the sofa.

She leaned forward, her elbows braced on her knees. "Court *her*? For two hundred years, the Horde hasn't allowed anyone in her caste to marry. They were only allowed to breed when the controlling towers put everyone in a mating frenzy, and the babies were taken and raised in a crèche. She grew up without family, without any concept of marriage. Eben, she won't even know what courting is."

"Families aren't always blood. You make your own." He knew that well; so did Yasmeen. "That's what they've done here for two hundred years. She'll understand that."

Yasmeen sighed and sat back. "You can't take her with you, regardless. Give her enough money to stay here. Tell her to wait."

Eben shook his head. "She'll run."

He was certain of it. She'd been frightened out of her wits, desperate to leave London. Had someone hurt her? He looked toward the door, ready to charge down the hall and find out. *Goddammit. Someone* would pay.

And he'd probably terrify her again. Jesus, her sweet little smile drove him *out of his mind.*

"Did she kill someone?" Barker wondered.

Eben took another long drink, glancing toward the door again. Maybe she had. Obviously not a lover and not for money, but he could name a hundred other reasons why a woman in London might resort to killing. And if she expected a police inspector to come knocking—or someone seeking revenge—it explained her desperation to leave.

Someone the Blacksmith couldn't protect her against? Eben couldn't imagine it, but it didn't matter. *He* would protect her.

Yasmeen yanked the bottle from his hand. "Eben. *Think.* You're sailing out tomorrow on an Ivory Market run. Will you risk having her on the ship?"

Hell. Pushing his hands into his hair, he shook his head. Sailing south along the west coast of Africa guaranteed *Vesuvius* would be shot at, boarded, or forced to outrun an airship. The market itself seethed with men who'd eat Ivy alive—some literally. If Eben lost her there, he wouldn't find her again. He couldn't take that chance.

"I'll change course," he decided. "I'll take her to Trahaearn's estate in Anglesey." The Iron Duke's Welsh holdings weren't as impregnable as those in London, but no matter what had frightened her, even Ivy would feel safe at such a place. *No one* crossed Trahaearn.

"You can't change course." Yasmeen's disgust showed itself in a curl of her lip over sharp teeth. "If she must leave town, buy her a seat on a locomotive and tell her to wait for you in Wales."

Eben shook his head. He wouldn't be satisfied unless he *saw* her settled in a safe location and persuaded to remain there. If he simply gave her money, she'd be gone—too afraid of him to stay. He needed at least a few days for Ivy to learn she had nothing to fear from him. If he changed course and took her to Wales on *Vesuvius*, he'd gain the time he needed.

"I will only be delayed a few days," he said.

Yasmeen's snarl deepened. "Which could easily become a week—or longer. Trahaearn's paid half up front. If you don't pick up the cargo on time, it'll go to another ship, and we'll lose the rest of our money."

"I care fuck all about the money—"

"Because you're a mad fool."

Eben stared at her. She didn't back down. Yasmeen never would when gold was at stake. "I'll cover the loss, pay you the same as Trahaearn would have," he offered.

"And Trahaearn will never hire me again. Will you pay for every loss?"

He couldn't. His pockets were deep, but not that deep. And there might be someone else he needed to pay off first. Mechanical flesh didn't come cheap—and if Ivy still owed the Blacksmith, he'd send his collectors after her.

In this fog, it'd take Eben twice as long to reach the smithy in the Narrow. Leaving now, he could return before Ivy awoke . . . if she ever managed to sleep. So he'd return before she got it into her head to run.

Eben stood. "I won't let her go, Yasmeen."

"Softhearted Eben." She sat back with a bitter hiss, her finger curled into claws. "You spitting idiot."

So he was. Eben turned to Barker. "Watch the stairs and don't let her leave. I'll return before dawn."

Somehow, he'd convince her to stay in Wales. And to wait for him.

Lying in the cloud-soft bed, Ivy was staring up at the darkened ceiling when she heard the tap at the window. An unmistakably feminine figure was silhouetted against the thick yellow mist.

Ivy sat up and swung her feet to the floor. Moving closer, she recognized the blue kerchief and the glint of gold hoops. Why would the woman who'd been in the parlor with Mad Machen be outside Ivy's window? And why had she climbed a ladder instead of simply knocking on the bedroom door?

Curious, Ivy unlocked the window—and immediately saw that she'd been wrong. Not climbed *up* a ladder, but *down*. The woman stood on the bottom rung, her hands wrapped around the rope rails.

An airship? They weren't allowed to fly this close to London. But as Ivy peered upward, she realized no one would see the ship. A few feet above the woman's head, the ladder disappeared into the fog.

"I'll take you as far as Port Fallow," the woman said. "You won't come to harm on my ship."

Startled, Ivy studied her face. Judging by the hardness of her green eyes, the offer to take Ivy to the notorious port city built on Amsterdam's ashes hadn't come from the kindness of her heart. And although Ivy sensed that this woman didn't often bother explaining herself, she had to ask, "Why?"

"It serves me and my crew."

Ivy glanced upward again. "The crew of what?"

"*Lady Corsair.*"

Oh, blue. For a moment, Ivy felt faint. The woman hanging outside the window was Lady Corsair. She had another name, maybe, but everyone knew her by the airship she captained. This woman had a reputation for killing anyone who questioned her, was a mercenary who would do anything for money.

Ivy didn't have any. "I can't pay you. I can only work."

"I don't want your money or your labor. A debt is far more valuable than coin."

And far more frightening when left unpaid. "What will I owe you?"

Lady Corsair grinned, flashing teeth that seemed too sharp. "I'll decide when I need it."

Ivy hesitated.

The airship captain shrugged and began climbing. "Mad Machen has returned. You can take his offer, instead."

Ivy's heart began to hammer. Turning her head, she strained to listen—and heard the heavy tread on the stairs. *Oh, blue heavens.* Mad Machen would take her if she remained here.

She glanced toward the bed, and the sight of the rumpled linens spurred her into action. He was too near to take the time and gather her things. Ivy scrambled through the window, grabbing on to the ladder. Exerting almost no effort at all, she let her arms carry her up the rope, and vanished into silence and the fog.

TWO

Two Years Later . . .

The jokes began as soon as Ivy ducked her head beneath the pianist's lacy pink skirts. Rolling over onto her back, she lay on the musician's raised wooden platform and looked up into the gears that formed the automaton's guts. Luckily, this wouldn't take long—just a broken tooth on the deadbeat escapement that timed the motion of the feet, and a worm gear out of alignment. She worked, trying to ignore the men doing their best to make the little town of Fool's Cove earn its name. By the time she'd repaired the escapement, every Hans, Stefan, and Jozef with two brain cells and a drink in his hand had joined in, offering tips for oiling a woman up—including Klaas, the tavern's owner.

She should have quoted him a higher price.

But they tired of it quickly enough. After a couple of minutes of tuning them out, she realized the tavern had gone quiet. Silent, even.

She paused. With her fingers wrapped around a pendulum rod, she listened to the approaching tread of a single pair of boots, painfully aware of her legs sticking out from beneath pink lace. The skirts lifted, and Ivy found herself staring into cat-green eyes under a ruby kerchief.

Lady Corsair said, "I've come to collect what you owe me, Ivy Blacksmith."

The woman's smile sent a tremor through Ivy's legs. *Run.* But she only came up on her elbows and asked, "Wasn't repairing every piece of equipment on your airship payment enough?"

The narrowing of Lady Corsair's eyes was her only answer.

Alright. *Lady Corsair*'s captain had never asked her to work; Ivy had simply needed to keep herself busy. "So I owe you the price of a passage from London to Port Fallow. I'll pay it now."

It'd take every bit of Ivy's savings, but she'd rather settle this debt with coin. She sat up, aware of the grease on her fingers, her cheek.

"I don't want your coin. We need you to build something for us."

Ivy's stomach dropped. *Building* didn't worry her as much as the other part. "Us?"

Lady Corsair straightened and stepped back, revealing the man behind her. Mad Machen—his face dark, eyes wild.

By the fucking stars, no.

Blood surged to her legs. Scuttling back, Ivy turned, got her boots under her and sprinted for the tavern kitchen. Past the stoves, she burst through the door and stumbled into a muddy yard full of white chickens. Feathers flew as they scrambled out of her path, squawking their alarm. She leapt over a gate, made it into the street.

Lady Corsair came out of nowhere. Catching Ivy by the hair with both hands, the aviator whipped her around to a stop, then yanked Ivy back against her.

Her voice was a terrifying purr in Ivy's ear. "You're fortunate I don't toss you to my men for that, blacksmith."

Almost blinded by tears of frustration and pain, Ivy spat, "You're tossing me to *him*."

"Two years ago, you cheated him out of a fare. As his friend, I'm only helping him claim what is rightfully his." Strong fingers tightened in Ivy's hair. "Look up."

Ivy blinked away the tears, fighting whatever was working

up from her chest—a scream or a sob, she didn't know. Half concealed by the low clouds, *Lady Corsair* floated above Ivy's shop, a long and shallow wooden ship tethered beneath an enormous white balloon. They'd come in under silent sail; her engines were off, the tail propellers still. A rope ladder had been lowered to Ivy's front door. They'd known *exactly* where to find her.

"I see," she choked out.

"Good. Now understand this: my aviators haven't had a good raid in months. You can keep fighting, and I'll let my crew run through this town instead of Port Fallow, which can handle them. So what say you, blacksmith?"

Ivy closed her eyes, clenched her fists. She had arms powerful enough to rip this woman apart. Instinct warned her not to try. There was strong, and there was deadly—and she feared Lady Corsair had the edge on the latter.

Her chest aching, she looked toward her shop again. "I have to gather my things."

Without a word, Lady Corsair let her go. Ivy trudged forward, avoiding the curious eyes of the townspeople coming out to look. Several sped back into the safety of their homes the moment they glimpsed the woman following her.

When they glimpsed the man, too. Though she couldn't make out the words, Ivy heard the rough anger in Mad Machen's voice as he questioned Lady Corsair. Felt his gaze boring into her back.

How stupid to hope she might have been safe here on the Norwegian coast, in one of the settlements populated by the descendants of families from eastern Europe who'd fled from the Horde centuries ago—and more recently, from England—but she'd never thought Mad Machen would sail into Fool's Cove. He *couldn't* sail into Fool's Cove. The shallow water hid jagged towers of stone that ripped out the wooden bottoms of every deep-keeled boat. Ice locked the town in winter. In the spring, giant eels seethed in an electric, twisted mating dance, and in the fall, the herring spawned in the fjord that drained into the cove drew young megalodons who churned the waters in a season-long feeding frenzy. The only route into the town was by airship or the fjord; only a fool would sail in by ship.

But he hadn't sailed. And the woman Ivy had assumed was his rival was his friend, instead.

She stepped around the rope ladder, resisting the urge to grab each rail and rip it down. When she opened the door, the bell's jingle welcomed her into the shop. A blue curtain split the ground level room in half. The small window in front showcased the automata she'd built—the practical egg-crackers and handwashers, the fanciful singing birds and jumping frogs—and the dresses sewed by her shopmate, Netta. Seamstress and blacksmith, they both pulled in more coin with repairs than with sales off the shelf . . . but even the repair money was barely enough to keep food in their bellies.

No thanks to bloody Mad Machen.

Only last month, she'd treated an emaciated man who still bore the marks of a whip. She'd made him a new foot, and listened to how Mad Machen had attacked his merchant ship, forced the man onto his crew, used him until he couldn't walk anymore, then left him to die in a dinghy. Mad Machen . . . who'd been tearing up the coast of the North Sea, searching for the redheaded blacksmith from London who'd cheated him.

The man had given her hair and guild tattoo a significant look. Though the work she'd done on his foot could have fed her for a year, she hadn't asked him to pay.

It wasn't the first time she'd heard the story, received that look, and hadn't been paid in return. Mad Machen had a habit of dropping men into dinghies near the cove. For months now, Ivy had suspected he knew she was there, and his revenge had been keeping her frightened and waiting. She should have run then—but she simply hadn't wanted to run again.

Black hair pulled into a bun at her nape, Netta came up to the front, and the friendly smile of greeting she wore warmed when she saw Ivy. "Back so early, and without a pint to show for it. That Klaas has a tighter fist than a sailor a year out to sea." She *tsked*, shaking her head, then moved over to the window. "We have a fish pie today, thanks from the widow Aughton. Now, look at all the busybodies standing about. What're they sticking their noses into today?"

"Me." Ivy ran her hand through her hair, trying to think. "I don't know when I'll return, Netta."

If she returned.

"What are you going on about? I—" Netta froze, staring out the window. "That man, is he . . . ? Oh, Ivy—run. Run!"

"I tried that," Ivy said, starting for the stairs. Every step was like twisting a screw through her chest. Downstairs, the bell chimed merrily as the door opened again. She didn't look back.

Full of light, with a window overlooking the cove, her room appeared larger than it was. She crouched in front of the chest at the foot of her narrow bed, retrieving a small steel box locked with a rotating combination. She dialed in the sequence, and the box unfolded, clicking as it reshaped into a fat squatting man, his left and right eyes reading a one and a six. Sixteen coins. She pressed his hand down, and thin electrum deniers spit from the smiling mouth into her palm one at a time. When the eyes showed a zero and an eight, she flicked the hand up—leaving half for Netta to pay their rent, so that she might have a shop to return to.

Someone began to climb the stairs—a heavy, uneven tread.

Ivy hurried to her wardrobe. She had a real satchel this time, made by Netta from mismatched pieces of fabric. Ivy filled it with her few changes of clothing, then looked around. Two tattered books lay on the nightstand—children's primers that Netta had taught Ivy to read. Taking those was like admitting she wasn't coming back. She left them where they were.

"Bring that with you."

Mad Machen's gruff voice came from behind her. Slowly, Ivy turned, her gaze sweeping up from the floor—stopping at his legs. From just above the right knee on down, he no longer filled out his trouser leg and boot. A prosthetic. One he'd had long enough that he didn't need a stabilizing cane, but he wouldn't be running after her soon, if ever.

She met his eyes. Dark and somber, they watched her face. His hair was longer, shaggier, and lightened by the summer sun. His cheeks were leaner, browner, and a new white scar cut cleanly through his flesh from his temple to his jaw.

Sometime in the past two years, he'd been through hell.

And because she couldn't take pleasure in it, she turned away so that she wouldn't feel compassion.

By some miracle, her voice was steady. "Bring what with me?"

"The dress."

It hung on the wardrobe door. Of pale blue satin, designed to gather beneath her breasts and cascade to the floor, the gown was a New Year's gift from Netta. A month ago, Ivy had attended one of the widow Aughton's socials wearing it with borrowed slippers, gloves over her gray arms, and ribbons in her hair. Only a few men had been brave enough to dance with her. They'd heard the stories about Mad Machen, too.

Her hands shook as she lifted the dress from the hook. That terrified her. The one thing she'd always been able to depend on was the steadiness of her hands.

When she turned, he was beside her bed, bending to slide his fingers over the rough woolen blanket. Anger suddenly rose up, stripping the thread of her fear.

The gown crumpled in her fists. "Why not here?"

His gaze flew to hers.

"Use me on the bed," she told him. "Take what you feel you're owed. Then leave me here, and let me continue as I was."

His brows lowered, and he slowly straightened. After an endless second in which he seemed to be holding on to his control, he said, "Our agreement was that you'd be in *my* bed."

"For passage. I didn't board your ship. I owe you nothing."

"But to pay your debt to Yasmeen, you have to board *Vesuvius*." He took a step toward her. "Bring the dress, Ivy."

She'd have ripped it. But Netta had spent hours sewing in secret . . . and Ivy loved the blasted thing. She shoved the gown into her satchel and turned for the stairs. She marched down and threw her arms around a weeping Netta.

"I left money. It's not much."

"I'll get by." Netta's strong arms squeezed her tight. "Take care, Ivy. And come back. Please."

Nodding, Ivy drew away. She heard Mad Machen on the

stairs—slow, careful. With her chin high, Ivy swept past Lady Corsair, through the door, and to the rope ladder.

And because it was the last time she could put distance between her and Mad Machen, Ivy climbed to her fate as fast as she could.

Lady Corsair's sails unfurled before Eben was halfway up the ladder. Within a minute, he was clinging to the swaying ropes, staring down into the shallow cove where small megalodons swam between jagged rocks, their dorsal fins cutting the surface. Yasmeen was furious with him, obviously.

His fury was directed right back. God damn her for keeping Ivy's location from him. For not telling him who the Blacksmith had sent them to find until after they'd stepped into that tavern.

And with every awkward step up the ladder, he thanked God that Ivy hadn't been on *Vesuvius* when she'd sailed from London two years ago—but he didn't need the sharks circling below as a reminder.

A gust buffeted him against the wooden hull. The impact rattled his teeth and vibrated painfully through his steel leg, into his thigh bone. Jaw clenched, he pulled himself up another rung and swung over the gunwale onto the deck. Most of the crew was at the halyards, hauling at the lines that drew the sails out along the horizontal spars, bringing the triangular canvas forward to catch more air. Yasmeen watched them from the quarterdeck.

He couldn't see Ivy anywhere.

A familiar tightness gripped his chest. Was she hiding from him? Christ, no wonder. He couldn't keep a rational head when he saw her, touched her. She twisted him up. Not a damn thing he said came out as it should. He'd wait before seeking her out, regain his wits—so that when she looked at him like a monster, he didn't heed his instinct and prove her right. That instinct had saved him more times than he could count, but if he wanted Ivy in his life, he couldn't give into it with her.

And he needed answers from Yasmeen first. Eben hadn't

expected that Ivy would be glad to see him. He hadn't expected her to flee in terror, either.

By the time he reached the quarterdeck, the airship had gained altitude, skimming below the clouds and bearing toward *Vesuvius*, anchored just beyond the mouth of the cove.

"Where is she?"

"I locked her in the officer's mess." Yasmeen didn't take her eyes off the men working the decks. "She looked ready to take a dive over the side."

"What the hell have you told her?"

"Only what you should have—" Her gaze narrowed when an aviator stepped into a coil of rope. Her voice rose, hard and sharp. "Mind that line, Ms. Pegg, or we'll be feeding your leg to the bleeding gulls! . . . again," she finished quietly, before glancing at Eben. "All of the men who came to me from your ship that were in need of a blacksmith, I sent to her with a story. I embellished."

Embellished. Enough that Ivy had thought he'd rape her. She likely imagined that once they reached *Vesuvius* she'd be whipped, abused, starved. Why not? Half the people who came off Eben's ship were.

"At every port, I heard that you were asking about her. And I heard the talk that had begun: men claiming that you'd weakened for a woman—and if you are weak in one area, you can be weakened in others. So I spread a different story." Yasmeen spared him another glance. "Both your ship and this blacksmith are better protected when everyone thinks that you only seek her because she cheated you. You've made destroying the Black Guard your crusade, but your first duty is to your men—and there are too many lives at stake for Mad Machen to become Softhearted Eben."

"I know," he said grimly. Christ, how he knew. The lives of his crew and the freedom of every person rounded up and chained into the belly of the Black Guard's slaver ships depended on the reputation he'd earned over the years. Fear was a more powerful weapon than the biggest rail cannon—and every terrified mercenary who'd rather give up his cargo than face Mad Machen saved more lives than a Softhearted Eben ever could.

"Then choose who you will be. You can't be both."

He pictured Ivy's face—a sight that had helped him fight through hell. And he felt the strange, cold presence below his knee, a constant reminder that there were others who hadn't been strong or lucky enough to break free.

Maybe he couldn't be both. But he could damn well try.

THREE

Twenty minutes passed before Mad Machen came for her. When she heard the door open, Ivy turned away from the porthole windows, Fool's Cove no longer visible behind them.

With dark eyes, he stared at her until a shout from the decks and a sudden decrease in the airship's speed sent Ivy stumbling forward. He started toward her, but stopped when she caught her balance. His gaze left her face, landing on the satchel she'd dropped by the door.

Bending, he grabbed up the handle, slung it over his shoulder. "We're almost above my ship. Come."

Ivy expected him to step aside to let her pass, but he didn't move out of the doorway as she approached. Ivy paused, wary. When his brows drew together with his frown, she fought the urge to scramble back.

His expression continued to darken. "Don't be afraid of me."

A disbelieving laugh escaped before she could stop it. Clamping her lips together, she lasted only a moment until the rest came out. "Certainly. I'll start doing that, right away."

To her surprise, he smiled before sliding the door open. Nerves fluttering in her stomach, she passed him quickly, entering the narrow passageway that led out from beneath the quarterdeck. Cold wind caught her full in the face. Shivering in her thin coat, she started toward the rope ladder at the side of the airship, already longing for the warmer air below. She'd forgotten how frigid even a slight breeze could seem as it blew across the airship's open decks.

Mad Machen came up beside her. Avoiding his gaze, Ivy looked down, where *Vesuvius* floated five hundred yards below. The ladder hadn't been lowered yet. As she watched, two aviators at a nearby capstan unwound a mooring cable toward the waiting ship. Within a few minutes, the crew below had tethered the airship to *Vesuvius*'s stern, the cable carrying enough slack to form a graceful curve between them.

She glanced over at Mad Machen. His hands braced on the gunwale, he was looking down at the ship with an expression that might have been anticipation. His gaze slid up the mooring line, then unexpectedly locked on hers.

"Put your arms around my neck, Ivy, and we'll head down."

Confused, she looked to the ladder, still rolled up near her feet.

Without warning, his arm circled her waist, hauling her back against his solid chest. Surrounded by the heat of his body, she tried not to stiffen.

"No? Then I'll hold on to you," he said against her hair, and reached for the mooring line. Snapping a large carabiner over the cable, he gripped the bottom of the steel loop.

Oh, blue. That was how they'd be going down? Spinning to face him, she flung her arms around his shoulders. Muscles bunched beneath her hands. Mad Machen swung them up and over the side, and then they were falling, bouncing and twisting, steel ripping along over the cable. Ivy squeezed her eyes shut, then popped them open again, staring over his shoulder. They dropped away from the airship at terrifying . . . *exhilarating* speed.

She laughed, suddenly loving this mad descent. His arm tightened around her back and Ivy abruptly became aware of how she clung to him, her legs wrapped around his thigh, her cheek against his warm neck—abruptly aware that she'd felt safe enough to let go of her fear, if only for a moment.

Then they were slowing at the bottom of the long arc of cable, leveling out. Ivy lifted her head and looked over her shoulder at *Vesuvius*'s approaching decks. Tall and imposing, *Vesuvius* was enormous. Wide at the waterline, the ship's black, rounded hull narrowed at the top, and the two rows of gallery windows built up the squared-off stern higher than the bow. Gunports lined the side, and more cannons took up space along the rails of the upper decks. From high above, the ship had appeared small and calm in the quiet waters, but closing in she could barely make sense of the crisscrossing ropes and furled sails, the timbers and spars—and twice as many crew members on the crowded upper deck alone than had served the entire airship, all moving about in chaotic activity.

"Zounds!" she exclaimed, and turned her head as Mad Machen chuckled, a deep rumble that she felt against her chest. The wind scraped his ragged hair back from his forehead, and when his short laugh ended, either the ship or the descent left a wide grin on his face.

Perhaps both.

Without glancing down at her, he said, "Hold tight," and let go of the carabiner, landing heavily on the poop deck. He stumbled, as if his right leg almost folded, but he wrenched upward and came to a halt, holding her against him. Breathing hard and still grinning, he pulled back to look into her face. His hair stuck up wildly in all directions. Amusement crinkled the corners of his eyes, softening his dark gaze. She waited for her fear to return, but could only think that *this* was the man she'd asked for help from two years before, the man she'd met at the Blacksmith's.

But her impression then had been wrong. She couldn't trust this impression, either.

Ivy pulled away. To her relief, Mad Machen let her go, turning to scan the ship. At a word, two men rushed to unfasten the mooring line. A shout from another deck sent hands scurrying up the masts, out onto the yards. Eight men around a capstan began hauling up the heavy anchor chain.

Watching them, Ivy took a few moments to find her breath—and her balance. The deck seemed to roll gently beneath her feet, a gentle rock from bow to stern. Gulls circled the topgallant masts, their raucous cries adding to the voices calling to one another up in the yards, to the orders shouted from below. Booted feet beat the decks as men hurried about, securing ropes. White sails unfurled with the rough scrape of canvas, and the timbers creaked when they filled with air.

Chaos, but a perfectly ordered one. Eyes wide as she tried to take it in, she followed Mad Machen to a lower deck, where Barker stood at a carved balustrade, overlooking the crew.

The quartermaster turned and spotted Ivy. His mouth fell open and his gaze darted to Mad Machen's face before returning to hers. His astonishment warmed into a smile.

"Well," he drawled. "Look at you, Ivy Blacksmith. You've color in your cheeks now."

All freckles. "A bit," she said.

"More than a bit. The blue skies suit you. Wouldn't you say so, Captain?"

"Yes." Mad Machen's slow perusal felt as if he was stripping Ivy down to her skin. "But so did London."

"That's true enough." Barker laughed suddenly, shaking his head. He looked to Mad Machen. "And so this explains why Yasmeen wouldn't tell us who the Blacksmith had named until after you'd fetched her. She knew you wouldn't strangle her in front of Ivy."

A gentle swell rocked the ship. Swaying, Ivy stared at Barker. "The Blacksmith?" So focused on the threat of Mad Machen, she'd completely forgotten what Lady Corsair had told her: they wanted Ivy to build something. "Why did he name me?"

Mad Machen glanced at Barker. The quartermaster's expression closed up and he nodded, as if that silent look had conveyed a message Ivy couldn't read.

The captain turned to Ivy. "He said you are best suited for the work."

"What work?" Of all her talents, her strongest was creating artificial limbs. Nothing like the Blacksmith's mechanical flesh, but far more precise and integrated than a typical prosthetic . . . *Oh.* Her gaze dropped. "Your leg?"

"No."

Mad Machen's abrupt answer told her not to pursue it. Why? She'd have to know eventually—and the sooner she began, the sooner she could return to Fool's Cove. "Then why am I here?"

His mouth tightened. For a moment, he seemed on the verge of speaking, but looked away from her, instead. He turned to Barker.

"Send for Duckie. He'll ready my cabin for Ivy's stay."

His cabin. Without a flicker of his eyelids, the quartermaster followed the order. Anger grated in Ivy's chest like a twisted gear.

The Blacksmith wouldn't have given her name if he'd known she'd be required to work in Mad Machen's bed, too. Ivy was certain of it.

"I don't owe you that service, Captain Machen. Tell your man to put me in another room."

"You're taking passage on my ship—"

"Not by my choice."

"—and you *will* sleep in my bed."

By the bleeding stars, she would *not* be forced. "You'll have to chain me down first, Mad Machen."

His smile was sudden and terrifying, a sharp flash of white against his tan. Ivy stepped back, abruptly aware that the only sound on the ship came from the gulls and the creaking hull. The crew had fallen silent. Barker's eyes had closed, as if he were praying. A blond, gangly boy with a red mark across his forehead rushed up the stairs onto the quarterdeck and stopped, looking uneasily between her and the captain.

Ivy swallowed. *Alright.* She shouldn't challenge Mad Machen here. When they had privacy, perhaps she could appeal to his rational side . . . if he had one. And if not, perhaps she could bargain with the mercenary in him.

Her heart pounding, she held still as Mad Machen crossed the distance between them. His dark face lowered, stopping with his lips a breath from hers. He murmured, "Here in front of my men, or in my cabin. *That* is your choice."

"Your cabin." Frustration shook through her whisper. "And damn you to a kraken's belly."

His brows rose, and a surprised laugh broke from him before his mouth suddenly covered hers, his callused palm cupping her jaw. Not a hard kiss, and not tender—it was a statement, she realized, for the men watching them. A claim, pure and simple.

A claim that went on until Ivy had to employ all of her willpower to refrain from biting him.

He finally lifted his head, and turned to the boy. "Duckie, escort Ivy Blacksmith to my cabin. See that she wants for nothing."

"Yes, sir." The boy gathered her satchel from the captain, and looked expectantly to Ivy.

Plastering on a smile, she pulled at her trouser legs and curtsied to Mad Machen. His laugh followed her to the stairs—and Ivy decided she could make a statement, too. A brass finial shaped like an egg decorated the end of the banister. Ivy closed her gray hand around it. Metal shrieked as she crushed the finial between her fingers.

His laughter stopped.

She released the mangled brass, and called over her shoulder, "I await your mighty prick, sir!"

Eben couldn't stop grinning. Judging by the way his crew kept their heads down and their hands busy, most assumed a storm was brewing, but Barker read his grin for what it was.

"Not so afraid now, is she?"

No, she wasn't. And not ready to trust him, but Eben knew it'd take time to *show* her that she could. The reputation he'd built couldn't be brushed away with a word—and he couldn't risk that it was brushed away from anyone's eyes but Ivy's. Yasmeen had been right about that.

But at least her fear had receded. He couldn't have borne it if she'd kept trembling at his approach or trying to run. The rest would come.

He eyed the stairs. Perhaps he could start—

"Meg!"

The shout came down from the crow's nest, where Teppers pointed out to starboard. Two hundred yards distant, a razor-edged dorsal fin sliced through the water, tall enough that if *Vesuvius* sailed next to it, the fin's point would reach halfway to the ship's upper decks.

"A big one," Barker said.

A damn big one. And with luck, it wouldn't come to investigate *Vesuvius*. Even under full sail, a megalodon was impossible to outrun. Altered and bred by the Horde until they were aggressive and territorial, a full-grown megalodon could leave a ship rudderless or damage the hull, even on a vessel as solid as Eben's—and the shark's armored plating made it damn hard to kill. The best course was just avoiding them, and if that failed, throw out bait—and then watch *Vesuvius*'s tail, because once megalodons caught a scent, they were hard to shake.

Out over the water, the dorsal fin turned toward them, then slid beneath the surface.

"Hard to port." Eben braced his feet and settled in. "Ready the chum."

It was going to be a long afternoon.

With a row of square windows that welcomed the pale, slanting sunlight, the captain's cabin was more spacious than Ivy anticipated. Though four cannons strapped to rolling platforms were lashed together at the center of the floor, enough room was left over for a dining table that could seat six, a teak desk piled high with maps and ledgers, two leather armchairs beneath the windows, a weapons cabinet, and a wardrobe. Chests with upholstered lids served as footrests or additional seats. A narrow door by the windows opened to a lavatory. Partitioning off one side of the room was a heavy green curtain—behind which, a blushing Duckie told her, was the captain's berth. As soon as he left, Ivy pushed the curtain aside, revealing a squat bureau topped by a ewer, a washbowl, and a mirror. A thick mattress lay on a waist-high wooden platform.

Blimey. The bed was *tiny.* Long enough to accommodate the captain's height, but almost as narrow as her bed in Fool's Cove. Certainly not wide enough for two people to lie side by side, especially if one had shoulders as broad as Mad Machen's. Even hanging off the edge would be impossible; a wooden rail guarded the side to keep the pitching boat from flinging the sleeper to the floor.

What in the blue blazes did he expect to do—lie on top of her all night?

Her stomach rolled. Perhaps that was exactly what he expected to do.

So she would reason with him when he returned. She wouldn't antagonize him, but lay out a rational alternative. With a blanket on the floor, she could sleep in the small space between the end of the bed and the chest of drawers. She wouldn't mind; she'd spent nights in worse places.

Ivy waited. When Duckie returned, she asked him for an extra blanket and made her spot on the floor. Eventually the sun dropped to the horizon, painting the cabin in orange light and purple shadows. Duckie brought her dinner on heavy plates: a thick fish stew swimming with carrots, leeks, and potatoes and sopped up with crusty rolls; melon slices bursting with juice; and a lemon tart made with French sugar. He didn't set a place for Mad Machen, who was "leading Meg on a grand chase." As she wasn't thrown about the room by a shark ramming the ship, or trying to cut her way out of its belly, the captain must have been doing a fine job of it.

When Mad Machen finally came, she was sitting in a chair by the windows, watching the stars appear against the coal black heavens—a view she never tired of, and that she'd never seen over London's hazy skies. The moon, sometimes, as a dull red glow through the smoke. Never the stars.

The captain's gaze found her in the darkened room. She couldn't see his expression, only the gleam of his eyes. After a long moment, he strode to the berth and slid aside the curtain. Her makeshift pallet made him pause.

Ivy filled the silence. "If I sleep on the—"

"No." He swept the blanket up and called for Duckie. Wearing only a nightshirt, the cabin boy came through the door an instant later. Mad Machen tossed the blanket to him. "If the nights are too cold, she can have it back."

"Yes, sir." Duckie left the cabin as quickly as he'd come.

With the flick of a spark lighter, Mad Machen lit the gas lamp on the bureau. In the dim glow, he looked toward Ivy. "You won't be cold."

Clamping her lips tight, Ivy faced the windows again. *Rational*, she reminded herself. He made it difficult.

And he'd stolen her view. Now that the lamp lit the cabin, his reflection appeared in the glass, instead. He stood at the bureau with his back to the windows, filling the washbowl with water. She glanced away when he removed his jacket, but looked again when she heard his shirt come off.

She'd spent years training at the Blacksmith's smithy, learning to build machines that ranged from tiny clockworks to enormous steam-powered locomotives. But before the Blacksmith had let her touch a single prosthetic, she'd had to study anatomy. For two years, she'd watched people wearing tight clothes and loose, observed the nude models brought in by the Blacksmith—and during quiet sessions at night, opening the drowned corpses brought in by the body collectors along the Thames—until she understood how every muscle, tendon, and joint within a human body affected balance and movement.

With sharply delineated muscle that moved smoothly beneath his tanned skin, Mad Machen had a form well worth studying.

Stripped down to his breeches, he washed his face, then wetted a cloth and wiped down the back of his neck, his chest, his underarms. He glanced around once, as if checking to see that she still faced the window. After a brief hesitation, he moved to a bootjack. Bracing his foot, he pulled off his left boot—but when his right came off, she turned in the armchair for a better look, frowning.

His breeches extended to midcalf, so she couldn't see his knee, but the mechanical leg looked to be a standard skeletal prosthetic, made of nickel-plated steel with basic movement at the joints . . . and a badly configured ankle.

"You have a load-bearing pneumatic where your Achilles tube should be." She stood and crossed the room. Crouching next to him, she fingered the wide cylinder above his heel. "Look at this. Shoddy work—"

She paused suddenly, looked up; he was staring down at her, his expression unreadable. "It's not by your ship's blacksmith, is it?"

"No."

His gruff response released the tension that had sprung through her. In London, there could be no excuse for work like this, but on a ship, there could be any number of reasons—a lack of equipment being the most likely. She didn't want to endanger a blacksmith's position over circumstances he couldn't avoid.

"Alright. Look here. Your Achilles tube is for balance and stability—it doesn't handle much weight, but prevents your foot apparatus from flopping around like a fish. But this . . ." She tapped her finger against the cylinder, shaking her head. "It's harder to compress, which limits the range of motion. You probably don't take note of it except for on an incline or stairs, or when you want to walk quickly—but then it's stiff. Yes?"

"Yes."

His voice had deepened, but Ivy didn't glance up to gauge his expression. She lifted the leg of his breeches and examined the knee. Rudimentary, but fine. Her fingers itched to build a more advanced joint, but fixing what he had would have to serve.

"If you show me to your smithy, I'll adjust the cylinder's valve so that it compresses under minimal weight. It won't be perfect, but you'll have a smoother stride until the pneumatic can be replaced."

"Not tonight."

Ivy closed her eyes as his answer sank through her. Pushing to her feet, she walked back to the window.

He might have sighed, but she wasn't certain. The creaking of the ship and the clank of his foot as he moved toward her covered the sound. He stopped by the table and glanced down at her plates. She'd eaten from all of them but one.

His brows lifted. "You don't like lemon tarts?"

She didn't know; she hadn't tried one. "Duckie said the sugar came from the Antilles."

Two hundred years before, the Horde had used cheap imported sugars and teas to infect almost everyone in Britain with their nanoagents. Ivy didn't know anyone raised under Horde rule who sweetened their food with anything but honey.

Sitting back against the table, he paused with his hand over the tart. "May I?"

"Yes," she said, grateful that unlike some descendents of the merchants and aristocrats who'd fled when the Horde had advanced across Europe—and who still considered themselves Englishmen, though they'd never stepped foot on British soil until after the Iron Duke blew up the Horde's tower—Mad Machen didn't try to convince her that she had nothing to fear from sugar imported from the New World.

Of course she didn't; she was already infected. She didn't reject sugar out of paranoia, but pride. Apparently, he understood that.

He ate quietly. She watched his reflection and hope began to rise in her chest. The downward cast of his shoulders told her that fatigue sat heavily on him. If exhausted, surely he wouldn't want to force her into his bed.

That hope died when her gaze slid down to his loins. She couldn't mistake the bulge that had formed behind the flap of his breeches. Though tired, he was obviously imagining what came next.

He finished the tart and straightened. "It grows late, Ivy. Let's go to bed."

Her teeth clenched. If he tried to force her, she would kill him. And if Ivy killed him, she wouldn't make it off this ship. Desperate, she cast around her mind for something—*anything*—that might appeal to him. She only had one thing. Unfortunately, she had very little of it.

She stood, digging into the pouch tied at the waist of her trousers and withdrawing a thin denier. She held the money out to him.

He frowned at the coin. "What is this for?"

"I'll sleep in your bed tonight. This is to sleep unmolested."

His gaze flew to her face. His dark brows drew together, and shadows moved over his expression. Ivy's hand didn't shake; the rest of her did.

After an endless moment, his fingers closed over hers. He took the coin. "Get into the bed."

She went quickly, before he could change his mind. Her knees sank into the thick mattress and she stretched out on her side, her back hard against the cold bulkhead. His uneven tread carried him to the bureau, where he snuffed the lamp, and she followed the sound of his steps to the bed. He rolled in beside her, a solid block of heat that almost flattened her against the side of the ship. His hands found her waist.

Ivy tried to shrink back and couldn't. "You agreed you wouldn't—"

"Crush you? Hold still." His rough voice brooked no argument. He hauled her against him, her head cradled by his shoulder, her leg over his thighs. "And relax."

Her laugh burst out, tinged with hysteria. He truly must be insane.

But as the minutes passed, the tension did ease from her body. Despite everything, she was comfortable—and warm. *So warm.*

Not that she wanted to become accustomed to this. "How long will we be sailing?"

He didn't answer for a long moment, and by the heaviness in his reply, she realized he'd almost been asleep. "Fifteen days."

She stared into the dark. *Fifteen.* And she had only eight coins.

Seven now.

Mad Machen stirred again. "And twenty days more for the return journey. We'll be sailing against the wind."

Five weeks altogether—and only coins enough for one.

Smoking hell.

FOUR

As always, Eben woke to the first of eight bells signaling the end of the middle watch. Four o'clock. On the deck above, the crew changed shifts, and the muffled thud of their footsteps told him the transition was smooth, with only one hand running late to his post. He listened to *Vesuvius*, to her familiar creaks and groans. The wind had picked up during the night, deepening each roll of the sea.

When the next bell rang in half an hour, Duckie would bring his coffee and breakfast, expecting to find Eben up and dressed. In two bells, Barker and Simms, the navigator, would meet with him to plot their course. Meg had pushed them far enough northwest that rounding the top of the British isle and sailing down the west coast might take them to Wales faster than turning back and sailing for the channel.

But Eben wasn't in a hurry.

Ivy had softened against him in sleep, her head pillowed on his chest and her fingers loosely curled beneath her chin. Her leg crossed over his groin. He hoped to God she didn't wake up. Holding her so close hardened his morning erection into an aching, solid length. If Ivy felt his arousal, Eben had no doubt she'd scramble away, certain he was bent on raping her.

The night before, he'd seen her terror as she'd offered the coin. It'd been all he could do not to haul her against him and prove that he wouldn't take her by force.

But this route was better. When she'd approached him with the denier, Eben had been planning to coax a kiss from her—and two years ago, a single touch of her lips had almost stolen his control. If he'd lost his head again, she wouldn't be sleeping soundly now, but lying tense and quivering beside him.

He'd already waited two years. So he could wait for a kiss—and hope that she soon exhausted her supply of coins.

Ivy had a vague memory of stirring awake in the dark, Mad Machen a shadow looming over the bed, softly telling her to sleep longer. She must have. When she fully opened her eyes, the sun was streaming into the cabin from the east.

Hot water filled the ewer on the bureau. She washed and quickly changed her clothes behind the closed curtain. A bell rang somewhere above, seven times. Men were up and about; she could hear footsteps and voices through the decks, a good-natured shout and a burst of male laughter.

She'd seen a number of the crew yesterday. They looked like a rough lot, and a few had a smell strong enough that dipping them in the ocean could have killed any megalodon in a thirty mile radius, but none had appeared starved or abused. They certainly hadn't looked like the four men whose prosthetics she'd rebuilt in Fool's Cove.

Perhaps she hadn't seen all of his men, though—or Mad Machen treated the captives he forced into labor differently than his regular crew.

A soft tap at the door was followed by Duckie's voice. She called him in, and marveled when she saw the meal he carried: black coffee, a bowl of porridge, honey and cream, round soda biscuits, and a thick slice of ham crowded a large tray. Though Mad Machen had been to sea these many years, he apparently still ate as if he lived in Manhattan City. No one in England made breakfasts such as this. The only item that Ivy consumed regularly was the coffee, made cheap and plentiful by the Liberé farmers in the southern American continent.

Perhaps everyone in the New World ate like this—and so would she, quite happily. But despite the growling of her stomach, she tried not to appear too eager. She'd had ham before. Twice.

Half an hour later, with her belly pleasantly full and the coffee mug warming her hands, she left the cabin. A short, low-ceilinged passageway led her from beneath the quarterdeck. Blinking, she emerged into the sun. Faint spray misted her face, and each breath drew in cold, clean air.

"And there she is." Barker's voice came from above her. Ivy glanced up, saw him leaning forward with his elbows against the balustrade, smiling down at her. "Had a bit of a lie-in, Miss Blacksmith?"

Her cheeks heated. She could imagine why Barker thought she'd sleep late. "No. I built an autogyro from the clock and the cannons in the captain's room, which I plan to fly off the ship tonight," she told the quartermaster. "What have you accomplished today, sir?"

Barker's smile vanished. He glanced quickly at Mad Machen, who stood beside him with feet braced and his arms folded over his wide chest, looking as if he owned everything he observed—including Ivy.

The captain's dark eyes met hers, and she read his amusement. "She would need more than a clock, Barker—and she's too clever to risk flying an autogyro anywhere a breeze might turn her over."

It was true. She'd have better luck trying to swim. But she was pleased Barker thought she might have built one and tried to escape.

Sipping her coffee, she turned and let her gaze skim the front of the ship. Though not as chaotic as when they'd weighed anchor the previous day, she counted over thirty men on the decks and up in the rigging, all busy. Beyond them, the sun gleamed over the sea's undulating surface. Ivy had to turn away. Though she'd adjusted to the rocking of the ship beneath her feet, watching the dip and rise of the bow against the horizon tossed her stomach about.

She looked up, unsurprised to find Mad Machen's gaze on her. "Where are we sailing to, Captain?" She supposed a fifteen-day journey from Norway might take them to . . . *Oh, blue heavens.* Dread speared like icicles through her chest. "London?"

"No. The Welsh coast."

Oh. Breathing became easier.

His voice low and rough, he said, "But if it *was* London, you'd have nothing to fear. Not with me."

Ivy stared at him. How did she respond to that? She didn't even know how to classify *her* response to his declaration. Her cheeks had heated again, and her belly tightened and seemed to pitch with the ship. But she wasn't queasy. Just . . . something else.

And of course she knew that the Horde hadn't returned to Britain in the past two years. She still didn't want to return, ever. London held nothing for her but suffocating memories she'd rather let go.

Mad Machen moved to the stairs, held out his hand. "Come up here."

Ivy searched for a reason to refuse, but aside from her reluctance to be so near to him, she couldn't find one. But she did not take his hand. She climbed the stairs and pushed her empty mug into his outstretched palm. Though uncertain of his reaction, the small defiance felt good.

"Thank you, Captain," she said.

The corners of his mouth deepened. Without a word, he turned and handed the cup off to a chuckling Barker.

Ivy bit her lip to repress her own smile, looking away from him. Though the quarterdeck was all but empty of crew, a hive of activity centered on the high poop deck at the stern of the ship. As she watched, two men cast a wide net over the side. Other men stood around barrels, holding machetes and shovels. The scent of fish was strong.

"They're replenishing the chum," Mad Machen said. "Distracting Meg yesterday cleaned out our supply."

Barrels of it, apparently. "And if she hadn't given up? Do you use your meat stores?"

"No. The crew draws straws, and we toss the loser over the side."

She glanced sharply around and saw his grin. She fought not to laugh, and nodded toward *Vesuvius*'s bow. "Why not use the rail cannon? Is the steam engine too unstable?"

If so, perhaps she could fix it. But Mad Machen was shaking his head.

"I haven't had one blow up yet. It's the vibrations. As soon as the engine starts up, Meg will ram us trying to get to it, and the engine noise would draw in others. So the cannon might kill her, but we'd be sitting in the center of a feeding frenzy around a bleeding shark." He gestured to the poop deck, at the white-haired man overseeing the fishing crew. "My engine master, Mr. Leveque."

"I see," Ivy said, and she did. The engine master's duty was making certain the engine would fire if the captain needed it . . . and to make certain he never needed to fire it.

And she saw that the responsibility for both ultimately lay on Mad Machen's shoulders.

The breeze picked up, cold and brisk. Pulling the edges of her coat together, she moved to the side of the ship to look over at the nets. She heard Mad Machen follow, and the snap of metal as he unbuckled his coat.

Heavy wool swept around her shoulders. Ivy stiffened before letting herself sink into the warmth of his big coat. Spite wouldn't keep her from shivering, and if Mad Machen's gesture meant he'd feel the bite of the morning air, all the better.

But he didn't look cold. The sun warmed his face, narrowing his eyes against the glare. The wind created by the ship's speed caught his collar, billowing through his shirt, and he stood solid as if the icy breath didn't touch him.

Her gaze fell to his throat, and the rough scar exposed by the wind. She'd heard several different stories about how he'd gotten it—and the "mad" in front of his name—but they varied wildly. Only one element remained the same: while serving as ship's surgeon, he'd crossed Rhys Trahaearn.

"Did the Iron Duke truly hang you aboard the *Terror*?"

He grinned. "So that's what you've heard?"

"Yes."

But she had her doubts—not that Trahaearn had been ruthless enough to hang him, but that he'd let Mad Machen live afterward.

"You've heard the wrong story, then. He didn't hang me *on* the ship. He hung me over the side, low enough that my feet dragged through the water."

Ivy gaped. She'd have thought he was joking, just as he had about the crew drawing straws, but the evidence circled his neck.

"Like bait?" When he nodded, she gasped, "Why?"

His grin faded, and he studied her face. Moving closer, he turned with his back to the sea and his elbows on the rail, watching the men. His voice lowered. "This doesn't go further than you and me. Alright?"

Her eyes widened. He'd done something so terrible? "Yes."

"Twelve years ago, we were on a run from Australia to the Ivory Market when we hit rough weather. What should have been a six-week trip had already stretched into three months, and we'd only just rounded the Cape of Good Hope and begun sailing up the west coast of Africa."

All Horde territory. And just as they had in Europe, the Horde had polluted the unoccupied territories with diseased nanoagents that took over the victim's will without use of a controlling tower. Mindless, the diseased humans only hungered and hunted.

"The crew had been living on reduced rations of salt pork and hard tack for almost two months," Mad Machen continued. "Those with bugs were getting along. The rest of us weren't."

"You weren't infected then?" The nanoagents couldn't prevent scurvy, but they'd delay the symptoms much longer.

He shook his head. "We had two weeks of sailing before we reached the Market. I informed the captain that we had to replenish our stores or a portion of the crew wasn't going to make it. And as the health of the crew was my priority, I'd studied the maps. I'd found a river delta a day's journey north. The river forked around an island—and the zombies don't usually cross water. So I asked him to drop anchor long enough to forage."

"He didn't agree?"

"It meant veering toward the shore. The waters along that shelf are kraken territory."

Ivy's heart thumped. The handlers at the crèche had used tales of the giant cephalopods to keep them in line as children. She'd been scared of kraken long before she learned they deserved the terror their name evoked, their long tentacles pulling apart ships or picking men from the decks and dragging them under.

"So he decided between losing a few men or losing them all," she realized.

"And furious that the island meant he had to make the choice. Not that Trahaearn gave any indication of it. I didn't realize then how ruddy pissed off I'd made him by pointing out that option—not until I had my own ship." Mad Machen paused, a frown creasing his brow. He met her eyes again. "Resigning yourself to losing men is easier than making the decisions that will kill them."

Uncomfortable, Ivy looked out to sea. She didn't want to think those decisions were difficult for Mad Machen. It didn't fit with the image she felt strangely desperate to hold on to.

"So he hanged you?"

"Not for that." A wry smile touched his lips. "The next morning, when he gave the helmsman the bearing that would take us to the Ivory Market, I told the crew to belay that order."

Ivy covered her mouth, staring at him. "You *are* mad."

His deep laugh creased his lean cheeks and wrinkled the corners of his eyes. He shook his head. " 'Mad' was accepting the bargain he laid out for me: he'd hang me over the side, and sail toward the island as long as I was alive. Otherwise, he'd shoot me where I stood."

"Why is that crazy? You were dead either way."

"Quick would have been easier." His gaze fell to her hands. "I think you know."

Yes. Even knowing what good would come of it, there had

been times during her surgery she'd wished for death just to end the pain. He'd seen that with Barker.

And Ivy hadn't had a Mad Machen to carry her home afterward.

He turned toward the sea again, so close that only an inch separated their arms, braced on the rail. When the ship rolled, her hip bumped lightly against his thigh.

Ivy couldn't catch her breath.

"So that's the story," he said. "Trahaearn avoided the kraken and sailed us to the island, the men foraged for fresh food, and I woke up a week after they hauled me back onboard, miraculously still in one piece."

Lucky to wake up at all. "And lesson learned: don't question the captain."

He shook his head. "My men question me often enough, but not in front of the crew. That, I won't allow. Tolerating one man who undermines my authority puts the entire ship at risk."

Her fingers tightened on the wooden gunwale. Perhaps she shouldn't have pushed that coffee mug into his hand.

Mad Machen must have read the sudden worry on her face. "You're not part of my crew, Ivy. When you challenge me, they understand you're challenging the man, not the captain—and that you aren't trying to take my command."

Relief eased through her. "I don't want your command."

"Or the man?" Stark emotion lined his face for an instant, stealing her automatic response. He didn't give her time to recover. "What *do* you want, Ivy?"

Clean air. A view of the stars. Work for her mind and her hands. "To build what I've come to build, and to return home."

He looked out to the sea. After a second, he nodded. "Then let's get you started."

She followed Mad Machen down a ladder into the dimly lit lower deck. He walked with his shoulders bent, ducking beneath low beams with an ease that spoke of long familiarity. He led her forward through cabins lined with cannons, past sailors who snapped to attention, around stanchions, past the galley were a tall, rawboned woman argued with slick-haired man over a bushel of potatoes, both of them gesturing wildly, paring knives in hand.

A narrow passageway terminated at a locked door. Producing the key from the pocket of the coat she still wore, Mad Machen opened it and showed her into a triangular cabin at the very front of the ship. Well-lit and stocked with tools, Ivy immediately saw that it served as a smithy. She started forward, but paused when she caught sight of the glass tank along the bulkhead near the door. Waist-high, reinforced at the edges with iron, the aquarium was filled with water, a few silver fish . . . and a small squid. It darted around the tank, eight arms forming a cone, tentacles trailing.

She turned to him, brows raised. "Supper?"

"No. The Blacksmith said you'd need it." He glanced around the room, frowning. "If I'd known it was *you*, I'd have put it in my cabin."

Because his was more comfortable or to keep her near his bed? Ivy didn't ask. "This suits me," she said, and it did. "What do I have to do?"

"Repair a submersible."

She laughed, looking around the cabin. Though not as cramped as some of the men's quarters, she certainly couldn't fit a submersible here—let alone fit it through the door. "In here?"

He smiled faintly. "No. It's in Wales, already constructed—and as-is, it's a complete loss. I need you to discover where my blacksmiths went wrong."

He strode past her to a chest constructed of steel. Ivy recognized that design—it was the Blacksmith's. Like her bank in Fool's Cove, it expanded and reconfigured when given the right combination. This one unfolded into a solid worktable. Long rolls of paper that had been hidden inside now lay on the surface.

Curious, Ivy smoothed out the paper, and stared at the first sketch. Not just a submersible—it was shaped like a kraken, with mechanical arms and maneuverable tentacles. This *had* to be a joke. "Someone built this?"

"Yes."

She tilted her head, struggling with her disbelief. It could be done, she supposed. A small, one-man craft that—

Her gaze skimmed over the dimensions. She choked. "This is longer than your ship!"

"Only the tentacles."

With a body as big as his cabin. "It can't be done. This is of metal, not . . . not"—she wiggled her fingers at the squid—"what *they* have. The weight of the tentacles alone would destabilize the entire structure. There's no counterweight."

"And you know that just from looking at the plans. My people had to build it first." Mad Machen studied her face, his gaze dark and unwavering. "Fix it, Ivy. You'll have mechanical flesh to work with. Yasmeen is traveling to London now to collect it from the Blacksmith."

She frowned at the plans, then at the aquarium. Using mechanical flesh *could* offset some of the weight, but the locomotion couldn't function like a squid's. The material simply wasn't that fluid. "It can't be done."

"It has to be."

"Why?" She couldn't imagine any use a kraken might have. "What do you plan to do? Frighten sailors? Tear apart ships?"

"Yes."

His implacable expression and the conviction in his voice stopped her. That *was* what he planned to do. Her chest tight, she looked down at the plans. "I won't build a monster for you."

His face darkened. He moved in suddenly, solid behind her, pushing her hips against the table. Her fingers clenched, crumpling paper. Trembling with shock and anger, she waited, but he only stood behind her, chest heaving. She felt his ragged breath against her ear, then her neck. Her stomach tightened as calloused fingers slid her hair aside. Warm lips caressed her nape. *Oh, blue.* A shudder wracked her bones, and she didn't know if it was anger or fear . . . or something else.

Tension hardened the body pressing into hers, and he pulled away. Wary, she turned to look at him.

His eyes were closed, his jaw clenched, his scars starkly

white against his skin. Then he was striding for the door, pausing at the threshold. "Fix it and I'll take you back to Fool's Cove. If you refuse, you'll never leave this ship."

He issued the rough threat without looking back. A moment later, he was gone.

Ivy stared at the empty doorway. He was absolutely and utterly *mad*. Her heart pounding, she looked to the tank, then at the plans. She picked up a pencil.

To return home, she needed to begin thinking like a madman.

FIVE

The ship's bell woke her. Silently, Ivy opened her eyes to the dark. Mad Machen's heart beat steadily beneath her cheek, his arm a solid brace of heat between her back and the cold bulkhead, his hand lightly resting at her waist. She'd curled into him during the night until she almost lay completely on top of him, all but straddling his left thigh.

She didn't move. The hard length against her hip told her that even if he hadn't roused yet, his body had. She closed her eyes again, pretending to sleep.

The previous day, she'd taken her meals in the smithy and worked until he'd come for her. Without a word, he'd taken her hand and led her to his cabin. She'd watched the stars while he washed and undressed, and he'd accepted her coin without comment. Their silence had been a swelling pressure that had grown as he followed her into the bed, but one she'd been unwilling to break, for reasons she couldn't define.

Ivy didn't want to break it now, either, but this time she could identify the reason: her body wanted his.

She'd felt this before—the hollow ache between her legs, the tightening of her nipples, the urge to crawl on top of another human and feed the hunger. It wasn't a memory she liked to revisit. Only a few months before the end of the Horde occupation, she'd been cleaning a factory's chimney when a rare Frenzy had struck. The two members of her sweeper team who were supposed to haul her out of the chimney had fallen on each other. For hours, she'd listened to their grunts and moans, compelled to join them—but trapped within the narrow pipe.

As terrifying as that had been, the alternative could have been worse. A good number of the women she'd known had gotten with child during the Frenzy. And although her hunger for Mad Machen originated from within her instead of from a radio signal, succumbing to it carried the same risk. She barely scraped by in Fool's Cove. How would she support a child? Netta would undoubtedly help, just as Ivy would her if their situations were reversed . . . but if Ivy had any choice in the matter, she wouldn't put that burden on her friend. Two years ago, when she'd offered Mad Machen her virginity, her desperation had outweighed any other fear. She couldn't take a similar risk now simply because her body *wanted.*

And she couldn't let Mad Machen take her simply because he wanted, too.

His chest rose and fell on a great sigh. So he *was* awake. Perhaps staring up into the dark, thinking whatever mad thoughts occupied his brain.

Or thinking of her. Ivy remained limp as he lifted his hand from her waist. His fingers stroked softly through her hair, and a light touch against her crown might have been a kiss. Turning onto his side, he began to ease away from her, his thigh moving deeper between hers as he rolled her gently onto her back. His erection brushed her hip and he froze, his breath hissing between his teeth.

Unable to continue pretending, she lifted her head from the pillow. A short groan escaped him, and she stilled when his big hand cupped her cheek.

"Ivy." Her name sounded low and rough.

What could she say? Ivy wet her lips. "Captain Machen."

"Eben."

Her stomach turned over, a frightening little flip. "I prefer 'Mad.' "

Judging by his voice, she thought he might have grinned. "Go back to sleep. There's nothing to do on a ship when it's dark." He paused, and amended, "That's not true. There is something, but you paid me not to do it."

Mad Machen must have felt her smile against his hand. He answered with a deep laugh.

After a moment, he said, "Before you head into the smithy, come topside. Your arms are strong enough to keep you safe climbing into the rigging. You'll enjoy the view from the crow's nest."

This, after threatening that she'd never leave his ship? She couldn't make sense of him—but she didn't want to pass up his offer.

When she nodded, his hand dropped from her cheek and he swung over the bed rail. His right foot clanked heavily against the deck. She still needed to adjust his pneumatic valve . . . but perhaps she'd wait until she had no more money to bargain with.

Only six coins left.

She rolled onto his part of the mattress, into the warmth left by his body. The memory of his hard thigh between hers wouldn't let her be. Clutching the blanket to her sensitive breasts, she squeezed her legs together until she shook.

Ivy didn't just enjoy the crow's nest—she loved it. She remained on the small platform for as long as she could stomach the swaying, using Teppers's biperspic lenses that brought the horizon to within an arm's length. She watched pods of whales, searched for icebergs and Megs. She held the lenses for so long that her sunburn formed white goggles around her eyes, and only left after she extracted a promise from Teppers that he'd show her how to skylark.

Her bugs had just healed the burn when she returned the next morning—and Teppers fulfilled his promise. She slid down the backstays from the top of the main mast to the poop deck, laughing wildly as she skimmed above Mad Machen's head. His grin when he met her at the quarterdeck flipped her stomach over.

He showed her every part of the ship, and gave her leave to explore on her own. She met the Lusitanian cooks, a husband and wife team whose passionate screams in Portuguese during their fights and lovemaking were legendary among the sailors. She learned that Duckie's name was Tom Cooper, and he'd gotten the nickname after shooting up six inches in as many months, and that the recurring red mark across his forehead came from his habit of running full tilt through the low-beamed decks. She discovered the ship's blacksmith had remained in Wales when the bosun approached her for help fixing a broken pulley in the rigging. She spent half of an afternoon with Leveque, the engine master, and though she couldn't understand a word of his French his love for the machine made perfect sense.

She didn't know the languages half the crew spoke. French and Portuguese were the trade languages, and she understood a few words, but the men from the New World also spoke Dutch, Spanish, Arabic, and the Liberé that gave Barker his musical accent. On a ship only a hundred and fifty feet long, she saw more of the world than she'd known before—and realized how much she hadn't yet seen.

And she'd never laughed so often. Had never felt as free. Yet she had to keep reminding herself that freedom was an illusion.

Every day, she came closer to building a monster. She dunked her arm into the tank and watched the squid attack her metal skin, imagining a mast or a person. The claws at the end of his tentacles couldn't bite into her arm. Wood and flesh wouldn't be so resilient. Yet Ivy used what she learned to improve the plans.

She wanted to believe that, despite what Mad Machen had said, the machine wouldn't be used to terrorize and destroy ships. She wanted to believe that the Blacksmith's involvement meant his intentions were good. But as brilliant as her mentor was, and despite the debt she'd always owe him for taking her into his guild, she knew the Blacksmith could be ruthless when someone crossed him—and there was much about him she didn't know. If the price was right, he might have agreed to help.

And every night, she slept next to Mad Machen, her body aching . . . and one denier poorer.

Eben braced himself before entering the smithy. The past few days, she'd left this small cabin sporting a surly temper. He thought that meant she'd been making progress on the kraken. If her ideas failed, surely Ivy would be pleased.

Still, she wouldn't be pleased to see *him*.

The previous night, when he'd come into his cabin, she'd been sitting at the window. She hadn't been looking at the stars, but the two coins glinting in her palm. She'd quickly put one away, and given him the other—not quite hiding her fear.

After tonight, she'd have no more coins left, but he wasn't certain if she was afraid that he'd force her . . . or because she wanted him. A few times, he'd caught her looking at him with heat in her eyes, and he didn't think it was anger. When her nipples pebbled under her thin shirt, he didn't always think it was the cold. He thought she might ache as much as he did—but he didn't know.

Not knowing was tearing him apart.

He stepped inside. Though a gas lamp burned brightly on the worktable, she wasn't sitting in front of it. Her expression clouded, she crouched in front of the squid tank, her hands braced against the glass and fingers drumming. Her silvery nails pinged with each beat.

Without glancing at him, she snapped, "Say what you've come to say. Then leave me be."

Anger fired through his veins. In front of his crew or not, *no one* dismissed him on his ship. Closing the door, he stepped toward her—and forced himself to stop. She still hadn't looked at him. Temper darkened her sharp features, her soft lips in a thin line, her green eyes stormy as she focused on something within the tank.

He glanced inside. The squid and several silvery fish darted about the water. At the bottom, a foot-long metal replica of a kraken lay on its side, its eight segmented arms waving about and tentacles limp, looking as pathetic as a beetle turned upside down.

Eben bit back his laugh, studying her face again. So that was it. She'd been angry at him often enough, but this time it had naught to do with him. He might as well not have even been here for all of the attention she turned his way. And given her dislike for the project, he'd have expected her to crow over her failure, but she was right pissed off that her prototype hadn't worked.

His practical, careful Ivy apparently had an artist's temperament.

"I had a friend at university who looked much the same when he couldn't find a rhyme for his poetry."

"Like a dying privy louse?"

Eben barked out a laugh. "I was speaking of your expression, not your kraken."

She snarled. He'd never wanted to kiss her so badly. Deliberately, he added fuel to her fire.

"It couldn't swim?"

"You've got eyes, don't you? Do you see it swimming about?" Disgusted, she pushed to her feet and dunked her arm into the tank.

His amusement fled. His heart jumped into his throat. Grabbing her waist, he hauled her back.

"Damn it, woman, that squid will . . ." He trailed off, staring at her gray hand dripping water.

The squid would do absolutely nothing to her.

She whipped around and stared at him as if he were a lunatic. Her brows drew together. She opened her mouth, then shook her head, pushing past him. "I can't reach the bleeding thing unless I stick my head in, anyway."

Eben turned to watch her. Muttering, she rummaged through shelves, pushing around Kleistian jars, tossing aside small gears and cylinders, and emerging with a coil of copper wire and an influence machine, its glass disks sealed inside a vacuum bell. Setting the machine next to the tank, she pushed up her wet sleeve and began wrapping the wire around her forearm. When she glanced at him, he saw curiosity had replaced her temper.

"You attended a university?"

"Yes."

A wistful expression softened her features. *Oh, hell.* Something in his chest tightened. He wanted to tell her that he'd hated every moment of society's rigid confinement and the blasted rules, but compared to the Horde, Manhattan City had been a bastion of freedom. So he only told her, "My parents disapproved of my choice of profession—both surgery and the navy. The only tolerable ship was a passenger ship, and it was best if you owned it."

"And now you are neither surgeon nor aboard a naval ship. Do they approve of you now?"

"They disowned me." And he still wasn't certain whether it had been because he'd remained on Trahaearn's ship, or because he'd voluntarily infected his body with nanoagents. Belief that the bugs would spread from person to person and eventually change them all into zombies still held strong through much of the New World; his family had been no exception.

"Disowned?" Ivy's brow had creased.

"They no longer claim me as their son."

"Oh." With pursed lips, she looked down at her arm, wrapped from her elbow to her wrist in copper wire. "I suppose I should not like it if my child became a pirate, either."

He grinned. *Their* child wouldn't be. "I consider myself a merchant."

"Do you attack other ships and steal their cargo?"

Unfortunately often. "Yes."

"Do you kill people?"

Also too often. "Yes."

"Then you're a Captain Cutthroat," she said, turning to crouch beside the influence machine. "Come and spin this."

His instincts bristled at the command. He squashed his first response before it left his mouth. His ankle was too stiff to crouch easily, but he sank slowly to his heels while Ivy attached two clamps to the long trailing wires coming off her arm. She fixed the connecting clamps to the nodes of the influence machine, then pointed to the handle that spun the disks, generating the static charge.

"Spin it fast."

Somewhat bemused, he began. The wheel clicked, the

metal plates attached to the glass disks rotating past the discharge brushes and collection combs. Ivy tapped the fingers of her left and right hands together, as if testing.

"Faster," she said.

The clicking became a whir. After a moment, her fingertips seemed to stick before she pulled them apart. She flattened the hand of her copper-encircled arm against the front of the tank. The metal kraken inside suddenly tilted and skidded across the bottom. It smacked into the thick glass opposite her palm.

"By da Vinci's blessed pen!" Eben couldn't contain his astonishment. His hand faltered on the handle.

"Don't stop spinning." Slowly, she began to slide her hand up the side of the tank. The kraken followed, as if glued to her palm. "If the current fails, she'll drop straight to the bottom again."

And she'd just made her arm into the most powerful magnet he'd ever seen, Eben realized. When the kraken was almost to the top, she reached over the glass with her opposite hand and plucked the machine out of the water. Eben stopped spinning and reached for the clamps.

She pulled away. "Mind the wire—it's blazing hot. Take this instead."

The wriggling kraken landed in his palm. He looked for the stop mechanism and didn't see one.

"How is this powered?"

Ivy began unwrapping the copper wire. "Electrostatic machines. When I have the mechanical flesh, it needs electrical input—but for now they're to power the propulsion pumps." When he looked at her blankly, she said, "The squid moves by squirting out water."

"Like puncturing an airship's balloon pushes it the opposite direction?"

"Much like." Her lips twisted. "It won't work when the squid is metal. It's too heavy."

"Kraken are armored."

"They have an armored *shell*. They aren't metal all the way through."

"Find a way to make it work, Ivy."

Temper reddened her cheeks, but if she snapped at him, Eben didn't hear a word she said. He'd found the hatch that opened the kraken's body, and was staring inside at three tiny automatons, each nothing more than a couple of gears and metal pegs made to resemble legs. They pedaled influence machines, the whir audible.

Jesus Christ. Everyone who came out of the Blacksmith's guild was skilled, but the short time she'd worked on this suggested a talent beyond anything he'd seen. Each arm and tentacle meticulously crafted, she'd created a near perfect, watertight submersible. Even something nonfunctional like this would fetch a hefty price in London or the New World, where automatons and clockworks were all the rage. Within a month or two, she could have been living like a queen anywhere she chose to go—yet she'd been creating egg-crackers and singing birds for a town that couldn't afford them.

The night she'd fled London, Eben had visited the Blacksmith, who'd said she'd already paid for her arms. Knowing how much Barker still owed for his leg, Eben hadn't understood how it was possible; looking at the automatons now, he suddenly did. The work she'd done for the Blacksmith must have brought him a fortune.

Yet she only had one damn coin. "What the hell were you doing in Fool's Cove?"

"Hiding from you."

His gaze snapped up, but she'd turned toward her worktable. His heart beat sickeningly for a few long seconds.

"And Netta's husband was killed when a steamcoach boiler exploded in Port Fallow. Netta and I pooled our resources, and we made it as far as Fool's Cove." She tossed the coil of wire onto a hook. "What did you come here for, Captain Machen. A progress report?"

For you. Like a lovesick fool. And now he found the flimsiest excuse to stay a little longer.

"No," he said gruffly. "My Achilles tube."

She hesitated for an instant, and he realized she hadn't forgotten, as he'd assumed. She'd delayed it, hoping to use it later—perhaps after her coins were gone.

Then he'd be damned if he left without her repairing it. She had one denier left. Tonight would be the last she kept him from touching her.

After a long second, she nodded and took the kraken from him, gesturing to his foot. "Remove your boot, then."

He did, without glancing down at the prosthetic. Though steel, the skeletal leg appeared thin and weak. He hated looking at it.

Ivy crouched behind him. "Brace your weight on your left leg. You'll lose your balance when I take this out," she said, and he heard her fingers loosening a bolt. "How did this happen?"

"Shark."

She gave a snort of disbelief. "What did you do—go swimming with one?"

"Yes."

She yanked out the pneumatic, wrenching his leg backward. Struggling to keep upright, he braced his hand on the worktable.

Cheeks flushed, she stood in front of him, the cylinder pointed at his face. "You're not that foolish. And I hope you don't think I'm foolish enough to believe that."

"No," he said. "I don't think that. But it's the truth."

She stared at him, as if waiting for him to explain, and finally turned away. He watched her rigid shoulders as she worked over the cylinder. A moment later, she was crouching next to him again, screwing the pneumatic back into place. Eben retrieved his boot, hauled it on. When he turned back to her, she was standing with her jaw set and her hand out.

"I'm not a member of your crew, Captain. And every man from this ship who has come to me for repairs has walked away without paying. No more."

The men Yasmeen had sent to Fool's Cove with their damned embellished stories. "Ivy, if I'd have known where you were, I'd have come to you myself."

Her lashes flickered, but other than that, she didn't move. Just held out her hand, waiting.

He wouldn't pay her in coin. Not when she'd use it to keep him away. But he only had one other thing that she'd want. Reluctantly, he dipped his fingers into his watch pocket and withdrew the bent iron disk he'd carried with him for two years. He placed it in her palm.

Her lips parted as she stared down at the ruined flange that had once been her elbow. A bullet had smashed into the center, filling in the hole and protruding like a mushroom cap through the other side.

"I was wearing it on a cord around my neck. The bullet still knocked me overboard." He tapped his hand against the side of his leg. "That's when the shark took it."

Her fingers closed over the iron piece. Her shining gaze lifted to his. "Thank you."

For the explanation or for returning the flange, he wasn't sure. He only knew that if he stayed any longer, nothing would stop him from kissing her. He left—and was amidships before he realized his right foot was moving as smoothly as his left, and he hadn't thought to thank her in return.

Ivy didn't know how long she sat holding the flange, staring at the plans on her worktable. Her mind was filled with stories: of a ruthless pirate who attacked passenger ships and made slaves of the crew . . . of a ship's surgeon hung over the side of a boat.

He'd asked her not to speak of that, and she'd assumed he wanted to hide the madness of defying his captain—perhaps to keep his crew from doing the same. But how could that be? Everyone knew that part. Now she wondered if he didn't want them to know he'd done it trying to save members of the crew, because that would make him seem soft.

Or perhaps he didn't want her to speak of it, because she might learn that he'd lied.

Of only one thing, she was certain: Lady Corsair had known she was in Fool's Cove, but Mad Machen hadn't. Ivy absolutely believed that he'd have come after her, just as he'd threatened in London.

Every other story, however . . . she simply didn't know what to believe.

With a sigh, she rubbed her forehead, trying to push away the ache. She turned her head to study the squid's tank. Its movements were a thing of beauty, but no matter how hard Mad Machen wished it, she couldn't simply do the same with metal. If she had something to counter the weight, perhaps, and give it buoyancy—and the buoyancy would have to vary, depending upon the depth needed. She'd never seen such a device, but it would be necessary for the right effect. It couldn't just be something that floated. A kraken always forced to float on its side wouldn't be terrifying; it would simply look dead.

Of course, that begged the question: how many sailors had actually *seen* a kraken, and knew whether it looked right or not? Surely the nightmare of one was worse than the reality.

Shaking her head, she glanced at the other fish in the tank. The small herring seemed to have no trouble remaining at one depth while still. A few weren't moving, yet they didn't sink or float to the surface. How?

And if she discovered how, could she replicate it?

Her heart gave a wild thump. She returned to the worktable . . . and gave the plans a quarter turn. *Oh, blue.* This could work.

No. This *would* work.

It was well after dark when Ivy finally made her way topside, but when she came up the ladder to the upper deck, she saw that Mad Machen hadn't retired to his cabin yet, either. He stood on the quarterdeck, his feet braced, his hands clasped behind his back. She climbed the stairs and joined him at the balustrade.

Standing close to him, she asked quietly, "Does it need to look like the real thing?"

The deck lamps cast feeble light across his expression, but she couldn't mistake his smile. "Give it giant eyes and tentacles, Ivy, and the rest won't matter."

Good. Hugging herself against the cold, she looked out over the water. The moon was full, throwing silver across the waves. She imagined a tentacle rising up from the surface, the suckers glistening like wet mouths, and gave herself a good scare. Shivering, she glanced back at Mad Machen. He'd been watching her.

"My leg hasn't given me any trouble," he said. "Climbing ladders and stairs is almost as easy as it was before. Thank you."

She nodded, then gasped when he pulled her in against his side, his arm circling her waist. His heat surrounded her. She let herself melt into it, but had to warn him, "I smell like fish."

He laughed quietly against her hair. "Cookie told me that you'd come and cut out fifteen fish bladders—and he asked that you be given galley duty. He said you handled a knife better than a Castilian assassin."

"Thanks to the bugs in the mechanical flesh." She lifted her right hand. Moonlight reflected in her fingernails. "They're so precise, I could engrave my name on a grain of sand . . . if my heart didn't beat, and I didn't breathe. Even I'm not as steady as they are."

"Nothing on a ship is that steady."

Mad Machen was. When he stood like this, big and solid beside her, Ivy felt as if she could lean against him forever and he'd never falter.

"Why are you out here so late?" The last time was when the megalodon had chased them north. Her gaze skimmed the water again. "Was there trouble?"

"No. I was waiting for you."

And her last coin. Ivy's throat tightened, and her heart drummed hard against her ribs. Not since her first day in Port Fallow had she been without any money at all. She'd barely been an hour off the airship when Netta's husband had spotted Ivy's guild tattoo and hired her to repair his cart's steam engine. She'd never had a lot of money, but she'd always had some. She'd always had a tiny bit of security.

Now she'd have none. And what would it gain her? A single day.

Mad Machen withdrew his arm from around her waist, gave her a little push toward the stairs. "Go and ready yourself for bed. I'll wait here until you've finished."

A single day, plus the time it took to prepare for bed. Ivy nodded and headed down. As always, Duckie had hot water ready—perhaps he'd been listening for her to come up from the smithy. The captain's soft soap erased the clinging scent of fish. She brushed her hair until it crackled with enough static to deliver a wiregram, and for the first time, she dressed in a nightgown instead of the trousers she'd been sleeping in. Clutching her last denier, Ivy climbed into bed and waited.

When he came in, she rose up on her knees and held out the coin before she could change her mind.

He smiled faintly, but it faded as he approached. His face darkened. "Your hand is shaking."

"Take it. Please."

"Goddammit, Ivy. I'm not—"

"Please."

His fingers folded over hers. With another curse, he took the coin and turned away.

Ivy sank down, hugging her knees to her chest. She closed her eyes and listened to him undress, to the splash of water and the scrape of a razor. She heard him return to the bed, but as the seconds passed and he didn't lie down beside her, she opened her eyes.

He stared down at her, his chest bare and his face a stark mask. "Earn it back."

Her heart thumping, she sat up. "How?"

The wary note in her voice spread shadows over his expression. He seemed to struggle, his lips paling as they thinned. Ivy fought not to shrink back, sensing that her fear would only make his reaction worse.

After an endless moment, he said gruffly, "You'll kiss me."

Oh. That wasn't so bad, was it? She frowned.

Mad Machen's brows drew together. "What?"

She rose up on her knees again and moved toward the rail. Anticipation fluttered in her stomach. She covered it with a light response. "I'm trying to decide what kissing a man in exchange for money makes me."

"I'm only a denier away from forcing myself on a woman. What does that make me?"

"Cheap," she said, and the warm flush building inside her heightened as he laughed.

His laughter stopped abruptly when she pursed her lips and raised her face to his. He drew back.

"Not a peck. A real kiss, so that you'll have a good taste of me."

Everything inside her tightened. *A good taste.* She knew what he meant. Not just touching lips, but a lick inside his mouth—and he'd taste hers.

Nervously, she wet her lips. Her gaze fell, and a deep hollow ache suddenly opened inside her. His thick erection jutted against his breeches. She wanted to feel him inside her. She wanted *him.* But she didn't dare risk a child, not when the only money she had was being earned with a kiss. Biting her lip, she averted her eyes. No need to look down. His mouth was temptation enough.

"I want inside you, Ivy. I can't deny that. But you don't have to worry that I'll take it beyond a kiss." Mad Machen came forward again, gripping the bed rail. "I'll keep my hands right here. You can touch me wherever you like, but I won't let go of this. Alright?"

"Alright," she whispered.

She scooted closer, until her knees hit the rail. His broad chest rose and fell as quickly as hers, each breath shallow and ragged—then stopping altogether as she pressed her mouth to his.

Oh. Warm and firm, his lips fit perfectly against hers. She waited, remembering how he'd shoved his tongue into her mouth two years ago, how her neck had hurt when he'd forced her head back, but he didn't move. The only sound between them was the creaking of the bed rail as his hands tightened on the wood.

And *her* hands . . . He'd given her permission to touch him, the chest and arms that were an anatomist's dream. Every night as he'd undressed, she'd admired him from across the cabin. Her eyes feasting, her hands empty. No longer.

Spreading her fingers, she slid their tips up the back of his hands, from knuckles to wrist. He breathed in sharply against her lips. The muscles in his forearms strained. Beneath his warm skin, nanoagents raced through his veins so quickly—as if his heart pounded. Hers did, too. His biceps bunched beneath her palms, and shook with effort, as if he carried a great weight rather than holding himself still. She parted her lips, and he froze, rigid as metal. But not beneath his skin. His blood raged like fire, nerves snapping with sensation, nanoagents enhancing it all and pulsing their messages to her fingers.

She tasted him—and suddenly she couldn't concentrate on her hands, only the heat of his mouth. Hunger wound inside her, tight as a spring. Again, she licked between his lips, searching. She couldn't define his flavor, not something she'd had before but just was *him*, slick and hot, and she wanted more.

Wrapping her arms around his neck, Ivy pulled herself higher, closer. Her nipples felt like small, tight rivets, and rubbing their tips against his hard chest started a throbbing ache between her legs.

Then Mad Machen kissed her back, his tongue sliding against hers, and the need burst through her. Her hands buried in his hair, nails digging into his scalp, the electrical storm of his mind like an ecstatic vibration against her fingers. She moaned low in her throat. His arms came around her waist, hauling her closer against him. Ivy kissed him deeper, loving the feel of him, the ache, the taste. All of it. This was worth more than a denier. She couldn't imagine any amount of coin that could match this.

He abruptly stilled. Chest heaving, he pulled away and looked down at his hands, his expression dark.

He'd forgotten, she realized. He'd forgotten that he'd promised not to let go of the rail.

So had she.

"You'll remember tomorrow," she said, her breath coming in pants.

His gaze lifted to hers. His slow grin made her want to leap over the rail into his arms again. She held steady.

"Tomorrow," he echoed.

"Yes." She moved back to make room for him. "The same trade."

And maybe tomorrow she'd get farther than his biceps.

"The same trade." This time, his echo sounded strangled. He stared at her for a long minute. "God help me."

Ivy took that as a "yes."

SIX

Six days later, Ivy lay panting in Mad Machen's narrow bed, hoping that he would pray for her, too. In all her life, the only name she'd invoked for help was the legendary Leonardo da Vinci's, whose war machines had halted the Horde's progression out of Asia and into Europe for almost fifty years. But da Vinci couldn't help her. He'd been dead for centuries. Mad Machen . . . very definitely . . . was not.

And he was as hideously clever.

She turned her head, confirming the pale sunlight streaming in through the gallery windows. Only half an hour ago, she'd been in the crow's nest, looking through the biperspic lenses toward Britain's western shores, pointing out other sails on the horizon. They didn't have to search for Meg here—fed by a warm Atlantic current, these waters weren't cold enough for the giant sharks or the kraken. She'd been thinking of that when she'd skylarked down to the quarterdeck, but Mad Machen hadn't met her with his usual grin. He'd picked her up and swung her facedown over his shoulder, and Ivy had only just recovered from her shock when she'd realized that he was taking her to his cabin. And for a short time, she'd been tempted to risk everything.

She hadn't had to. Mad Machen had only been a few steps from the bed when he'd asked, "Won't you pay me to stop?"

Which meant that she'd have to earn her coin back with a kiss.

And so she'd ended up on her back in the bed anyway, fully clothed, Mad Machen's mouth fastened to hers and his hands fisted beside her shoulders. With her legs around his hips and his heavy weight cradled between her thighs, he'd rocked until the needy ache had broken inside her, until she'd cried out as it shattered her hunger and rattled Ivy to the core. Then his mouth had become slow and languid on hers, as if he'd taken the wet heat from between her legs and alchemized her arousal into a kiss.

Once again, she'd been tempted to risk everything—and once again, she hadn't had to. Mad Machen had only just lifted his head when Duckie had knocked at the door, calling through that Barker needed him topside.

And so now she lay alone, wishing for someone to whom she could pray. Only two days remained of their journey—and twenty days to return. She could not hold out. With every hour, her hunger for him became its own desperation, and she would not take a risk simply because she *wanted* . . . but this desire had become something more like *need*, instead.

Turning away from the windows, she buried her face in her hands. She knew the danger of this, could remember so clearly Netta's grief and devastation when she'd lost her man. If Ivy carried on in this manner, she'd be returning to Fool's Cove the same way. She needed to find some defense, because her fear of Mad Machen had not proven to be enough of one. Two weeks on his ship, and she'd seen little to justify his reputation. He could be hard and gruff and uncompromising, but not once had she witnessed any cruelty.

Now she risked more than a child. And she didn't even need to take him inside her body to risk her heart.

With a sigh, she sat up—and was almost thrown out of the bed as *Vesuvius* canted steeply to port. Ivy grabbed the rail, suddenly realizing that the shouts and running footsteps on the deck above weren't from the usual shift change. They came more often, were more urgent, and Mad Machen's voice rose above the rest. *Oh, blue.*

She leapt to the deck just as someone knocked at the door. Duckie waited outside the cabin, his face flushed and eyes wide. Beyond him, men hurried about, climbing rigging and hauling line.

"Miss Blacksmith, the captain requests that you follow me to the engine room. Mr. Leveque needs your assistance."

No, Leveque didn't. The engine room was simply the most secure location on the ship. She nodded. "Lead the way, Mr. Cooper."

She walked beside him down the passageway leading from beneath the quarterdeck. As soon as she emerged, Ivy glanced up. Standing at the balustrade, a grim-faced Mad Machen met her eyes before tipping his head toward the ladder that would take her below. She didn't argue, but paused for an instant at the ladder's head, looking forward.

They were sailing toward a sinking ship. Almost as large as *Vesuvius*, her masts tilted drunkenly forward, the bowsprit almost parallel with the waterline.

Ivy's heart lurched. Were they going to help it—or attack it?

Duckie called up from the lower deck. "Miss Blacksmith!"

She hurried down into pandemonium. The gun captains shouted orders, directing teams of men who shoved cannons toward open gunports. Boys raced about, placing buckets of water near the guns, spreading sand on the deck. Men began tying their neck scarves around their ears, and instinctively, Ivy covered hers.

She followed Duckie down another ladder, and the next deck was marginally quieter. Ivy shouted, "Why the cannons? That ship is foundered!"

Duckie shook his head. "It's a slavers' trick!" he shouted. "They took the captain in once—they won't get him again. Quickly, Miss Blacksmith!"

He raced along the passageway to the engine room, and Ivy hurried after him, her mind spinning. She'd heard something like this before. Aboard the airship that had taken her to Fool's Cove, the crew had been abuzz with reports of ships that used inflatables to lift their stern. When another ship answered their signals for help, the crew was ambushed and boarded, passengers taken as slaves. But like the tales of clockwork armies in Europe and tribes of warrior women in South America, like the stories about giant worms on the Russian steppes, or humans that the Horde had bred to animals—no one had actually seen it for themselves or known someone who had, and so Ivy had dismissed it.

She wouldn't have believed Mad Machen if he'd told her, either.

Duckie pounded on the engine room door, yelling a stream of French. She heard locks opening from the other side, then Leveque poked his balding head out. He smiled at Ivy and gestured her in.

Quietly, he sat at a small desk and picked up a pipe, puffing out rings of blue smoke. The expensive scent of tobacco filled the room. The engine lay silent. Around them, the hull creaked. Fewer boots trampled the deck above, as if all the men were in position and waiting.

Her heart leapt as a cannon fired, a single shot followed by a muffled cheer. Leveque spoke, and though she didn't understand anything he said, she gathered by his tone that he was telling her everything would be alright.

She'd have to take his word for it.

Only twenty minutes passed before Leveque stood and moved to the door. She looked at him wonderingly, and when he pulled a white kerchief from his pocket and waved it, she understood: the other ship had surrendered.

He unlocked the door and, with a bow, gestured her through ahead of him.

On the main gun deck, the men hadn't stood down from their positions, though they'd obviously relaxed. Several wiped the sweat from their faces and necks with their scarves. Others laughed and talked quietly. Ivy climbed the ladder to the upper deck, emerging amidst a cluster of Mad Machen's men armed with pistols and swords. Their eyes were trained starboard, and Ivy followed the path of their gaze. Her stomach lurched.

Mad Machen stood at the rail, holding a man by his neck over the side. His face purpled, the man struggled for air, clutching at Mad Machen's wrist. His ship floated fifteen feet from *Vesuvius*'s side, grapplings and gangways stretching across the distance. That single cannon shot must have destroyed the inflatable, sending the stern crashing back to the surface. Both the mizzenmast and main had broken, the heavy timbers fallen aft, sails and lines trailing in the water behind the ship. At least a hundred men had been gathered on the decks—the ship's crew, Ivy realized.

Mad Machen's deep voice was loud enough to carry to the other ship, and full of deadly threat. "I ask you a final time, Captain. Which of these men is your employer?"

When the captain waved his hand, Mad Machen brought him in. Falling to his knees on the deck, the mercenary gasped for air and wheezed, "The . . . hold. With . . . the cargo."

Mad Machen's face darkened, and for an instant, Ivy thought he would kill the man. But he turned away from him, calling out, "Mr. Areyto, lead your men across and secure the hold. All men with bugs remain on *Vesuvius* until she's clear."

"Aye, Captain."

Eyes wide, Ivy watched the master-at-arms step onto the gangway while half of his men lined the rail with weapons aimed toward the other deck. Why only those who weren't infected? They weren't as strong, wouldn't heal as quickly.

A sudden murmur ran through the men surrounding her. Mad Machen shouted, "Hold! Return, Mr. Areyto."

Ivy strained to see what had caught their attention. But there were only the men standing on the other deck, unmoving . . . some of them unnaturally rigid. The ship lifted on a swell. Several men toppled over, as if they were stiff boards caught in a wind.

As if their bugs had been frozen.

Horror crawled up from her belly. Ivy stifled her whimper, trying to push away the memory of lying in her bed, of hands prodding at her body.

On the other ship, a man slowly climbed up onto the deck. Blond and handsome, his skin as tanned as Mad Machen's, he held a bloody knife in his right hand and a gleaming metal box topped by a spike in his left.

No—not a spike, Ivy realized. *A miniature tower.* Her gaze flew back to his face, to his pale hair. But this man wasn't one of the Horde.

He began walking toward the rail, smiling. "Perhaps you will kill me, Captain Machen, but the Black Guard will endure. We will never be defeat—"

A loud crack rent the air. In a burst of red, the man's forehead exploded. Ivy jolted back into one of the crew, her hands flying up to cover her shriek. The men steadied her.

Mad Machen lowered his pistol and looked aft. "Retrieve the device and shut it down, Mr. Areyto. Mr. Barker, call for the surgeon—" He broke off as his gaze met Ivy's. She stared at him, hands clasped over her mouth. With a rough note in his voice, he continued, "And ask him to meet me in the hold."

A chorus of *Aye, Captain* sounded. Ivy stumbled back to the port rail, and was sick over the side.

When the last person had been unchained and led—or carried—out of the hold, Eben returned topside. He glanced across the water at *Vesuvius*'s decks. He wasn't surprised to see that some of the men and women the Black Guard had meant to sell as slaves had remained above decks, lifting their faces to the sun. He wasn't surprised that Ivy had gone.

It didn't matter. He could still see her. Her white face and the horror in her eyes were etched in his memory—as was her rush to vomit over the side.

Why the bloody hell did she have to come above decks *then*?

He found the ship's captain on the quarterdeck. The man took one look at Eben's expression and paled.

Eben felt no pity for him. "Order your men to lower the launches. You have ten minutes to abandon ship. Make certain that you, Captain, are the last one into the boats, or my master-at-arms will shoot you off the ladder."

The captain's face flushed. Forgetting his fear, he sputtered with indignation. Eben cut him off.

"Ten minutes." He turned toward the rail. His crew had already hauled all but one gangway back to *Vesuvius*. "I suggest you pull hard for shore. Word is, a kraken hunts these waters."

He crossed over to *Vesuvius*. Barker met him at the rail. Quietly, the quartermaster said, "The bastard gutted more than a few. The bugs are slowing the bleeding, but Jannsen says he needs more hands or he'll lose half of them."

The surgeon had too much experience with the Black Guard's last-minute vengeance to be mistaken. Eben nodded and started toward the ladder.

Barker called after him, "And the ship, sir?"

"Ten minutes." Eben began rolling up his sleeves. "Then blow her out of the water."

SEVEN

Mad Machen's crew had done this before. Those who weren't still manning the starboard cannons rushed about the lower deck, clearing space for more than fifty newcomers. Pallets went down for those too weak or with too many prosthetics for a hammock. Boys distributed clear broth, holding the cup for those who needed it. Ivy commandeered linens and hot water, and started in cleaning wounds and repairing damaged prosthetics—broken so that they couldn't use the tools to escape the chains—and listening to their stories.

Most had come from London slums: areas of Southwark, usually, but Ivy wasn't surprised to hear a few name Limehouse, which included the Blacksmith's territory. From London, they'd been smuggled west and held until the ship had come, then loaded aboard at night.

But they hadn't all been taken from London. And although the others spoke in accents too heavy for Ivy to decipher, their pulverizing hammers, drills, and shovels told her just as well—they were all coal miners, likely taken from the colliers in Wales. The Horde had gone, but the men still needed to work, and they'd kept the equipment grafted to their bodies.

That same equipment made them more valuable to the New World slavers.

But not all of them would have been laborers; some had been headed for the skin-trade. And looking at the emaciated women and boys, Ivy understood that she hadn't been too skinny for them to take, as she'd always thought: her guild tattoo had kept her safe. Even the Black Guard, whoever they were, knew better than to cross the Blacksmith.

But the Black Guard must have angered him . . . because the Blacksmith was helping Eben build a monster designed to frighten and destroy them.

And bless the bright stars—so was Ivy.

Midnight had long passed before Eben finally left sick bay. For the first time, he hoped that Ivy had already fallen asleep. Everything inside him was scraped raw. He couldn't bear it if she looked at him in fear and horror again.

The sliver of yellow light beneath his cabin door dashed his hope. He girded his heart before entering.

He expected to find her by the gallery windows, but she sat in her nightgown at the dining table, frowning down at the pieces of the Black Guard's freezing device. She'd wound her hair around her head like a crown, each braid a coppery red in the soft glow of the lamp. Shadows formed half circles below her eyes.

She glanced up at him, her solemn gaze lingering on the blood staining his shirt. Stiffly, he turned toward the bureau to change and wash. He heard her sigh.

"This device isn't like anything I've ever seen," she said. "The power source—it's a battery, but I'd need a thousand Kleistian jars to equal a few seconds of activation. And the circuitry, and these . . . these . . . I don't know *what* they are. It's like looking at a nanoagent. Somehow, commands are being processed, and I don't know *how*."

The last word came out muffled. Eben turned, saw that she'd put her hands over her face. She drew deep, steadying breaths. "The Blacksmith might know," she added quietly.

"We'll send it to him."

Opening her hands, she looked at him through the brackets of her palms. "It's Horde technology. But that man wasn't Horde."

"No," Eben said. "None of the Black Guard have been."

Ivy studied him for an endless moment. Then she nodded and stood, gathering the pieces into a small bin. "You were in the surgery a long time."

"We lost two," he said gruffly.

"I heard. I'm sorry." Her searching gaze swept over him again. "Did you eat?"

"Yes."

With her nightgown skimming the floor, she walked to the bed and lay down. When she awoke tomorrow, *Vesuvius* would be anchored near Trahaearn's estate, and she'd be heading ashore to build the kraken. And although Eben had intended to stay with her, now he'd be sailing into the port at Holyhead, returning those who the slavers had abducted from Wales, and then on to London. He'd be away from her for almost a month.

Christ. For two weeks, he'd done everything possible to show Ivy he wasn't a monster. One day had ruined all of that—and as soon as she left his ship, he'd have no way to prevent her from running.

Again.

His heart heavy, he finished cleaning off the sweat and blood. He looked toward the bed, then snuffed the lamp so that if she turned away from him, at least he wouldn't see it.

But as soon as his head hit the pillow, she curled against his side and laid her cheek over his heart. His throat tightened. Eben stared up into the dark, trying to remember any moment in his life when a single action had affected him more. He couldn't.

By God, he loved her.

And he'd kiss her now, if she would just give him the denier that they'd passed back and forth the past week. He waited, wondering if she held it in her hand—but he could feel her left palm flat against his arm, her fingers gently stroking his biceps, and her right was tucked loosely beneath her chin.

"You forgot the coin."

"No." Her warm breath whispered over his chest. "I know you'd never force me."

He couldn't respond for almost a full minute. Then he said, "I wish you'd figured that out *after* you'd earned your denier back." Her laugh left him as full and light as an airship. "Tell me, Ivy: do I have to pay for a kiss?"

"I should charge you five hundred gold sous. I'm furious with you."

She had an odd way of showing it. "I know what shooting that bastard looked like. But—"

"Not him. Good riddance to him, the murdering bum-chute." She lifted her head. His eyes had adjusted to the reflected moonlight coming in through the windows; there was no mistaking her fierce expression as she looked down at him. "I'm speaking of how you let me think you were stealing cargo and killing men. You didn't mention that the cargo you stole was people, and the men were slave handlers."

And that painted a fine picture of him. But as much as he'd have liked to leave her with that impression, he couldn't. "I've still killed plenty of men, Ivy. The seas aren't kind to anyone, and the jobs I take on for Trahaearn are usually the ones nobody else wants, because it puts a target on my ship. There's been many a time that I've had to shoot first—and I can't regret any of them. It just happens that in the past two years, I've been shooting at the Black Guard."

She was silent, taking that in. Finally she asked, "What do they want?"

"I don't know. They've always got a man on the ships they hire, but every time I've run into one, I've either had to kill him, or he kills himself after reciting the same speech that slave handler started up today. But I can tell you how they're financed."

Ivy beat him to it. "Selling slaves."

"Yes. To the Ivory Market, or the Lusitanian mines in Appalachia."

"Blue." Her forehead dropped to his chest. "That night in London, they came into my room. I thought they were the Horde."

Good Christ. And Eben wouldn't have known that she was gone. The thought of it opened a hollow pit in his chest.

"Duckie said they tricked you," she added.

Damn that boy. "He shouldn't have. It doesn't do me any good for people to know that I was taken in."

She lifted her head. Humor lightened her expression. "It damages your reputation?"

"Yes." Eben didn't mind Ivy knowing the truth. He trusted her. But it still put a dent in his pride. "That reputation keeps my ship safe—but Duckie probably thought you already knew."

"How would I?"

"Because it happened when I was looking for you." When she frowned, he said, "I returned to the Star Rose that morning, and I assumed you ran to another ship. Searching from port to port would have been impossible. But Trahaearn owns those docks, and keeps a record of every ship docking and leaving—and a destination for most. I got that list, and tracked them all down."

Her mouth had fallen open.

"So when I came up on that foundered ship . . . hell, I'd planned to board her anyway. Except it wasn't you in the hold, and I stayed down there for a good bit of time with the others they'd taken from London. Duckie was one of them. Chained up right next to me."

"Truly?" At his nod, she asked, "How did you get out?"

"They'd told Barker not to follow or they'd kill me—but if I don't pay Barker, then he can't pay the Blacksmith. He took the risk of following."

"What'd they do?"

"Try to kill me. When Barker sailed in close, they counted on him slowing down to collect my body. So they took me topside, shot me in the chest, and I went over. I was just at *Vesuvius*'s hull when the shark took my leg."

Her hand flattened over his heart. "My elbow really did save you."

In more ways than one. He'd held on to her small flange in that stinking hold, his only thought of escaping and continuing to search for her. But he hadn't. He'd gone after the slavers instead.

"I caught up with them—and that's when I first heard of the Black Guard. The slave handler on that ship had been one, too."

"Before you killed him?"

"Yes. And stranded most of the crew."

Her gaze was troubled—but not by the fate of the slavers' crew. "Have there been so many taken?"

"Probably more. I only found them because I went looking. Most of them don't come through London—Trahaearn watches his docks too closely, and most of the mercenaries the Black Guard hires are too afraid of him to risk it. So the majority of the people taken have been smuggled out of Wales and Cornwall."

"But Trahaearn's the Duke of Anglesey. He has holdings in Wales. They aren't scared of him there?"

"It's easier to smuggle along the coast than the Thames." But he agreed, "It damages his name that they're doing it under his nose—even if he's in London."

Realization slowly spread across her features. "I see."

He smiled a little. "Do you?"

"Yes. Scaring sailors and tearing ships apart—but above all, keeping the mercenaries too afraid to approach the coast. Whose idea was the kraken?"

"It was mine." He didn't mention that he'd been drunk at the time. Trahaearn had liked the idea well enough.

"And who is paying for it?"

His grin broadened. "The Iron Duke."

"So this is all about you and the Iron Duke destroying the Black Guard?"

"Just taking one source of their money. They'll no doubt find another."

"And then?"

He pictured the people in the hold of that first ship—and all of them that had come after. "Then I'll find them again."

"But with the Horde gone, Britain has a navy again. Why can't they—"

"Because after two hundred years, the navy is nothing but

muscle for the Manhattan City merchants." Pirates in fancy uniforms. "And the people being taken are too poor to matter to them—and they've no interest in patrolling this coast."

"So you're going to do their job with a monster."

"Yes." But he needed to tell her, "The crew doesn't know about the kraken, Ivy. Barker does—but the others, they assume we're being paid by Trahaearn to recover his people, and I'm in it for the money. And I can't afford them or anyone else thinking I've gone soft."

"And so that's the reason behind the stories." She studied his face. "*Have* you gone soft?"

"The crews of the Black Guard's mercenary ships wouldn't think so."

"No, they wouldn't," she said quietly, and he knew she was thinking of the slave handler he'd shot, of the barrage of cannon fire that had destroyed the ship. Looking into his eyes, she lifted her hand to his jaw. His heart sledgehammered against his ribs.

"One denier," she said. "And I'll kiss you."

Anticipation became tearing pain—and anger. He still had to pay?

By God, he wouldn't. He'd take the kiss and every goddamn thing he wanted from her, and she'd beg for more.

He let himself imagine it, only for a second. Then the red haze cleared from his vision and he saw her pale face, her rounded eyes. Fear? *Christ, no.* But he didn't know what his expression had shown her—and he didn't know what she thought when she looked at him. He only knew he had to put some distance between them.

"Eben," she said.

He tried to shrug her off as he sat up, but she clung to him, her strong fingers clamped over his shoulders. "Move away, Ivy."

"Eben."

His name. For the first time, his name. He stopped, met her searching gaze.

"I don't mean to—" She cut herself off, and started again. "I need a limit. Something tangible. Something that prevents us from taking this beyond a kiss . . . or very far beyond it."

He struggled to take in her meaning. "You want to set terms—and back them up with the denier?"

"Yes."

"Why?"

"Because if we make an agreement, you'll honor it. And I can't afford . . . I can't *risk* more." Her gaze dropped to his mouth, and a wistful note softened her voice. "No matter how tempted I am."

Risk? What did she risk by—

Oh, hell. Eben closed his eyes. God, what a fool he was. Under Horde rule, only one result came from a coupling between a man and a woman, and most didn't remain together afterward. Then the child would be taken and raised in a crèche.

But Ivy would have kept her child. And when she'd come to *Vesuvius*, she'd only had eight deniers . . . all of which he'd taken.

Quietly, he told her, "I wouldn't risk it either, Ivy. A ship is no place to raise a child, and I'm not a man who'd be content visiting the family I've made four or five times a year. When I return to land permanently, maybe then. Not while I'm out to sea."

"Oh." Confusion furrowed her brow. "You never meant to shag me?"

Eben had to laugh. Of course he had. Even now, hearing that word from her lips left him as hard as a cannon.

"I mean to, Ivy. Every night, and twice in the day. And each time, using a lambskin sheath that will catch my seed."

Disbelief widened her eyes. "You have such a thing?"

"Yes."

When she gave a delighted laugh, he determined to buy a crate more the next time *Vesuvius* put into port.

"And it does not fail?"

He almost lied. Then he admitted, "Yes. But only rarely, Ivy. *Very* rarely."

Her face fell. She looked away from him, biting her bottom lip.

Her disappointment was simultaneously the most heartening and the most torturous response he'd ever witnessed. She wanted him—but she wouldn't risk having him.

Unless Eben convinced her it wasn't a risk at all.

Yasmeen had warned him that Ivy wouldn't know what courting was, and he hadn't forgotten that—but he hadn't truly understood it, either. He'd hoped that she would accept him as a partner. But it would probably never occur to her to imagine him—or anyone—in that position, even if she began to care for him.

He touched her chin, made her meet his eyes. "If it failed, I wouldn't leave you alone, Ivy. I'd come with you to shore. I'd see that you and the baby had everything you needed. And I'd stay with you, always."

Surprise, hope, and doubt warred across her features. "Eben, I think . . ." She trailed off, staring at him, as if searching for an answer within. Whatever she found drooped her shoulders and softened her mouth into a sad curve. "I just don't know."

Though he recognized that her response indicated uncertainty rather than rejection, he had to fight the hollow ache in his chest. Determination soon filled it. She'd already come to believe he was man enough not to force her; she would come to believe he was man enough to care for her, too. Until then, he could pleasure them both without risking a child.

"Let me up, Ivy."

She let him go—reluctantly, he was gratified to see. After lighting the gas lamp, Eben retrieved a heavy gold coin.

Her eyes widened when he placed the coin in her palm. "A sous?"

"I'll only kiss you," he promised, then guided her hand to the juncture of her thighs. With his fingers over hers, he tucked their hands between her legs. He watched her lips part, heard her soft gasp. "But only if I kiss you here."

EIGHT

Oh, blue heavens. As Ivy stared up at him, the pressure of his palm increased until her hand firmly cupped her most sensitive flesh. Wetness seeped through the thin cotton of her nightgown onto her fingers.

Need roughened Eben's voice. "This can be my mouth, Ivy."

And she wanted that kiss beyond measure. Heat unfurled through her belly. She dropped the sous to the mattress, reaching for him. He caught her wrist and tugged her toward the side of the bed.

"Come to the window."

Her choppy breaths, the clank of his foot, and the creak of the ship were the only sounds in the cabin as he led her to the leather armchair. So many times, he'd come in to find her watching the stars. Had he imagined doing *this*?

At his urging, she sat, perching at the edge of the seat. Eben loomed over her, his back to the window. The glow from the lamp cast soft gold over the right side of his face, leaving the other half shadowed. Just to look at him was a pleasure—but her hands would have known him, even in the dark. They'd memorized his lean features, the breadth of his shoulders, every line and hollow of his chest and stomach, packed with muscle.

His gaze burned with intensity. "Lean back, Ivy."

Slowly, she sank deeper into the chair. Her hands slid along the tops of her thighs, a whisper of metal over cotton. When her shoulders rested against the leather back, Eben knelt before her. His fingers caught the hem of her nightgown and began to draw it up to her knees. Ivy shivered.

"Cold?"

A breathless laugh escaped her. *Hardly.* She was burning up from the inside. Cheeks flushed, she felt faint perspiration across her brow, but it didn't soothe the heat building beneath her skin.

She caught the hint of his smile before he bent his head. Her toes curled against the deck. She trembled again when his lips brushed her right knee.

"I need to spread you open for my mouth. But I won't force you."

Oh. Beneath her hands, her thighs were clenched together, as if she was uncertain. She wasn't—and Ivy wanted to be bold. She wanted Eben to know she didn't fear him. Gathering her courage, she let her legs fall apart and opened for him until her knees hooked over the arms of the chair. She hiked her nightgown hem to her waist.

Eben froze, his dark stare fixed on her exposed flesh. Her name came out strangled. "Ivy."

Her courage almost failed. "This isn't what you meant?"

"It is. More than I . . . *God.* You're already wet for me." He suddenly palmed the underside of her thighs as if to hold her open to his hungry gaze. His thumbs stroked the sensitive tendons of her inner thighs. "Do you know what I plan to do now, Ivy?"

He would put his mouth on her. She couldn't imagine any further, but the very thought set her body quivering in anticipation. Her fingers bunched in her nightgown.

"You'll kiss me."

"Yes." His right fingers smoothed into the crease of her thigh and followed it up to her hip. Gasping, Ivy rocked toward him. His hand flattened over her lower belly, holding her in place as his thumb slid through red curls. Gently, he began to circle the slick bud at the apex of her sex. "I'll kiss these pretty pink lips, Ivy. And I'll spread them with my tongue and lick inside you, tasting you all over."

Ivy couldn't form a coherent reply. Only panting breaths as his thumb stroked harder, the tip wet now, slippery over her flesh. The maddening circles were both bliss and torment, wringing a moan from deep in her throat.

"Then I'll suck on your clit until you come for me." His voice roughened in response to another tortured moan. "But I'll tell you what I won't do—look at me, Ivy."

Her fingers clenching on the arms of the chair, her thighs trembling, she lifted her gaze. Need had hardened his face, his eyelids heavy as he watched her. His left hand rose, tugging down the neckline of her gown, baring her right breast and tightly budded nipple. Yearning for his touch, she arched into his palm.

He drew his hand away, pinning her right knee against the chair arm. "I won't suckle your sweet tits." His thumb circled faster. "I won't lick every inch of your skin. I won't push your thighs together and guide my cock through your wet slit, pumping my shaft across your clit, making you scream for me to come inside you. I won't fuck you with my fingers and my tongue until you're riding my hand and my mouth. And you won't be touching me, either."

"Eben, please." She didn't know what she wanted. Only that she wanted all of that, and that the tension winding tighter and tighter inside her needed to break. Helplessly, she rolled her hips against his hand. "Please. *Please.*"

"Not until you return to *Vesuvius.*"

His words barely penetrated the fever clouding her mind. Until she returned . . . ?

The shadows on his face deepened. "I won't be with you as you begin building the kraken, Ivy. So I want you to wait for me. Just three weeks. Then I'll join you at Trahaearn's estate—and I'll give you everything you want while you finish your work there, and again on your way back home."

Back home. And before that, almost a month without him. A sharp pain speared through her chest, stealing her breath.

When she didn't reply, his expression darkened. "You'll wait for me." Not a request now, but a harsh command. His thumb stroked harder. Long fingers pushed between her slick folds to press against her opening. Ivy turned her face into her shoulder, gasping. *"You'll wait."*

"Damn you, Mad Machen. Yes!" she burst out. "Now kiss me like you promis—"

He swooped down. Ivy's demand melted into a moan as his hot mouth covered her, tongue sliding over swollen flesh. She cried out, her back arching, her shoulders jammed against the seat back.

"You taste . . . so good." His voice was a growl between licks that ravaged her senses. His fingers tightened on her thighs. "Won't . . . let you go."

Ivy didn't want him to. She reached for him, burying her fingers in his thick hair. His stiffened tongue delved through her folds. His big hands wedged beneath her bottom, lifting her for a deeper kiss.

Blue, blue, blue. Almost sobbing with pleasure, Ivy heard his answering groan. Her hips swiveled of their own accord, and his mouth moved with her, lapping at her clitoris before suckling the tender bud between his lips. His tongue flicked as he drew on her, and Ivy's muscles suddenly locked as she strained toward that shattering precipice. Eben didn't stop, each lick painful now, too much, too intense. Then he suckled again and she broke, crying out as she bucked against his mouth.

His tongue softened. He gently licked her as she came down, then pressed a kiss to her quivering belly. He lifted his head and his gaze ran over her, from her flushed sex to her perspiring face.

"My God, Ivy. You're beautiful."

Did he truly think so? He looked at her as if he did—he was the *only* person who'd ever looked at her like that. She blinked away the stinging in her eyes. "You're suffering from a loss of blood to your brain, Eben."

"So I am." He laughed and dropped another kiss to the inside of her knee. Lifting her still-shaking legs from the arms of the chair, he helped Ivy to her feet. She swayed against him, her belly bumping into his engorged shaft. Eben groaned, closing his eyes. "I'm a fool for saying that you can't touch me until I return. Will you ease me then?"

She wanted to now. "Yes."

"Sweet Ivy." His big hands cupped her jaw, thumbs sweeping over her cheekbones. "I also said I'd only kiss you one time in return for the sous. But if I break my promise and kiss your lips before we sleep, will you forgive me?"

"I won't forgive you if you *don't* kiss me."

Eben grinned as he lowered his head, and she was breathless by the time he lifted her into his arms and carried her to the bed.

When the eighth bell of first watch rang, Ivy opened her eyes. Eben lay quiet beside her, his erection against her hip. Before he could speak, she covered his mouth with a kiss—then took him in hand and stroked until he came, awakening all of *Vesuvius* by shouting her name.

NINE

Six Weeks Later . . .

Autumn had already come to Anglesey; yellow and orange warmed the low, rolling hills in the distance. Eben had thought that the sight of the island's shores would lessen the frustration and dread that had built with every passing day, but when Anglesey appeared on the northern horizon, he was struck by the devastating certainty that Ivy had already gone.

Between weather and repairs that had forced him into dry dock, he'd been delayed too damn long.

Ivy might have worked on the kraken for three weeks, as she'd promised. But he'd forced that promise from her, just as he'd forced her to fix the machine—and why would she have remained in Anglesey for God knew how many months to repair a monster?

She didn't have reason to stay. Although she'd wanted him, she doubted he could take care of her. The damned irony was that by giving her a sous—hoping to show her that he could provide for a family, that he would be generous—he'd offered her an escape route. That much money could take her halfway around the world.

So he'd just have to find her again.

Dread hardening into determination, Eben handed the

telescope over to Barker and braced his hands on the quarterdeck's balustrade.

"Captain!"

The shout came from the crow's nest, where Teppers pointed over the port bow. Eben narrowed his eyes against the sun. The water's calm surface had been disturbed by a small eruption, as if a pocket of air had broken underneath. A few moments later, there was another, almost one hundred yards closer to *Vesuvius*.

He glanced at Barker, holding the telescope to his eye. "Anything?"

Barker shook his head.

Another shout came from the bosun's mate, at the starboard rail amidships. "Captain!"

Eben had only a second to glimpse the enormous dark form just below the surface, a rounded body plated with interlocking iron segments. Another pocket erupted fifty feet from *Vesuvius*'s side, disturbing the water—when it faded to a ripple the creature beneath had gone.

Barker looked to him with wide eyes. "Would Ivy have had time enough to rebuild it?"

"No." And thank God, because otherwise she might have been in the sea with the real thing. "Hold steady on course. Ready the axes."

And pray that they could sail on past it. If the tentacles got hold of them, their only option was to chop away until the kraken let go.

A film of sweat popped out on the quartermaster's brow. Barker nodded and shouted to the crew, "Man the axe stations, and look sharp! Keep your eyes out—"

Terrified shouts sounded from the poop deck. Eben pivoted to look aft. His blood froze.

Dark and glistening, as thick as his waist at the tip, the tentacle rose over the quarterdeck. Plate-sized suckers covered the pale gray underside, the pink flesh seeming to open and close like hungry mouths as the kraken sought prey . . . and it came straight for Eben.

He reached for his weapon—too late. Heavy muscle wrapped his upper body in an unbreakable coil, pinning his arms to his sides. *Jesus Christ.* The oily stink filled his desperate breaths as the tentacle lifted him off his feet. He felt the suckers pulling at his legs, his back. Barker shouted and came at the thick arm with an axe. The blade skidded off the oily skin in a shower of sparks.

Mechanical flesh.

Barker's mouth dropped open. Eben met his gaze for a second, and saw his astonishment reflected in the other man's eyes. *Ivy had done it.*

But what the hell was she doing now?

Eben didn't have time to ask. The tentacle carried him over the side of the ship. He pulled in a final breath before it dragged him beneath the freezing water. The shouts and screams from *Vesuvius* vanished into a swirling, watery quiet. Overhead, *Vesuvius*'s keel formed a long, dark shadow. He looked down into a nightmare.

Ivy's giant machine churned the water below, its enormous staring eyes lit like a furnace. Steam boiled from the tips of the eight arms spread like rays beneath an enormous rounded body, as if the hell inside couldn't be contained. Wrapped in the tentacle, he dove past the plated body, between two arms, toward the underside of the submersible—where a kraken's beak would be. A rounded hatch opened instead, revealing a gaslit chamber. The tentacle shoved him toward it, until his head broke the surface and he hauled in a deep, ragged breath. The tentacle loosened.

Kneeling by the rim in a white shirt and trousers, Ivy laughed and dragged him from the icy water into a steam bath. Eben lay on the metal floor, coughing and sputtering, staring up at her. Red hair was plastered to her head with sweat, her face flushed. She was utterly beautiful.

"Can you breathe?" she asked.

Chest heaving, he nodded. He wasn't sure about talking yet, but—

Ivy bent over, gripping his wet hair to hold him still, and ravished his mouth with a kiss. When she let go, he couldn't speak, breathe—or think. He'd never been so astonished in his life.

She grinned down at him. "Do you think the machine is frightening enough?"

He barked out a laugh, which sent him into another fit of coughing. Patting his back, Ivy looked around.

"Circle beneath *Vesuvius*," she said, and climbed to her feet.

Still catching his breath, Eben rose, shoulders bent to avoid the low ceiling. Three men—one his former blacksmith, Lambert—and two women manned the submersible from seats surrounded by forests of levers, and every surface on the bulkheads and ceiling was packed with valves and controls. A low hiss and the clacking of the four pedaling automatons sounded strangely hollow, as did his voice.

"The heat in here—is it from a steam engine?"

He couldn't hear one, but it might have been shut down. He hoped to God she never fired one, not while in the water.

Ivy shook her head. "Just a boiler and valves to circulate steam around the gas bladders in the arms—and to keep us from freezing."

Eben struggled for some response. What she'd put together here . . . he'd told her to do it, but he hadn't known if *anyone* could. And it was beyond words.

Ivy continued, "It needs a crew of five. Your blacksmith and Trahaearn's steward helped me choose. They can all keep a secret, and know the area well enough to leave the local fishermen and traders alone. And they are each loyal to you or the Iron Duke." She glanced toward a short, blond man looking through a periscope. "I've trained John Davies to take my place."

Eben recognized him. Eight months ago, Davies had been chained in the hold of a slave ship, his arm drill smashed beyond repair.

Davies pushed the periscope up into the ceiling, and turned with his hand extended. "Good to see you again, Captain."

Automatically, Eben shook his hand—then looked down in surprise. It was a prosthetic shaped exactly like a hand, but it wasn't mechanical flesh. Instead, it had been created of interlocking machines, each operating individually to resemble lifelike movement. He could feel the difference in pressure and strength in each of the man's fingers, just as he would if the hand were flesh. If not for the hardness of the metal, Eben wouldn't have known he was gripping a prosthetic. He'd never seen anything like it before.

Davies grinned and lifted his chin toward one of the women.

"My lady, Mary, and I have an ongoing debate. Between this and the kraken, I say this hand is the more amazing. She doesn't agree. And Ivy won't give her opinion, citing bias as the maker."

Eben felt as if he'd been dunked underwater again. He looked to Ivy, who was standing beside one of the crew, checking a valve. "You did this?"

"It was a trade. He needed an arm more than he needed a hook, and I needed his two-seater balloon to get around the island." She glanced over her shoulder and met his gaze. Her green eyes were bright with amusement. "You were gone more than three weeks. I had to do *something*."

And she'd done something . . . incredible. He glanced down at the prosthetic, then around the chamber. *Hell. Beyond incredible.* Though the primary structure of the kraken had remained mostly the same, the modifications she'd made had turned it into *this*. Functioning. Frightening.

Yet she'd been hiding from him in Fool's Cove. He didn't think she would have, now. Her face shone with animation and joy—but also confidence. She'd always been secure in her work. But he thought that she, too, recognized just how amazing her talent was.

How amazing *she* was.

She moved to the hatch in the center of the floor. "Mary, will you bring in the tentacle?"

Eben joined her, looking down into the circle of water. "So I'm to go back?"

"Now you can add surviving a kraken's belly to your reputation." She smiled up at him. "As soon as we've docked, I'll ask Mary to fly me out to *Vesuvius*."

Thank God. The six-week knot of frustration and dread that had built up in him suddenly unwound. He nodded and stepped to the edge of the hatch. Ivy's voice was the last thing he heard before the waters closed over his head.

"I'll see you soon, Captain."

She'd missed him.

Since Mary had flown her out to *Vesuvius* in the two-seater balloon, Ivy hadn't left Eben's side. For weeks, she'd feared something terrible had happened, and had forced herself to keep busy rather than dwell on the worst.

She'd loved showing him what she'd done. She remained with him throughout the day, telling him everything she'd seen on Anglesey, all of the ideas she had for new automatons and machines. He spoke as little as usual, but she could tell that he'd enjoyed being with her.

And she could tell that something was wrong. That there was something new about him—a certain distance, as if he were looking at her through biperspic lenses and seeing her in a new way. It made her nervous, and so she only talked more and more.

By the end of the day, anxiety had taken up residence in her stomach, made worse when he left her alone to wash and prepare for sleep. Now she waited in the bed, her heart pounding, and every passing second felt like another week of not knowing where he was.

She came up on her knees when he returned to the cabin. He smiled when he saw her, but his expression darkened when his gaze fell to her hand, fingers loosely curled to conceal the small package in her palm.

"No." He strode toward the bed, pulling off his jacket and tossing it to the floor. "No more money between us, Ivy. You have my word that I won't take you too far—and you'll trust me on that alone."

"It's not—"

His mouth cut off the rest. Oh, blue—she'd missed this, too. Lifting to him, she wrapped her arms around his neck, opening her lips to his kiss and moaning at the first, heady taste. Relief and hunger roughened Eben's answering groan. He dragged her nightgown up her legs and filled his hands with her bare backside, kneading in time to the thrust of his tongue.

Ivy's head swam. One kiss chased away every thought, and it wasn't until she buried her fingers in his hair and felt the crinkle of parchment against her palm that she recalled what she'd tried to tell him.

With effort, she tore her mouth away. She held him in

place with her hands in his hair, preventing him from lowering his head to hers again. Chest heaving, she tried to catch her breath.

"It's not a coin," she managed between pants. She brought her right hand down, opening her fingers. "I looked through your drawers until I found one. I'm sorry I didn't ask, but I wanted to surprise you."

She'd managed that, at least. He stared down at the square oiled-parchment envelope, the red wax seal broken when she'd glanced inside to confirm the contents. The sheath had been shockingly thin, but pliable, and prepared with clear oil infused with a light fragrance that had reminded her of freshly cut oak.

Eben's burning gaze rose to search her face. "You're certain?"

Her heart pounding, Ivy nodded. And though she *was* certain, she still had to fight to keep her voice steady. "I built a kraken, Eben. Surely I can support a child, no matter where I go when I leave *Vesuvius*. So this is a risk I'm willing to take."

His face seemed to pale. "Where do you intend to go?"

"Since our agreement was that you'd take me home after I fixed the kraken, I'll return to Fool's Cove, first." And she'd promised Netta that she'd come back. Perhaps her friend would like to leave that small town with her. "After that, I don't know."

She didn't want to think beyond that time. Weeks ago, Eben had told her the return voyage would take twenty days. Those days were all she could focus on now. She'd missed him so much, even knowing he would come back. She couldn't imagine how deep the ache would be when she couldn't look forward to his return.

Eben's throat worked as if he had to force himself to swallow. His gaze fell to the sheath again, and a bleak expression moved across his face. Ivy only had a moment to wonder about it before determination firmed his mouth. "Alright, then. Hold on, Ivy."

He gripped the bed rail and hauled back. Ivy grasped his shoulders for support as the mattress suddenly jolted forward several feet. She heard the clacking of gears from inside the platform beneath the bed, and when she glanced back, saw a second mattress rising into the space he'd made.

No, not a second mattress—it was *the other half of the bed.* Her mouth dropped open.

She whipped around to face him. "All this time?"

"Yes." He yanked off his left boot, tossed it to the floor. He hesitated after he pulled off the right, and glanced up at her. "Do you want me to keep my leg covered?"

Oh, heavens. Wordlessly, Ivy held up her metal hands. A smile softened the corners of his mouth. He pressed a kiss to her fingers before cupping her nape and coming in for a long taste of her lips. A moan worked up through her throat, and her need built with each hot stroke of his tongue. Tugging his shirt from his breeches, she rediscovered muscles too long unexplored by her hands.

Her nails scraped over his chest. Eben broke their kiss, his lips tracing a path over her jaw. Heat seared her nerves as he nipped the tender skin above her guild tattoo, soothed it with a lick. She cried out in surprise as he dipped his head to her breast and suckled strongly through the thin nightgown. Her hands shook; her head fell back. The world seemed to spin about, her body the center. Then his right hand skimmed up her inner thigh, and the center shifted and contracted to the rough glide of his skin, the bold caress through her slick folds, the press of his fingers against her entrance. Her nails dug into his shoulders.

He lifted his head and his dark gaze locked on hers. "You'll take me, Ivy. First like this. And when you're ready, you'll take all of me."

"Yes." Anticipation shivered across her skin. "I'm ready now."

"Are you?"

His gaze didn't leave her face as his fingers curled into her. Delicate flesh yielded to his penetration, sending ripples of pleasure beneath her skin. Ivy gasped, her hips rocking forward, her eyes glazing. *Oh, blue heavens.* This was . . . so good.

And not enough. *"More."*

Eben groaned her name, burying his face in her neck. His

fingers stroked deep and slow. "This first time won't go easy. I want you to come like this, so you'll enjoy at least part of it."

She'd love all of it, even if it hurt. But this didn't. Ecstasy was quickly unwinding through her, twisting and loosening with each pump of his hand. She barely felt the slide of cotton down her arms. Then he licked her nipple and all that she could feel was his tongue and his strong fingers, pushing her higher. With a gruff sound of pleasure, he sucked the taut peak into his mouth, his thumb caressed the swollen bud of her sex and she was there, shaking and clenching—and ready for more.

Her hands dove to the front of his breeches. A strangled noise came from his throat, something like *Wait*, but her nimble fingers had already unfastened the buttons and found him, thick and hot in her palms.

"Ivy—"

He broke off as her fingers slid over the wide tip, spreading the drop of his seed. Her gaze lifted to his. "Come into the bed now. Come into *me*."

His throat worked. "Yes."

At his rough reply, she scooted back, pushing the nightgown past her hips and kicking it away. Eben shoved his breeches down and looked up at her. His gaze stilled on her legs, jumped to her breasts, and fell to the curls between her thighs before rising to her face.

"You take my breath, Ivy."

And he would make her cry if he didn't stop that. Reaching forward, she drew him to her—skin to skin, for the first time. He lay at her side, his mouth finding hers, his hands stroking her back toward the edge. She trembled with need as he unwrapped the sheath, smoothing it over his heavy shaft. Finally, he settled between her spread thighs, elbows braced beside her shoulders, and looked down at her.

Sweat sheened his skin, dark gold by the light of the gas lamp. He brushed a stray hair back from her forehead. "Tell me if it becomes too painful. I swear to God, I'll stop."

She could feel him, the blunt tip wedged between her slick folds. Anticipation was driving her insane. "I ache now."

His mouth lowered to hers. "Then take me."

The muscles in his back flexed beneath her hands. Pressure built at her entrance, followed by tearing pain. By the starry sky—it *did* hurt. Biting back a scream, she turned her head, squeezing her eyelids shut. Eben gently kissed her cheeks and her lips; his cock split her in half below. He murmured her name, sipping away the tears gathering at the corners of her eyes. And still he drove deeper, until she felt as if a heated piston had been grafted inside her.

He finally stopped, his hips pinning hers and her thighs open wide, the weight of his upper body supported on his forearms. "Ivy?"

She couldn't look at him. Only moments before, she'd begged for this. Now she just wanted him to get on with it and then get off her.

"Have you finished?"

"No." He kissed the corner of her mouth. "We'll wait a few minutes while your bugs heal you up around me. You won't have to go through that again."

"Good." The burning pain had faded. Now she was just *full*. She couldn't decide if it was uncomfortable or not—but she definitely didn't like this.

She could see that Eben liked it, though. His breathing was quick and shallow, the muscles in his chest and arms straining with the effort of keeping still. Beneath her hands, his nano-agents raced like fire, sparking across his nerves. His heart pounded. Experimentally, she lifted her hips.

Though she only managed to nudge him, his reaction was everything she could have hoped. He sucked in a sharp breath, his spine bowing as he jerked upward. His hands fisted beside her head. As if gratified by his response, her inner muscles clung to him when he began to withdraw.

"No, Ivy. Wait until—"

Her fingers digging into his firm ass, she hauled him back. The impact rocked Ivy to her toes, little ripples that seemed to reverberate in the slick channel hugging his length. Eben shouted in surprise and pleasure, his head falling forward, teeth clenching. A deep groan tore from him.

"I can't, love . . . I can't—Ah, *God.* I'm sorry. I have to—" Muscle bunched beneath her palms. He rose above her, bracing his left hand beside her shoulder and sliding his right hand between them, the tip of his middle finger brushing her clitoris. "I'll try . . . to go slow."

He pulled back. Ivy stiffened, preparing herself—and wishing he'd go fast. If he finished quickly, then she could . . . she could . . . *Oh, blue heavens.* He pushed into her, and though his thick length stuffed her too full, the stretch wasn't painful, and the movement of his finger flicked little sparks into her belly, a fire building higher and higher.

She still didn't know if she liked it. But she wanted more. Her palms smoothed up over his back. She hooked her leg over his hip, and cried out when he suddenly thrust deep.

Eben froze. "Did I hurt you? God, Ivy. I didn't expect you to wrap your leg—"

"No." Her back arched. She couldn't stop moving, writhing against him. "More. *More.*"

Tension shook through his big body, sweat gathering on his skin and glistening in the lamplight. His gaze fixed on her face, he worked leisurely into her again. And again. She bit her lips to stop herself from crying out, but her moans were almost as loud. At the end of each long stroke, she stiffened and trembled until his fingers on her clit pushed her into motion again, and she twisted her hips, trying to take more. He slowly slid in to the hilt, and she was as desperate as before. Helplessly, she spread her legs wide.

"Eben, I need . . ." She didn't know. Her chest heaved with her labored breaths. *"Please."*

With a tortured groan, he paused with his cock lodged inside her and closed his eyes, as if gathering strength. He withdrew his hand from between them and slid it beneath her hip, tilting her pelvis up.

In a low voice, he said, "Tell me if it's too much."

He slammed forward. Ivy gasped, tried to catch her breath, but he was already there again, deep and hard. Her hands spasmed. Afraid of hurting him, she grabbed the sheets and twisted, crying out as he pounded into her.

"This?" Letting go of her hip, he buried his fingers in her hair, as if to anchor her for each heavy stroke. "Is this what you need?"

Too overwhelmed to speak, Ivy nodded. Then his mouth covered hers, hungry, searching. Her legs wrapping him tight, she found his rhythm and met each powerful lunge. Her breasts swayed with the force of his thrusts, their stiffened tips brushing his chest in a maddening tease. Need spiraled, like a screw turning tighter and tighter with every desperate plunge. Her limbs suddenly locked, her body straining and rigid. His kiss deepened. His mouth caught her cries as she shuddered around him, her inner muscles clenching on his shaft. Then he was pumping into her again, hard and fast, gripping her backside to hold her still. He was finally letting go, Ivy realized, and she moved with him, urged him on until he shoved deep, shaking as he pulsed inside her, groaning against her lips. She clung to him, panting, sweating.

And decided that she'd liked it, after all.

Unable to sleep, Eben rose long before the end of first watch. He dressed in his breeches and shirt, and crossed the cabin as quietly as his leg would allow. After pouring a brandy, he sat at the window and looked out into the dark sky.

He tried not to think of Ivy. He tried not to think about twenty days from now, when she would leave his ship. He tried not to think about how proving that he was a man of his word meant *keeping* his word . . . and that meant he had to take her home as he'd promised. He tried not to think about the risk she'd taken by accepting him into her body—not because she believed he'd care for her, but because she would be fine without him.

In the few minutes that he managed not to think of those things, he drank his brandy, and tried to think of what might persuade Ivy to call *Vesuvius* her home.

But there were places Eben didn't dare let his mind wander, where lurking terrors might rise up and swallow him whole. And so he didn't let himself think about how Ivy deserved so much more than his ship—and how loving her meant that he might have to let her go.

TEN

Ivy had never taken a bath with a revolver at an arm's length away before.

Though if she were to pick at nits, she hadn't taken that many baths before—at least, not fully submerged as she was now. A cloth and a bowl of water had always sufficed. But this was better.

With a blissful sigh, she leaned back in the steaming tub, trying to block out the noises from the tavern downstairs. Eben had assured her this Port Fallow inn had the best rooms and food, despite the rough and tumble patrons. Considering that Ivy had never stayed at an inn before, she'd had to take his word for it—and she'd have been happy sleeping in a shanty near the city wall, as long as Eben shared the dirt floor with her.

She glanced at the gun again, then at the door, solidly locked. Eben hadn't said whether he'd worried more about the patrons or the odd chance that a zombie might make it over the wall and across Amsterdam's old canals, but he'd been adamant about keeping the weapon with her at all times. Knowing this city, she had to agree. Though she'd only been here a few weeks before she and Netta had flown north to

Fool's Cove, she'd heard about more murders and theft than over the course of a year in London.

And within six days, she'd be in Fool's Cove again.

A familiar ache settled in her heart—and though she sat in the bath until the water cooled, the pain still hadn't faded. Every day, it remained for a longer time. She feared that by the time she reached home, the ache would have taken up permanent residence in her chest.

With a sigh, she left the bath. The blue dress that Netta had made for her hung in the wardrobe. Ivy didn't know what Eben had planned for the evening, but he'd requested that she wear it. She slipped it over her head, and though it fastened in the back, a design that usually required assistance from a maid—or a friend—Ivy had no trouble bending her arms around and maneuvering the tiny hooks. She looked inside the small bag that Eben had given her before he'd left the room. . . .and had to sit on the bed when her knees went weak.

Her heart pounding, she withdrew a pair of silk stockings. *Her* silk stockings, the pair she'd left behind at a London inn, two years before. He'd kept them all this time?

And her elbow, too—but she understood that better. The flange had saved his life. Why keep these?

She fingered the satin ribbons, and hope filled her chest. He'd kept her stockings aboard *Vesuvius* for two years. Perhaps . . . perhaps he'd want her to stay, too.

But what would she *do*? Ivy didn't want to be part of his crew. And though she'd gladly cover the blacksmith's duties, she knew the work would occupy her only for a few hours a week—at the most—and provide no challenge at all. Within three months, she could outfit every crew member who needed one with a new and better prosthetic . . . but what then?

The room's door clicked shut. *Eben.* Facing the wardrobe, Ivy composed herself. She would ask him if she could stay, but . . .

A shiver ran over her skin as realization set in: she hadn't heard the door unlock and open—and she didn't hear his distinctive tread.

Oh, blue. The revolver lay on a chair across the room.

Ivy carefully kept her gaze from touching the weapon as she turned, hoping that the intruder wouldn't look that way, too. Her heart racing, she glanced toward the door.

Lady Corsair stood with her back against the wall, frowning as she took in the blue gown. Her green eyes met Ivy's. "Barker was right," she said. "Mad Machen plans to openly court you."

Ivy's mouth dropped open. *That* was what this evening was about? Eben didn't need to do that.

"You didn't know." The other woman's lips pursed. "It must be a last resort. All else has failed, so he tries the old-fashioned method. And the softhearted fool will ruin himself and destroy his crew in the process. God*damm*it, Eben."

Though Ivy bristled at the insult tossed at him, she couldn't mistake the emotion behind Lady Corsair's speech. The woman cared.

So did Ivy. "What would ruin him?"

"You would, Ivy Blacksmith." A hard smile curved Lady Corsair's lips. "On the sea, you can never show your belly or your throat, because someone will rip them out. And you are the soft spot that Mad Machen is about to show the world."

"I see," Ivy whispered. And she did. Too well.

Lady Corsair studied her face before swearing again. She turned for the door.

"Captain Corsair," Ivy said, and waited until the woman glanced at her. "You sent four men from your airship to my shop in Fool's Cove, and failed to pay for my work. I expect to be paid now."

Black eyebrows arched in disbelief. She laughed. "You're a cheeky one, blacksmith. But you're not funny."

She opened the door. Ivy said, "If you don't pay me, I'll head down to the tavern, and spin a story about how you generously offered to pay for your aviators' prosthetics, and were so pleased with my work that you gave me double. But if you pay me now, I'll only say that you fooled me, and that I haven't been able to coax a single denier from your purse."

Green eyes narrowing, Lady Corsair snapped the door closed and stalked across the room, fingering the handle of the knife sheathed at her thigh. Ivy's heart careened against her chest with the woman's every step, but she held her ground, lifting her chin to meet the woman's gaze.

"I know it'd be easier to kill me," Ivy said. "Except that Eben's your soft spot, isn't he?"

Lady Corsair's sudden grin should have terrified her—but Ivy knew she was right. She held out her hand.

"Pay me."

The woman's grin became something more like a smile. She reached beneath her belt, withdrew a small leather purse, and dropped it into Ivy's palm.

"It's all I have with me," she said. "But it should be enough."

Ivy couldn't respond. Her nanoagents had automatically measured the weight in her hand, and she knew exactly how much Lady Corsair had given.

The woman's sharp smile widened. While Ivy stood dumbstruck, Lady Corsair cupped her hand between Ivy's legs.

"Funny. I thought for certain the Blacksmith must have added a pair of balls." She backed toward the door, saluting Ivy as she went. "You'll do well to keep using those, blacksmith."

Perhaps Lady Corsair got by using her balls. Ivy preferred her brains.

Her fingers closed over the purse. How strange, to have enough money to buy anything she wanted—and to realize what she wanted most, no amount of money could buy. Mad Machen's reputation could only be built through stories, though action . . . and it took years.

But there must be *some* way to have him. She just had to figure it out.

Ivy was sitting on the bed, staring at the pile of gold coins on the bedspread when she heard Eben's key in the lock. He halted halfway through the door, his gaze drinking her in.

"Look at you, Ivy."

Even with her heart aching, he could make her smile. She smoothed her hand over the blue satin skirt. "Netta is a wonderful seamstress."

"Perhaps," he said, closing the door. "But Netta isn't wearing it. And soon you won't be, ei—" His step faltered when he saw the pile on the bed. "What is that?"

She heard the rough note in his voice, the worry. She didn't know what would soothe it, so she told him the truth. "Fifty livre. Lady Corsair paid me for my work. Overpaid me, actually."

He barked out a hoarse laugh at her understatement. "Why?"

She'd spent the past thirty minutes trying to understand it. "I think . . . so that I wouldn't ruin you. So that I could go anywhere I wanted to—as long as it was away from you. She said you meant to court me, that you'd be torn apart for being soft, and that it would also destroy your crew. Is that true?"

His skin paled beneath his tan. Jaw clenched, he turned away from her.

"It *is* true," she whispered. She hadn't been completely certain before—not when the story came from Lady Corsair. But Eben's reaction said that it was. "Why would you take that risk?"

"Ivy . . ." He shook his head, and the sound that came from him seemed like a laugh, but pain or fear was sculpted into his posture, his expression. But when he faced her, there was only need and hope. "Because you're worth more to me than anything else in this world. Because I want you to make *Vesuvius* your home. And because. . . I love you, Ivy."

Her heart filled, followed by a stabbing pain. His love, her love—it changed nothing. Lady Corsair was still right, and more people than Eben would be hurt. So would his crew . . . and the slaves that Mad Machen could potentially save.

Eben's eyes closed. His voice was bleak. "You don't have to say it, Ivy. I can see your answer in your face. Where will you go?"

"I don't know. Perhaps I'll buy equipment for a blacksmith's shop, in another city. Maybe in the New World. With this much money, I can go anywhere, do anything." Except what she most wanted. Her vision blurred as she glanced down at the coins. "Fool's Cove, first. I promised Netta I'd come back."

"And I promised to take you there. *God.*" He fisted his hands in his hair, staring at her in utter torment. Then he lost all expression, and his hands fell to his sides as he turned to leave. His voice was flat as he said, "We'll sail in the morning."

He closed the door quietly. Ivy wished he'd slammed it. *She* wanted to slam it. She remained on the bed instead, rocking back and forth, refusing to cry—and refusing to give in to impulse and throw the money as hard as she could across the room.

Love, money. None of it changed the problem of reputation. Mad Machen saved people for coin, not because he cared. He chased a woman because she'd cheated him—not because he loved her. And the woman who stayed would have to be . . . would have to be . . .

She'd have to be *mad.*

Ivy's lips parted. Her heart pounding, she rose from the bed, and collected the money—then she crossed the room and collected the gun. She counted the number of bullets and removed three.

She'd reached the door before realizing that only stockings encased her feet. Spotting her worn black boots, she pulled them on.

They'd work well enough. Money could buy her slippers. Only crazy would get her a man.

Men and women packed the tavern. From somewhere in the back, automaton musicians badly in need of repairs to their instruments played a jaunty song. Ivy pushed through the crowd, and she supposed it said much about the patrons here that not one glanced a second time at the revolver she carried in her right hand, though a few did stare at her guild tattoo. Rising up on her toes, she tried to scan the tables and the bar, but there were too many people, most of them taller. She debated for an instant whether to circle the room, looking for Eben—but now that she'd resolved to do this, she decided to go full bore.

Hiking up her skirts, she clambered atop the nearest table

and stood. A single fierce look silenced the protesting men whose drinks sloshed wildly in her wake—though she noted they were amused rather than afraid.

That would do, too.

She spotted Eben at the bar, and her heart clenched. He sat alone with his shoulders slumped, his expression desolate. He held a small glass loosely in his hand. When he lifted it toward his lips, Ivy raised her gun, aimed, and pulled the trigger.

The glass exploded. The deafening crack of the revolver faded to silence. Even the song died, which hadn't been played by broken automatons, Ivy realized—just very bad musicians. She found herself facing a roomful of pistols, but she only had eyes for the one in Eben's hand. It pointed straight back at her.

His face whitened. A glass shard had cut his lip; blood spilled over his jaw. She saw his mouth form her name, and she shouted over him.

"Mad Machen!" She aimed for his heart even as he lowered his gun—as did everyone around them. No longer concerned for their lives, they cleared a path between Ivy and Eben, and settled in to watch. "You heartless brigand! You've tracked me to the ends of the earth to have your revenge, and you've used me in your bed. You've forced me to work in *Vesuvius*'s smithy. No more. I demand that you set a course for my home, Captain. And you will do it now, or I will put a bullet through your mad brainpan."

Eben's expression darkened. Slowly, he rose to his feet and wiped the blood from his mouth. His voice was low and dangerous. "So you think you'll take command of my ship, do you?"

"You have forced me to this point, Mad Machen. Do you think that I will stay in your smithy forever? No longer will I watch as you make a fortune with my windups, forcing me to slave away on your ship and selling them at every port."

"You'll do whatever I say, Ivy Blacksmith. You're mine, as is every coin you earn."

She adjusted her aim when he stalked toward her. "Stay there, or I will shoot your leg from under you!"

She planned to make him a better one, anyway.

He didn't stop. Ivy fired. The bullet slammed into solid steel just below his right knee. He stumbled forward to keep his balance. A murmur ran through the crowd.

Jaw hardening, Eben straightened. The look he gave Ivy sent the men around her table scrambling for distance. He approached, and when he was within a few feet, Ivy pointed the revolver at his groin.

"Next will be your prick, sir. And you know that my hands are too steady to miss."

His grin was a mad thing, filled with blood and wild laughter. "Then I will force you to graft on a new one. Perhaps something smaller, that you can take more easily."

He continued forward. Ivy pulled the trigger. The hammer fell with a loud click. She only had time to shriek before he swept her feet from the tabletop. Tossing her facedown over his shoulder, he strode for the door. She pounded her fists against his back, screaming for help.

Thank the blessed stars, not a single patron came to her aid. And she was gratified to hear, just before Eben pushed through the exit,

"She's as bleeding mad as he is!"

Ivy found herself in the nearest alley, up against the nearest wall, with Eben kissing her as if he'd never stop. She didn't want him to. Threading her fingers into his hair, she tasted his sweat and his blood—but the tears were hers.

"I love you," she said against his mouth the moment he gave her a chance to breathe. "I love you. Did you know?"

His eyes closed and he shook his head. "Not until I saw you on that table. You *are* mad. And, my God, I love you for it."

Laughing, she kissed him again. After a moment, she said, "You have to punish me for challenging your command."

"By forcing you to set up a shop aboard *Vesuvius*?"

"By keeping me with you forever." She wrapped her arms around his neck. "And I will have clean air, a view, work for my mind and my hands—and you. Everything I want. So take me home, Captain."

"That's an order I'll follow." Lifting her up, Eben cradled her against his chest and turned for the docks.

Ivy smiled and lay her head on his shoulder. "Would you have let me return to Fool's Cove?"

"No. When courting fails, the next step is abduction."

She laughed into the night—until she caught a glimpse of his face. His expression was serious. Her mouth fell open. "Weren't you joking?"

His sudden grin didn't make her any more or less certain. Alright. She'd let him have that one.

"Do you know," she told him, gently touching the almost-healed cut on his lip, "that I've never once held a gun before today?"

His grin remained only until he glanced at her features. He came to a stop. "Now *you're* not serious. That glass you shot was an inch from my head."

"But it's true." She wiggled her fingers, silvery in the moonlight. "I knew my aim would be perfect. And it was, don't you agree?"

He studied her face a moment longer, before starting toward *Vesuvius* again, a smile deepening the corners of his mouth. "God help me," he said.

Once again, she took that as a "yes."

Keep reading for a preview of
Virginia Kantra's next
Children of the Sea novel

Immortal Sea

Coming September 2010 from Berkley Sensation!

Morgan looked down, arrested, at the woman clinging to his arm. Was she aware what she invited? His kind did not touch. Only to fight or to mate.

His blood rushed like water under ice. Perhaps tonight he would do both.

He had not come ashore to rut. He was not as abstemious as his prince, Conn, but he had standards. Unlike his sister Morwenna and others among the mer, he did not often waste his seed on humankind.

The woman's throat moved as she swallowed. "Sorry," she said, and dropped his arm.

She was very young, he observed. Attractive, with healthy skin and glossy brown hair. Her face was a strong oval, her jaw slightly squared, her unfettered breasts high and pleasing. There was even a gleam that might be intelligence in those brown eyes.

It would be no great privation to indulge her and himself.

"Do not apologize." Grasping her hand, he replaced it on his sleeve. Her nails were clean and unpolished, her fingers tapered.

He imagined those short nails pressing into his flesh, and the rush in his blood became a roar. *No privation at all.*

He glanced around the narrow buildings fronting the street. He would not take her here, in this filthy human warren. But there were other places less noxious, and nearby. Adjusting his stride to hers, he led her away, seeking green ways and open water.

The lights and noise of the city at night eddied and ebbed around them, the amber pool of a streetlight, the green glow of a bar sign, a lamp in a second-floor window.

At the next intersection, she hesitated, her gaze darting down the street toward a café where trees strung with tiny lights canopied a cluster of empty tables. "Don't we want to go that way?"

She did possess intelligence, then. Or at least a sense of direction.

"If you like." Morgan shrugged. "It is quieter toward the harbor."

Her brow pleated. Her eyes were big and dark. He watched the silent battle between feminine caution and female desire, felt the moment of acquiescence when her hand relaxed on his forearm. He fought to keep his flare of triumph from his face.

"Quieter," she repeated.

"More . . . scenic," he said, searching for a word that might appeal to her.

"Oh." Her tongue touched her lower lip in doubt or invitation. "I haven't seen the harbor yet. This is my first visit to Copenhagen."

"Indeed." Warmth radiated from her hand up his arm. Anticipation flowed thick and urgent through his veins. She was not part of his purpose here. But she was a respite, a recompense of a sort, for long years of trial and frustration.

Her bare shoulders gleamed in the moonlight, sweetly curved as the curl of a shell. The night swirled around them like seaweed caught in the tide, the smell of beer and piss and car exhaust, a waft from a flower box, a breeze from the sea.

"I almost didn't come," she continued, as if he had expressed an interest. "Not part of The Plan, you know?"

He did not know and cared even less. But her voice was

low pitched and pleasant. To hear it again, he asked, "There is a plan?"

She nodded, touching the ends of her hair where it brushed her smooth shoulders. He observed the small, betraying gesture with satisfaction. Consciously or not, she was signaling her awareness of him as a male.

"I start med school in the fall," she said. "My dad wanted me to stay home and do a post-bacc program, get a leg up on the competition. And my mother wanted one more summer of tennis and Junior League before I slip from her grasp forever."

He had no idea what she was talking about. "And what do you want?"

Her eyes crinkled. "A break," she said with such rueful honesty that he almost smiled back. "Everything always revolves around school. Like I don't live my own life, I just prepare for it. I wanted . . . something different. An adventure, I guess."

He could give her something different, he thought. He would even make sure she enjoyed it.

The barred storefronts ceded ground to cobblestone streets and narrow houses with cramped garden plots. The scent of standing water and of lilies carried on the breeze. *Not much farther now*, he thought.

"What about you?" she asked with friendly interest.

He glanced down in surprise.

"What brings you here?"

His purpose was bitter as brine in his mouth, deep and cold as the sea.

For Morgan was warden of the northern deeps, charged by a lost king to fight a losing battle.

For a thousand years he had served the sea king's son, battling demons in the deep, defending his desmesne from the sly encroachments of the *sidhe*. But his powers had proved useless against the depredations of humankind. For more than a century, the overflow from this city's streets and canals had polluted the sound and the sea, turning the port into a shit house. Only now, when the humans had finally learned to curb their waste, could Morgan begin the slow process of repair. Recovery of the seabed would take centuries.

He did not blame this girl—much—for what her kind had done. She was here and female and willing. Under the circumstances, he was prepared to overlook a great deal.

"Business," he said.

Her deep brown eyes assessed him. "You don't dress like a businessman."

He wore the black and silver of the finfolk, subtly altered so he could pass for a man of this place and time. "No?"

"No."

He did not respond. The sky was thick with moisture, glowing with the lights of the city and the promise of dawn. The moon wore golden vapor like a veil.

"You don't want to talk about it," she guessed.

He smiled, showing the edge of his teeth. "You did not seek my company for my conversation."

She stopped on the sidewalk, her chin tilted at a challenging angle. Despite her earlier signals, he had been too blunt. Women, human women, required some preliminaries. Or perhaps her female pride was offended. "Really? What is it you think I want from you?"

Her cheeks were flushed. Her scent filled his nostrils. Beneath the sharp notes of her annoyance, he could smell the sweetness of her body readying itself for his. His shaft went hard as stone.

"My protection," he offered.

She nodded once, her eyes big and wary. "Yeah," she admitted. "Okay."

He stepped closer, watching her face carefully. "And perhaps . . . an adventure?"

He heard the betraying intake of her breath. Her small, round breasts rose. And suddenly he wanted this, wanted *her*, beyond habit or reason, instinct or expedience. The intensity of his lust surprised him.

She was only human, after all.

KEEP READING FOR A PREVIEW OF
MELJEAN BROOK'S NEXT NOVEL

THE IRON DUKE

COMING OCTOBER 2010 FROM BERKLEY SENSATION!

By the time Mina and Newberry reached the Isle of Dogs, the nip of the evening air had become a bite. Not a true island, the isle was surrounded on three sides by a bend in the river. On the London side, multiple trading companies had built up small docks—mostly abandoned. The southern and eastern sides held the Iron Duke's docks, which serviced his company's ships, and those who paid for the space. In nine years, he'd been paid enough to buy up the center of the isle and build his fortress.

The high wrought-iron fence that surrounded his gardens had earned him the nickname The Iron Duke—the iron kept the rest of London out, and whatever riches he hid inside, in. The spikes at the top of the fence guaranteed that no one in the surrounding slums would scale it, and no one was invited in. At least, no one in Mina's circle, or her mother's.

She was never certain if their circle was too high, or too low.

Newberry stopped in front of the gate. When a face appeared at the small gatehouse window, he shouted, "Detective Inspector Wentworth, on Crown business! Open her up!"

The gatekeeper appeared, a grizzled man with a long gray

beard and the heavy step that marked a metal leg. A former pirate, Mina guessed. Though the Crown insisted that Trahaearn and his men had all been privateers, acting with the permission of the king, only a few children who didn't know any better believed the story. The rest of them knew he'd been a pirate all along, and the story was just designed to bolster faith in the king and his ministers after the revolution. That story and bestowing a title on Trahaearn had been two of King Edward's last cogent acts. The crew had been given naval ranks, and *Marco's Terror* pressed into the service of the Navy . . . where she'd supposedly been all along.

The Iron Duke had traded the *Terror* and the seas for a title and a fortress in the middle of a slum. She wondered if he felt that exchange had been worth it.

The gatekeeper glanced at her. "And the jade?"

At Mina's side, Newberry bristled. "*She* is the detective inspector, Lady Wilhelmina Wentworth."

Oh, Newberry. In Manhattan City, titles still meant more than escaping the modification that the British lower classes had suffered under the Horde. And when the gatekeeper looked at her again, she knew what he saw—and it wasn't a lady. Nor was it the epaulettes declaring her rank, or the red band sewed into her sleeve, boasting that she'd spilled Horde blood in the revolution.

No, he saw her face, calculated her age, and understood that she'd been conceived during a Frenzy. And that, because of her family's status, her mother and father had been allowed to keep her rather than being taken by the Horde to be raised in a crèche.

The gatekeeper looked at her assistant. "And you?"

"Constable Newberry."

Scratching his beard, the old man shuffled back toward the gatehouse. "All right. I'll be sending a gram up to the captain, then."

He still called the Iron Duke "captain?" Mina could not decide if that said more about Trahaearn or the gatekeeper. At least one of them did not put much stock in titles, but she could not determine if it was the gatekeeper alone.

The gatekeeper didn't return—and former pirate or not, he

must be literate if he could write a gram and read the answer from the main house. That answer came quickly. She and Newberry hadn't waited more than a minute before the gates opened on well-oiled hinges.

The park was enormous, with green lawns stretching out into the dark. Dogs sniffed along the fence, their handlers bundled up against the cold. If someone had invaded the property, he wouldn't find many places to hide outside the buildings. All of the shrubs and trees were still young, planted after Trahaearn had purchased the estate.

The house rivaled Chesterfield before that great building had fallen into disrepair and been demolished. Made of yellow stone, two rectangular wings jutted forward to form a large courtyard. Unadorned casements decorated the many windows, and the blocky stone front was relieved only by the window glass, and the balustrade along the top of the roof. A fountain tinkled at the center of the courtyard. Behind it, the main steps created semicircles leading to the entrance.

On the center of the steps, a white sheet concealed a body-shaped lump. No blood soaked through the sheet. A man waited on the top step, his slight form in a poker-straight posture that Mina couldn't place for a moment. Then it struck her: Navy. Probably another pirate, though this one had been a sailor—or an officer—first.

A house of this size would require a small army of staff, and she and Newberry would have to question each one. Soon, she'd know how many of Trahaearn's pirates had come to dry land with him.

As they reached the fountain, she turned to Newberry. "Stop here. Set up your camera by the body. I want photographs of everything before we move it."

Newberry parked and climbed out. Mina didn't wait for him to gather his equipment from the bonnet. She strode toward the house. The man descended the steps to greet her, and she was forced to revise her opinion. His posture wasn't rigid discipline, but a cover for wiry, contained energy. His dark hair slicked back from a narrow face. Unlike the man at the gate, he was neat, and almost bursting with the need to help.

"Inspector Wentworth." With ink-stained fingers, he gestured to the body, inviting her to look.

She was not in a rush, however. The body would not be going anywhere. "Mr.—?"

"St. John." He said it like a bounder, rather than the two abbreviated syllables of someone born in England. "Steward to his grace's estate."

"This estate or his property in Wales?" Which, as far as Mina was aware, Trahaearn didn't often visit.

"Anglesey, Inspector."

Newberry passed them, easily carrying the heavy photographic equipment. St. John half turned, as if to offer his assistance, then glanced back as Mina asked, "When did you arrive here from Wales, Mr. St. John?"

"Yesterday."

"Did you witness what happened here?"

He shook his head. "I was in the study when I heard the footman—Chesley—inform the housekeeper that someone had fallen. Mrs. Lavery then told his grace."

Mina frowned. She hadn't been called out here because someone had been a clumsy oaf, had they? "Someone tripped on the stairs?"

"No, inspector. Fallen." His hand made a sharp dive from his shoulder to his hip.

Mina glanced at the body again, then at the balustrade lining the roof. "Do you know who it was?"

"No."

She was not surprised. If he managed the Welsh estate, he wouldn't likely know the London staff well. "Who covered him with the sheet?"

"I did, after his grace sent the staff back into the house."

So they'd all come out to gawk. "Did anyone identify him while they were outside?"

"No."

Or maybe they just hadn't spoken up. "Where is the staff now?"

"They are gathered in the main parlor."

Where they would all pass the story around until they were

each convinced they'd witnessed it personally. Blast. Mina firmed her lips.

As if understanding her frustration, St. John added, "The footman is alone in the study, however. His grace told him to stay there. He hasn't spoken with anyone else since Mrs. Lavery told his grace."

The footman had been taken into the study and asked nothing? "But he has talked to the duke?"

The answer came from behind her, from a voice that could carry his commands across a ship, without shouting. "He has, Inspector."

She turned to find a man as big as his voice. Oh, damn the news sheets. They hadn't been kind to *him*—they'd been kind to their readers, protecting them from the effect of this man. He was just as hard and as handsome as they'd portrayed. Altogether dark and forbidding, his gaze was as pointed and as guarded as the fence that was his namesake. The Iron Duke wasn't as tall as his statue, but still taller than any man had a right to be—and as broad through the shoulders as Newberry, but without the spare flesh.

The news sheets had shown all of that, but they hadn't conveyed his power. But it was not just size, Mina immediately recognized. Not just his looks. She'd seen handsome before. She'd seen rich and influential. Yet this man had a presence beyond looks and money. For the first time, she could see why men might follow him through kraken-infested waters or into Horde territory, then follow him back onto shore and remain with him.

He was terrifying.

Disturbed by her reaction, Mina glanced at the man standing beside him: tall, brown-haired, his expression bored. Mina did not recognize him. Perhaps a bounder and, if so, probably an aristocrat—and he likely expected to be treated as one.

Bully for him.

She looked to the duke again. Like his companion, he wore a long black overcoat, breeches, and boots. A waistcoat buckled like armor over a white shirt with a simple collar reminiscent of the Horde's tunic collar. Fashionable clothes, but almost invisible—as if overpowered by the man wearing them.

Something, Mina suspected, that he did not just to his clothes, but the people around him. She could not afford to be one of them.

She'd never been introduced to someone of his standing before, but she'd seen Superintendent Hale meet the prime minister without a single gesture to acknowledge that he ranked above her. Mina followed that example and offered the short nod of an equal. "Your Grace. I understand that you did not witness this man die."

"No."

She looked beyond him. "And your companion . . . ?"

"Also saw nothing," the other man answered.

She'd been right; his accent marked him as a bounder. Yet she had to revise her opinion of him. He wasn't bored by the death—just too familiar with it to be excited by yet another. She couldn't understand that. The more death she saw, the more the injustice of each one touched her. "Your name, sir?"

His smile seemed just at the edge of a laugh. "Mr. Smith."

A joker. How fun.

She thought a flicker of irritation crossed the duke's expression. But when he didn't offer his companion's true name, she let it go. One of the staff would know.

"Mr. St. John has told me that no one has identified the body, and only your footman saw his fall."

"Yes."

"Did your footman relate anything else to you?"

"Only that his landing sounded just like a man falling from the topsail yard to the deck below. Except this one didn't scream."

No scream? Either the man had been drunk, asleep, or already dead. She would soon find out which it was.

"If you'll pardon me, Your Grace."

With a nod, she turned toward the steps, where Newberry tested the camera's flashing light. She heard the Iron Duke and his companion follow her. As long as they did not touch the body or try to help her examine it, she did not care.

Mina looked down at her hands. *She* would touch the body,

and Newberry had not thought to bring her serviceable wool gloves to exchange for her white evening gloves. They were only satin—neither her mother's tinkering nor her own salary could afford kid—but they were still too dear to ruin.

She tugged at the tips of her fingers, but the fastenings at her wrist prevented them from sliding off. Futilely, she tried to push the small buttons through equally small satin loops. The seams at the tips of her fingers made them too bulky, and the fabric was too slippery. It could not be done without a maid, or a mother.

She looked round for Newberry, and saw that the black powder from the ferrotype camera already dusted his hands. Blast it. She lifted her wrist to her mouth, pushed the cuff of her sleeve out of the way with her chin, and began to work at the tiny loops with her teeth. She would bite them through, if she had to. Even the despised task of sewing the buttons back on would be easier than—

"Give your hand over, Inspector."

Mina froze, her hackles rising at the command. She looked through her fingers at Trahaearn's face.

She heard a noise from his companion, a snorted half laugh—as if Trahaearn had failed an easy test.

The duke's voice softened. His expression did not. "May I assist you?"

No, she thought. *Do not touch me, do not come close.* But the body on the steps would not allow her that reply.

"Yes. Thank you, Your Grace."

She held out her hand, and watched as he removed his own gloves. Kid, lined with sable. Just imagining that luxurious softness warmed her.

She would not have been surprised if his presence had, as well. With his great size, he seemed to surround her with heat just by standing so near. His hands were large, his fingers long and nails square. As he took her wrist in his left palm, calluses audibly scraped the satin. His face darkened. She could not tell if it was in anger or embarrassment.

However rough his skin was, his fingers were nimble. He deftly unfastened the first button, and the next. "This was not the evening you had planned."

"No."

She did not say this was preferable to the Victory Ball, but perhaps he read it in her voice. His teeth flashed in a smile. Her breath quickened, and she focused on her wrist. Only two buttons left, and then she could work.

She should be working now. "Were the dogs patrolling the grounds before the body was discovered?"

"No. They search for the point of entry now."

Mina pictured the iron fence. Perhaps a child could slip through the bars; a man could not. But if someone had let him through . . . ? "Have you spoken with your man at the front gate?"

"Wills?"

She had not asked the gatekeeper his name. "If Wills has a prosthetic left leg, and often saves a portion of his supper in his beard for his breakfast, then we are speaking of the same man."

"That is Wills." He studied her with unreadable eyes. "He would not let anyone through."

Without my leave, Mina finished for him. And perhaps he was right, though of course she would verify it with the gatekeeper, and ask the steward about deliveries. Someone might have hidden themselves in one.

His gaze fell to her glove again. "There we are," Trahaearn said softly. "Now to—"

She pulled her hand away at the same time Trahaearn gripped the satin fingertips. He tugged. Satin slid in a warm caress over her elbow, her forearm.

Flames lit her cheeks. "Your Grace—"

His expression changed as he continued to pull. First registering surprise, as if he had not realized that the glove extended past her wrist. Then an emotion hard and sharp as the long glove slowly gave way. Its white length finally dangled from his fingers, and to Mina seemed as intimate as if he held her stocking.

Her sleeve still covered her arm, but she felt exposed. Stripped. With as much dignity as she could, Mina claimed the glove.

"Thank you, Your Grace. I can manage the other." She

stuffed the glove into her pocket. With her bare fingers, she made quick work of the buttons at her left wrist.

She looked up to find him staring at her. His cheekbones blazed with color, his gaze hot.

She'd seen lust before. This marked the first time that she hadn't seen any disgust or hatred beneath it.

"Thank you," she said again, amazed by the evenness of her voice when everything inside her trembled.

"Inspector." He inclined his head, then looked beyond her to the stairs.

And as she turned, the trembling stopped. Her legs were steady as she walked to the steps, her gaze unflinching, her mind focused.

"You were to assist her, not undress her," she heard his companion say. Trahaearn didn't reply, and Mina didn't look back at him.

Even the pull of the Iron Duke was not stronger than Death.

LOOK FOR THE NEW PSY-CHANGELING NOVEL FROM

NEW YORK TIMES BESTSELLING AUTHOR

NALINI SINGH

Play of Passion

As Tracker for the SnowDancer pack, it's up to Drew Kincaid to rein in rogue changelings who have lost control of their animal halves. But nothing in his life has prepared him for the battle he must now wage to win the heart of a woman who makes his body ignite...and who threatens to enslave his wolf.

Lieutenant Indigo Riviere doesn't easily allow skin privileges, especially of the sensual kind—and the last person she expects to find herself craving is the most wickedly playful male in the den. Everything she knows tells her to pull back...but she hasn't counted on Drew's will.

Now, two of SnowDancer's most stubborn wolves find themselves playing a hotly sexy game even as lethal danger stalks the very place they call home...

penguin.com

M696T0510